THE KNIFE!

Sky ignored Readn, shifting and huffing air and then, finally, unexpectedly, nickering a greeting.

To *what*?

Out of the darkness, over light footsteps on the road that were just now audible, Rethia's voice said, "Dan? Danny is that you?"

"Goddess damn," he breathed, not believing what his ears told him, though the rest of him had already known. "Rethia. . . ?"

Her answer was to quicken her step, while Readn ducked under the lead rope and headed for the road. He met her in the middle of it, and got nothing more than a glimpse of her face before she caught him up in a hug so sudden and fierce it literally knocked an *oomph* out of him. "What?" he said, when her indistinct words met up with his jacket and turned incomprehensible, and then didn't give her a chance to repeat herself, but took her by the shoulders and set her back a few steps. "What are you *doing* here? Why are you alone?"

She didn't answer any of those things, but what she said was infinitely more important. "They have Kacey," she said breathlessly. *"The Knife has Kacey."*

Wolf Justice

DORANNA DURGIN

WOLF JUSTICE

Copyright © 1998 by Doranna Durgin

A Baen Books Original

Baen Publishing Enterprises
P.O. Box 1403
Riverdale, NY 10471

ISBN: 0-671-87891-3

Cover art by Larry Elmore

First printing, September 1998

Distributed by Simon & Schuster
1230 Avenue of the Americas
New York, NY 10020

Printed in the United States of America

To Ann: *thank goodness for Free Fridays*

with thanks to
Judith, First Reader Extraordinaire

Answers Questioned

Rethia dreamed of unicorns. Their hooves evoked thunder, the flash of their horns begat lightning. *Dust swirling through bright sunlight, musky sweat filling the air, thick currents of magic drifting on the breeze of their mad dance, their unicorn winds* . . . Amidst it all sat a young girl, dazzled and terrified, afraid to watch and afraid not to—and so she saw the unicorns leaving her world for some other place. Tired of being hunted, captured and killed for their fierce, wild beauty, they simply left her Keland behind, taking their magic with them.

Almost gone. They were almost gone. . . . Blue eyes huge with awe and suppressed panic—eyes that Rethia now watched, and once had seen through—that little girl stood her ground as the last of the unicorns approached. *Rhythmic huffing breath, huge round hooves, a giant muzzle of crisply dark walnut points, nostrils open wide with exertion, wider yet to inhale her scent* . . . Boldly, she reached up—far up—to touch the beast.

Even in sleep, Rethia knew what would happen next, after she saw herself crumple, bespelled, to the ground. She'd had this dream often enough, and she'd lived it before that. Later, half a day and a whole night later, the little girl would open eyes that never looked at the world in the same way again. From the inside looking out, she would discover it difficult to gather her thoughts past the faint inner call she could never quite hear and never quite ignore. From the outside looking in, those eyes had gone deep brown around the outside edge of the blue, and never quite seemed to focus on whatever she was looking at.

Keland's magic was gone . . . except for the quiet heart of it, left to dwell within a confused young girl.

Rethia woke feeling like there was something she'd forgotten to do, and she couldn't quite remember what; she waited in the thrall of the dream, lying in the quiet loft of her father's house and healing clinic. The night's noises pressed in on her like a muffled lullaby. Kacey, moving quietly around in the main house, tidying as she was wont to do on a sleepless night. An owl hooting in the woods tucked up close behind the house, and the rattling of the cold, late winter wind in the trees, slipping through her cracked-open shutters.

Not that long ago, there would have been other things—snow in the winter, insects in the summer—slipping through those shutters as well. Back when Keland had lost its magic, leaving the wizards of the land mystified—and searching for something else to do with themselves. Back when the people had learned to live without the convenience of spells to send messages, spells to protect themselves and heal themselves, and spells to keep bugs out of the house.

Back before Rethia, finally clarifying that mysterious, distracting inner call, had followed it to find the unicorns . . . and to open the door for them, to invite them home.

The magic had come with them, carried in by unicorn winds. But between their departure and their return—newly appreciated and newly protected—a generation grew up without magic; the generation before that had known only a diluted echo of that which they now lived with. Rethia often thought that learning to live with magic again was turning out to be much more difficult than learning to live without it. She herself had gloried in the unicorns' return, finding herself completely whole again for the first time since that day in the meadow. Though she still drifted easily into a vague state of contemplation, she also had moments of preternatural clarity, and an intuitive understanding of magic that no wizard could hope to learn. And though the unicorns did not often deign to show themselves to others, Rethia had memorized the soft feel of their muzzles, the coarse, thick profusion of their manes, and the smooth, cool and curious feel of their horns.

It didn't seem so simple to the other people in her world; the magic which had seemed to answer so many of the questions about her life created only confusion in others'. There were older wizards who'd been experts so long ago, suddenly expected to step into their old roles as though they hadn't lost a day of practice—and as though there were enough of them left alive to fill the ranks as they'd once done. And there was a chaos of people who'd suddenly felt full-strength magic thrumming through their souls for the first time in their lives—and who now suddenly had to struggle to control their abilities without the lifetime of practice and childhood experience that would have made doing so second nature.

And there were, in larger numbers, the people who didn't feel any difference at all, and whose reactions ranged from eager acceptance of the new resources and magical services, to those who wanted it regulated and banned and altogether out of their lives.

It made for an uneasy mix. Especially for the man who'd also been tangled up in magic's return, a man who was not only dangerously reactive to it, but who had watched his wife die by dark, stolen magic, and who'd lost a son to it before that. Who had, in the end, lost an entire way of life. Reandn, too, struggled to adjust to the magic he'd tried so hard to destroy, and which now threatened his life through its very presence in this world again. It seemed to her he was finally gaining ground in his fight against the bitterness and anger that had once permeated his every move, but Rethia still wished his transition had been as joyful and painless as hers. Lying in the overwarm loft, glad for the draft of cool air from the cracked shutters, she tried to imagine her life if she'd never recalled the unicorns or understood what had happened to her that day so many years ago, that which made her so different and so otherworldly.

And suddenly she wondered if she'd been the only one.

What if there were others, security against the risk that Rethia would die in childhood as so many children did, or that she'd simply never figure out how to open that door when the time was right? What if those others were still out there, still unfulfilled and confused about their own otherworldliness?

She needed to know, she realized. She needed to find them, if they were out there.

She just wasn't sure how to start.

Chapter 1

Teya dove behind a bush in panic as the enemy loosed one last volley from bow and sling, cringing as an arrow rattled through bare branches. With a strangled but heartfelt squeak of fear, she flattened herself closer to the wet, leafy ground cover of late winter. *Ardrith keep me for her own*— With Arval's wizard to hide the Wolf patrol in an illusion of silence and invisibility, and Teya to keep the enemy wizard distracted, the outlaws should have been surrounded, should have been overwhelmed, should have been *defeated*, dammit! Anything but this . . . this . . . *massacre*.

Another arrow hit the tree beside her, imbedding inches into the wood with a solid *thwack*. Teya screamed, flinging her arms protectively around her head—as if it would do any good—and had the sudden feeling she'd wet herself—but as long as she'd been hugging the sodden leaves, couldn't tell for sure. When the Hells had this gone so wrong? When she'd felt her wizard partner falter, bobbling the threads of the protection he'd woven for the Remote Wolf Patrol? When the first arrow had found its suddenly vulnerable mark, and the patrol Wolves, caught exposed in the dip between two hills, had been rushed from above by the outlaw leader's men?

Or maybe their crushing defeat had begun the moment Teya realized their wizardly opponent was at least as strong as she, and her sudden sweat tingled on equally sudden goosebumps of fear. This wasn't her specialty, this sparring with magic. She was expert at truth spells and detection spells, at the subtle forms of magical defense and at spinning her magic so quietly she caused no alarm in a citizenry just becoming used to having magic to spin. More than anything, she was adept at protecting others from the stir of magic her spells created, and it was this skill that had earned her the position of Patrol Wizard—not her ability to trade magical barbs of hate between two hills. Guilt settled around her as, across the battered slope, her comrades cried out in agonized death throes. And still she hid, because she'd barely been a Yearling in her Wolf training before magic's return snatched her away to wizardly schooling in Solace. No spell she could spin would help the dying patrol now, no physical bravado could turn the battle their way . . . it was far too late for that. Hide, hide and hope to live, that was her only choice. Hope the outlaws got tired and went to collect their own wounded while the surviving Wolves dragged themselves away from defeat.

A tiny remaining shred of common sense broke through Teya's guilt. The true first step of this defeat had been taken by those in ultimate command of this patrol—the Wolf Leader, Saxe, and the Prime, Ethne, who coordinated Keland's armed forces of Wolf, Hound, Fox and Dragon—when they'd given Minor Arval the authority to remove Reandn from leadership for the duration of this assignment.

Reandn had fought the assignment, he'd railed against its heavy reliance on magic, as he always railed against magic, even hers. He wouldn't have let the Minor's man position his Wolves into such physical vulnerability, relying only on magic for their safety. Teya was certain of it, even though she didn't really understand Reandn, didn't really know the man after only six months of service with him.

She wasn't even sure if she merely disliked him, or if she *intensely* disliked him.

But even Teya understood the reasons Saxe and Ethne had overridden Reandn's objections. With the Resiores struggling more than ever against the yoke of Keland's sovereignty, and inner Keland still in social turmoil two years after magic's return, King's Keep needed Highborn support from Minors like Arval. And they needed the confidence of Keland's people that the Keep could guide them safely through this chaotic time.

So when a wizard-driven band of ruthless outlaws started plundering Arval's hills, no wonder the Wolf leaders had decided that a fully cooperative effort to destroy the band was more important than heeding Reandn's well-known aversion to magic, even law-enforcing magic.

No wonder she was in this mess.

Teya risked a peek through the outer branches of the bush. Downhill, there were only bodies, ill-concealed by the leafless trees. A gasp caught in her throat as she recognized Apalla, one of Teya's closest friends, collapsed over the body of her partner, one hand loosely wrapped around the arrow that had killed her. To the side Teya discovered Sannat and Kessin, and below them, half hidden in the trees, three other bodies in quick succession.

No one was moving. Teya slowly stood up, exposing herself to danger but aware only of the dread caught in her throat, feeling like a scream that had gotten trapped halfway out and that might just kill her when it exploded free. Her new vantage point revealed a number of other bodies in Wolf colors, and one feebly thrashing form. "Oh, Tenaebra," she whimpered, but none of the sound made it past that trapped scream. "Oh, graces . . ."

A rustle of noise splintered grief into terror. She

whirled to face it, to the side that had been blinded by
the very bush and tree she hid behind, and found herself
staring at the enemy. An outlaw, blood dripping from
his hands and smeared in his untrimmed beard, his knife
covered with—

Teya stood frozen in shock. The man grinned at her.
"Giving 'em all the death stroke, I was. Didn't expect
to find a whole one amongst you. Must be a magic-user,
ey? All used up, are you?"

She just gaped at him, while a dim little voice in her
head screamed *run*, you idiot, *run*! But she didn't have
so much as a trickle of energy left even if she'd been
quick-witted enough to use it. It wasn't until he reached
for her, until his bloodied hand closed around her arm,
that her body woke up and reacted. The scream, trapped
in her throat so long, erupted at full volume, and she
snatched at her belt for her knife, finally falling back
to unfinished Wolf training.

He reacted before she had the weapon fully out of
its sheath, pulling her downhill a step or two and then
using the momentum to swing her against the tree. Teya
braced herself for the impact, but felt herself slip through
his bloodied grip; she crashed through the bush and
whiplashed around the tree with her shoulder as the
fulcrum. The joint gave way, and she cried out more at
the sound of it than the pain, crumpling at the base of
the tree. Dazed, she realized she'd dropped the knife,
and frantically patted the ground around her.

His foot came down on her hand, pinning it; she
whimpered as he shifted his full weight onto it. "Please . . ."
she said, looking up at him. It seemed a very long way.

"I think we'll keep you," he said. "You've got just
enough fight in you to make it fun."

Fear turned to horror. She tried to force her injured
arm to move, to find that knife—and couldn't. She tried
to muster the grit to fight him, at least to force him
into killing her, and couldn't do that, either. As if he
saw the conflict within her, he laughed.

But the laugh choked in the middle and turned into a grunt of amazement; awkwardly, he clawed at his own back. Teya jerked her hand free as he swayed, and scrabbled to get away from him. Still in utter lack of comprehension, he fell heavily and slid a short distance down the hill. Teya stared at the arrow protruding from his back and tried to understand it herself, for the fletching was undyed quill, the same as the outlaws had been using.

"Teya!" Dakina emerged from cover and scrambled along the hillside, limping badly and tossing an enemy bow aside. Relief washed over Teya along with the pain of her torn shoulder; she wasn't alone out here, not the only survivor high on the hill above where the outlaws collected their wounded. It seemed a good occasion to faint, and when the world greyed out, she didn't fight it.

Reandn paced the length of the Minor's great hall, scowling peevishly at the lavish use of wood and thinking just as peevishly that Arval would have done better, much better, to have thickened the walls of his keep with additional stone. He stopped and favored an ornate cornice with an especially grim look.

"Come now," Arval said from over his afternoon snack, his voice booming across the all-but-empty room. "What has my poor hall ever done to you?"

Reandn didn't respond, at least not outwardly. There was nothing wrong with the keep, he realized. Oh, it wasn't stonebound King's Keep, with its thick defensive walls and towers, but it didn't need to be. And the wood was cheap enough, in this part of Keland.

No, his building anger was more properly aimed at the Minor himself. "We should have heard something by now," he said, moving up to Arval's raised table. "You're sure that little keepmaster's apprentice can receive from your wizard?"

"He's not precise," Arval said, amiably enough, "but he manages the job."

Well he might be feeling amiable, given how quickly the Prime had jerked Reandn's authority over his patrol and handed it to Arval instead. *Amiable* was far from Reandn's reaction to it all. But Saxe had warned him to keep a tight rein on his mouth—Reandn could almost smile, remembering the look on Teya's reddened face when she'd had to relay that message—and Reandn, well aware of the Keep's need for Arval's confidence and support, had done his best to remain respectful.

It was getting harder by the moment. His patrol was out there under someone else's command, and his wizard was paired with Arval's, under the orders of someone who knew little of her personal strengths and weaknesses. Tenaebra's tits, he'd fought the idea of having a wizard in his patrol, even a fledgling one. But the Prime had insisted—and found him one who'd not only had a taste of Wolf training, but who excelled in shielding Reandn and his allergies from the very magic she worked. She bided by his rules and tried to hide her resentment at them, she never forgot to protect him when there was magic around, and she never ignored it when he felt the whisper of magic before she did.

And she was in *his* patrol, dammit—like the regular Wolf pairs, she was his to protect from the little stupidities that kept an already dangerous job from being unnecessarily life-threatening. And the big stupidities, too, Reandn thought, shooting a covert glare at the table. He had no idea what Arval's final strategy had been. He knew only that the man had planned to use the Wolves to snare a local magic-using outlaw while Teya and the Minor's own wizard flung prodigious magic around to ensure the ultimate success of the mission. That's all it had taken to get his hackles up and guarantee his initial refusal to cooperate.

Reandn knew better than to trust magic. As long as there was magic around, there was the potential that someone would try to use it against you, just as Ronsin had used it to kill Reandn's wife and son. And he'd learned quickly enough that the newest generation of wizards was only half-trained; even when they were using magic to help, it was almost bound to go awry and make things worse. Best to depend only on what the Wolves had always used—a quiet foot, a quick hand, and the wits they'd been blessed with.

They should have been back by now. Arval's wizard—Reandn had never even learned his name—should at least have sent word.

"Would you sit *down*?" Arval said, irritation creeping into his voice. "You're upsetting my digestion."

Might do you some good, Reandn managed not to say, thinking of the man's girth. Ah, well, there was a reason he'd rarely entered the main keep when he was Wolf First at King's Keep. Even when he'd kept his mouth shut, his opinions of some of the Highborn leaked out through the expression in his grey eyes.

He dropped off the dais and hooked the end of the lower table bench with his ankle, pulling it out to sit as Arval asked—but ended up right back on his feet when he heard someone approaching the entrance at the far end of the hall. Arval shot a quick glare at him, snapping, "Sit—"

Reandn raised a hand that cut Arval off—by the pure effrontery of the gesture, to judge by the strangled noise he made. By then the young keepmaster's apprentice was in the vast doorway, out of breath and struggling to maintain the appropriate dignity. "Meir!" he said, starting off well enough, though the rest of the words simply tumbled out of him. "One of the Wolves to see you, meir, right now, she says, meir, and it don't look good, meir—"

Arval came to his feet, rounding the main table and coming off the platform with his heavy-footed stride. Reandn was way ahead of him, though he stopped short when Teya—why Teya, out of all of them?—came up from behind the boy and around him, not waiting for permission to approach. She ignored Arval and fastened her eyes on Reandn, aiming herself straight at him, stumbling on the way. She was bruised and battered, her torn clothes grimed with blood and dirt. She held her right arm protectively against her body, and winced at the sight of Reandn's hand reaching to steady her elbow. He let the hand drop.

"First," she said, and got stuck there, unable to do anything but hold his gaze, her light brown eyes full of so many unspeakable words that he got stuck there right along with her. "Reandn—"

Arval stepped up beside Reandn and demanded, "Where's Yanwr? What are you doing here?"

Yanwr. The other wizard. Reandn gave Teya a fraction of a nod and she told Arval, "Yanwr's dead. I tried contacting the apprentice . . . I couldn't. So I came." She looked up at Reandn and her voice broke. "I'm the only one left who can ride, Reandn. Hells, I'm practically the only one—I mean, the rest are—most of them are . . ."

Reandn closed his eyes. *Dead*. They were dead. It didn't matter that she couldn't say it. He'd been on that hillside; he knew it. In his mind's eye he saw them there. In that instant, the grief that always lurked in him, the black chasm from Adela's death, loomed big enough to swallow him whole. His Wolves were gone, led into death by Arval's man. *His* Wolves, *his* responsibility—only Ethne had made it impossible to keep them out of magic's way.

He should have gone anyway. He should have done *something*, should have—

"What happened?" Arval demanded. "Come *on*, woman! Tell me!"

"Seveyga sent them out ahead, down between the hills . . . they were supposed to outflank the outlaws, and Yanwr was supposed to keep them unseen." She stopped, and gulped a hesitation. Reandn didn't have to open his eyes, to look at her expression; he heard what she wasn't saying clearly enough: *because otherwise there was no cover at all.* Seveyga had trusted the magic, magic alone. "I was supposed to keep the outlaw wizard's attention, but he was strong—he was so strong . . . he felt what Yanwr was doing anyway, and he stripped the spell away." Her voice fell to a whisper. "They didn't have a chance, they were caught at the bottom of the hill—"

Her voice broke off in a cry of pain as Arval shouted, "You let the outlaw past your defenses? It's *your* fault?"

Reandn's eyes snapped open; his grief flared into temper. Arval had a cruel grip on Teya's injured arm, and she had gone grey, unable to do anything more than clutch at the pain. Reandn instantly clamped down hard on Arval's forearm, digging his fingers into the clenched muscle there. Voice low and gravelly, he said, "You sent my Wolves out to a slaughter."

Arval dropped Teya's arm and turned on Reandn, florid in his anger, shoving himself up close. "Your Wolves were supposed to be the best!" His finger stabbed at the Wolf Pack patch on Reandn's shoulder, and at the lacings of rank below it. "They should have been able to handle these untrained outlaws!" *Jab, jab, jab* went the finger against Reandn's shoulder, hard enough so Reandn had to take a step back to maintain his balance.

Barely audible, Teya half-sobbed, "Oh, no, don't push—"

"And this wizard of yours! She left them wide open to outlaw magic!" *Jab, jab.* Reandn's face hardened, and his eyes grew dangerous. Saxe's remembered voice whispered restraint at him.

"No, *please* don't push hi—" Teya said, moving to put herself between Reandn and the Minor.

Arval turned on her. "*You!*" he said, and gave her a shove. "Mind your place!"

Teya stumbled a step backwards, bounced off Reandn, and fell, sprawling awkwardly, crying in agony.

Saxe's imagined voice of restraint disappeared in the roar of Reandn's fury.

❖   ❖   ❖

"Danny," Saxe said—Saxe's very own voice, along with Saxe's very own self, magicked from King's Keep for the occasion, "you broke his *nose*."

Reandn didn't answer. He and Saxe were in the nicest of what might genteelly be called the Arval Keep holding cells. It was clean and not too clammy, and had a hole in the corner instead of an unemptied bucket. Reandn suspected there were other cells somewhere on the grounds, and that they were kept less fastidiously.

"*Reandn.*" Saxe leaned against the vertically barred cell door, his voice growing tight. Lines of fatigue etched around his eyes, and there was a sprinkling of premature grey in his dark, short-cropped hair.

Reandn shrugged, his shoulders moving against the chill stone wall behind him. Remorselessness. His thumb rubbed across Adela's ring.

"Goddess damn, Reandn!" Saxe exploded, slamming the flat of his hand against the bars of the door. "When the *Hells* are you going to learn you can't keep doing this sort of thing? It's not what Wolf Justice *means*."

Reandn growled, "He lived. Most of my patrol didn't."

"And are you going to come after me, next? It was my voice in Ethne's ear—*my* call to keep you out of this one."

"It was a mistake!" Reandn snapped at him. "How did you think I would react when you set me aside? Those were *my Wolves*, Saxe, and you let Arval send them to be slaughtered!" He flung his words like a weapon, and they hit Saxe dead center.

The Wolf Leader's fatigue shifted into something more, and his eyes looked more haunted than angry. He rubbed a hand across his face and took a moment before meeting Reandn's gaze. His eyes held regret, and sorrow, and a certain resignation. "They're not your patrol anymore, Danny."

Reandn snorted. "No, they're mostly *dead*!" His anger turned into an anguished plea. "I haven't even *seen* them yet, Saxe—for Ardrith's sake get me out of here so I can *see* them, and see who's left alive."

"Dakina," Saxe said, absently rubbing the hand he'd slammed against the bars. "Teya, of course. Sahan should live, though he'll never work patrol again. Maybe Dreyfen . . . we don't know yet. Same for Maccus."

Reandn waited a moment for Saxe to continue before he realized that was the end of the list. *So few of them* . . . And suddenly he wasn't alone; he felt the soft whisper of a touch on his face, an equally soft whisper in his mind, murmuring comfort. *Adela*, drawn by his distress; how long had it been since he'd felt her presence? Closing his eyes, he set his jaw against the raw pain in his throat and after a minute was able to ask out loud. "So few?" His voice sounded every bit as raw as it felt.

Saxe nodded; he seemed to be searching for words and finally gave up, moving on to things more practical. Things easier to talk about. "There hasn't been a loss this great in the history of the service. I'd really like to talk to Yanwr; it was his failed spell that exposed them all, and Teya isn't sure just what happened. But of course Yanwr's dead with the rest of them, so we may never know." He looked straight at Reandn and repeated, "They're not yours anymore."

"We *do* know what happened. Seveyga put them in an indefensible position and then counted on magic alone to keep them safe. You should have made Arval reveal the details of his strategy before you turned him loose with my Wolves, Saxe, you should have kept him on a leash!"

"They're not your Wolves anymore."

This time, Reandn heard him. *Not his* . . . He found the edge of the cell's rickety cot and sat, stunned, staring blankly at Saxe. Former partner. Wolf Leader. Friend?

Saxe didn't seem to be able to meet his eyes anymore. "Arval wanted you celled until you turn green with mold. Ethne and I managed to talk him down to dishonorable dismissal."

"Ethne's here?" Reandn said, though the shock of that

barely left an impact after what he was certain he'd just heard.

Saxe nodded. "I could hate you for this, you know," he said, and Reandn looked at him in surprise, trying to match the words with the deep regret on his friend's face. "We trained together, we rose through the ranks together . . . Hells, we've been in this so long together that I'm practically in the *habit* of saving your Wolf neck after you pull something politically stupid. But . . . I can't do it this time." He shook his head. "You *idiot*, you've forced me to oust the best partner I ever had!"

It had been years since they patrolled as partners, since they'd each risen to the rank where they commanded the patrols instead of participating in them. But miles and years apart, they'd ever been tied to those days when they were paired in Wolf Patrols. Reandn cleared his throat. "Well," he said, "I . . . guess I . . ." *don't have any idea what to say, that's what*. He closed his mouth, tried to think about what it all meant, really *meant*, and failed.

Saxe said wearily, "You shouldn't have hit him, Danny."

Reandn tried to summon anger, and failed at that, too. He said simply, "Arval deserved what he got and *more*. Far more."

"That he did," Saxe agreed readily. "Oh, that he did. But sometimes we have to make trade-offs, Danny. Think about it. How are you going to protect them now?"

Elbows on knees, Reandn rested his face in his hands, suddenly recognizing where the bulk of his anger lay. He was their patrol leader. He should have marched them off the grounds of Arval Keep, orders or no; he should never have let them go out under Seveyga and Yanwr.

Saxe's voice was quiet. "Hindsight is a wonderful thing, Danny. This time, damn you, *learn* from it. I won't be around to smooth the ruffled feathers you cause. Not anymore."

Reandn's grim smile remained hidden. He knew what

Saxe meant to say. *Hold your temper. Think before you
act.* But what he'd actually said was something else
entirely. Reandn would learn from hindsight, all right.
The biggest mistake he'd made in this mess was in letting
rank and politics override his instincts about what was
best for the people he cared about.

Teya sat on the floor in front of Dakina's sickbed,
carefully keeping her own injured shoulder away from
Dakina's badly wounded leg. Dakina slowly ran a brush
through Teya's long, light brown hair, stopping to fuss
at every little snarl she ran into. It had taken only
moments for them to come to their new temporary
arrangement, and now Teya ran foot errands for Dakina,
while Dakina did two-armed jobs for Teya. At least for
a while.

In truth, Teya could almost certainly have brushed
her hair one-handed, but there was something about
the activity that comforted them both, and Ardrith knew
they both needed comforting in this makeshift sick house,
with the remnants of their patrol fighting for life around
them.

Both women were from the eastern edge of Keland,
a swampy land of hunters and fishers and a great many
recipes for frog meat. Not to mention poisonous snakes
and hidden spots of swamp sludge so soft and deep that
few ever escaped its grip. The very land had a way of
making one slow and careful, and prone to deciding
one's decisions twice.

Teya a'Apa and Dakina a'Pael were years apart in
age; Dakina had made her adjustments to the ways of
King's Keep and its Wolves several years before it had
occurred to Teya that being a Wolf meant learning to
make the snap decisions of folk who fought and stalked
their way through life. But their common homeland
meant that they understood one another, and that when
a fellow Wolf did something particularly grating to their
swampland sensibilities, they could roll their eyes at

one another and not have to add a single word to make
themselves understood.

Teya had been the best of the yearling trackers, but
in her heart, she understood that she wouldn't have made
it through final training, that she'd never have been able
to rely on her own instantaneous reaction, or to trust
it. That she'd been fortunate when the magic came along
and swept her away to Solace for a new kind of training.

Reandn's ability to act and react so swiftly set her back
each time she saw it, and reminded her of her failure
to do the same. If she'd been faster on the hill, could
she somehow have stopped the slaughter? All she
remembered was feeling confused and battered with
visual and magical input. She was, deep down, certain
that if it had been Reandn wielding the magic that day,
the patrol would have survived.

Then she snorted. Reandn, wielding magic. Now *there*
was a likely thought.

"What?" Dakina asked. She'd separated Teya's hair
into sections and was placing them here and there, as
if experimenting with how she wanted to braid it today.

"Just thinking," Teya said. "Just . . . thinking."

"I try not to do that," Dakina said dryly. "At least for
now." She pulled the hair up high on the back of Teya's
head and began braiding it from there. "Ribbons. We
need ribbons, don't you think?"

Teya snorted. "The pairs would laugh me right out
of the patrol."

"Maybe. It'd give them something to laugh *about*, at
least."

"Maybe we *do* need ribbons."

From the doorway of the small shed, Reandn said,
"I'll see to it."

Both women jumped. "Ow, *ow*," Teya complained as
Dakina twisted around, taking her hands—and Teya's
hair—with her.

"Sorry," Dakina muttered. "I wish I knew how he can
be so damned *quiet*."

"It balances out the rest of the time, when you can't possibly ignore him," Teya muttered back.

Dakina swiftly finished off the braid as Reandn came inside the roughly finished outbuilding, and Teya's first glance at him inspired another, more narrow-eyed examination of her patrol leader. Fatigued, unshaven, the short, thick scar along the angle of his jaw standing out more than ever. He'd obviously slept in his clothes, and his hair, its length recently cut to a much shorter style, had fallen into place without the benefit of brush or comb. It was to his eyes she looked when she was trying to gauge his mood, the grey eyes that were so compelling beneath the contrast of dark brows and dark blond hair.

This time, she couldn't read them. Neither, to judge by Dakina's look, could she. And the others . . . well, Sahan was asleep, dosed into a stupor by Arval's healer. With any luck he'd stay that way for a while; his mangled arm kept him in agony otherwise. Dreyfen and Maccus were unconscious, fighting for their lives. A young woman sat between them; not the healer, but a sensitive—someone without much power to wield magic, but enough perception to sit vigil, and to call the healer if anything went wrong. At the moment she was watching Reandn, her expression guarded.

Reandn nodded at her, and moved a few steps closer to the wounded men, regarding them silently for a moment. She shouldn't be watching him, Teya thought, she should give him a little privacy. But she watched anyway, thinking at first that he was callous and unreacting, and then seeing how his thumb worried the ring on the little finger of the same hand. His dead wife's ring, his worry stone. The thing that always gave him away. His breath caught in his throat, just like hers had done so often in the last day.

That's all it had been. One day.

When he turned back to the women, Teya suddenly realized how weary he looked. Not just tired, but worn down, almost . . . defeated. He shifted his jaw sideways ever so slightly, an ear-popping gesture—the unconscious habit that meant the magic was troubling him. She wanted to say something to him, *anything* . . . but her mind remained blank and uncooperative.

After all, what could she say? Nothing but the same hollow words she'd tried on herself, and she simply wasn't used to casual conversation with him.

"They'll get you out of here soon," Reandn said, as if he hadn't been breaking an awkward silence, but had been in the middle of a conversation all along. "As soon as the men are strong enough to take the Wizard's Road, you'll be sent to King's Keep, where you'll stay somewhere better than an emptied storage shed."

"King's Keep?" Dakina said carefully. "What about . . ." She trailed off and looked at Teya, who in turn looked at what was left of their patrol and finished asking the question.

"What about the Remote? Are we being disbanded?"

"Arval already managed that, I think," Reandn said, and his face hardened. "If you heal well enough, you'll be put back in the Remote. Saxe'll save a place for you, and they're going to be adding a second Remote to the Maurant-King's Keep Road as well. You'll get priority for placements in either of them." He eyed Teya. "I've been told you'll be going to Solace for a while."

Teya glanced up at Dakina, feeling herself close down into cautiousness. "That's good, I suppose. I can learn a lot while I heal." It wasn't like they'd pronounced her a fully trained wizard when she'd left the school there, after all—they'd been quite clear that she'd been chosen for her particular strengths, and that she'd be expected to continue schooling at every opportunity. "But . . . will you . . . want me back?"

There—it had happened again. Another swift expression that Teya just couldn't decipher, abruptly replaced with a layer of the assertiveness Reandn usually projected.

"Teya, what happened was not your fault," he said,

an edge to his voice. "Have any of Arval's people said anything to you? Because if they have—" He stopped suddenly, ducked his head for a swift, if fleeting, grin, and finished, "Well, I guess I won't break any more noses. But I *will* have Saxe set a guard on you all. In fact, I think I'll do it regardless. There's no need for Arval's people to have access to you, aside from the healer."

Teya just frowned at him, trying to understand the undercurrent of his expressions. There was something going on here that she didn't know about, and it was as if she didn't quite know him anymore—or as if he didn't quite know himself.

He watched her for a moment, and said, "I couldn't get here any sooner. It's taken since yesterday evening to get things settled with Arval."

Yesterday evening. That's when Saxe and Ethne had arrived, Teya knew. They'd come to talk to her, and had asked her the details of what had happened—which had turned out to be a good thing, because she could tell from their faces that what she was saying was considerably different from Arval's report. She said, "Saxe told us it might be a while before you made it here."

He relaxed a touch. Relief. Now *that*, she could recognize. "I've given the patrol's personal gear to Saxe. He'll make sure it goes to the right families, along with the commendation pay you all earned. Tomorrow . . ." he hesitated only an instant here, but Teya knew what was coming. "Tomorrow in the main hall, there'll be a ceremony honoring our dead. I'll make sure you get there if you want to, but . . . I won't be there. Obvious reasons. Saxe and I are holding the Binding come nightfall, a private one. If you want to come . . ."

"Oh, yes," said Dakina.

"Yes," Teya whispered. She couldn't care less about Arval's empty ceremony. But she wanted to light a torch for each of her fallen pack members, to be part of the ritual that came after any encounter where the Wolves lost more than one pack member—the Binding. However many torches there were, they'd end up bound together, an offering to Tenaebra. If the goddess listened, then it would be that much easier for the fallen Wolves to find one another in the many layers of Tenaebra's heavens.

Wolves seldom went to Ardrith's heavens. Ardrith gathered the souls released by old age and disease, and left those who died in violence to her sister.

Reandn looked away from them. It was a deliberate evasion, and Teya felt her old exasperations with him coming to the fore. He wasn't telling them something, and she was halfway to blurting out a demand to hear it. He said, "After the Binding . . . I'm going up to Little Wisdom. We've all decided it's best if I don't stay on here."

"But what about those outlaws?" Dakina asked. "We took a bite out of 'em, but nothing that'll stop 'em."

Reandn shook his head. "Not our problem anymore. If Arval is smart, he'll ask Solace for help—that's what he should have done in the first place. Cut the wizard out of that crew, and the rest'll be as easy to nail as any band that's gotten too predictable."

"*We* could have done it," Teya muttered, smarting a bit over that one. Either he was saying he hadn't trusted her to handle them from the start, or he was saying the Remote wasn't up to handling wizards in the first place.

Dakina looked at her, puzzled. "Of course we could have done it. If the man had just let us go in there like we always do, with you checking it out for us and Reandn calling the orders."

He gave Dakina what might have been a grateful look. "Keep that in mind," he said. "What happened out there wasn't your fault, either of you."

He'd said that before. Teya looked back to his eyes, still trying to decipher what she saw there. On impulse, she said, "It wasn't yours, either."

That got a reaction. His shoulders drew back, his expression shuttered down, and all he left to her was the slight gathering of his eyebrows—the edges of anger. She'd overstepped the bounds of rank with that one, and Teya waited for cold, quick words that would tell her so. She'd certainly heard them often enough, and usually over the use of her magic.

He said nothing. He eyed the three unconscious men again, and then deliberately turned away, walking by the two women without saying anything. Dakina touched Teya's shoulder, catching her eye for a minute and giving a familiar shrug. *Don't mind him.*

To Teya's surprise, Reandn stopped in the doorway and turned back to them, hesitating. Then he offered them a Wolf salute, his closed fist just touching the base of his throat. Teya returned it without thinking, as did Dakina beside her, and by then Reandn was gone.

Teya suddenly found herself wondering about all the unspoken words of the last moments, realizing just how many there had been. She wondered just what Reandn wasn't telling them.

And she wondered why she suddenly had the impulse to label that look in his eyes as *loneliness.*

Chapter 2

Sky laid his ears back and looked at Reandn from the corner of his eye, nostrils wrinkled in excessive irritation at the sight of the bridle in Reandn's hand. The notion of being bridled before he'd finished the last wisps of his morning hay! Reandn offered a pat in apology and tried not to laugh out loud.

Sky. Dark bay racking horse, back hock scarred enough to limit his flexion and give his rolling gait a slight hitch. Oversensitive, defensive, wanting nothing more than a rider who could see through it all and give him the steadiness he needed. Sky, the horse who'd run himself to death at Reandn's request, racing to keep Ronsin away from the magic that would make him more dangerous than ever.

And Sky, the horse who'd then been healed by unicorns. A walking testament to Rethia's success in returning both unicorns and their magic to a magic-barren land.

A testament who hadn't finished his breakfast, thank you very much, and who didn't have the slightest interest in maintaining the dignity his unique status conferred to him. He flattened his ears, flared his nostrils, and tilted his head warningly, his teeth all but bared.

Reandn poked him gently in the shoulder. "Stop that."

His bluff called, Sky's ears flipped forward, and he waited for both bridle and the treat that would follow. Just as well he never cared how withered the winter-stored carrots were, considering the abuse Reandn took in order to filch them from the various kitchens he had access to at any given time.

He bridled the horse and gave him his expected chunk of rubbery old carrot, untangling Sky's forelock and mane from the bridle crown piece with careful fingers and an affectionate pat. There was no true guile in the bay; he was as easy to read as a signpost, if somewhat less consistent.

His saddlebags packed and bulging, winter gear stowed over them—for while Reandn intended to stay at roadhouses for the eight days' travel to Little Wisdom, he wasn't taking any chance of getting caught unprepared in the changeable late winter weather—and Sky finally bridled and amiable, Reandn led his horse out into the cold morning wind. His goodbyes, such as they were, had been said, his patrol honored in the Binding ceremony, and his back pay dispensed.

Somehow he wasn't surprised to find Saxe waiting for him by the keep gate. That gate had probably never been closed, but at least it had a guard—not that the guard would have enough time to sound a useful warning, with the way the tree line had been allowed to creep up on the keep wall. Arval was depending on some kind of perimeter spell to warn him of trouble, Reandn imagined. He'd have been mighty uneasy in the guard's shoes.

The guard stepped away from Saxe as Reandn approached, his expression an interesting mixture of curiosity and disdain. Reandn had seen a lot of that expression in the past few days; Arval's small collection of keep guards and strongarms seemed to regard him as stupid for hitting their Minor, but at the same time they wondered about the mettle of the man who'd dared to do it.

Saxe stood in the lee of the gate, his wool-lined collar flipped up to cover his neck and ears, his hands shoved deeply into his pockets. Reandn felt the wind more strongly just looking at him, and shivered, hoping for some sun once daylight fully arrived. He hunched inside his own wool-lined jacket, Wolf-issue minus the patch that declared it so, and tucked his neck cape more snugly under his chin. He asked, "Come for some parting I-told-you-sos?"

Saxe shook his head, but didn't seem to take offense. "There aren't any told-you-sos that are worth this wind to make." He shrugged inside the jacket. "Just came to say goodbye to a friend, and wish him well."

"I'll be around," Reandn said. "Probably causing you just as much trouble, one way or the other."

"Going to Kacey's place for a while?"

Reandn lifted an eyebrow at him. "Most people call it Teayo's." Kacey's father still supervised the healing at his home sickroom, and still made most of the house calls, though his age and girth were finally starting to slow him down.

Saxe shrugged again. "She's the one I first met there; she's the one I think of. Besides, she's got a memorable personality. Hells, when you two are in the same room, the words must fly as sharp as knives. Not much like you and Dela."

"Nothing is like me and Dela," Reandn said, his words just as sharp as the ones Saxe imagined. That comment earned him yet another shrug, and Reandn knew he'd been unfair. Saxe might not miss Adela like Reandn did, but she'd been his friend, and he missed her all the same; he wasn't truly equating the two women.

There was no equating Kacey to anyone, Reandn was learning. She was too much . . . her own person. Which was why, he supposed, they did indeed trade more than the ordinary number of edged words—although between and even *during* such moments, the depth of her affection for him usually managed to peek out. Well, they'd see what happened once he was around more often. He couldn't go too far from the healers' clinic in any case, because Rethia—Kacey's foster sister—was there, and it took Rethia's unicorn-gifted touch to keep his potentially fatal reaction to magic at bay.

Reandn twisted in the saddle, looking back at the small outbuilding that housed his—no, *not* his anymore— surviving patrol members. "I wish you'd let me tell them." To really say goodbye, he meant, instead of neglecting to mention he wouldn't be back from this particular visit to Little Wisdom.

"I'm sorry," Saxe said, and meant it. "They need something to hold them together while they deal with the shock of this. By the time they learn the truth, they'll already be separated, and able to deal with the fact that they won't be reuniting under your command."

"I think that's a mistake, too," Reandn said, and at Saxe's frown added, "splitting them up, and keeping them that way."

"Teya's the least injured of them, and she's got to take the chance to learn more about magic."

"But the rest of them? And you should keep Teya and Dakina together. They understand one another as well as pairs that have been together for a dozen years."

"As well as you and I?" Saxe said wryly. "I suppose you're right. I've seen that in them, these last few days. I'll keep it in mind—but that's all I can promise."

Reandn scowled; Sky shifted beneath him, lifted a hoof to paw the ground, and thought better of it. "What's going on with the Keep these days, Saxe? You never used to sacrifice your Wolves for anything, always had the good of the pack in mind."

Saxe raised his eyebrows, then shook his head, careful to keep his collar closed to the wind. "Nothing changes, does it, Danny. You've never paid enough attention to Keep affairs."

Nothing changes? Reandn snorted, and might have put it into words, but Saxe spoke right over him.

"That's not really just, I suppose, given that you've been Remote for so long. But you should have kept better track. The Resiores are a mess."

"Nothing new about that. Things have been that way since before I left the Keep."

Saxe shook his head, still hunched within his collar. "Not like this. Not like it's been since the magic came back."

"Surprise," Reandn said dryly, and suddenly, for a moment, they were a team again, commiserating about the way Keep affairs made a Wolf's job harder.

Saxe gave him a rueful grin. "Half of the Resioran Highborn embrace magic and Keland, and half of them want to break away for Geltria, where the unicorns run thin and so does the magic. The people fall just about evenly on both sides, and the merchants—who are, as ever, fussing over Keland tariffs and taxes—do a good job of keeping them all stirred up."

"We've got good people in the Resiores, Saxe. They'll get things settled."

"Maybe." Saxe shoved Sky's head away as the gelding decided to inspect Saxe's left ear. "But no one really believes it. Otherwise, we wouldn't have taken in that unofficial Resioran representative last fall."

Reandn absently lifted a rein, recapturing Sky's attention. "Why did you? Two factions, one representative . . . sounds like trouble, to me."

"I wish you'd gotten around to asking me earlier, when I was standing somewhere *warm*," Saxe said pointedly. "You're right. It could be trouble. But we had to do something, and accepting an official ambassador seemed like the best thing. Once the pass opens up again— which it ought to do within the moon's change—we're going to have to do everything right if we're to avoid war. War with the Resiores, or civil war in the Resiores themselves . . . Goddess grace, so far Geltria is just waiting to see how things play out. Sooner or later, they'll join the fray."

Saxe closed his eyes, shook his head, and the tension in his red, wind-bitten face gave Reandn a glimpse of the difficulties his friend had been facing. Difficulties he certainly hadn't made any easier. *Not that I wouldn't do it again* . . . Saxe said, "Do you really think we'd have given Arval authority over your patrol if his—and every other Minor's—support wasn't absolutely crucial right now? We've got enough going on, trying to manage the changes in Keland itself. We're not going to be able to handle both Keland and the Resiores if men like Arval don't do everything—and I mean every damn thing—in their power to help us."

Reandn grinned, one-sided and wry-around-the-edges. "Sounds like I'm lucky not to be still stuck in that cell, if the Keep is courting its Minors that seriously."

"Don't forget it," Saxe said, meaning it. "I fought for you, Danny. But there's just too much at stake."

There didn't seem to be anything to say to that. Reandn lifted one gloved hand for a salute, and Saxe took his hand out of his pocket to return it. "Take the quiet roads, Danny. If you can find them."

There was only one road to Little Wisdom from here, and it wasn't to it that Saxe referred. "If I can find them," Reandn repeated into his neck cape. Sky flicked back an ear in response, and Reandn gave him the infinitesimal squeeze of leg that meant *go*. Gratefully, Sky popped forward in the odd hop-start he used in deference to his scarred hock, and settled into a quick, steady rack.

Kacey fought the laundry, grappling with the sheets in the stiff breeze of the afternoon. Now was the only time of day the sun hit the clothesline, and the only time in the last ten days they'd had sun at all, and she'd be bloody-damned if she'd miss the chance to get things clean *and* dry. At least, dry without hanging things all over the house; quite a sight when they were full up from the results of late winter ills. Thank the goddess—either one, Kacey didn't care—that as her father Teayo had slowed, they'd hired a part-time cook along with their new healer apprentice. Maybe it was even time to get someone to help with the chores around here, so Kacey could devote more energy to healing. She knew she'd never be a gifted healer like her father, or inspired like Rethia. But she excelled at running the sickhouse, and in mixing medicines and herbs—and she knew her limits. All crucial skills to have in a healer's house.

Rethia, too, was more help than she'd once been; she still walked around in her own private fog half the time, but when she came back to Kacey and Teayo's world, she was much more apt to notice the practical aspects of life. She was inside right now, stirring the next batch of sheets in the giant cauldron that served to warm the water.

Her father's wizard friend Farren had just given them a new spell to make fireless heat, and then spent days tutoring their young and fumbling healer-mage, Tellan, to use it. It was, Kacey thought, one of the few truly useful spells to reach their household since magic's return. Not that she didn't enjoy seeing chameleon shrews and unicorn sign, and watching the odd stream of thick magic bubble past in the breeze, but none of that was much help when there was laundry to wash and not quite enough wood gathered to do the chore properly.

The noise of wind-snapped sheets and bandages filled her ears and left room for little other sound; her hair blew into her mouth and eyes and her wet fingers grew clumsy in the cold. Rethia, slender to the point of too thin, would be shivered into uselessness by now. Kacey herself was chilled enough, despite two layers of sweaters over her tunic, topped off by one of her father's huge wool shirts, and the long-legged underwear under her loose trousers. Unlike Rethia, she had plenty of her own padding, but she was still glad enough when the last long bandage dangled from the clothesline. She left the basket where it was and turned to run back into the house—only to discover that she wasn't alone, and probably hadn't been for some time.

There, in the lane that wound through the trees between the main road and the large open yard of the house and barn, stood Sky. Reandn sat on him, reins long and looping, hands stuffed in his jacket pockets, grinning that lopsided grin that always made Kacey go a little soft inside—though at the same time she had to fight the urge to shake the expression right off his face. She'd never really come to understand that one.

"Damn Wolf!" she cried at him, nonetheless closing the distance between them with some speed. "*Always* sneaking up on people."

Reandn dismounted, keeping the grin. "Only the ones who aren't paying any attention. No matter how I ask him, Kacey, Sky does insist on putting his feet down. Never fails to make noise."

"Damn noisy laundry then," she said promptly, and gave him a hug. His arm settled comfortably around her shoulders, giving her a little squeeze as he flipped the reins over Sky's head and they walked up toward the barn together. "We weren't expecting you," she said, and stopped, giving Reandn a narrow-eyed look. "You're all right, aren't you? You haven't done anything to get your allergies flared up?"

"I'm fine," Reandn said, lifting both hands in a mercy plea despite the fact that one was still over her shoulder and the other was in Sky's face. The horse snorted in irritation.

Kacey didn't reduce the intensity of her gaze. Something was up; it showed in his eyes, where everything always showed.

Rethia came running out of the house, her face reddened by the heat of the laundry cauldron, her body covered by nothing more than the light tunic and kirtle she'd donned for the chore. "Reandn!" she cried. "I *knew* I felt you coming!" She flung her arms around his neck, gave him a quick kiss on the cheek, and then stepped back to give him space. One of her wise moments, Kacey thought. Reandn had never quite reconciled himself to the fact that Rethia had returned the magic he'd fought so hard to keep out of Keland—or to the fact that he'd considered killing her to prevent it. Such irony that it was Rethia and Rethia alone, with her unicorn-gifted magic, who could soothe Reandn's allergy to the magic that otherwise would have killed him.

Rethia knew of his conflict, Kacey was certain. But she was never one to let things get in the way of the happiness of a moment.

"What do you mean, you *felt* him coming?" Kacey asked, suddenly hearing the words. Rethia had felt him from the steamy kitchen, when Kacey hadn't known he was practically within arm's reach? That hardly seemed fair.

"Just that," Rethia said. "Like a scent on the current of magic. An aura. Everyone's is different; I can feel where Father is right now, if I think about it. Can't you?"

"Of course we can't," Kacey said, and felt Reandn's arm tighten around her shoulder. She glanced up at him and discovered he was laughing, laughing and shaking his head.

"Just another one of those Rethia things," he said.

As if *he* had to tell her about Rethia things. She'd been living with her foster sister since she was fifteen and Rethia was six, dammit. But she sighed and closed her eyes and nodded, recognizing that her snappishness came from being unable to reach out to her father— no, be honest, to Reandn—when Rethia did it so easily that she took it for granted and had never until this moment mentioned anything about magical auras. No, it *wasn't* fair. So be it. "Rethia," she said, "you're going to freeze."

Indeed, Rethia was already shivering. "Come inside," she said. "I'll have some hot tea waiting."

"Make sure Tellan makes a sickroom check, too," Kacey said. "Some of them will need a trip to the bathroom by now, and help getting there."

"He was doing it when I left," Rethia said over her shoulder, already heading for the house, hugging herself for warmth. "Oh, I never thought I'd miss that laundry! Hurry!" She ran the rest of the way back, heading straight for the door that led to the kitchen at the back of the house.

"I'm colder just from looking at her shiver," Reandn said, removing his arm from her shoulder to tug Sky's girth loose. "Late spring we're having this year."

Kacey gave him a push toward the little barn. "Stall that strange horse of yours and let's get inside then."

But Reandn just looked at her a moment, easily absorbing the nudge. Then he carefully reached out a hand to extract the hair that had blown into her mouth— yet again—and tucked it behind her ear. "Don't change," he told her, and led the horse away.

Kacey stared after him, and wondered just what, under the surface—for there was so much of Reandn that was under the surface—that was supposed to mean.

"Well," Rethia said, looking at Reandn with a little frown, "it really hasn't been all that long since I did this, especially if that medicine is doing any good. Is it?"

Reandn shrugged. "It could be. Then again, I haven't been exposed to all that much magic of late, so it's hard to tell."

They sat before the long table at one end of the kitchen, the one place in this house where Reandn truly felt at home. It was a huge kitchen, and always busy—full of pungent boiling herbs, cooking meals, stewing laundry— and it served as the informal social center for the house. At the other end of the long room, there was a closed-off area for bathing, set close to the stove for warmth and convenience. Compared to this kitchen and the sickroom, the rest of the house was quite small—a great room with two tiny sleeping chambers off the back, and the loft where Rethia slept. Below the kitchen was a dug-out storage cellar where Reandn was certain he could find at least a few shriveled old carrots, and that was just about it.

There was the small barn, of course, and the several outbuildings, all of which held tools with which he was more than familiar. It seemed to Reandn that Teayo made a serious effort to save up chores for Reandn to handle in his regular, if infrequent, visits. Reandn found that he never really minded—which didn't keep him from muttering when he was repairing shingles on a hot day, or from contriving to look as miserable as possible when he helped fork new hay into the barn and the intense dustiness bothered the faint, all-too-normal allergies that everyone seemed to have when immersed in hay.

That was how Kacey had thought to try mixing thick herb extracts for his magic allergies—after she'd dosed him because of one particularly dusty wagon, half of which had been thrown out because of mold, and he'd noticed a slight effect on the undertone of magic thrumming in his head.

The undertone was always there, now; it had become a permanent part of his life the day Rethia retrieved the unicorns. Untreated, it grew into a disorienting, dizzying roar, while his chest tightened and his lungs labored, until eventually, he could no longer breathe at all. It had happened once; once he'd almost been in the Heavens with Adela and their adopted son Kavan. Thoughtfully, Reandn fingered the fine white line that slashed diagonally across his left palm, a reminder of that day. For a while, he'd all but sought out a death that would reunite him with Adela, Tenaebra's death. Life had eventually recaptured his attention, but death no longer scared him, and that made him more reckless than he might have been.

Rethia gently appropriated his hand, tracing her finger along the scar. "She doesn't come back so often any more, does she."

Reandn didn't even ask. Of course Rethia knew. She always knew. He took his hand back and curled it around the warm tea mug, feeling the clink of Adela's ring against the fired clay. "Not so often, no." She'd warned him that it would be like that, during those last few sweet moments together the time he'd almost died.

Kacey shifted on the bench seat opposite him, never comfortable at the thought of Adela's presence. Her face was red with warmth, though she'd already stripped off all her extra layers—as had he. Tendrils of hair curled damply on her cheeks, escaping from the tie that had captured the rest of the curls since their arrival into the kitchen warmth. She was pretty, Kacey was, though Reandn didn't think she knew it; it was the sort of pretty that didn't strike him right away, but crept up on him slowly until one day it suddenly seemed obvious. But she was always too busy glaring at her short stubby fingers, and hiding her figure—quite well-padded, but hardly shapeless—under the oversize shirts and loose trousers she habitually wore, and he doubted it had ever seemed obvious to her.

Rethia was watching him, watching as if she knew . . . *something*.

"Better do it before your sheets and underwear boil to mush," he suggested to her; she gave him a wiser look than he liked before putting her hands on either side of his head. Reandn closed his eyes for the moment when the world would give a sudden little *lurch*, and then the noise in his ears retreated to a faint whisper he heard only if he went looking for it. Opening his eyes to Rethia's inquiring expression, he said, "I don't think you can ever do that often enough. Especially now . . . I've gotten too accustomed to having a patrol wizard who can shield me from things." Even now, he felt the spell on the cauldron working against his body; it was only then he noticed that the thing was boiling without a fire in the pit beneath it. And then he saw the look on Kacey's face, and realized that she hadn't missed the import of his words.

"I knew something had happened," she said. "I knew it. Is she dead, Dan? What was her name—Teya?"

Reandn gave a short and bitter laugh. "No. She's one of the very few left alive."

Kacey stiffened. Back by the cauldron, Rethia dropped the claw-footed clothes handler, ignoring the fact that it immediately sank along with the garments she'd been retrieving.

"Tellan," Kacey called into the house, not taking her eyes off Reandn, "come turn this heat off." In a more normal tone, she added, "I have the feeling we're done with laundry for the day."

The cook arrived, was introduced to Reandn as Lydda, and promptly set about cooking a bland supper for the sickhouse occupants. Neither Kacey nor Rethia seemed to have reservations about speaking freely in front of the woman, but Reandn found himself watching her until he realized she was simply too absorbed in her task—and making too much of her own noise—to care what they were saying at the other end of the long kitchen.

And so he told Teayo's daughters what had happened. Rethia simply watched him with the even, unnerving blue and brown gaze to which he'd finally grown accustomed; Kacey frowned most of the time. She'd met most of the patrol—though not Teya, who'd gone on to Solace—when Reandn brought them in to get rid of the head lice with which they'd managed thoroughly to infect one another. That had been midway through winter . . . not so very long ago.

When she frowned over Arval's broken nose, he knew what that was about, too, though she had the wits not to say anything out loud. And as the kitchen filled with the smell of baking bread and the cook propped open the back door to let the heat out, Reandn told them he was no longer a Wolf, and let the statement settle into silence.

After a moment, Kacey narrowed her eyes at him. Big and brown and often full of sparks, those eyes were entirely too perceptive. "You're just sitting there," she said. "It's obvious how you feel about your patrol, and about Arval, and I'd have thought I could've predicted how you'd feel about getting kicked out of the Wolves. But you're just sitting there, and I *can't* tell. How *do* you feel about it?"

Reandn caught himself just short of rolling his eyes. Trust Kacey not to make the obvious assumption, but to ask the same question he'd been asking himself ever since he'd finally understood Saxe's words. Rethia just smiled her quiet smile, and that figured, too.

They'd both know if he was lying, so he gave them the only truth he had. "I'm not sure."

Rethia nodded, as if it made perfect sense to her, and got up to join the cook. For her, the conversation was over; she knew what she needed to know. Whatever that was.

Not so Kacey. "You don't *know*?"

Frowning, Reandn looked at the bottom of his empty mug. Escaped tea leaves plastered themselves to its rough glaze, and gave his eyes something to do while his mind wandered off. No, he didn't know, and it somehow seemed that that honest answer should be enough for now. His life as a Wolf had changed so much since those days in King's Keep, when he'd had Adela and Kavan, his secure rank as Wolf First, and a predictable pattern of days and seasons. When Adela had once challenged him to imagine what it would be like if he suddenly lost his place in the Wolves, he'd been unable even to consider it.

Kacey sighed loudly, and Reandn looked up at her in surprise, only then realizing he'd ignored her question entirely. Well, perhaps not entirely. Just out loud. "I . . ." he said, and then got lost again, unable to find words he was willing to say.

"*You*." Kacey repeated dryly, half mocking him but

mostly just giving up. "Fine. Try this one. What're you going to do now?"

For the first time Reandn realized how he'd come to take Teayo's little haven for granted. "I was hoping . . . I've got some thinking to do, and it's safe here."

From the magic, he meant, for even if he inadvertently exposed himself to too much of it, he'd have Rethia's healing touch nearby. Besides, he'd lay odds they had another round of chores heaped up and waiting for him.

Kacey *did* roll her eyes, then. "Of course you can stay here," she said. "Rethia'll come sleep with me, and you can have the loft—considering how full the sickroom is, and what it's full *of*. That's not what I *meant*."

"No," he agreed, understanding that, now. She was asking another one of the things over which he hadn't been able to gather his thoughts.

"Be natural enough to hire out at a private keep, and do just the things you're good at now, I suppose. If you could find someone who didn't mind blunt words."

He showed teeth in a not-smile, an expression that had once taken her aback but to which by now she was well accustomed. "I'm more concerned about finding someone who hasn't been seduced into flinging magic around."

She scowled at him, but it wasn't at *him*. "That . . . won't be easy."

Rethia, dipping into the conversation from where she was stirring what smelled like bean soup, said, "People with your allergies used to be a great asset, Farren told us once."

"That was in court, Rethia," Kacey said, tucking her hair behind her ear again, her face less flushed now that Lydda's open door kept the heat down. She glanced at Reandn; he looked away, feeling an unaccustomed chagrin. Born of a camp follower, shoved in as kitchen help in King's Keep as soon as he was old enough to turn a spit, teased and scorned until he'd proven he could fight back and then mostly ignored until he'd earned his way into the Wolves—a happenstance rare enough to be called unheard of, for the Wolves came from higher born blood than that—how was he *supposed* to feel about the Highborn? And, more importantly, how was he supposed to change those feelings now, when he was a man grown and in his prime?

He wasn't. He couldn't. And Kacey knew it just as well as he did. He glanced at her, finding exasperation— but finding it tinged with affection.

"I know," Rethia said. "But still . . ." And then she tilted her head, looking toward the sickroom as if she could see through walls. "Kacey," she said, putting the long-handled soup spoon aside.

Kacey stood up. No one was surprised to hear Tellan calling for her an instant later, his adolescent voice breaking midway through her name. "You'll stay here for as long as you want, that's all you need to know for now. My father will tell you what needs doing." As she left the room, Rethia on her heels, Kacey gave him a little grin and said, "You can start by checking that laundry. In this wind, it just might be dry!"

Reandn jammed the narrow, pointed post-hole shovel into the ground long enough to take off his jacket and toss it over the fence section that was still standing. Rethia's horse, Willow, stuck his head out of his end stall and stretched it almost to the barn door, longingly eyeing the sunny paddock. From within, Sky snorted impatiently. The immediate clamor of hooves followed: Kacey's little black mare, just as displeased to be stalled on such a calm and sunny day, and taking out her own impatience on the stall partition. Sky kicked back.

"Watch that hock!" Reandn hollered at the barn. "It's your own fault you're in there!" Which it was. Sky had never quite come to terms with the fact that he was gelded late in life, and he'd been pestering the black mare mercilessly since she'd come in season. A little flirt, a little posturing from Sky, and a squeal or two later the sound of splintering wood—and the horses were trotting free through hanging laundry, quite pleased with themselves.

The laundry survived. The fence post didn't.

Reandn was just grateful that the ground had thawed enough to take the bite of the shovel. He jammed the blade deep into the hole and twisted, breaking up the dirt, and then peered down to decide enough was enough. He could barely reach the bottom of the hole to clear the dirt as it was.

Dropping in the new fence post, he held it upright and trickled rocks in around it, then slipped the rails into place before kicking the dirt back in the hole and tamping it down. This work was just the sort of thing he'd done for Teayo these past ten days, the kind of thing that kept his body moving and his mind more or less free.

Not that the thinking time had done him any good. He still didn't have any answers, any new direction for his life. He was an anomaly, a man trained to elite standards of physical arts who couldn't travel far from this clinic and Rethia's healing touch—who, if he took a direct hit from strong magic, might not even make it back to receive that touch. Yet staying here, trading off chores to slink around behind Rethia's protection, didn't set well at all.

Even so, when he stood, pulling his shoulders back in a stretch, he eyed the other posts in the fence. It'd be a good thing to pack stones into the softening dirt around them, and make sure they didn't wiggle enough to stress and break. Otherwise, the way Sky and the mare had been acting, he would be right back out here digging post holes. He slipped out of the paddock and away from the boot-sucking mud the horses had churned up, and walked the outside of the fence line.

He hadn't gotten far when he felt the first sly buzz of magic in his ears. He stiffened, stopping where he was, realizing not only that someone worked magic nearby, but that they were working it on *him*. Not a great magic, not something that posed any real threat to his allergies, but *magic*. Just the thought of it kicked his anger into dangerous territory; eyes narrowed, he turned a slow circle, searching. From the woods beyond the paddock to the dark entrance of the barn to the lane and front clearing of the house to the bulk of the sickroom, nearly all he could see of the house from here to—

Movement caught the corner of his eye. A medium-sized figure darted from the corner of the barn into its darkness; the horses snorted and the little mare kicked her stall again. The magic flared into something strong enough to make Reandn stagger a step before he pushed past the sudden disorientation it caused, but it didn't slow his silent approach to the barn. The spell, whatever it was, had no discernible effect.

But the clamor of magic . . . it beat at him, and he fought back, reaching the barn with only one thought— *get it stopped*. Stumbling into darkness with eyes that were used to bright sunlight and barely able to focus in the first place, he followed the magic straight to its source with no thought or care for the fact that the spell-user might be armed with something other than magic. Past the stalls he went, and into the niche of storage at the other end of the barn. By the time he saw the revealing flash of light-colored tunic, Reandn moved on the energy of his anger alone, and when he grabbed that tunic, he brought them both to his knees in a clatter of falling pitchforks and shovels.

To his astonishment, the spell-user loosed a near shriek of fear that hit his ears almost as hard as the magic. "Shut up!" Reandn bellowed back, while the magic crescendoed around them. The spell-user babbled incomprehensibly, the magic spiraled into agony, Reandn's chest tightened—and his anger exploded. He jerked the spell-user into the barn aisle and then slammed him against a stall without ever bothering to get up off his knees. *As if he could.* The feel of magic bobbled uncertainly—and then the irritated mare slammed her hoof into the stall behind the spell-user's head.

With a strangled grunt, the spell-user went limp, and the magic flickered away. Reandn let the unresisting body fall to the packed dirt of the aisle floor, and ended up on his hands and knees, waiting for the effects of the magic to fade.

"Dan?" Kacey called, her voice close. "What's going on? Tellan? Danny? Where *are* you?"

"In here," Reandn told her, not knowing or truly caring if he was loud enough to hear. Evidently he'd gotten her attention, for her voice was suddenly much closer.

"Tellan!" she cried, running the last few steps into the barn. Reandn looked up at her, discovering that his eyes had adjusted to the dim light. Yes, Tellan. The youth made a disoriented noise, alarm and apologies all at once, that gained him little sympathy from Reandn.

"Tellan," Reandn growled, while Kacey crouched over the apprentice, quickly checking him for injuries. "You're lucky I didn't kill you, you little idiot. What the Hells did you think you were doing?"

"*You* did this to him?" Kacey said, her quick glance accusing. Then she frowned, and looked back at Tellan. "You were using magic out here?"

Reandn's voice came out as a low growl. "He was using some kind of spell on me."

"*On* you?" Kacey looked down at Tellan again, but whatever she meant to ask, she cut short; instead she frowned at the vague way Tellan looked back up at her. "What did you do to him?"

"Nothing. Not really. Scared him." Reandn sat back on his heels, letting his head tilt back while he took a deep breath and waited for the last effects of the magic to fade. "Your mare kicked the stall behind his head. I think that's what's befuddled him."

"Wonderful. Help me get him outside—I want to take a better look at him."

Reandn grumbled, but he climbed slowly to his feet as Kacey pulled Tellan up far enough to shove a shoulder beneath his arm. Reandn grabbed the apprentice by the back of his trousers; between the two of them, they hauled Tellan to the bright splash of sunshine outside the barn doorway. Reandn dropped his half of the apprentice and slid down the side of the barn. The light made his head hurt, and he closed his eyes and decided there would be no more fence-post repairs this day.

Kacey ran her fingers through the hair on the back of Tellan's head, feeling more than looking for problems. "Not even any swelling," she said. "With any luck he's just shaken up. You look worse than he does, Dan, you're as pale as the sunshine."

"He ought to have known better," Reandn said, fighting the urge to rest his head against his upraised knees. His legs felt a little too long, and not in the least capable of holding him up again. "Didn't you tell him to keep his magic to himself around me?"

"Only ten or fifteen times," Kacey said, and added pointedly, "about as often as I've told you to keep your temper around me."

"Am I losing my temper at you?" Reandn raised an eyebrow at her and then decided it wasn't worth the effort.

Kacey didn't hesitate; her words were sharp. "That's not what I said, Reandn."

He covered his face with his hands and said through them, "Just find out what he was doing, will you? He was using magic on me and I want to know why. And I want to know why it got so out of hand." From the moment he'd been introduced to Reandn, the apprentice had found ways to avoid him . . . and now this? Not only stalking him, but throwing a spell at him? Reandn glanced at Kacey's frown and saw that she, too, was at a loss to explain such atypical behavior from the boy.

"Did you hear that?" Kacey said, her voice just as sharp as she turned to Tellan. "I know you've had the wind knocked out of your thoughts, Tellan, but you're all right, and you're certainly listening—do you think I can't tell? So speak up!"

There was no brooking Kacey in this mood; even Reandn knew better than that. Moving his hands just far enough to shade his eyes rather than cover them, he looked over at the boy. Tellan was pale, all right, but then, he always looked pale to Reandn. He was an awkward youth, and his was not the sort of awkwardness he could outgrow. His turned-out feet were too big, his shoulders were narrow, and his movements were graceless and often downright clumsy. He had the patchy beginnings of a beard which needed to be shaved, but far too many active blemishes on his face to do it. He struck Reandn as the sort who would never excel at his craft, but who would be quietly indispensable, always functioning in the background.

Reandn leaned toward him and said, "If you don't talk, boy, I'm going to put you in the stall with that mare."

Kacey made a face at him but didn't counter the threat, and Tellan opened his eyes, scooted away from Reandn until he bumped into Kacey, and realized, with visible shock, that she wasn't going to protect him. His words a blurted mumble, he said, "I was just painting you."

Reandn exchanged a glance with Kacey, and she looked as puzzled as he felt. "You were doing *what*?"

"Painting you." Apparently realizing that Reandn wasn't really about to haul him into the mare's stall, Tellan straightened a little, and his voice steadied out. "So I'd know where you were all the time."

Kacey looked at Reandn, and all he could do was shrug. "But Tellan, *why*?" she asked. "You have strict orders not to work magic near Reandn—and here you were, working it *on* him."

"It was only a little spell," Tellan said, mumbling again. "I didn't think he'd even know."

"You thought wrong," Reandn said, puzzlement leaning back toward anger again. "And what the bloody Hells were you thinking, throwing all that magic at me? Don't try to tell me *that* was any little painting spell."

Tellan quickly shook his head. "I didn't mean to do that, I really didn't. Something happened in the middle of the spell, I lost the structure of it, and then it got out of control, and you were chasing me and I—"

"That's all right, Tellan," Kacey said, her voice brusque, cutting off the inquisition altogether, as though she'd suddenly gotten full. "I know the look he had on his face when he felt the magic, and it's enough to frighten anyone. Go inside, why don't you, and lie down for a few moments. Get yourself pulled together; my father's coming back for a midday meal, and he mentioned something about taking you with him this afternoon."

Tellan's face brightened, though plenty of wariness remained as he glanced over to Reandn. Reandn suddenly realized the boy was waiting for his permission as well. He nodded.

Considering the alacrity with which Tellan moved, he wasn't all that stunned by his experience after all. Reandn stared after him, and leaned his head against the barn, resting his forearms across his knees. Kacey shifted around to put her back to the barn, sitting on the damp ground beside Reandn, their shoulders almost close enough to touch. She said, "I guess he can't scent people out like Rethia does. Maybe no one can."

"Why the Hells was he trying to keep track of me in the first place?" Reandn grumbled.

Kacey made an indecipherable noise, and Reandn glanced at her to find an expression of mixed affection and exasperation. "Why do you *think* he wanted to keep track of you, O Wolf-who-stalks-where-he-will? You frighten him!" She shook her head when he just looked at her. "You've got a reputation, Dan. You've earned it, too."

"For goddess' sake, I'd never hurt that boy."

"You just almost did."

Reandn stared off toward the sickroom door Tellan

had just made hasty use of. He'd never have harmed the apprentice, but Tellan was afraid of Reandn, so he'd tried the paint spell, which had gotten out of hand—the results of which meant Reandn had only confirmed the boy's fears in the first place . . . Reandn groaned, dizzied anew by it all. "I can't *not* protect myself."

"I didn't mean that. I just meant . . ." she trailed off, frowning. "I don't know what I meant. Just try to understand sometimes, will you?" She climbed to her feet, brushing off her visibly damp posterior; her knees and shins bore soggy splotches as well. "Besides, if you pay attention, you'll see it's when you're protecting someone *else* that you get yourself into so much trouble."

She left him then, walking back to the house as if she didn't have a care in the world. Frustrated, Reandn stared at her back until she was nearly to the sickhouse door, and then shouted after her, "I can't not do *that* either!"

"I know," she said over her shoulder, far too airily to suit him. "That's why we all love you anyway." And then the door closed behind her.

Reandn let his head fall against the barn once more, groaning again and glad there was no one to hear it. *Women.* What made it worse was that he was certain that the entire exchange had made sense to *her*.

From inside the barn, Sky blasted a mighty whinny at him, demanding the mare, demanding to be outside, demanding *something* other than what he had. Reandn waved him away, as if the horse could see or care, and suddenly realized just how much of the damp ground had seeped through the seat of his pants to his skin. The day, he thought, was definitely turning out to be something he'd just as soon have slept through. Might as well take a look at those other fence posts after all.

Chapter 3

Kacey stood by the big windows of the sickroom, looking out at Reandn bent over a fence rail and trying for an easy angle to tamp down new stones at the base of a listing post. The *easy* angle was to climb in there amidst the muck, but she didn't blame him for avoiding it. Besides, it afforded her a rather pleasant view from here. The seat of his pants had dried, though there were mud-leeched edges tracing the damp spot, following Reandn's form.

No, not a bad view at all.

Rethia came up behind her, looking out the same window and seeing something else entirely. "If the sun holds, I'll go out looking for early greens tomorrow . . . cattail shoots are up . . . and wild oats." The vagueness of her voice meant that in her mind, she was already there, searching her favorite spots and taking time to stroke the unicorn or two that inevitably showed up when Rethia was about. Anyone else from Little Wisdom, the village that was less than a day's walk away, would be considered lucky to see the glint of a horn or the whisk of a tail, but Rethia never gave her unusual relationship with the unicorns a second thought.

Now that the creatures were back, and now that the people understood their gift of magic to Keland, they were protected and honored—and no longer hunted and captured and coveted, the very human behaviors that drove them to leave this world in the first place. Other lands had unicorns—massive creatures, to move so quietly across wood and field, and hardly what one could call safe or tame—but Keland was their home, and the place they concentrated their numbers and their magic.

It would be a good thing when the first generation of new wizards was fully trained, instead of fumbling around with half-learned spells. Tellan, for instance, was effective enough in his apprenticeship duties; he went to Solace every month to take in more classes and to discuss what he'd learned, and in the meanwhile he was perfectly suited for easing pain and helping to clear infection and stop bleeding. Those were the things he'd learned well, and practiced often. But his other spells, like that spell this morning . . .

Kacey shook her head. What a disaster that episode could have been. Poor Reandn, sitting up against the barn, pale from his brush with strong magic—and utterly befuddled at Tellan's need to keep track of him. He obviously had no idea how much the anger still showed on his face, and how intensely his eyes blazed when he felt it.

Kacey liked his eyes, actually. She'd seen them laugh, and she knew what few others realized—that his laughter was just as intense as his anger.

Rethia bumped up against Kacey, a deliberate touch. "He *does* care," she said. "It's just too confusing for him to look at it head-on."

Kacey didn't even turn to look at her sister, who often knew far more than she ought about who was thinking what, and when they were thinking it. "That's the thing, then, isn't it?" She made a small, huffy noise and said, "Really, I ought to find myself some nice older man who's gotten *over* losing his first wife, and who'd be happy for some companionship."

"It's more the way it happened than the fact that he lost her," Rethia said. "Besides, the important thing is for you to be happy, and you really don't need to have a man at all for that. *I* don't."

You could if you wanted to, Kacey thought. She didn't say it out loud, and she didn't know if Rethia somehow understood the unspoken words anyway. She glanced at her sister. Rethia had those striking eyes, as attractive as they were odd. And she had thick hair, the fairest of blondes and just tinged with strawberry red. She was pretty, and much hardier than she looked. She laughed full and often, and judging by how she doted on the little ones who made their way to Teayo's sickroom, she'd be happy with a family of her own. She probably could have had most any man she wanted . . . and she didn't.

But Kacey did. She looked out at Reandn—he was stretching his back out now, shaking out his shoulders and shrugging off the tension, but in the midst of it, he stiffened, looking over his shoulder at the far end of the lane.

"Visitors," Rethia murmured. There was something in her voice that made Kacey look at her more closely, but she couldn't read what she saw in her sister's face. Resentment? *That* was unusual. She grabbed the jacket she'd flung over the stool behind her herb storage workbench and marched out of the house.

Reandn met her midway between the house and the barn, in front of the hitching rail set there. Kacey could barely hear the hooves that had alerted him, but it was enough. There was more than one horse on its way, enough to account for Reandn's extra attention. Absently, she straightened the collar of his hastily donned jacket, and then did the same for herself. By then the horses were in sight, moving at an easy canter—and while the men she saw meant nothing to Kacey, Reandn's face closed down hard.

"What?" she asked.

"Saxe. The others, I don't know."

She instantly wondered if Minor Arval had changed his mind about seeing Reandn jailed, and from the look on his face, Reandn was thinking the same. And as the riders pulled up before them, she did recognize Saxe—whom she'd once met two years earlier—but not the other two.

Saxe didn't make any attempt at pleasantries. "Dan. Need to talk to you."

"Introduce us." Reandn's request was pleasant enough, but Kacey heard the steel that meant it wasn't really a *request* after all.

So, apparently, did Saxe. Kacey reminded herself that this man had known Reandn much longer than she, and that they'd been close friends all that time. "Raley and Paton," he said, nodding at one and then the other. "Both are King Hawley's men." Both looked it, too; their clothes were just a little too fine for extended riding, and their faces a little too pale from lack of sun.

"Who don't they trust?" Reandn asked. "You, or me?"

Saxe grimaced; Kacey read his expression as either a plea or a warning, but she couldn't tell which. "Neither. They have an interest in this conversation. If you've a mind to invite us in, we can discuss it."

Looking at Reandn, Kacey had the impulse to take them all into the kitchen and watch Hawley's men wilt. But she sighed inwardly, and instead said, "Of course you're welcome to come inside. I hope you keep in mind that this is a healer's house, and we have no need for the luxuries of a court."

Saxe grinned at her, a sudden and welcome change. "I like it better, myself, meira, unless you've changed it greatly since last I was here."

"No, it's pretty much the same," Kacey said, somewhat ruefully. "I can't get my father to get rid of that old chair no matter what. Don't worry, I'll sit in that one."

Raley said, "Our conversation is for Reandn."

Reandn smiled at them. "Kacey is meira of this house.

If you want this conversation to happen, you'll include her."

Kacey gave him a surprised but grateful look, though she suspected he was acting from a desire to be contrary as much as to consider her. And she had to admit satisfaction at the irritation that crossed Raley's face before he nodded. Saxe remained utterly unreadable, and Kacey placed a silent bet with herself that he wasn't all that happy to be saddled with these men, whatever their purpose.

But she knew something, now—they weren't here after Reandn. Otherwise they surely wouldn't bother to accommodate his contrariness. More cheerfully, she waited as the men dismounted and hitched their horses, and then led them in through the front door, straight into the great room. She dropped her coat on her father's sagging, cushioned chair, and left them to sort out the other seating while she got a tray for tea. Rethia poked her head out of the sickroom and Kacey just shrugged at her, unable to offer any answers. Yet.

When she returned with tea and mugs, she found Reandn standing, leaning against the doorway with his arms crossed. He shook his head at her gesture with the tea tray, and said, "Saxe wants me to go on a little trip."

Paton's lips tightened; he exchanged a glance with Raley, who tilted back in Kacey's rocking chair and eyed her. She said, "He's only going to tell me anyway, so you might as well have me hear your version of it. Would you like some tea?"

From the straightbacked chair by the fireplace, Saxe snorted, and Kacey raised an eyebrow at him, meeting his quiet disbelief. The truth, of course, was that Reandn was perfectly willing to keep anything from her he felt she didn't need to know, but she held her bluff.

Raley cleared his throat. "Tea would be welcome, meira."

"Kacey," she said, and poured it for them. Both Reandn

and Saxe abstained, exchanging glances that said they'd
rather have this conversation alone. Kacey set the tea
tray on the little footstool before her father's listing chair,
and sat in the chair itself. "A trip to where?"

"The pass." Reandn watched Hawley's men as he
spoke. "They need an escort."

"For whom?"

Paton set his tea aside. "I really do draw the line here,
meir."

Reandn grinned at him, that grin where he showed
his teeth and didn't look the least amused, unless it was
black humor. An intimidating expression, no doubt about
that. "Someone important," he said to Kacey. "That's
all they were able to blurt out while you were gone."

Kacey gave Saxe the coldest look she could muster.
"Have you forgotten that you dismissed Reandn from
your Wolves, meir?" The honorific was a slap to someone
she'd once received in her house as *friend*, and Saxe
winced from it. *Good.*

"That *is* an interesting point," Reandn said, sounding
much more casual than Kacey was sure he felt, as if
her own acerbic response left him the room to back
off.

Saxe cut through it all. "Let's do it your way, Dan,"
he said. "No Highborn finessing." One of the other men
made a strangled noise of protest, but cut it off before
Kacey could tell who it came from. "I don't want you
out of the Wolves, and you don't want to be out. If you
can accomplish this thing, I can put you right back where
you were. All of the current Remote postings are
temporary."

Hope leaped in Kacey's chest, but suspicion followed
hard on it. Reandn voiced them for her. "And did you
know about this when you sent me off without telling
my patrol what was going on? Do they know even yet?"

Saxe hesitated, and then shook his head, short and
sharp. "They don't. And I didn't. This just came up a
few days ago, and there's been plenty of lost sleep over

it. As you can imagine, coming to you was the last thing on Ethne's mind."

Kacey blinked, hurt on Reandn's behalf, but Reandn only laughed. "That's more like it. Exactly what's going on?"

Paton would have spoken then, but Saxe's look stilled him. "We've discussed some of this, but humor me. The Resiores infighting has solidified into two major factions—those who embrace magic, and those who don't. The magic-lovers, the Allegients, want to renew their ties to Keland, and the others want to use it as the excuse to secede, which they've been preaching for years anyway. That faction calls itself the Shining Knife, and they're overly fond of burning warehouses and rigging accidents."

Kacey just stared at him. She hadn't known any of it. Well, that there were plenty in the Resiores who wanted to declare independence, yes. And everyone knew how crucial their supplies of coal and timber were to all of northern Keland. The voices crying for independence had once all said the same thing— that their region was being stripped of precious resources without enough in return, and that they were more isolated from Keland than they were from their other bordering countries. Now, with a zealous hatred of magic in the mix . . . no wonder the problems were mounting.

Well, she wasn't surprised not to have heard of the troubles. So much could happen over a winter of isolation, and even with the reviving systems of magical messages, Keep news took a long time to reach Little Wisdom—assuming someone bothered to pass it on in the first place. "Why hasn't King Hawley sent some Dragons over there to deal with this problem?"

"And risk the permanent loss of the Allegients?" Paton said, frowning at her as if either the answer were obvious, or the question highly inappropriate.

Raley said, "We are readying the troops, meira. When necessary, they will be used."

"Kacey," Kacey corrected again. "So you want the Resiores to return like a babe to the breast, and not like a son sent out to the woodshed to await the belt." Raley looked offended, but Kacey heard Reandn's quiet snort. When she looked at him, he was grinning.

"You can come with me the next time I'm flung in amongst the Highborn," he said. "Translate for me."

Even Saxe had cracked a smile; he leaned back in the straightbacked chair and took a casual stab into the fireplace with the poker beside it, sending sparks flying up the chimney. "You've got the gist of it," he told Kacey. "Things are a mess, Geltria is sending their own ambassadors into the Resiores— wouldn't that be something, for the Resiores to be Geltrian, sitting as they are so handy to King's Keep!—and we've got something crucial that needs to be done. Reandn can do it."

"Which brings us back to Kacey's point," Reandn said. "I'm no longer a Wolf, so why me?" He gave his former partner a sardonic look. "More expendable?"

Saxe grimaced. "Not a reason I had thought of, no. Look, Dan, the, ahh, visitor—her name is Kalena—" At Raley's noise of outrage, Saxe shook his head. "It's a common enough Resiore name, meir, and I'm not going to waste time hunting out secretive ways to refer to her. Kalena and her supporters are too damn aware of Resiore pride. The pass is a dangerous place at the best of times, and you can be certain there's at least one political faction strongly opposed to the visit. But the word is, the Resiore party will be providing its own guards, and they want nothing from us but a token honor guard." His expression made clear his opinion of the decision. "We've already got a couple of Hounds picked out for it, but what we *need* is half a patrol of Wolves. We're definitely not willing to do this job without more assurance of Kalena's safety."

"Half a patrol of Wolves. And you want me to take their place?" Reandn shifted against the doorframe. "That's a lot to ask."

Complacently, Saxe said, "I never said you weren't one of the best Wolves we had. Just that you didn't know how to deal with the Highborn."

Reandn snorted. "*The* best," he said. "And I know how to deal with the Highborn."

"You'd better," Saxe shot back at him, complacence vanished. "Because Kalena is nothing if not Highborn."

"I haven't yet said I'm interested in doing this little job of yours," Reandn reminded Saxe. Paton and Raley exchanged a grim look; Kacey glanced up at Reandn to find him tenser than she would have expected.

"Reandn," Paton said, as if he was just now trying out the shape of the word in his mouth, and it didn't quite fit. "We can't protect Kalena as well as we ought, and her safety is paramount. The best we can do is slip in a man as the party's remount wrangler—someone who knows the dangers of patrol, but who won't be recognized even by the Hound escort. And someone who knows the pass area, as we hear you do. Everyone else with the skill level we need is well known around King's Keep."

Reandn seemed to consider his words. "I've worked with plenty of Hounds, and I've been gone only two years."

"Almost two and a half, now," Saxe said. "Trust us to have picked two Hounds who won't know you."

Raley gave Reandn a swift look, one Kacey didn't like at all—calculation and impatience wrapped up into a patronizing delivery. "Don't forget what we're offering you."

Reandn straightened in the doorway. It was a casual move, with nothing overt about it, and yet it made Kacey feel like scooting out of the line of fire. He said evenly, "How could I?"

Paton caught Saxe's eye. "I'm not sure this was a good idea."

Saxe just shrugged. "It's the only one we've got." Raley all but rolled his eyes, while Paton stiffened and carefully looked at no one. Saxe gave them both a smile, cheerful enough. "Don't forget, meirs, I too am a Wolf. I'm not interested in letting you play games with my former partner."

Reandn didn't bother trying to hide his grin; it was one of the real ones, the ones Kacey generally savored. But at the moment she had other things on her mind. All well and good for these two to play with thwarting subtle Highborn manipulations, but *someone* had to maintain common sense. "And how long would this assignment take?" Raley, distracted from his annoyance with Saxe, gave her another one of those *what's she doing here* looks, and she snapped, "Oh, just answer me!"

Reandn caught on right away. But then, he would. "About three quarters to get to the pass, if I've got Wolf's Rights along the way—or if one of our friends there gives me the coin to provision myself as I go, instead of packing along a mule. I'd say maybe four to get back, since we'll be slowed by Highborn notions of travel on the way back to the Keep."

"Sounds right to me," Saxe agreed.

"Then I ought to be fine, as long as no one's working major magics within my reach. And if they are . . ." He didn't need to finish. Kacey knew well enough what he meant, and by the Highborn sighs she heard, so did everyone else.

"That's way too close to your limit, Dan," she said, knowing he wouldn't want to hear it. But two full months between Rethia's treatments was the longest he'd ever gone, and he'd been pretty sick at that. Then again, if their new elixir helped to prolong that time . . .

"We've thought of that," Saxe said. "We've still got a guide to add to the party, remember. We're looking for a wizard who will be an added layer of protection for the Resiore party, and who can also protect Reandn."

"Teya?" Reandn said instantly.

Saxe shook his head. "She knows you as her patrol leader, Dan. She's not seasoned enough to keep that fact from showing. No, the wizard we choose will be just like the Hounds—he'll have no idea you're a Wolf."

"He—or she—is going to wonder why you bother to have me along at all, then, considering my weakness to magic," Reandn warned.

Raley said, "We'll deal with that." And then his face changed, shifting back into the exasperation this whole situation seemed destined to bring out in him. He was looking at Reandn, and Kacey glanced up behind Reandn to discover the true object of his displeasure—Rethia. Reandn didn't look aside as she settled in next to him, directly behind Kacey. He'd known, of course. Kacey gave him a brief little frown. Once, just *once*, she'd like to get there first, and not be the one who was surprised.

Not likely. Besides, it was what kept him safe on patrol, and that meant she had less to worry about.

Rethia said, "That's not enough."

Kacey blinked, stumbling over the way Rethia's comment fit into her thoughts, but for once her sister was talking about something else entirely.

"Not enough?" Raley repeated. "What do you mean, *not enough*?"

She said it slowly, so he could understand; as was often the case with strangers, she kept her head tilted down slightly, looking at him through the thick fringe of her bangs. "That isn't enough protection. He's going to be too far away from me. If something happens—"

"What could happen?" Raley said. He looked as if he wanted to sweep Rethia away from the room like a bug before a broom.

"Listen to her," Reandn said softly. "I am."

A paragon of patience, Rethia said, "What if something goes wrong, and they're attacked by magic? Will your wizard be able to respond to the magic *and* protect Danny?"

Paton said slowly, "The wizard's first priority will be to protect Kalena and her party."

"The point," Raley interrupted, "is that by including

Reandn in the escort, we're hoping to avoid or prevent that kind of trouble."

"*Hoping* isn't *doing*," Rethia said.

"It's a risk Reandn will have to decide if he wants to take."

Reandn seemed to be more amused at being spoken of in the third person than he was alarmed at Rethia's words, but Kacey read the tension in his body and knew better.

And Rethia lost patience, lifting her head to lock gazes with Raley, using her startling eyes like a shout to get his attention. "Do people from the Keep always make things so hard?" she asked. "All you have to do is give Danny a way to reach me. If I know he's in trouble with magic, I'll go to him."

"You'll—what?" Paton asked, as taken aback by her eyes as was Raley.

Rethia looked at Kacey, a plea for help. Kacey said, "Meirs, you yourselves took the Wizard's Road to speak to us— unless you want us to believe that you rode all the way from the Keep within the three days since you heard of Kalena's arrival. All Rethia's saying is that if Reandn is endangered by your wizard's inability to protect him, we want to be able to reach him just as quickly. I'm sure there are details to work out, but then, that's why you're here, isn't it? Work them out!"

"It could be dangerous for Rethia," Saxe said. "We can't be sure of what she'll be coming into. We can't ask that of her."

"No, you can't," Kacey said, not trying to hide the heat behind her words. "She's *offering*. We're *healers*, Saxe, and while we may not be in your precious Wolf Pack, we *do* protect our own."

"Danny is family now," Rethia said, her quiet voice a marked contrast to Kacey's hot words.

Silence followed, but Kacey didn't miss the quick look Saxe sent Reandn. When she checked, Reandn hadn't moved at all, but there was a quiet hint of a smile on his face. For once, he knew when enough was enough; Kacey and Rethia's words would stand on their own.

Kacey's face warmed in a sudden, unaccountable flush; it took her a moment to understand why. *Danny is family*, Rethia had said. And Reandn had just smiled—no uncomfortable shifting, no objections, no evasions. Kacey, too, smiled, turning her head so Reandn couldn't see any sign of it. For the first time she felt that whatever turn his life was about to take, he would make an effort to keep them a part of it—and not just because he needed Rethia's healing touch.

Reandn spent the evening outside, doing chores in the chill moonlight until well after dark. Teayo returned, sensed Reandn's taciturn mood, and exchanged only as many words as it took to accept Reandn's offer to unharness and feed his mare. His arrival home meant supper would be served, but Reandn had no interest in food just yet, not if it meant sitting through explanations of what had occurred at the house that day—or in his quick discussion with Saxe, afterward.

That's when he'd learned who Kalena was—the first officially sanctioned ambassador from a region whose dependence had previously been so taken for granted that the notion of an ambassador would have been laughed out of court. For their first, the Resiores had chosen the daughter of a Highborn timberlands Minor, a young woman well known to the current unofficial Resioran representative, Malik.

"Malik made this happen," Saxe had said. "He's borderline Highborn, in coal. Odd thing, since most of the coal people lean toward Geltrian affiliation, but apparently he's a friend of the family. Paton's been working with him to prepare things for Kalena—though Malik knows nothing of you. Like we said . . . no one else does."

Wonderful. A new Resioran ambassador, too hills-proud to accept a proper escort—and the Keep was desperate enough to call on Reandn, dismissed and disgraced, as their clandestine security measure, just one of the many Wolves who should have been there in the first place.

"It's not that bad," Saxe had said, reacting to Reandn's dark expression. "No one knows when she's coming—we've deliberately seeded rumors it'll be midsummer. And a small escort is less likely to be noticed on the road. If we did send a true formal escort, *everyone* would know something was up." And then he grinned, a grin of old, when they'd been partnered and equally ranked. "It's your way back into the Wolves, Dan."

His way back into the Wolves. Why, then, did it seem more complex than that, and enough to kill his appetite and keep him out here, working . . . distracted.

Because, he told himself. He had a lot to think about, and sometimes that kind of thinking was best done by not thinking at all, but just *doing*, until his mind wandered back to the matters at hand and he discovered he'd come to a decision. Usually, working around the horses did that for him.

But not always. And not tonight. As he returned to the abandoned kitchen, he hoped Saxe was having better luck with arrangements for Rethia—because Reandn himself, while he had quickly decided on the issue of whether or not to join Kalena's escort, couldn't manage to shake some feeling of wrongness about it all.

So he ate the food that was waiting for him in the unstoked warmth of the oven, grateful when the others left him in peace. Kacey came in briefly to revive the fire under the teapot, and then again to take tea out to the sickroom. Reandn recognized the odor of one of her soothing concoctions, and decided it was later than he'd thought; she was putting her patients to bed for the night. He ducked into the little wash area and took off his shirt to sponge away the day's dirt and sweat, then rinsed the shirt out in the lukewarm, ever-present cauldron.

He'd have to come up with new clothes for the escort duty; almost everything he owned was Wolf issue. He'd let Saxe or the Highborn take care of the cost, he decided, wringing out the shirt and hanging it by the stove to dry overnight. Quietly, he moved into the short hall that sprouted the sickroom off one side and the great room off the other, their doorways just slightly offset from one another.

Rethia and Teayo had already taken to the sleeping alcoves; the light of a single lamp shone on Kacey's workbench, picking highlights out from the curves of her face and throwing her curls into chiaroscuro jumble. She bent over paper with pen in hand. Some kind of list, then—probably how much of which herbs she needed Rethia to gather. He moved to the doorway and hesitated there.

She glanced up at the movement, saw who it was, and sat up, carefully putting her pen aside. Her lips pressed together in disapproval of some sort; Reandn knew her well enough by now to guess it was at something she was thinking, and not anything he'd done—although no doubt she was surprised to find him wandering around shirtless. She'd figure it out.

What she did was put a finger to her lips and nod toward the beds that were out of his sight. Apparently even Tellan was asleep.

He kept his voice low. "I . . . just wanted to say thanks."

She screwed her face up in a questioning expression he couldn't possibly misinterpret, even in the poor light.

"I'm glad you were here this afternoon," he said simply.

It seemed to take her by surprise, and Reandn didn't give her time to gather her thoughts. It had rather taken him by surprise, too. He bid her good night and drew himself up into the loft at the end of the great room, not chancing to lower the ladder when it might wake Teayo and Rethia, and moving quietly under the extremely low ceiling for the same reason. His floor was their ceiling, and the stone chimney neatly bisected the length of the loft, radiating warmth. Tucked in behind it was a thick, straw-filled pallet, and he rolled onto it, feeling for the blankets. Something gave a squeak of protest and scuttled away across the floor. Damn chameleon shrews, they were everywhere now.

Too tired to think of anything more than getting a cat for this house and grateful for the fact, Reandn fell asleep.

But *sleep* and *rest* are two different things. The evasive feelings he couldn't define when he was awake invaded his dreams, leaving him angry and confused but with no answers. He finally woke with a start, full of fury with no outlet, and banged his head on the abrupt slope of the roof boards above the pallet. *Lonely Hells!* The curse resounded in his thoughts almost loudly enough to take form in the close space of the loft; for a moment he thought he'd spoken out loud.

No, just dream befuddled, a suitable finish to a day of waking befuddlement. After his breathing calmed, he fell quickly back into the sleep that had never quite let go of him.

This time, he wasn't alone.

Someone else's gentle breath crossed his cheek, just enough warning that when lips settled lightly on his own, he was prepared. Adela's herb-washed hair brushed the side of his face. "Danny . . ." she said, barely loud enough to call a whisper. "It's been a long time since you called me so strongly."

Reandn, stunned to feel her touch again after so long, tangled his fingers in the hair on either side of her face and pulled her close, kissing her long and hard, reveling in the taste and feel of her. He finally released her to bury his head in that long dark hair, right at the sweet curve where her neck joined her shoulders. His breathing was ragged and his heart pounding and—*and it's only a dream.* Really Adela, and truly a conversation, but it would all disappear once he woke.

"My," she said. "I'd almost forgotten what that was like."

"I haven't," he said, his voice as rough as his breathing. Slowly, he became aware of his surroundings—in these rare moments with Adela, he could find himself anywhere. But tonight, adding to the illusion of reality, he discovered he was right where he'd fallen asleep. Gently, he moved back from her, propping himself up on one elbow to regard her. She mirrored him, running a finger over her lower lip as if to remind her of his touch. Her bare shoulder peeked out from beneath her hair.

Bare shoulder. Bare arm. Bare *everything*. "What are you trying to do?" he said, his voice all but breaking like a boy's. "Torture me?"

She looked at herself and laughed. "I wasn't thinking. Here, is this better?" Abruptly, she wore one of his old shirts, as was often her habit when they were together at King's Keep.

"Well, maybe not *better*," he said grudgingly. "But easier."

She laughed again, a loving sound. "Danny," she said, still smiling at him, "What's got you all muddled up? I know what's happened; I know you grieve for your patrol. But your grief isn't what I feel." She eyed him a moment, and he waited until she added, "It takes a lot to call me, these days. I don't even feel them as days, Danny, I just always find myself surprised by how much time has passed since the last time I touched you . . . and each time, I wonder if it's the last. It might be. You know that, don't you?"

A sudden cold hand wrapped itself around Reandn's heart, but he nodded. He knew. He'd felt it happening. Kavan was already gone, as bright and inquisitive in death as life had never allowed him to be, and too busy to worry about old ties from a previous existence. "He loves you," Adela said then, letting Reandn know how loudly he'd been thinking.

He wished, in this dream world, that he could pluck the thoughts from her mind, too, and know—really *know*—what it was like for her. But all he could do was swallow hard and nod.

"Things change, Danny," she said. "Things change, and it's not always for the worse. I will never, ever stop loving you." She ran her fingers down the side of his face, and whispered, "But I may change the way I do it."

"Haven't things *changed* enough?" Reandn asked, unable to keep the rough note from his voice. Hadn't they? Not so long ago, he lived in a world without magic. He was Wolf First at King's Keep, second only to Saxe, with a wife he adored, and a foster son who filled the gap of childlessness in their lives.

Then came the magic; it took everything away, and gave back only deadly allergies. King's Keep, aware of his inability to stay near heavily populated, magic-using communities, created a Remote Patrol, the first step in reestablishing Wolf presence outside of the Keep, and set him at the head of it. Teayo's family, the healers who had once saved his life after an ambush, continued to save it by helping him manage his allergies. And Kacey—she was so good, and she tried so hard, but her feelings for him showed in her eyes whether she was laughing with him or lashing him with her tongue. Yes, despite what Saxe had said at Arval's, things *had* changed.

And now he'd lost the patrol and the Wolves—or had he? And was he helping Saxe out of knee-jerk loyalty, or because he truly wanted to regain his place with the Wolves?

"It's too *much*," he said, shaking his head at Adela. "I don't know what I am . . . I don't know what I want."

"You won't know until you *know*," Adela said. "It's not something you can just *decide* to know."

"I lied." Reandn closed his eyes. "I do know. I want *you*."

"Things change," Adela said. She leaned over and kissed him again, just as long and hard as the first time. Reandn made a protesting noise deep in his throat as she left him—not pulling away, but *leaving*—and then she was gone, her touch lingering on his lips and her voice in his ear. *However I can, I'll always love you*.

He thought he was awake, then. His breath came fast and hard, catching at his throat both in and out. The loft was warm, too warm, and yet his skin still ran goosebumps from Adela's touch. He *was* awake, wasn't he?

Teayo's massive snore broke the silence of the night, and Reandn's doubt disappeared. He lay there a moment, perfectly still, listening to the snoring—and then suddenly couldn't get out of that loft fast enough. Too warm, too close, too *Adela*. He snagged the blanket and lowered himself to the great room. Once in the kitchen, he flipped the blanket into a fold, and wrapped it around his shoulders.

The chill night air hit his face like a slap, erasing his Dela-caused goosebumps and replacing them with commonplace ones. He breathed deeply, his bare feet walking on their own volition, cold mud oozing between his toes. He was halfway down the lane to the road before he realized it, and before the cold really began to seep in.

There he stopped. For long moments, he stood there, fighting the need to *do* something, to make a decision, *any* decision—and feeling the inexplicable desire to run, just run, until his legs gave out from the effort.

Running away, he suddenly realized. That's what it would be, it's what he really wanted to do. But there was no running away from the way he felt, and the confusion wouldn't settle until he somehow managed to face it head on. No matter what the Prime said, in his heart Reandn would always be a Wolf, and this confusion was just as much of an enemy as anything he'd ever faced.

And a Wolf did not run from the enemy.

In the morning, Reandn stumbled through the great room somewhat later than was his norm but not late enough to have gotten sufficient sleep; no four people could ever be moving about and yet be quiet enough for that. Kacey was in the sickroom with someone's family, giving directions for the patient's care at home, and Teayo's cart—presumably with Teayo inside—was gone. Tellan was outside; from the hallway, Reandn caught a glimpse of him through the sickroom window, and heard snatches of his voice—uncertain, worried—as he helped someone out of a wagon. There seemed to be plenty of blood in evidence; Reandn guessed it was a gruesome farm accident and knew it was likely he'd be called on to hold someone down. Tellan's improving ability to sedate patients would be well tested today, too, if Reandn was right.

Might as well get some food in his stomach first. If he recalled correctly, someone had bartered honey for herbs the day before, and it just might be out with the oat porridge—ah, yes. Warming by the stove. The porridge itself glopped into a bowl, past its prime, but the honey would make up for it. Reandn slid the bowl onto the table and discovered his neatly folded shirt waiting for him there. He pulled it over his head and commenced to scooping food into his mouth. Just a normal day, he thought, and a deadly ironic contrast to his night.

Rethia came in from outside as he was finishing up, her face flushed and muddy spots on her loose trouser knees. "It's beautiful out!" she said happily, depositing her basket of greens and herbs by the dry sink next to the stove. "You slept through the most interesting sunrise."

"I guess I did."

Something in his voice must have alerted her—but then again, this was Rethia, so who knew—for she looked down at him a moment, her eyes clouded. "Did you talk to her last night?"

Reandn nodded without saying anything. Rethia sighed, and moved on, retrieving a small brazier and filling it with some of their precious hard coal. She shoveled already-flaming wood chunks from the stove in on top of it all, carefully fanning it so the coal would catch and burn. "I thought, maybe," she said, still in their conversation and responding to Reandn's nonverbal reply. "When you didn't get up before I did, I peeked up in the loft and saw how muddy your feet were."

Reandn glanced under the table at his feet, distinctly remembering that he'd wiped them off so he wouldn't track mud. He discovered he'd forgotten about the mud that had squished between his toes and settled along their upper edges. Oh, well. "Whups," he said.

"You don't want to talk about it, though," she said, making the statement an invitation to do just that.

"What do you think?"

"I think not." She peeled her coat off; it was long enough that it, too, had brushed the ground as she knelt, and mud fringed the edges. "I think Kacey's going to need your help. Tellan tries, but he's just not . . ."

Her words trailed off into nothingness and Reandn didn't hesitate to finish it for her, knowing she'd never get around to it herself; she was probably thinking about that sunrise. Or Adela. Or their new patient—or all three. "Not strong enough, I know. What do you do when I'm not around?" For Teayo was always expected elsewhere, and counted on them to handle the sickroom without him.

She looked at him, vaguely surprised. "Struggle." And then she was gone again, there but not there.

Reandn eyed what was left of the porridge and decided against a second serving. Helping in the sickroom wasn't something he wanted to do on an overfull stomach. Nor with a clean shirt, he thought, and pulled it back off again. Kacey would shove one of her father's oversized old workshirts at him if she cared.

She cared. The first thing she did when he entered the sickroom was point an imperious finger at the wall behind the workbench, where several such shirts were generally available. She did not, however, hesitate with what she was doing, which was calming her patient. Reandn eyed the situation, glad to see that the family waited outside, even if they did crowd around the window. On the bed nearest the workbench—he always thought of that bed as his, considering the time he'd spent there—was a crying child, and under all the blood it was hard to see just which sex the child might be. Kacey sat on one side of the bed, murmuring soothing words, and Tellan sat on the other, looking pale as he bit his lip and tried—evidently without success—to calm the child with magic. "It would help," Kacey said to him through gritted teeth, "if you could at least slow the bleeding."

"I'm *trying*," Tellan said. He was holding three pads of bandages on the thrashing figure, and Reandn could well imagine that between the squalling child, the appalling amount of blood, and the nearly impossible task of keeping a grip on the slick, squirming child, Tellan had no chance of achieving the concentration he needed for his magic. There was certainly no trace of it in the air.

"I can't get sweet syrup into her while she's this upset," Kacey said shortly, her hand clamped down over the sopping rag wrapped around the child's forearm. "Goddess, I can't see a thing with all this blood. How cut up *is* she?"

Shirt in hand, Reandn stuck his head out the door and said, "You're blocking the light." Startled, the confounded family only stared at him. Too upset and panicked to quite understand what he wanted, it seemed. "Leave one person to watch," he said, patient but unyielding, "and the rest of you wait by the wagon."

This brought protest, but the oldest person there, a grandmother or aunt, started rounding them up. Eventually, only the oldest son stood by the window, and the rest of them huddled together at the wagon, comforting one another.

"Thank you," Kacey said when Reandn came back inside, her strained voice barely loud enough to hear over the girl's shrieks. "Now help me keep this child still! I have *got* to get her sedated if I'm going to stitch her up before it's too late."

They didn't have a chance, Reandn thought, not unless someone did something fast. At first he'd wondered why they weren't trying to tie her down, but now he could see the deep cuts on her arms and legs that made it impossible. He did the first thing that came to him; he moved in, stepping right up on the bed and sliding down against the wall at its head—splinters and all—and picked the girl up to settle her in his lap. He laced his arms under hers, clamping onto his wrists where they met over her chest, and then crossed his legs over her hips. She was just a little too small to fit snugly in his grip, and she continued flinging blood around along with her arms and legs—but she was effectively immobilized throughout her body.

"Perfect!" Kacey said, quickly turning to her little cup of sweet syrup. Using a tiny spoon, she left her hand poised by the girl's face until just the right opportunity presented itself, then darted in to deliver the pain-killing sedative. As much was on the girl's lips and chin as in her mouth, but Kacey immediately refilled the spoon and tried again.

"What the Hells happened to her?" Reandn asked, loud above the noise of the child herself. Beside him, Tellan used the opportunity to tie down his bandages and move on to other injuries.

Kacey was grim, her voice steady as she got another spoonful into the girl. "I'm not entirely sure, they were all talking at once. Something about all their farming tools being sharpened for the season, and the girl taking a fall from the barn loft."

Plough, scythe, saws, reapers . . . Reandn winced. And Kacey said in frustration, "This just isn't fast enough! C'mon, sweetie, just be still a moment—"

But she wasn't. She was beyond hearing them, trapped in her own pain and terror and fighting them as hard as she could. Reandn readjusted his grip and bent his head to her ear—or as close as he could get without getting his nose broken. Sharp and loud, he whistled, the call he used to get Sky from the other end of a pasture.

Startled, the girl froze—just for an instant, but long enough for Kacey's quick hands to get more sweet syrup into her. As the girl gathered her breath to renew her noise, Reandn whistled again, not quite as loud, and then crooned into her ear, soothing nonsense.

It only held her a few moments before she started crying, more weakly this time—but by then Kacey was sitting back on her short bedside stool, satisfaction on her face. Behind her, Rethia whisked into the room, carrying the brazier in a small frame and carefully setting it within Kacey's reach. From one of the drawers of the workbench, she retrieved a clatter of instruments, none of which Reandn could see—except for the minuscule flat-ended poker that she stuck into the hottest part of the brazier coals.

All of a sudden, Reandn regretted his breakfast altogether. Realizing he'd stopped murmuring to the girl, he picked it up again, but in truth she wasn't struggling very hard anymore, anyway. It hadn't been long enough for the syrup to take effect, as he knew all too well. He looked up to catch the despair in Kacey's eyes. "Tellan," she said. "*Please.*"

Tellan looked up from the girl's shin, where he'd found a cut shallow enough to slather comfrey salve on and bandage up. "I—" he said, and his gaze darted to Reandn and away again. Reandn was not slow to see the fear there.

"Stop the bleeding," he said, as much of an order as he could make it.

"Will you be all right?" Kacey asked, as if suddenly realizing the ramifications of her request. She looked at Reandn with worried eyes, blood smeared across her face, and then at the soaked cloth around the girl's arm. "It may be too late already. . . ."

"Do it, dammit!" Reandn said, holding on to the girl a little more tightly.

Tellan did. Reandn concentrated on the feel of his own fingers digging into his wrists as he held the child, setting his teeth against the magic in his head, his body. Not as bad as the day before, he told himself, and not near as bad as what he'd endured in times past. Just something to live through . . . he'd learned long ago how far sheer determination could take him, past the thrumming buzz that filled his head, past the tightening of his chest, driving his body to do as it must.

When it faded, all he heard was the rapid sound of his heartbeat in his ears—and then, finally, Kacey's faint, "Goddess bless."

He realized he was slumped over the girl, though his grip had not slackened. Slowly, he took a deep breath, straightened himself, and opened his eyes. Looking at the girl, he couldn't tell much difference; she was limp in his grip now, and breathing in short, shallow gasps. But when Kacey wiped one of the cuts clean, it no longer welled right up again with blood. "That's wonderful, Tellan. Now go in and keep her under, will you—don't forget how much syrup we've put in her, don't overdo it—and I'll look at this arm." She glanced down at the brazier, where the coals still glowed red-hot. "I just hope we can save it."

Tellan worked in silence a moment, much more subtle magic this time. Rethia set a tray on the end of the bed with a number of fine curved needles, already threaded, lined up and waiting, and immediately began washing down the girl's legs. Tellan, his voice faint, opened his eyes and said, "All right. I've got her. She's very weak, Kacey."

"I know," Kacey said. "We'll . . . we'll do what we can." She looked up at Reandn and asked, "Are you all right?"

but didn't hesitate before returning to the bandage she was carefully unwrapping.

Reandn said, "I will be," and shifted beneath the girl. "What's her name?"

"I don't even know. Tellan has her now; you don't have to stay."

"Sophi," Rethia said.

"I'll stay." But Reandn uncrossed and straightened his legs, easing the girl into more of a reclining position even as Kacey worked. He stroked her hair; she couldn't be more than eight years old, and it seemed to him that someone should be here just to tell her everything was going to be all right, even if she appeared not to hear. There were a lot of things *he* remembered from his time under Kacey's sweet syrup, after all. "I'll stay with you, Sophi."

Tellan, still remote with concentration as he monitored her wakefulness, offered Reandn a pair of bent shears and said tentatively, "Maybe you can get her shirt off?"

Maybe. Reandn took the shears, and when he was done with that, Rethia handed him a cloth and warm water and asked him to wash what he could reach. He thought it would take a good dunking before the child was actually clean again, but he did what he could, speaking to her all the while and doing his best to ignore what Kacey was up to, she with thread and needle and the lingering odor of burnt flesh.

Eventually, it was over. Reandn climbed off the bed and left a pillow to cradle Sophi's head instead, and Rethia took the brazier away, and Tellan tiredly started seeing to the handful of other patients, some of whom had sickened at the sights before them.

"We need to get a separate room for this kind of thing," Kacey sighed, looking at the other patients. "Thank Ardrith it doesn't happen very often." And she went out to talk to the family members, who were by this time crowding around the window again.

Reandn pulled off his borrowed shirt, feeling as worn

as though he'd just worked an entire patrol shift, and went to hunt up his own. Boots, too, he thought, and finally took the time to get the rest of the mud off his feet. The horses hadn't been fed, and after an entire morning trapped in their stalls, they were probably mighty peeved.

He'd just finished hauling water for them and was standing at the paddock fence, watching them take out their frustration on each other, when Kacey came up beside him. She was well bundled in her characteristic layers of jackets, but she had her arms wrapped around herself as though chilled despite the sun that shone strongly on her. "Must be spring," she said, kicking at the mud under the lowest fence rail. "Looks like this might actually dry up someday."

Reandn didn't respond. He rested his elbows on the upper rail and turned his face to the sun, closing his eyes in its brightness.

Kacey sighed, and stood in silence for a while. Then, altogether unexpectedly, she said, "I'm always surprised to find you so good with children."

Oh? He gave her a little frown.

She frowned, too, but it was at herself. "That . . . didn't come out very well. I mean to say . . . that is . . . well, graces!"

"Just say it, Kacey," Reandn told her. "You're generally pretty good at that."

He'd gotten her ire with that one. "I just meant, well, life went on after you lost Adela. It'll go on if you lose the Wolves, too. We can use your *help* here, Reandn. Since Rethia brought the magic back, so many more people have realized we're here, and we're always shorthanded."

"I'm not meant for cutting away clothing and washing off blood," Reandn said sharply, trying to remember that Kacey had no idea what he'd been through the night before, and no real concept of Adela's visits at all. Life had gone on without Adela, but it hadn't been easy—

and until now, he hadn't realized just how hard he'd been hanging on to those infrequent visits of hers. He heard her again, her gentleness as she told him, *Things change*.

"I didn't mean that, I meant—well, no one *else* thought of handling Sophi like you did. We may lose her yet, but she'd surely be dead already without your help. There are so many reasons we'd be happy to have you stay—" Her words were running together a little, a sure sign that she was upset and trying to hide it. "Tellan can learn to protect you from his magic, I'm sure he can—" She cut herself off as if suddenly hearing how she sounded, and risked a look at him. There were tears welling in her eyes.

Reandn looked away from them.

"It's just," she said, and he could hear those tears now, "it's just I'm worried about you. This sounds so dangerous, sending you out with no authority, among magic and politics and some spoiled Highborn who won't even let herself be properly protected. It'd be so much safer here—"

He took it all wrong, too full of anger at *Things change* and his helplessness to do anything about most of it to make the effort truly to understand her. "Do you really think Saxe would ask this of me if he didn't think I was good enough to handle it?"

"That's not what I meant," Kacey stammered.

No, what she meant was that she cared for him too much, that she wanted him to stay so he wouldn't leave her—for the Wolves, or for the consequences of the risks he was about to take.

They knew each other well after two years, no matter the sporadic nature of his visits. Another time, perhaps, he would have put his arm around her shoulder—not offering her what she wanted, but sorry to see her upset.

But not now. He'd had too much thrown at him, too many decisions he'd had no part in, too many events he'd been powerless to affect. The only thing he knew was how to fight back. Suddenly things didn't seem so confusing anymore, and all the feelings he'd wrestled during the night now solidified into the same sort of determination that had gotten him out of the kitchen and into the Pack, the same determination that saw him through the ravages of magic. He was a Wolf. And he was going to make sure he stayed that way.

Chapter 4

Drip. Drip. Teya covered her ears with her hands. The wizard schools had been so poorly maintained, for so many years. . . . Things were better than, say, two years ago, but—*drip!*—not as good as they could be.

There was so much more to magic than people supposed, more than just memorizing gestures for different elements. Most people never felt those individual elements at all, but only the generalized hum they made when thrown together. But the students . . . they learned to isolate the elements, and then to associate gestures with each—over and over again, until invoking will and crooking a finger *just so* immediately drew forth a tendril of precisely defined power. Only then, after endless hours of drills and repetition, did they start recombining the elements into spells.

Some people felt the elements as touch, or tasted them, or even saw them in their mind as indescribable colors. Teya heard them in subliminal notes, and usually had no trouble blocking out the noise of the world—*drip!*—to concentrate.

A rumble of the season's first thunder drowned out the noise of rainwater plinking into the old chamberpot Teya had appropriated. That's what she got for being an interim student—the rooms in the top floor of the

old stone and wood building. But how in the Hells was
she supposed to study with that infernal drip mocking
her in the background?

Aurgh. Teya pushed her notes away and left the austere
little study desk to do stretches in the middle of the
room, following the orders of the school's healers. Her
assorted bruises were nearly healed, but her dislocated
shoulder was another thing altogether, and remained
stiff and sore. At this rate, she'd never get back out on
patrol. She wondered what Reandn was doing with his
substitute wizard, and her mouth quirked into a wry
little smile. Knowing how difficult he could be to work
with when it came to magic, she could easily imagine
Reandn stalking around like one of the thunderclouds
now overhead, with the frustrated wizard grumbling
loudly every time Reandn's back was turned.

She wondered how long it would take the substitute
to realize Reandn heard a lot more than it seemed he
ought to, grumbles especially. My, how her own face
had burned when she'd learned that lesson herself. But
now, as she'd healed, and as she'd worried about her
future in the Remote Patrol, she discovered she was at
least used to Reandn's ways, and that she wanted that
position *back*. It was better, she thought, than starting
all over with another patrol leader, someone who might
not appreciate her strengths, and who might rag her
endlessly about her weaknesses. Reandn, at least, did
not do that, whatever his other faults.

Drip.

She was done with lessons for the day. Since her return
here, she'd had several assignments on which to
concentrate—a few pointedly effective offensive spells,
a refined and more powerful scrying spell—but at her
own request, the bulk of her time had been spent in
schooling her reaction times. Her assigned tutor, Rainer,
spent hours in verbal battle with her, throwing out
situations and heckling her—"Hurry up, Teya, people
are dying, Teya, you've got to be faster, Teya"—while

Teya searched for the responding spell she wanted. At the same time, she spent far too many hours in this lonely room, drilling herself with cards of her own devising. Flip a card, read the spell, and quickly display the mnemonics for it, moving her fingers in the wizard's language without actually calling the magic behind them.

She'd thought she was getting faster, that the spells were coming to mind more easily all the time, and that her response time to Rainer's verbal battles had improved. Then, yesterday, he'd added the mnemonics to his exercises; now she had to come back with the name of a spell and finger-twist out the mnemonics just as quickly. Within moments she was stuttering with both words and fingers.

Maybe she just needed a break. A day or two when she didn't think about it at all, but spent her time stretching and reading and exploring Solace.

Thunder rumbled at her; in a childish impulse she stuck her tongue out at it—and then jumped at the sudden knocking at her door, certain she'd somehow been seen.

"Stupid," she told herself. Kneading her aching shoulder, she opened the door.

The woman standing there was no one she knew. A tall and slender—or maybe downright thin—woman, dressed simply in a plain blue kirtle over a soft white shirt—and were those old, faded bloodstains on the sleeve? Her hair was thick and blonder than anyone's ought to be, hanging damply below her shoulders with the crimped look of recently released braids.

It was when she met the woman's eyes that Teya suddenly realized who she was. Someone Teya'd heard much about, and never seen, for she'd always come to Solace when Reandn went to Little Wisdom. "Rethia," she said—no, admit it, she blurted the name more than anything.

Rethia turned her eyes away, hiding them beneath thick lashes. "I found the right door, then . . . Teya?"

"Yes," Teya said, lost in the question of why in Ardrith's name this woman was here. And then she realized she was still looking out from a mostly closed door, and that Rethia stood out in the drafty hallway with plenty of evidence of the rain on her clothes. Hastily, she opened the door. "Please, come in. They're only temporary student's quarters, but I did do a little warming spell a while ago."

Rethia smiled, and Teya thought it looked like a relieved expression. What did this woman have to worry about? she wondered. She was the one who'd brought back the magic!

Rethia appeared not even to notice the plinking drip into the chamber pot, or the austere little chair Teya gestured at by way of invitation. She fumbled at the side of her kirtle until she found the seam pocket, and withdrew a note. "From Reandn," she said. "Though I wrote it for him, so if it doesn't quite sound like him, that's why."

Teya took the note, absently remembering her surprise at the discovery that Reandn didn't read, and didn't write beyond scrawling his name. Most Wolves came from good solid trade families at the least, and entered pack training with both their numbers and letters learned. Teya herself was the daughter of a successful net merchant, and had once helped keep both the family's books and their correspondence.

Even without the knowledge of his scholarly shortcomings, she'd have known right away that this hand wasn't Reandn's, not this precise and delicate script. Teya could all but see Rethia writing it.

But then she read the words, and forgot about the scribing altogether. Reandn, discharged? The patrol, all but disbanded? Then where was Dakina? How would she ever discover the fate of the three injured men? And how could she pass on Reandn's regards and final goodbye, the request he made of her? She gaped at the letter a moment, and then gathered herself to send Rethia a sharp look. "What do you know of this?"

"All of it," Rethia said, seeming to understand perfectly well that Teya was asking about the unspoken details behind the brief note. "But he isn't supposed to have told you *any* of it. Please don't ask anyone else about it."

"I won't," Teya assured her. "That is— I won't, unless I don't get any more answers from you."

She expected irritation, or hesitation, or even stubborn refusal. Rethia just looked at her, standing damply in the middle of the room with the chamberpot-echoed drip behind her, and said, "I told him."

Teya stared at her, and after a moment, shook her head as if to clear it. Rethia was striking, and once you were used to her eyes and hair, perhaps even beautiful, but . . . she was also quite strange.

But apparently willing to talk. "What happened?" Teya said. "Why did they kick him out of the Wolves?"

"Arval's nose," Rethia told her.

"Arval's—but he was only defending me!"

Rethia asked, "Does Danny make you angry?"

Teya was completely taken aback, and spent a few moments in confusion before she realized Rethia was referring to Reandn. Danny—of course. It had never occurred to her that he would ever be called by such a nickname. And even then, she had no idea what Rethia was getting at. In the end, she simply answered the question honestly. "Yes, sometimes. Or, I suppose . . . ofttimes."

Rethia said, "Ignoring the *oughts*? Not listening to your *shoulds*? Stepping all over your *let's do it this ways*?"

"He makes his own rules when he wants to," Teya said, feeling the heat in her face for the implied—no, outright—disrespect in those words. But goddess damn, it was true!

Rethia *looked* . . . Teya wasn't sure. Elsewhere, perhaps. "A few days ago," Rethia said, her gaze most definitely *not* taking in the chamber pot she looked at, "we had a little girl come in, so badly cut up that it was days before we knew we'd saved her, even if she won't ever have the use of one hand again. She was so frightened, and in so much pain . . . we couldn't even begin to treat her. Danny was the one who held her, and talked to her, and calmed her enough so we could save her life. We hadn't even thought to do the things he did. I guess he broke our rules, too, in a way."

Teya waited a moment, and then frowned. Rethia had said that like it actually had something to do with this conversation. "Rethia . . ." she started, and then stopped short, horrified at the patronizing tone in her own voice.

Rethia's little smile said she'd heard it too; she suddenly sounded more practical, as if some part of her had closed itself off to Teya. "The Prime kicked him out of the Wolves for attacking Minor Arval. He wasn't allowed to tell you. Ethne wanted things to settle down first, Danny said. And even then he wasn't sure what they might actually tell you, so he wanted to set things straight before he left." She answered Teya's next question before Teya even had a chance to open her mouth. "They've offered him a deal, now—handle a special assignment for them, and they'll give him back the Wolves. He left this morning."

"For where?"

Rethia shook her head. "Nowhere near here."

Teya suppressed a flash of annoyance, sensing that where Rethia had spoken of other things readily enough, she would not be swayed when it came to this one. "What about his allergies?" she asked. "Nowhere near here means he won't be able to come to you. And it means I won't be around to shield him from magic. I may not be so good at some spells, but I'm not being prideful when I tell you I've never met anyone in my generation of wizards who can shield Reandn as well as I can."

"He trusts you," Rethia said in agreement, words that hit Teya like a little shock, though Rethia gave her no time to think about them. "I'm worried, too. I don't usually . . ." She stopped, and looked straight at Teya with a self-deprecating smile. "Maybe you can tell. But people like you and Reandn, you see something you want, or something you think is important, and you fight for it. I see those things and I . . . well, I don't. Fight, I mean. There are usually other ways. But this time . . . they just don't understand, you know. They haven't seen how sick magic can make Danny. You haven't, either. So I made . . . a fuss."

Teya found that hard to imagine. Soft-spoken. Reserved. Even withdrawn. Those were the words she'd have used to describe this woman. She fought the impulse to ask, *Did you actually shout?* because she'd already been rude enough. "What," she asked instead, "what happened?"

Rethia reached beneath the gently scooped neckline of the kirtle and pulled out a small, asymmetrical disk. An amulet. "Danny has one just like mine. Farren made them for us yesterday. If Danny's in trouble, all he has to do is break it; it'll resonate in this one. I'll be sent out on the Wizard's Road and I'll help him."

"Great swampmuck, woman, that's no guarantee at all! What if you can't find him in time?" Teya *knew* they'd send Rethia not straight to Reandn, but only to the nearest location that the sending wizard was familiar with. "Besides, if he's in trouble with magic, chances are too damned good that there's a whole lot else going on, too. You're either going to walk straight into it, or you won't even be able to get close to him!"

"You're right," Rethia said, looking more sad than upset by Teya's ire. "But it's Danny's choice to take the risks ahead of him. This is just the best *I* can do to make sure the magic doesn't kill him while he's at it."

For a long moment, Teya could only stare at her. Then she gathered herself together, took a deep breath, and offered Rethia a Wolf's salute. "Goddess grace, Rethia. And my gratitude . . . for telling me what you could."

"You're welcome," Rethia murmured. "I wish . . . it were more." And she ducked her head to give Teya one more look from beneath her bangs and lashes before she departed, leaving Teya with the notion that there were unspoken words ringing loudly around her.

Drip.

Teya snarled an oath at the chamberpot and snatched up her cloak. Bloody damned if she wasn't going on that walk anyway.

The amulet felt strange and cool against Reandn's skin, as though it were magic that hadn't quite happened yet, but wasn't far away. After a day or two of that, he left the thing hanging outside his shirt. Plenty of people wore amulets these days, though the fact that there was very little true use for them meant they were mostly fakes.

His clothes were as unfamiliar as the amulet. They'd already seen plenty of use by the time Saxe handed them to Reandn; they were sturdy and not disreputable, which was all he asked. This job was going to be difficult enough—a veteran, ranking Wolf slinking around in the guise of a remount wrangler—and he at least needed to look like someone the Keep trusted to handle horses for Resiore Highborn. The tunic was long, modestly embellished with embroidery, and belted over baggy pants.

When he stood still in them, if there was no breeze to make the roughly woven material brush his skin, he felt alarmingly close to being without pants at all. Thank Ardrith's mercy he had a pair of half-chaps—plain ones, and battered, but perfectly serviceable—to hold the pants in tight against his lower legs, or after half a lifetime of riding, he'd be sporting blisters again.

At least he still had his boots. And he still had Sky. And the weather was finally fairing up for spring, still raining plenty but not quite as cold. Add the luxury of sleeping at inns and stabling Sky with plenty of feed and hay, and Reandn didn't have much to complain about. The days on the way to Norposten, the small town just north of King's Keep, were as good as a vacation. Sky didn't even contrive to throw a shoe.

Perversely, Reandn found his thoughts lingering on his time at Teayo's home, where he'd left before finishing his work on the fence, and where the well needed dredging. He didn't think about Adela in her journey through Tenaebra's Heavens. And he didn't think about his surviving patrol members, or whether Teya would manage to convey his words to them. He didn't wonder about Sophi's recovery, and he definitely didn't think about the way he'd just thrown his hands up at Kacey's pinched annoyance at his departure. Or about the way her deep brown eyes had revealed the worry the rest of her had hidden.

Definitely not.

When he returned, he'd be a Wolf again, and that was the important thing. Everything else would pass. But he was relieved to reach Norposten all the same; from here on, he'd travel with more than his own thoughts and one eccentric horse for company.

In town, Reandn found the livery that was holding his remounts, and while he was looking them over, one of the Hounds found him, obvious enough in the browns of his boots, trousers, and marked and rank-laced vest. Unlike the Wolves, he had no half-chaps, and chose his own color of shirt—in this case, deep green to offset his violently red hair. "You're either Dan," the man said, coming to rest beside Reandn at the livery corral, "or you're his twin. From the description I got, anyway."

Dan. Just a tad too familiar for Reandn, who drew his lines deeply around him. But the Hounds *had* heard his name, even if they'd never seen him, and Saxe decided it would be best to avoid using it. "That would be me," he told the man. "Hired on special for this one."

"Ethne said you've worked with the Keep forces before."

Reandn nodded. "I've done some training for your Wolf mounts," he said, which was perfectly true.

"I'm Damen," the man said. "My partner—that's

Nican—is around here somewhere; we've been expecting you. And Elstan is at the inn."

"The wizard?" Reandn guessed.

Damen shrugged. Relaxed and confident, he struck Reandn as the kind of man who was good enough at what he did that he didn't carry around a lot of worries. "The wizard, yes. Officially he's our guide, and no one from the Resiore party is to know any different—I'm sure someone told you that." His eyes slid to the horses, and then back to Reandn, as if carefully and quietly gauging Reandn's reaction to his words. "As it happens I'm the one with the map. Of course, this whole thing would have been a lot simpler if Resiore pride had let the Keep send a Wolf patrol to escort them. Wolves are better at slinking around the countryside."

Probably not the last of the subtle digs he'd hear about Wolves; there'd always been a friendly rivalry between the two closely related branches of Keep security. Reandn let the comment about Resiore pride pass as well—that one had surely been deliberate bait—and simply said, "I've been there myself. That's better than any map."

Damen watched him a moment—Hounds were ever intent at sniffing things out from what people said—or what they didn't. "It is, and I'd heard. I'd heard, too, that you've some problem with magic. Frankly, at first I didn't much like the idea of having you along, given that. But the Prime requested you, and Elstan's spells will be minimal. Communications, mostly, if our luck holds. Elstan knows your problem and I'm assured he can deal with it. Can you?"

"There's magic around me whether or not I take this road," Reandn pointed out, unable to completely hide the bitterness. With effort, he lightened his tone. "No one can slip a spell over us unknown if I'm around, not even a spell quiet enough to sneak up on a wizard."

"Well, then," Damen said, offering him a smile. "Maybe the Prime knows what's best after all."

Reandn wasn't sure of that; he offered a noncommittal

response. "I wouldn't be here if she hadn't asked for me."

Damen glanced askance at him. Damn Hounds—he ought to know better than to play word games with one. But this Hound let it go, and nodded at the corral. "These horses are all retired Wolf mounts—mustered out early because they didn't have what the Wolves want in a horse. We shouldn't have any trouble with them."

Didn't have quite the fire, is what he meant. That meant well-trained, athletic horses with temperaments a child could handle. "Except that palomino," Reandn said. "That mare's too fine for patrol work. She's a gift for Meira Kalena, then?"

Damen raised a thick eyebrow at him. All of his hair was plentiful, red and wiry, and looked somewhat at odds with his easy composure, as did his profusion of freckles. "You *have* worked with Wolf horses before," he said, then grinned, the sort of apology he clearly expected would do the trick—and it probably always had. "Not that I doubted you. But there's wranglers, and then there's wranglers. You'll know what I mean."

Reandn just nodded. This man was used to having things his way, but not to being heavy-handed about it. Good news for a Wolf who had most likely outranked this Hound not too long ago.

"Your own horse settled?" Damen asked. At Reandn's nod, he said, "You might as well come along to the inn, then. There's good food, and a Tits-fine bard, and we'll have an early start tomorrow."

Reandn watched the bard—a middle-aged woman with a schooled alto and a handful of children who scampered to catch the coins flung her way, cheering the loudest after her songs—who held her hand up to her throat and said, pitifully hoarse, "I'll play more later, gentlefolk, but I've a thirsty voice to feed just now."

The crowd's response was good-natured disappointment, for Damen had not exaggerated her skills. But she favored the sort of heartbreaking ballads Reandn did his best to avoid—Adela's favorites, of course—and he barely hid his relief at her departure.

"Didn't I tell you?" Nican—darkly resplendent in a red shirt beneath his Hound brown—crowed to Elstan. "Damn fine!" As partners, he and Damen were a study in contrasts. But Damen—tall, deep-voiced and easygoing—seemed completely adjusted to Nican, who was several inches shorter than Reandn but not the least bit smaller. He was, in fact, a burly man who looked like he'd somehow lost track of the height that had surely been allotted to him. But his words came fast, and his gestures were generous and frequent. Sitting at the same table in the busy tavern below the inn rooms, he was a little more than Reandn cared to deal with. Out on the road, it would be better.

He hoped.

Elstan merely shrugged; Reandn already had the impression that the cynical quirk of his lips was more or less permanent.

"Man, have you no heart?" Nican declared. "Have you ever heard 'Ciara's Ride' sung with such feeling?"

"Some men put their feelings on rations," Damen suggested. "What say, Dan, sitting over there so quietly? You rationing along with Elstan?"

Reandn's first impulse was low and growly and not meant for a remount wrangler to say to a Hound. After an instant's hesitation, he managed a slow and somewhat wicked smile. "I've just been put to sleep. Give me a good randy sing-along anytime."

Not the least put off, Nican said, "Oh, she'll do those when she comes back. Then we'll see if Elstan sings as well as he drinks down that ale."

"Wine," said Elstan. "Maybe the last fine vintage I'll have until we return from this journey, but wine nonetheless."

"Ah," Nican said. "A taste for the finer things. What brings you on this trip, then, if it's the court life you prefer?"

If Elstan had any sense of humor, it didn't show; he scooped his light brown hair out of his face and fixed his eyes—light brown to match his hair, and his stare without the impact he probably thought to inflict—on Nican. He might have thought his age gave him some advantage. Where Nican and Damen were more or less of Reandn's thirty-two years, Elstan appeared older by at least another five.

But no one else appeared impressed, not by his seniority or his connections. He said, "Malik himself requested my presence."

"Ah," Nican said again. "Then no doubt you're right to be here. Well, boyo, we won't make faces at your wine, long as you leave us our ale."

Elstan said nothing; Reandn thought he saw some color flush the man's neck, though in this poor light it was difficult to tell. But he had no doubt about the magic—it whispered against his ears and started to build, and he threw the wizard such a glare that Damen gave him a startled glance. Elstan never looked his way, but the magic fizzled away much less gracefully than Teya's ever had, like boiling water suddenly without a pot.

Randy sing-alongs, that's what they needed. The sooner the better, and then tomorrow they'd be out of these close quarters and on their way, bringing the hope of peace from the Resiores—and bringing Reandn back to the Wolves.

Teya stood at the top of the stairs and looked pensively down the hallway. She was on the second floor of the school, where the masters—the older wizards, who had learned their skills a generation earlier—did individual tutoring in their own dedicated rooms. Farren's room was here.

Teya had never formally met the wizard, who'd been there when magic returned. Reandn had mentioned him only in terms of the wizard's work with Saxe, and never commented about the man himself one way or the other.

From the few encounters she'd had with Farren, Teya could well imagine the two men wouldn't get along well, even if magic were no issue at all. Both had—and here Teya structured her thoughts to keep them reasonably respectful—unusually strong personalities. No doubt they'd spent a lot of their time together snarling at one another.

Saxe, however, seemed to get along fine with the old wizard. Maybe, Teya thought, because he'd been introduced along with his rank, which Farren respected. Reandn had met Farren while sickened by translocation and crazed with grief for his slain wife—and not as a Wolf at all. Just once, Teya had seen them together— the day she was posted to Reandn's patrol—and even though she'd barely known either of them, she'd seen the difference in how Farren treated Reandn. Peremptorily, with an assumption that his own words were the final ones. Oh, yes, there was a lot of tension there.

She wasn't comfortable with the thought of going to Farren for anything, never mind a favor.

Fortunately, Saxe was here as well; Teya was surprised at how often she'd seen the Wolf Leader in these halls recently. He and Farren were working hard to develop standards and policies for a new branch of the King's Service—wizards, trained to keep vigil on other magic-users. Teya's position as the first wizard in a Wolf patrol was the initial step in the process, but she had no illusions about making it into the new wizard patrol itself.

Not anymore.

She walked quietly down the quaintly detailed hallway—the entire building was a product of its time, a generation before the loss of magic itself, and at that point only one of many mage school buildings clustered in the center of Solace—and stopped beside the ornate curlicues that framed Farren's door. Up until this moment she'd been half-resolved to knock on the door, but suddenly doing so seemed entirely inappropriate. Interrupt a meeting between the Wolf Leader and the school's liaison to the Keep? Maybe on another, bolder day, but certainly not on this one. She'd just have to hope they came out for some fresh air before she had to run to the privy—for the moment she stepped away from this door, *that's* when the two of them would emerge.

She was somewhat startled when, after only a few moments of abstract thought, she discovered that the door was open and Saxe was looking at her with amused patience.

"Quick eye and quiet foot, Wolf," he said. "Even here."

Teya blushed. Not a good start. "I don't mean to interrupt," she said, rushing the words too much. "I—I just wanted to talk to you, and I figured here would be the best place to wait."

"Well, come in, then. I suspect I would benefit from a few minutes of *not* thinking about the ramifications of this particular project."

"In there? Me?" Silently, Teya groaned at herself. What an impression she must be making. But Saxe only nodded and opened the door wider.

The room was just as she remembered it—neat, organized, completely walled with bookshelves, uncluttered with the numerous and usually strange mementos the other masters tended to collect. She'd heard Farren ran a tailor shop in Maurant during the years between magic, and she could well imagine it, and imagine his precision with the details of such a business.

Farren sat behind a desktop strewn with notes, although even there, Teya thought she detected some semblance of order. He, too, was as she remembered— not a big man, old enough to be her grandfather but still straight and trim, with none of the thin-skinned frailties that would make her think of him as truly aged. He nodded to her, pleasantly enough, and leaned back in his chair, giving her tacit permission to carry on her conversation with Saxe.

"What can I do for you, Teya?" Saxe asked, seating himself beside the desk.

"I have some questions," she said. "About my patrol. Or what's left of it, I suppose."

Saxe winced. He had honest, square-cut features around a nose that ought to have been a little smaller, and even with her knowledge of his part in Reandn's current situation, she couldn't help but trust him. No wonder he'd made it to Wolf Leader. "Dakina's doing very well," he said. "And it looks like Dreyfen will heal well enough to stay on active duty. Maccus . . . that head wound of his . . ." Saxe shook his head. "He's not back with us yet. Don't get your hopes up for him, Teya. Without magic, he'd be dead now."

"Thank you," she said. "But that's not what I wanted to ask about."

Saxe raised an eyebrow in invitation. "What is it, then?"

"I was just wondering . . ." How to put this so she didn't reveal the information she already had? "I'm here, Dakina and Dreyfen are at the Keep, and the new Remote Patrols are forming out in Keland. No one's said anything to me about returning to Reandn's patrol, so I thought. . . . Will I be punished, Saxe? Is that why I haven't heard anything about returning to the Remote? And what about Dakina? Her partner was killed, and we'd really like to be paired when we go active again."

There. It was a long speech, but it said what she wanted to. She'd left a clear opening for Saxe to admit Reandn had been kicked out of the Wolves—and for him to tell her she wouldn't work with her patrol members again.

His expression was grave, and he swapped a glance with Farren, who said, "There are factors involved here that you know nothing about. It would be best if you didn't concern yourself with anything but healing and learning for now. Rest assured, we intend to use your unique abilities to their fullest extent."

With no little trepidation, Teya mustered her next words. "I say this with all respect possible, Meir Farren, but . . . this is a Wolf matter. I am asking, Wolf to Wolf."

Farren's blue eyes sparked, and Teya braced herself for his response. But Saxe, quiet but firm, said, "Farren," and drew the wizard's stern gaze. "That was a just statement. She was waiting for me; I was the one who invited her into your study. And," he added, raising a brow at the older man, "as I recall, it was to me she put the question."

Teya stood absolutely still, hoping that somehow neither of them would notice she was still in the room. Little chance of that, of course. As soon as Farren gave a short nod, Saxe turned back to her, and renewed their conversation as though it had never been interrupted.

"I didn't realize you felt so strongly about pairing with Dakina," he said, with the kind of regret that told her it was already too late.

Panic of a sort edged her voice. It was true, what Reandn's note implied was really true. "We figured we could handle it once we were reunited in the patrol. Reandn probably would have paired us up that way without even having to ask." That, she suddenly realized, was also true. As angry as Reandn made her, he was fully aware of the small social currents within the patrol, and considered them in his decisions.

Saxe shook his head, ever so slightly. "We can't afford to have you all in the same patrol, never mind paired," he said. "You went through the same horrifying experience; it's going to affect you no matter how you try to fight it."

"It'll just make us stronger," Teya said, unable to say the words as loudly as she'd like.

"In some ways," Saxe agreed. But he shook his head again anyway. "It's no punishment, Teya. But this is the way things have to be. You'll all have separate assignments."

"Will I even be put back out with the Remote?" Teya didn't dare to look at Saxe, but fastened her gaze on the indecipherable, upside-down scribbling on Farren's papers. They seemed a little blurry, and she blinked quickly, struggling to find a more professional composure. Somehow, what they'd been through hadn't seemed as bad when she thought she'd still have at least two of her patrol mates with her, and Reandn to lead them. That last notion was enough to startle her pressing grief away; she hadn't realized she'd actually come to depend on him.

Saxe said, "We're not sure yet. I . . . wish I could give you answers. The best I can do is tell you that we consider the experiment, the addition of a specialized wizard into a Wolf patrol, to be a successful one." He smiled at her; it didn't even seem forced. "If it worked with Reandn, it'll work with anybody."

Teya dutifully smiled back. She said carefully, "I hope, at least, that if you return me to the Wolves, you'll consider assigning me in Reandn's patrol. Right now I'm the only one you've got who's trained to make absolutely certain my magic doesn't affect him." She knew it wouldn't happen; she no longer had the unmitigated trust she'd once put in her Wolf leadership. Saxe and the Prime might well be doing what they thought was best for all, but that didn't mean they were doing what was best for *everybody*. The most her words could do would be to trickle through Saxe's mind when he was trying to sleep at night, and considering the look on his face right this moment, that might even happen.

Teya cleared her throat, and gave Saxe a salute, waiting for his nod of dismissal before she turned to go. She gave Farren a salute as well, but before she'd reached the door, something else occurred to her, and she turned back to them both, at a loss. "If I'm not really a Wolf anymore, and I'm not fully a student, then am I in any service at all?" Goddess, what if they decided to channel her to the Hounds, where her swamp upbringing would be all the more obvious, or to the Foxes, whose clandestine ways appealed to her even less than the Hounds' courtly domain?

Clearly, neither of them had considered the question at all. After a glance at Saxe, Farren said, "It would be unwise of the school to lose someone of your field experience at this point. Certainly, you should stay and learn what you can while you have the opportunity."

Slowly, Teya nodded. "I—yes, thank you, meir." Just as slowly, she left the room and returned to her own. Students came to this school of their own free will; they vied for the available slots, which as of yet were seriously limited. Some failed; some decided it wasn't the life they wanted. But no one, not even the successes, was forced to stay.

When she'd signed on with the Wolves, she'd agreed to stay for the years of her training and three years beyond, to pay for that training. But they'd gladly released her to the school when she'd shown such obvious signs of wizardly talent. And she'd signed nothing upon return to them, although she drew Wolf's pay like any other patrol member.

Now they had terminated that position with the Wolves. And, she thought, they were making far too many assumptions about her willingness to let them guide her life.

The thought rocked her. Here she'd just been *waiting* to hear what would happen next, when in truth she was able to make some of her own choices.

The first thing that occurred to her also scared the wits out of her.

Teya paced the room, shoving the chamberpot under her bed with a foot when she reached it. But pacing got her nowhere, so she put herself cross-legged on the middle of her bed and closed her eyes. She was swamp bred. One thing she was good at was standing in front of a decision and looking it up and down.

She drew Rethia's visit to mind; she'd thought about it for many days afterward, trying to understand some of the more obtuse things the woman had said. She was an odd one, all right, but Teya had the feeling that nothing she said or did was without purpose, no matter how obscure it might seem to someone else.

Does Danny make you angry? Rethia had asked. And of course the answer was yes, all too often. Because he was stubborn, and sometimes talking to him was like running face-first into a stone wall. Because sometimes he did things his own way, no matter what anyone else did to change his mind.

He'd handled Arval his own way, and look where it'd gotten him. *Yes, and he did things his own way to help that little girl*, Teya's quiet inner voice told her, and she grew absolutely still on the bed. But hitting Arval hadn't done *anyone* any good.

It stopped Arval from pushing you around.

Swiftly, she searched her memory, going past her sense of who and what her patrol leader was to the specific incidents that created that image. Her first patrol under his command, when he refused to let her use magic to subdue several ruffians the patrol had cornered. "Not yet," he'd said. "Not until I know you can do it." Humiliated, Teya instantly assumed he didn't trust her, simply because he didn't trust magic. Now she tried to look at the situation through his eyes. *Untested fledgling wizard, a spell to take the fight out of two burly outlaws who were tightly hemmed in by the Wolves . . .* Her eyes flew open. What if she'd misaimed that spell? She'd never even considered the possibility, but then, she knew the procedure behind it. He hadn't.

And how many times have you used that spell since you proved your aim was precise?

Plenty.

She sorted through similar incidents—the ones she had seen, the ones she was part of, the times his notorious temper was quick to rise, and the times he'd dug his heels in against Highborn orders.

Not all because he was just plain hard to get along with, or recklessly unheeding of the consequences. But because he thought it was best for the patrol. Or whoever had come under their jurisdiction. "Let the burning Minor *have* the thief," she remembered muttering under her breath on one brittle-cold day that winter, as Reandn and the Minor argued authority. In the end, since the Wolves had the thief held in the midst of them, they'd also walked away with him. Teya had rolled her eyes while her teeth chattered, knowing the patrol would hear about it from the Keep, and all for Reandn's willingness to take on a fight of any sort.

It suddenly occurred to her that since then, she'd heard bits and pieces about how harshly the Minor in question treated lawbreakers. And that the thief was young and cold and scared to death. Oh, he'd spent some time in jail, but in another Minor's area, and under the King's Justice. As far as Teya knew he still had all his fingers, and could still make an honest living if he cared to.

And after all of that, she recalled her own panicky thoughts during the bloodbath on the hill. *Reandn wouldn't have let this happen.*

Teya got up from her bed and moved over to the window, trailing her fingers down the thick, wavy glass. Reandn made her angry, he kept a strict hand on her use of magic, he usually did things his own way no matter what anyone else said. That was all still true. But she had the uncomfortable feeling in the pit of her stomach— like she'd swallowed a cold, raw potato whole—that she'd been just as quick to judge Reandn as she'd thought he'd been to judge her. And of the two of them, she thought he was probably closer to the mark.

That's where her impulse had come from, then. The scary one, the one she didn't even really want to think about, but that kept nudging at her anyway. The need to make it right between them. And the obvious way to do it. The thing that had been behind Rethia's last, veiled look, all its words unspoken.

She was no longer a Wolf—at least, not quite. She was no longer formally a student, either. She could make her own choices, though she doubted not that both

Farren and Saxe had made certain assumptions about those choices. They wouldn't be happy to know she was even considering this one.

To find Reandn, and join him, and protect him from the magic as no other wizard could do. To give him back some of the loyalty he'd been showing her all this time, and her unaware of it. And to be just as stubborn as he was about doing it.

After all, she'd been a key part of his dismissal from the Wolves. It seemed only fair that she play a part in getting him back in.

Chapter 5

Reandn balanced his small battered shaving mirror in the crook of a tree and thought again about just letting his beard grow. Unfortunately it was a decidedly scruffy sort of beard. In the past, he'd stayed clean-shaven for Adela. Now he couldn't quite seem to break the habit of pleasing her.

Well. Maybe next winter. Carefully, he set blade to skin and went to work on the several days' worth of stubble that looked back out at him from the mirror. Instantly, his breath fogged the thick glass. One of *those* mornings, then. All right; he knew the drill. A simple matter of holding his breath at the right time . . .

Reandn fell into the careful rhythm of shaving—but only until the unexpected blast of magic shattered his concentration; he yelped, slicing a fine line next to the whitening scar along his jaw. What the Hells? Another wave of magic hit him and he grabbed the tree for support, wondering if he'd missed something in his morning scout through the area, but not hearing anything over the magical chaos in his head to indicate anyone was in trouble.

Then his watering eyes saw Elstan, his fingers twisting away in a quick spell, his own shaving kit propped up on the sideboards of the supply wagon. The magic faded away, replaced by the hum of a spell still in place, and Elstan hummed along with it, setting his blade against his throat. Reandn scrubbed what was left of the shaving oil from his face and stalked up behind the wizard.

"What," he said darkly, waiting until Elstan started the next stroke of the razor, "is going on?"

Elstan jerked in surprise, and then hissed as a spot of blood spread out on top of the oil on his neck. "What are you trying to do, kill me?"

"I might ask you the same." Reandn came around to drape an elbow over the sideboard, the other hand hooked into his belt, his expression more intense than his body language would imply. Damen and Nican looked over from the breakfast fire they'd built, watchful but silent. "You were told about using magic around me. If you're going to use it, shield me. If you can't shield me, don't use it."

"*That* little spell? Don't try to tell me you felt that," Elstan snorted. He looked at the razor as if he'd like to finish his shave, but apparently decided he'd only court more nicks until he was out from under Reandn's scrutiny. By then, Damen had had enough, and was on his way over. "I really don't know why they couldn't have found a wrangler without so-called allergies to magic."

Damen stopped by the corner of the wagon and said, "I hate to put my nose in your business, but this sounds like it's about to become *my* business."

Reandn squelched a flash of annoyance—appropriate from a Wolf Patrol Leader but not from a wrangler. "I think we've handled it."

"We most certainly have *not*!" Elstan said. "I'm not here to be menaced by our *wrangler*. How am I supposed to handle outside threats if I'm worried about the one right beside me?"

"Don't recall that we've run into any outside threats," Damen said, but his eyes went to Reandn, who said nothing. "I heard enough of it," the Hound said. "What kind of a spell were you using, Elstan?"

The wizard, unaccountably, looked a little sheepish. "One I've been working on. To keep me from getting nicked when I shave."

Damen nodded. "Fine. If you're going to use incidental magic, then shield the rest of us from it. You agreed to that when you took on this assignment." He eyed Reandn again. "Don't let things get out of hand. Hear?"

Reandn hesitated, assessed Elstan's resistance to his orders to be on a level with his own, and knew nothing had been solved here. He gave a short nod.

Damen looked at Elstan's throat, humor drifting across his face. "I wouldn't bother with that particular spell again. It doesn't seem to do you much good."

Elstan waited until the Hound had returned to the fire before shooting Reandn a dark look, though his words were a mere mutter. "It works just fine, when there's no interference."

Reandn ignored him. It looked like he was going to need the practice.

Kacey stood with her sister in the darkness of the front yard, watching the cart lantern recede down the lane; Rethia wrapped her arm around Kacey's waist and leaned her head on Kacey's shoulder. The chill around both of them had nothing to do with the weather, for the fine, clear night hinted strongly of the summer to come.

"We did our best," she told Rethia, but her voice came out tight and unconvincing.

"I should have been able to do something for her." Rethia shook her head gently against Kacey's shoulder. "That's what I'm best at, poisons and infections."

Kacey's response was sharper than she intended. "Sophi fell on a whole farm's worth of newly sharpened tools. Goddess knows what filth we couldn't get out of those wounds."

Rethia knew her too well to take hurt; she merely held her sister more tightly for a moment.

The child had seemed well on her way to recovery when Rethia and Reandn left for Solace, but by the time Rethia had come back, Kacey was entrenched in a battle for Sophi's life. Three of the deepest cuts had taken infection, and none of their healing, magic or otherwise, had the strength to do the job. Looking back on it, Kacey felt like they had merely prolonged the girl's suffering, that it would have been better had she died when she first came to them.

"We *did* do our best," Rethia said, though she, too, sounded like she was only trying to convince herself. "I just keep thinking, what if I hadn't been in Solace? What if I'd caught the infection when it first started?"

Kacey scowled at the pain in her sister's voice. "What *if*," she said. "What if Reandn hadn't gotten her calmed in the first place? Might as well start there if you're going to play that game."

Rethia just nodded, but Kacey's own words kicked her thoughts off in another direction. "I hate the thought of telling Reandn we lost her," she said, looking at the last place where she'd been able to see the cart. "I hate worse thinking we might not get the chance."

"He'll be all right," Rethia said. "And if he's not, I can help him. Anyway, he's all right, now."

Kacey couldn't quite keep the accusing note from her voice. "How can you tell?"

"Just a feeling."

"You can still . . . what did you call it, feel his magical aura? From *here*?"

"No." Rethia lifted her head, sounding distracted and looking small and fragile in the moonlight; she, too, was staring down the lane the cart had taken, with its small, sad burden. "Just a feeling." After a moment she added, "Anyone can do it, you know."

"Do *what*?"

"Recognize magical scents." Rethia glanced over at her sister, and the moonlight glanced off her eyes. "I asked, when I was in Solace. Farren says it's not *using* magic at all, just . . . well, listening to it. Most people just do it with those that they care about most."

"*I've* never felt anything like that," Kacey said, not surprised. She had little if any feel of magic; she likened it to being color blind.

"Maybe you will," Rethia said. "Now that you know it's possible." She glanced back at the house. "I'm going for a walk, I think."

"Wait." Kacey hastily peeled off her top layer, a wool shirt. "Take this." Not that it was all that cool, but somehow she'd feel better anyway.

Rethia absently pushed her arms through the sleeves, almost lost in the garment, and wandered off toward the barn. No doubt heading for the well-worn trail that led to the meadow where she'd brought the unicorns back. Kacey watched her go, lost in her own thoughts, until she heard her father's breathing—Teayo was acquiring an audible wheeze as he aged—behind her.

"Come, my girl," he said, putting his hand on her shoulder. "Come inside." He took her hand, and Kacey let herself be led back inside, wishing for a whole host of reasons that she was truly a girl again, and still believed in her father's ability to make everything all right.

Close to the first of the roads that turned off toward the pass, the escort party stopped in Pasdon, the small town nestled in the foothills of the mountains. Amid the numerous small shops that claimed to be the last chance to buy this or that—always an absolutely crucial item, to judge by the signs that Damen, chortling, read for Nican and Reandn—there were a number of truly essential services.

In the livery, Nican stored the wagon and rented a smaller, more maneuverable cart for the pass roads. Reandn took the opportunity to tighten all the nail clenches on the horses' shoes, and left Elstan's bridle for repair. By the time they'd all run their respective errands—for Elstan and Damen were off resupplying

their foodstuffs—and then gathered by the livery, dusk
was turning to dark and they were all interested in dinner.
Elstan kept muttering something about a bath, and
Reandn thought that for once, the wizard had a good
idea.

"Sounds good to me, too," Damen said, once Nican
joined them. "Remember, we'll be stopping here on the
way back, too. Keep your eyes open for potential
problems." One red eyebrow askew, he looked at Reandn.
"We'll need all the help we can get to carry this trip off
without a hitch, so that goes for you, too, Dan."

That goes double for me, Reandn thought, but only
nodded. Besides, the Hounds specialized in guarding
individuals indoors and in crowds; Reandn's strengths
lay in the ways of forest and path, tracking and
apprehending. Up until now, he'd done little more than
play the part of the wrangler he was supposed to be,
keeping quiet, dodging Elstan instead of facing him
down, closing his mouth on any comments he might
have made while the Hounds discussed this assignment.
Once they hit the pass rendezvous, once they had
Kalena—who, as well as playing the part of the Resiores'
first official ambassador, was also supposed to find a
suitable husband to solidify political ties between
Keland and its rebellious Resiore offspring—then his
job would start in earnest.

Nican tapped his foot with impatience—the shorter
man's thick body seemed to be in constant motion no
matter how still he actually stood—and said, "Let's eat,
then talk. Did you hear my stomach just then? I can't
think with that sort of noise so close to my ears!"

Damen just grinned, but held out his hand in a grand,
darkness-obscured gesture for Nican to lead them on.
Off the group marched, heading for the Silver & Silk—
the town's finest inn—and glad of the need to check it
out. Nican had early suggested that the only thorough
way to do so was actually to stay there, on the King's
coin.

Of course, in the darkness they passed their turn and had to backtrack, giving Damen plenty of opportunity to make much of how Nican had indeed lost his ability to think. Reandn trailed behind them, shifting his saddlebags on his shoulder, thinking of days when he'd been able to joke the same with Saxe.

Magic washed over him, a weak stirring; Reandn recovered quickly from his stumble, confirmed it wasn't Elstan's by the way the wizard jerked around to face the threat, and dropped his saddlebags to the ground, whirling to plant himself on the balls of his feet, ready for anything.

The figure behind them was almost indiscernible in the darkness; pale glimpses hinted at his finger-twisting. Reandn, feeling nothing but the angry buzz of magic in his ears, moved in on the threat. "Dan!" Damen snapped from behind Elstan, a demand for restraint, but the street was narrow, and clogged with barrels and baskets, and Damen couldn't move quickly enough to interpose himself between them.

The figure mumbled spell elements and Reandn felt Elstan responding with his own magic, filtering through the incomplete shield he'd erected for Reandn. The anonymous wizard barely faltered, and demanded, "What pass road are you going to use coming down?"

And oddly enough, Reandn felt perfectly comfortable with telling, with saying *the long road* even though it hadn't been discussed, because he knew it was the logical choice. Behind him, he heard Nican choke off his own reply.

"*Compulsion*," Elstan said in a strangled voice, barely loud enough for Reandn to hear the noise in his head. Compulsion . . . he still felt like talking, but moved in on the wizard instead.

The figure took a step back and, sounding strained, demanded, "*Which road*? Which shortcuts?"

"Elstan!" Nican made the name into an order; Elstan's muttered reply meant nothing to Reandn's ears, fast filling with magic as they were, and despite his growing desire to talk, he had nothing to say. He stalked the wizard, who lost the threads of the spell, giving Reandn just enough relief so when she—he?—snapped an indecipherable command, Reandn knew instantly that the wizard had help.

The quiet scrape of boot leather against rough wooden barrel staves, the flurry of dark-upon-dark movement, Damen's cry of warning—Reandn took it all in, whirling to face the new threat. A thick weighted cudgel slashed down at his head, and he bounced away from it, rushing right back in to grab that arm, using his momentum to drive the man up against the nearest building. For the first time he had a feel for the man's excessive size, but new magic surged up around him, blinding him to anything else—and the arm twisted out of his grip. The man shoved him back, pummeling him with a few quick blows from a heavy fist that might as well have been the cudgel itself.

He might have been lost, then, if the magic hadn't ebbed for a moment, just long enough for him to block the next blow, operating more on instinct and long-drilled defenses than on a clear picture of what was happening in the magic-scourged darkness of the narrow street. And it was instinct that saved him when the magic crashed down again, leaving him with just enough clarity to realize he was going to die if he didn't end this right *now*—

A hazy fugue of tumult later, the magic cleared completely, leaving Reandn gasping, stumbling backward, the cudgel falling from one hand and the building behind coming up to smack him between the shoulder blades.

"Sweet Tenaebra!" Elstan cursed, unwisely revealing how close he was to Reandn. "You killed him!"

Distantly, someone was shouting; Reandn raised his head with effort and discovered someone on the run toward them, lantern in hand. He discovered, too, that his ribs ached where he'd taken blows he didn't feel at the time, and that one shoulder must have taken at least a glancing hit from the cudgel. Bruises, nothing more.

"He's not dead yet," Damen said, "but give him a moment." Between his words, Reandn heard a faint gurgling noise, the noise of death. "Damn these barrels, Dan, I just couldn't get through to you in time."

"What'd you kill him for?" Elstan said, incredulous. "We could have questioned him!"

Nican slid between them and out to greet the lantern bearer, a shopkeeper who was babbling about Locals on the way and how they ought to stay right here, and what in Tenaebra's Hell had happened—Nican inserted a calming phrase here and there, but went largely ignored. Reandn heard it all with only the fringes of his awareness; the rest of his attention was focused right on Elstan, whose accusing expression caught the light from the lantern and all but glowed in the darkness.

"Why'd I kill him?" Reandn repeated, so incredulous at the words he had to repeat them to make sure that's what he'd heard. "Because you didn't do your job, that's why! You left me wide open to all that magic!" Unthinking, he took a step toward Elstan, who flinched.

"Dan." Damen's voice came unruffled and full of true authority. Reandn unclenched his fists and stepped back again. "He's right about one thing. That magic-user got clean away; we definitely could have used the chance to question this man."

As if Reandn didn't know that. "I didn't mean to—" he started, and then stopped, because it sounded so absurd. *Whups, I didn't mean to kill him.* In fact, he wasn't entirely sure what he'd done, only that training and muscle had taken over when his mind had succumbed to magic.

Damen looked sharply at him, having latched on to those aborted words. "You didn't *mean* to? You *accidentally* disarmed him and laid that cudgel up against his throat?"

"Call it luck," Reandn said shortly. "With Elstan's magic

in my ears, I'm *lucky* I came out of it alive. It'd be me on the ground there if I hadn't been . . . lucky."

Damen frowned, making no effort to hide his skepticism. Reandn didn't blame him. Luck like that generally had endless hours of training and experience behind it.

"I've heard enough," Elstan said. "If it weren't for my magic, we'd have spilled our plans to that wizard, and then where would we be?"

"Right about where we are," Damen said, standing with an expressive grunt. "Considering we haven't *decided* which of the roads we want to take. Except that if you'd left Dan some space from the magic, we might very well have a prisoner left to question." He glanced down the street, where Nican spoke to someone in a Local's uniform, and moved in on Elstan so they could talk in a semblance of privacy. Reandn listened anyway.

Elstan's response was one he had tried before. "It's absurd that we have to work with a wrangler who needs that sort of pro—"

"Shut up," Damen said, but kept his voice low. "It doesn't really make any difference, does it? The Keep chose him, and they did it for their own reasons. Don't forget that you're only *playing* the role of guide—he's the only one who's actually traveled the pass area. Elstan, when you signed on for this little trip, you agreed to protect him. Now, what's the problem here? Won't you, or can't you?"

Elstan gave Reandn a furious look, but Damen waited with a patience that meant he'd stand there for as long as it took, and the wizard finally muttered, "It's a new spell. I'm working on it. I didn't honestly imagine he could be so sensitive. And I *can* find our path—using my magic."

Lonely Hells, the man doesn't know *how to keep his magic away from me.* "There's a lot more to getting through this area than not losing the path," he told the wizard, and then ignored him. It was a better option than tearing his head off, which was starting to sound far too tempting. "Damen, I didn't realize that you had no instruction on the route. I thought you simply weren't ready to tell me."

"Nope," Damen said, moving back from Elstan. "Didn't want to have anything set in stone—for just this sort of reason." He nodded at the dead man. "Here's not the place to talk about it, though. Nican will handle the Local; let's get us to that hotel, and get them started heating water for us."

Now *that* sounded like a good idea. Finding his knees steady again, Reandn followed Damen up the street. Elstan stood where Damen had left him, looking like he still wanted the chance to muster up some scathing argument. His face had started this journey too pale and had put on something of a permanent sunburn flush ever since, but now he stood out in the darkness like a ghost. Reandn hesitated as he passed the wizard, just long enough to say, "Ambition's no bad thing for any man—but your ambition stops when it starts to step all over me. You can't keep your magic to yourself, then shut it down."

Elstan crossed his arms over his chest. "That sounded an awful lot like folly, my friend. What chance has a wrangler got against a trained wizard?"

Reandn grinned at him, and jerked his head to indicate the large lump of what had been a confident fighting man. "Same as I had against him, Elstan." He tipped a finger at Elstan's throat. "Wizards bleed—or don't you remember?"

Elstan batted at his hand. Reandn avoided the contact and instantly returned his hand to a hair's breadth away from Elstan's throat; the wizard froze in consternation. "Think about it," Reandn said, and went off to get his dinner.

"I saw that," Damen said, scrubbing a thick towel over his wet hair. Thick and clean, and smelling of herbs. This inn was no mean place, and would be able to host their Resiore Highborn in style. Reandn sat immersed in the high-sided tub, debating himself over whether he'd gotten the soap out of his hair, and decided to go under one more time. When he emerged, snorting water out of his nose, Damen had planted one hand on the side of the tub, waiting. He might have been imposing if the towel wrapped haphazardly around his hips wasn't slipping.

Reandn pushed water out of his eyes and said, "Saw what, in particular?"

"What you did to Elstan." Damen straightened and adjusted his towel. His clothes, like Reandn's, dried by a roaring fire, draped over an elaborately carved mantle made from Resioran chokenut wood. The rest of the room was just as lavish in its appointments, from the thick feather mattresses with their embroidered linens to the filigreed iron sconces holding lattice-windowed lanterns. A Wolfish wrangler could feel quite out of place.

Reandn groped over the side of the hammered copper tub and found his own towel. "Nican's going to have a nice cold bath if he doesn't get himself back here."

Damen waved a hand. "Don't you worry about Nicco. He's building good cheer with the Locals somewhere, and enjoying himself doing it. We were talking about you."

"I thought we were talking about Elstan. I've plenty to say about him."

"I'm sure you do." Damen's tone was dry; he'd settled on putting his hands on his hips, which served to hold the towel up as well as to emphasize his point. Reandn stood and sluiced water off his body, stepped out of the tub, and started in with the towel. Ah, luxury—stopped short by Damen's sudden comment. "Hells, he *did* get in a few good hits."

Reandn glanced at him; he'd said as much, after all. "I think we should talk about the pass," he said. "*Before* Elstan returns." Elstan had elected to pay for his own separate bath out of his private purse, and waited in the dining area while the water heated for it. "He's enough of a problem for me; he's only going to get worse if he has to listen to this."

Damen snorted, padding over to check his clean, drying clothes. "You've already taken it too far for that, threatening him like you did. Not," he added, glancing over at Reandn, "that I blame you. No man should claim to strengths he doesn't have, especially when the lives of others ride on it. We can only hope he's as good with the rest of his magic as he seems to think he is." His voice seemed to indicate there would be more, so Reandn waited where he was, with water from his wet hair dripping slowly down his back. "Dan, I *understand*— but I can't have it. We've got enough to deal with on this trip. You're a good wrangler and I'm glad for it. But stay out of Elstan's way. Come to me with it if he doesn't shield you with his magic."

Reandn just stood there. It was a long way from being Wolf Remote to being a wrangler who had little say in anything that went on around him. He should have acquiesced, and acknowledged Damen's command. But the best he could do, after closing his eyes to remind himself just why he was here—the Resiores . . . Kalena . . . *the Wolves*—was to nod, and say, "I hear you."

Damen looked at him for another long moment, the firelight licking at the edge of his crisp red hair so it looked red-hot. "Good. Your clothes are dry. Catch."

It could have been much worse. Reandn might have been traveling with two Hounds with no tolerance at all for a wrangler who stepped out of line instead of these two easygoing men. He snatched his clothes out of the air and wasted no time donning them; they were still warm from the fire, and that, too, was a luxury.

"Now," Damen said. "About that pass."

Reandn changed subjects just as easily. "There are two main ways to go, with a lot of little options on the longer branch—most of them are choices we can make as we get there; I know them all. The short route is a rough climb; it can be done in a day but it's better at one and a half. No one'll be able to trail us closely without being seen, but the cart won't make it up that way. The longer route—two or three days of riding—is easier, and right now, we've got plenty of time to get there before Kalena does. We've got to go down that way, regardless—Kalena probably won't be able to handle the short route, unless Resiore Highborn are different from ours. Going up it would give you a chance to check out the different routes—most of them just split and join up again, going around outcrops and the like—and spot the most likely places for trouble." He knew the worst ones, himself, but that wouldn't be enough for the Hounds.

"I see," Damen murmured, though none of it seemed to come as a surprise—and shouldn't have. This much, he would have been briefed on. Testing his wrangler, he was. "Been thinking about this, have you?"

"A wrangler," Reandn told him, "is always thinking about the safest way to take his stock." And grinned. Let Damen think of that what he might.

It had been easier than she had expected to get this far. Teya looked at the road before her—the road to Pasdon—and took her thoughts back to Solace, back to the very beginning of this trip.

In Solace, she had sat on her bed and stared at the short coil of hair in the palm of her hand. Dark blond hair, medium-fine, all too familiar. It had given her no answers.

With a sigh, she slipped the hair back into the small silk bag where it belonged. In her pack, along with her day-to-day gear, she had silk bags for every member of the Remote. Gathering them had been amongst the first of the things Reandn had allowed her as patrol wizard; as long she had the hair samples, she could locate any of the Wolves.

For the first time, it occurred to her just how many of those samples would lead her back to Minor Arval's Tenaebra-damned hill. With a quick shudder, she dumped her pack out and sorted through the bags, shoving aside those from her dead comrades. She'd dump them in a fireplace just as soon as she could, no doubt about that. She stared at the bags a moment and shivered. So many dead.

Then you might as well think about the one who's still alive. She knew where he was, now; the finding spell had shown her that much, pinpointing a spot on the crude map she had chalked on the floor. So far away . . . he must have gone almost immediately upon leaving Arval's. Even if she'd had a horse and enough coin to keep them both fed, she didn't know if she could catch up to him. If only she were one of those who'd shown talent for translocation, then she could—

Teya stopped those thoughts short. Who said *she* had to do the translocation? There was no way she would get authorization to have the spell invoked for herself, but—wasn't Saxe returning to the Keep in the morning? It didn't take so much more magic to translocate two or three than it did to do the same to one. Reandn wasn't so far from there, not yet. And at the Keep she'd find Dakina and Maccus, to whom she needed to say her own good-byes now, as well as pass on Reandn's. Starting from the Keep would make up all those days of travel she trailed him; she could worry about getting a horse once she was there. Surely, Teya had thought, Saxe would understand her need to say good-bye to her patrol mates, and sympathize enough to let her come along.

As it turned out, she'd been right. But visiting Dakina had turned out to be harder than Teya imagined. They'd cried a lot, the two of them had, for just seeing each other brought back all the pain of what they'd lost together, all feelings that had gone vague, almost booted out of their lives, by their quick separation and the move away from their patrol area. They had distracted themselves by talking about Reandn's message, and that had been hard, too, for Teya had promised not to tell the extra that she knew.

Maccus greeted her with less enthusiasm; that hurt, but soon enough Teya figured out that it was the memories he wasn't glad to see, and not her at all. And while Dakina was healing enough for very light duty, Maccus still had a long time to wait. Hearing Reandn's news hadn't helped his mood any, though Teya noted how his voice got all gruff when he realized the effort she'd gone to to deliver the message, and that Reandn had defied so much to write it for them in the first place. "He always did watch out for us," he'd said, and then turned stony and silent.

Teya didn't blame him, not really. She'd had more time to think it out, and knew more about how the Keep had been willing to use their patrol, and how they'd dealt with things afterward.

So, patting the neck of the sturdy *borrowed* creature beneath her, she didn't feel all that badly about deceiving Saxe, though she wondered what the consequences might be. "I'd like to go for a ride," she'd told him after several days at the Keep. "May I borrow one of the Wolf mounts?" And Saxe had nodded, no doubt little suspecting that the ride Teya had in mind might last quite some time. But this course was one way of standing up to the Keep, to Saxe and Ethne and whomever else made the kinds of decisions that had so wracked their patrol this spring—and of showing them the kind of loyalty the Remote Wolves had for each other, and what Reandn, as frustrating as he was, could inspire in them.

You were wrong, she told them firmly in her head, wondering if she'd ever have the nerve—or chance—to say it for real.

Of course, if she never caught up to Reandn, if she came limping back to the Keep with nothing to show for what she'd done—well, things would be a little harder then. She doubted she'd be able to talk her way out of that one.

The thought strengthened her resolve to do this job, and do it right. She'd done a recent location check on Reandn, and knew he was north of her, undoubtedly on this same road. She'd have to ride steadily to catch up with him, and earn provisions on the way. She didn't worry about that; wizards were not so plentiful that her skills would go unheralded, and she knew many more spells than those she used regularly on patrol. "I hope you're ready, Reandn," she said, "because what's left of your patrol is on its way."

Nican returned to the inn with chagrin on his face and bad news on his lips. "Local wants us here while he tries to get the dead man identified," he informed them, picking through the food that Elstan had brought back up to the room, his stomach growling more loudly than ever.

"I doubt the dead man's from around here," Damen said, voicing Reandn's thoughts. "Look, Nicco, did you tell him we're on a schedule?"

"Sure." Nican shrugged. "But short of telling him just what we're up to, he won't be convinced of its importance. Besides, it's just an excuse. He really wants us here while he tries to confirm who we are. He's pretty edgy—we're lucky he didn't come right out and detain us."

"Not many Hounds outside of the Keep," Reandn said, his fingers busy at the long lead rope he was splicing from two newly ragged pieces back into one. "If you were Wolves, now, you might have a chance."

Damen flicked his fingers at his own shoulder, where the Hound emblem—his own worn enough to show frayed threads around the edges—proclaimed his status, and below it, where patterns of leather lace identified his rank. "How's he think we came by these patches?"

"Stole 'em," Nican said, cheerfully enough, depositing

cleaned rabbit bones back on the plate. "Not to worry. Don't forget that the Keep just sent a mage out here for messages. Not that the fellow can do anything *but* messages . . . it's enough for our purposes. They'll sort it out."

Reandn raised an eyebrow. "The Keep's that worried about things here near the pass?"

"Not that you know about," Damen said, and left it at that. To Nican, he said, "Well, then, we ought to have this problem cleared up by tomorrow morning at the latest. We won't lose that much time."

" 'Fraid it's not that easy," Nican wiped his greasy fingers on the inn's finely woven linen napkin and left it crumpled by the food, casting an apologetic look at Damen. "Messenger's sick right now—running a fever, mumbling a lot. Not casting spells of any sort, that's for sure. Local wants to know what's our rush, anyway. I didn't push—had the feeling it would only make things worse."

Damen grumbled something unintelligible, echoing Reandn's own inner curse. "Nicco, you're supposed to be able to charm your way out of anything. This is a fine time to lose your touch."

"Speaking of charm," Elstan said, "I could try to—"

"No!" the Hounds said in emphatic unison. Nican looked at his partner and shrugged. "If we run out of time, we leave."

"One day," Reandn said, "and we won't be able to take the long way. Three days, and we'll have to push hard to make it the rough way. Even then, someone'll have to take the cart around on the other road."

"I'll do it, if it comes to that," Damen said. "Dan, we want that palomino waiting for Kalena along with Nicco, so you two'll be going the rough way. And Elstan, because we want him there to watch for magic."

"Makes more sense to take the remounts the long way," Reandn said, more because he thought he ought to than because he wanted to. Given the choice, he wanted to be with Kalena's party as soon as possible.

"I suppose it does, to a wrangler," Damen said, a note of apology in his voice. He scrubbed a hand down his short wiry beard. "But it'll be bad enough not to have the extra supplies there, and only one of the supposed Hound honor escorts."

Reandn shrugged, staying in wrangler role. "It's up to you."

"Exactly." Damen nodded. "All right then. We give the Local a few days, and then we leave regardless. If we have to straighten things out on the way back through, so be it. Say, Nicco, now that I'm nice and clean, I can tell just how bad you stink. Elstan's bath water is still warm enough—have at it, why don't you."

Nican made a melodramatic face to indicate much offense, and within moments, the leftover food had found its way into the silliest of battles, while the wizard protested loudly and hastened to put himself out of the way.

Reandn ducked a gleaming bone and it sailed by to land in the bath; before long Damen had Nican in the tub, clothes and all. It was the camaraderie of two men who served together with the kind of intensity that demanded an equally fervent release of tension, and Reandn was well familiar with it. *Soon enough*, he told himself. He was here, after all, to regain both the duty and everything that went with it.

Except that it suddenly occurred to him that since leaving the Keep, since losing Adela and his ability to serve as Wolf First, he'd already been shut off from this, the camaraderie and the Wolfish byplay, stuck in the role of Remote First with no one near his rank or experience to relax with. He stiffened where he sat, his hands stilling on the complex weave of the splice, and wondered if it would always be that way. And then his thoughts crept back to the hot day he'd sneaked into Teayo's sickroom with a bota full of cool well water and taken clear aim at the back of unsuspecting Kacey's neck. The patients had cheered them on from Kacey's first outraged shriek, and then of course, she'd retaliated with nothing less than her usual spirit. Not the same as being with a bunch of rowdy Wolves, no, not the same at all.

Reandn went back to splicing his rope, but the images persisted.

The following day, Reandn, with patience that Saxe would have applauded, sat in the Local post building and told the Local everything he remembered from the attack. Everything, that is, but his own reaction to magic; no one around here needed to know about that. Once, twice, three times, he went over the moments of the fight, shifting to ease the throb of his bruises, until finally that patience frayed just a tad and he asked his own questions. The Local, an older man with a larger force under his command than the size of the town seemed to merit, readily admitted that he could find no wrong in what Reandn and the others had done. "Doesn't mean there's not something going on here that I maybe ought to know about," he told Reandn. "I've been at this job too long to ignore my gut when it tells me that's so. And if it is, you'd best come right out and tell me, because if I find out about it on my own, I won't be happy with you. Believe me, you'll know it."

Reandn liked him. But all he could do was shake his head, and eventually the man made a noise of disgust and turned him loose.

He knew the Local's frustration. His own gut feelings, the hunches that had saved his life more than once and usually meant trouble for everyone, were unhappily bumping into each other. How had the attacking wizard and his—or her, they still weren't sure—accomplice known why they were in town? Even if they had known for sure that Kalena was on her way—and Reandn figured that information was harder to hide from the Resiore end of things—how had they found her intended escort so quickly after their arrival in Pasdon? Two

Hound uniforms among them meant they were hardly incognito, but to have been accosted so quickly meant that someone was spending far too much time and energy looking for an escort in the first place.

The Hounds, he suspected, had already discussed this question between them, and had rightly not considered that their wrangler would have any need to participate. In fact, he didn't even know what Damen and Nican were up to. He'd see if they were at the inn, he decided, and then take one of the remounts out for a quick ride through the area—a one-Wolf patrol.

Just outside the inn, the usual mixed currents of magic in the background of Reandn's thoughts made way for the louder tone of a spell in progress, flavored with the discordant feel of Elstan's magic. He paused there, wondering if perhaps he might ought to take that ride *before* he checked for the Hounds, and trying not to feel the resentment that welled up in him. Elstan could hardly be expected to shield him when the wizard didn't even know he was within reach of it, but goddess *damn*, he was already weary of dealing with this man and his magic, and their journey together wasn't even half over.

After a moment he realized his thoughts must be showing on his face, as yet another inn patron on the prowl for a midday meal hesitated at the open door beside him and then too quickly ducked inside. Consciously, he shook the Wolf out of his posture. No true wrangler under Hound orders would take himself out of reach for several hours, especially not without trying to check in first. Even if there *was* a wizard finger-twisting nearby.

All the same, he stopped outside their room, swallowing hard against the magic and fighting the overwhelming urge to shake his head clear—it would, he had learned, only make him dizzy for real as well as from magic. When he opened the door and stepped through, it was with the quiet, stalking steps that were more than second nature to him now.

Elstan sat cross-legged on one of the several beds,

his eyes closed; he muttered words in a conversational pattern—though in the gaps meant for a reply, there was only silence. As Reandn closed the door behind him, the wizard's voice grew louder, loud enough to decipher through the noise of magic bouncing around in Reandn's head. "Of *course* the Local is suspicious! After the way that wrangler killed—"

Reandn thought it was time to clear his throat.

Elstan stiffened in response, his eyes flying open; his fingers clenched in a quick, spastic gesture, and the flow of magic in the room abruptly vanished. "How dare you sneak in on me!" he said, literally sputtering the words; Reandn was tempted to hand him a washrag for his chin instead of dignifying the wizardly outrage.

"I wasn't sneaking anywhere," he said. "You ought to lock the door if you don't want people coming in while you're not paying attention. What was that all about?"

"I don't report to you, wrangler."

Reandn said nothing.

Elstan shook his head, and his clearly defined lips thinned. "I was checking in with the Keep, as is my job, and I imagine that if you bother the Hounds about it, you'll learn that they asked me to attend to it promptly because of last night's encounter."

Reandn leaned back against the closed door, considering the wizard for a moment. Elstan's flushed face, pale around his mouth and eyes, becried more than simple anger at being interrupted. All the same, the little that Reandn had heard fit neatly into Elstan's claim—and he didn't imagine that the wizard was particularly adept at a cunning lie. So he merely said, "As long as my neck is in danger along with yours, Keep business *is* my business."

"This is pointless." Elstan jabbed his finger toward the door. "I've got work to do—out!"

If nothing else, Elstan had just provided him with a perfect excuse to ride the area. *Out*, Reandn had been told, and *out* was where he intended to go. He gave

Elstan a dryly executed salute—the more common Dragon salute, which was a touch to his right shoulder to indicate his weapons and his ability to wield them were at Elstan's disposal—and left the room.

He had, he decided, considering Elstan's harried expression, a lot to think about.

The escort waited as long as they could, and then prepared to go. The livery owner had been instructed not to release their stock, but Nican cheerfully bribed him to go take in a leisurely morning meal, and they were left alone with the horses, cart, and mule.

Reandn unknotted the rawhide lacing that wound through the thin braid in the bell mare's tail, taking a dozen chiming bells with it. The other horses would be hobbled at night now, instead of going free to forage with the mare's familiar bells keeping them close. Just her presence, tied at camp, would be enough to keep the little herd from testing the limits of hobbled travel.

"Ah," Nican said, joining him at the town corral beyond which sat their cart, loaded and ready to go, the mule looking bored in its harness. "Just on my way to ask you to do that. Last thing we need when trying to be inconspicuous in the pass, ey?"

"True enough. Even if there wasn't any sign of unusual traffic at the base of the pass roads." For that's where Reandn had gone on his ride, sitting the unfamiliar canter of one of the remounts to examine the turnoff area at both roads. With traces of snow left on the muddy roads and the pass just barely open, the road wasn't hard to read. A few hardy souls had been through, but not many, and no one left tracks leading into the sparse woods around the base of both roads. The rocky incline of the short road, with its abrupt and steep twists, would be almost impossible to read; Reandn knew that the trees at its base quickly gave way to thin, hardy foliage, bushes that could grow from a crack in vertical rock. Unleafed at this time of year, they would offer no cover. The longer road wound lazy zigzags amid the widely spaced conifers, and Reandn had examined it as far up as he could, finding nothing that alarmed him despite the incident with the unidentified wizard. If someone was lurking in numbers, or taking serious stock in the lay of the land, there wasn't any sign of it.

Or else they were damn good, and in that case, Kalena and the escort could find themselves in real trouble. Reandn hefted the string of bells and said, "I'd almost feel better if we'd *found* some sign." At least then they'd *know*, and the wizard's attempt to gain information would make more sense.

"Assumed we'd find nothing more than you did, I see." Nican didn't seem to take any offense at it, just a certain amount of amusement. The Hounds, too, had checked the roads, riding out the day after Reandn, both impatient as their travel time shrank and the Local placidly waited for his wizardly messenger to recover—which hadn't happened yet. The Hounds, as planned, were moving on without sanction.

Reandn said cheerfully, "Not unless you two started seeing things."

Nican snorted. "Damn cocky wrangler. We ought to send you the long way around, and on foot."

Reandn grinned. "You really want to be tied to that palomino while you do Hound duty up the short road? Damen's not going to make it to the head of the pass in time to meet Kalena—you damned sure want to see that that horse makes it."

"That means you come with me, I suppose," Nican said, but his gloomy mien was an act. "Well, if nothing else, I need you around for relief from our self-important wizard." For they no longer had the option of the long road, if they were to arrive before Kalena at the pass. Damen opted to take the cart the long way, giving at least one of them the chance to scout their return route. Reandn's remounts would carry a few light packs, just enough to supply them until Damen arrived.

Reandn glanced across the corral to where Elstan wrestled with his saddle girth, and his feelings must have gone straight to his face.

"Tsk," Nican said. "You and that wizard. You might as well be Knife, the way you two set each other off. Though he's agreeable enough this morning—he's not even rubbing magic in your face."

"Not a peep," Reandn said. "He's probably put it aside for his favorite morning entertainment." That entertainment would be watching Sky—or, rather, the first few moments after Reandn mounted Sky, when the horse teetered between obedience and flat-out running away.

"I'm kind of fond of that particular diversion myself," Nican said. "Wasn't until I felt that racking gait that I figured out why you put up with him." His ride on Sky had been brief and speedy and had left Damen snorting with laughter, but Nican had handed back the reins with new respect for the horse. Or maybe it was for Reandn, for handling the creature at all.

"Oh, Sky's earned his place with me," Reandn said. "But the truth of it is, once you've got his trust, he's no trouble." *Usually*. He gave the gelding a fond glance; Sky, tied to the corral rail, was making deep-chested manly noises at the bell mare. Scarred hock, gelded late, full of quirks and eccentricities, the horse had still given his life once because Reandn asked it. Yes, he'd earned another lifetime of forbearance.

"I notice," Nican said quite somberly, "that you always make sure he's facing a clear path before you so much as put a foot in the stirrup."

"Hells, yes," Reandn said. "I'm not betting he won't just try to go through anything in his way. Would you?"

Nican's somber expression cracked into the grin that had been hiding beneath. "Hells, *no*."

Damen looked up from the other side of the corral, where he conferred with Elstan and the map. "Nicco, quit bothering him—we want to get out of this town sometime before noon!" And before the ranking Local was up and around.

Little chance of a problem with that—dawn had just moments ago brightened into true day. But Reandn tied the last horse's halter to the horse in line before him, and picked up the bell mare's lead rope. "All ready," he said. "Just let me get Sky sorted out and we can go."

Sky, pawing dramatically for the bell mare, clunked his foot against the corral rail, startling himself into a wild shy against his lead rope. Instantly, he humped his back and popped his hind feet up in an annoyed buck, his ears flattened and his nostrils flared with such exaggeration that Reandn rolled his eyes.

"No trouble at all," Nican said, and snickered.

Rocks loomed around them, sometimes over them, and always beneath them, dotted in the shadows with blobs of the season's last snow and jutting out to make the trail twisting and complex. Sky's breath puffed out with frosty little grunts, and Reandn leaned far forward in the saddle, leaving the horse his head and staying off his bunched, hard-working quarters. Just past this steep rise was a flat area big enough for all of them, and with any luck, Nican, who was leading, would call a halt to let the horses blow. Reandn wiped his face—sweaty despite the higher altitude's chill—and decided he could use a rest himself.

Behind him, the string of remounts clattered up the trail, moving more easily without the weight of riders, barely hindered by the two light packs among them. Ahead, Elstan lurched on his own mount, struggling with the rough ride but not complaining, and too distracted to play with his magic. Reandn knew he'd already been far too exposed on this trip, and suspected that if it weren't for the effectiveness of Kacey's nasty elixir, he'd be in trouble long before he made it back to Teayo's little clinic.

Oh, bloody damn. He'd counted his blessings too

early. Elstan was at it again, though how he had the concentration to work magic, Reandn didn't know, for he was struggling with his horse, trying to guide it to a slightly different path than Nican's—a treacherous path with a jumble of rocks for footing. *Why—?*

And then Reandn realized that Elstan had his hands full of reins, and no fingers left to twist in magic. *Someone else*— Sudden strong spell-noise flared and faded, blurring Reandn's vision and snatching the warning from his throat. Elstan cried out in fear and surprise as man and horse went down, falling away from each other. The horse screamed in a too-human expression of pain. Stunned, Elstan lay just within reach of the horse's flailing hooves as the animal tried to regain its feet.

Reandn flung himself off Sky, dropping the bell mare's lead as he scrambled over rocks to reach the horse and throw himself on its neck. Struggling with the creature, his nose full of its sweat and his hands slipping over its slick hide, he spent interminable moments trying to still the horse without getting tossed among the rocks himself.

By the time he got a good grip on a rein and jammed it under his foot, Nican was dragging Elstan away— and Elstan, despite his dazed expression, protested the rough treatment almost immediately. A good sign that he hadn't cracked his head open, at least. Reandn left Nican to check the wizard over, and turned back to the horse.

Ah. Not much point in doing anything but slitting the animal's throat, not with its foreleg splintered, white bone gleaming—although if he was slow enough, it'd be dead before he got the chance, the way its blood drained into the rocks from that leg. It lay still now, its entire body heaving with labored breathing, its eyes glazed with shock. Reandn looked up to find Nican's gaze upon him, and he shook his head. Kneeling half next to, half on top of the horse's neck, he stroked it while it died.

By that time he'd had plenty of chance to look over

the track Elstan had taken, and to see that the horse had had no chance at all, not from the moment it set foot among those rocks. *Damn*. He gave the horse one last pat and let it lie. *Damn*. What had that been about? Elstan, at least, was sitting now, no signs of blood or bone. Reandn caught Nican's eye and put a question into it.

"He'll be all right, I think." Nican looked from the horse to Elstan and back again. "Goddess knows how long he'll hurt from this, but bruises aren't usually fatal."

"Not usually," Reandn said, his voice hard. "Why the Hells did you force that horse over there, Elstan? You as good as killed it."

Elstan's hands shook; he put them in his lap and only muttered, "Trust the wrangler to see to the horse before checking to see if I was even still alive."

Nican snorted. "Wouldn't have made any difference *how* alive you were if he hadn't kept that horse down. It was trying to get up, Elstan my boy, and just who do you think it would have gotten up *on*?"

Elstan stayed silent for a long moment, long enough for Reandn to assess the other horses and find them waiting patiently, glad for the break. Above them, Nican's mount seemed to be wandering uphill, but not at any speed. Finally the wizard pushed his hair—long enough to fall in his face, not long enough to tie back, and not anything Reandn would have put up with—away from his eyes, took a deep breath, and spoke the first honest, albeit puzzled words that Reandn had heard from him. "I don't know why I went that way," he said. "I just *did* it. I didn't even think about it."

"You thought about it enough to fight your horse," Reandn said, but there was no accusation in his voice.

Elstan didn't deny it. He shifted, wincing, and rubbed the side of his leg. What they needed, Reandn knew, was a good stream, still frigid from the snow pack; a few cold compresses would go a long way toward keeping those bruises manageable. Elstan, unfortunately, would do without. He was at least truly beginning to regain his wits; a few more deep breaths and he said, "I . . . yes, I just really *wanted* to go that way."

"What about the magic?" Reandn asked.

Nican said sharply, "There was magic?"

Elstan's mouth fell open and stayed that way; his eyes searched the rocks as though he'd find the answers there. At last he said, "I . . . I guess there was. Not much of it, though."

"Enough," Reandn said, pointedly looking at the dead horse.

"Somehow it didn't seem important at the time. I suppose that was part of the spell." Elstan's normal confidence, the slightly supercilious tone of voice that set Reandn's teeth on edge, crept into his words again. "It was a compulsion spell, of course. And it must have been set for me."

Yes, the wizard was recovering quite nicely from the shock of his fall.

"The same reason someone came at us in the street the other night," Nican said. "Doubt me not, set by the same wizard."

Elstan nodded. "We certainly know he likes to deal with compulsion spells."

"Why not set a spell for all of us?" Reandn exchanged a puzzled glance with Nican, not much interested in Elstan's suppositions.

Elstan answered anyway, prefacing his words with a snort. "That's obvious. If someone else triggered a spell before I got to it, I'd be able to counter it—and I *am* the one they need out of the way so their own wizard can work unfettered."

You'd try *to counter it*, Reandn thought. So far he'd been unimpressed with Elstan's wizardry, but he reminded himself that his early exposure to Farren's skilled finger-twisting had left him jaded to wizards of more average ability. And Teya, he'd kept on a tight enough rein that she'd never had the opportunity to flaunt spells in which she wasn't well rehearsed. He said to Nican, "They didn't try to kill us the first time, either. They could have."

Nican nodded, his brows set in a thoughtful line, but Elstan scoffed. "What are you talking about? Have you forgotten it was *you* that man went after? If you hadn't been so lucky, you'd be dead right now!"

"No," Nican said to Elstan, with a glance at Reandn to see that his wrangler wasn't rising to such bait. "Dan's right. They didn't intend for that meeting to be physical at all—it went bad when the spell didn't work."

"I countered it," Elstan said. He shifted his weight, testing his bruised leg.

"Whatever," Nican said, casually waving away the interruption. "Point is, they didn't mean for anyone to be hurt. Which means that they weren't ready to stop us—and that they still *aren't* ready to stop us, not all of us."

"Which means," Reandn finished, "that they want Kalena on this side of the pass."

Elstan frowned. "How do you figure that?"

Nican eyed Reandn as if wondering the same thing of his remount wrangler, though he'd clearly followed Reandn's thinking. He told Elstan, "If we don't show up at the pass to meet Kalena, she's simply going to return to the Resiores in a big huff, insulted. If we meet her as expected—supposing we were none the wiser about that little compulsion spell, and they have no reason to suspect that Dan can feel that level of magic—then she'll be traveling Keland roads. So if they don't want to stop us, then they *do* want her traveling in Keland. Follow?"

"It seems like a lot of supposing to me."

"Just common sense," Reandn said. He stepped away from the conversation, moving to the dead horse. A few moments of staring at it confirmed the thought roaming around in his mind. "Nican . . . Kalena might be better served if we *didn't* meet her at the pass."

Nican moved up beside Reandn. "Maybe so. But we've got our orders, and Damen's headed for the apex of the pass with or without us. Doesn't leave us with any choice no matter how you look at it." He paused, and Reandn waited, watching him try to come up with the right words. "Dan, the Prime figured you were up to this sort of thing, or you wouldn't be here."

Reandn snorted. "I'm fine. It's Kalena I'm thinking about. Which will make things worse—failing to meet her, or losing her to the outfit that caused this accident? If this incident was caused by the Shining Knife, they won't give up." He nudged the horse with his foot.

"It's *Kalena* you're thinking about?" Elstan said.

Reandn closed his eyes. *Think Wolves. Think patience.*

But Nican's own patience had dissolved in a flash of anger. "Elstan, goddess' sake, watch your mouth!" When angry, his penchant for motion turned into short, abrupt gestures; he glared at the wizard until it became obvious that Elstan wasn't going to do anything more than examine his bruises further, as though Nican hadn't spoken at all. The Hound turned back to Reandn and said under his breath, "Damn cocky wizard. First one I've worked with, and I hope the last."

"They're not all like that," Reandn found himself saying, much to his own surprise—but then he couldn't help adding, "They're each annoying in their own charming way." He crouched by the horse, running a hand along its shoulder. "Let's just count ourselves lucky we came this way—for we're on to them now, whether they're Knife or not—and hope that Damen's not in any trouble." Bracing himself on the animal's shoulder, he leaned over its neck, stretching out to undo the bridle buckles one-handed. He pulled the bridle from its head and tossed the tangled leather at Elstan's feet. "Go on down and bridle up one of the remounts."

"Damen's probably fine," Nican said. "He's not a wizard, after all, so he's not who they want right now. Say, maybe you should put Elstan up on Sky. He seems to be a nice sure-footed beast for the trail." He grinned, a wicked expression.

"Not fair to Sky," Reandn said, struggling to loosen the girth; the awkward angle gave him little leverage. "And don't forget that Damen's route is the one with all the cutoffs and places for unfriendly folk to lurk—and I'm betting they're there. All the same, I imagine they'll leave him alone when they see he's not the wizard."

Nican gave him an unexpected comradely slap on the back; Reandn started, losing his grip on the leather girth strap, and looked back to find Nican grinning. "You do have a bit more to say than *go easy on the horses*, don't you?"

Just so it only amuses you. With a grunt of effort, Reandn got the girth buckles loosened; pulling the saddle off was another thing altogether, since the far stirrup was caught under the animal's body and too wedged in rock to slide out. In the end all three of them worked to free it, sweating and straining; Reandn would have left Elstan to saddle the horse then, but the wizard didn't look like he'd have the strength. "Long day ahead of us yet," he warned Elstan as he hefted the saddle and headed for the placid chestnut the wizard had chosen.

For once, Elstan said nothing.

They made it to the head of the pass—the wide, flat spot where one step put you in the Resiores and the other in Keland proper—just before full dark, in night air growing colder by the moment. Altitude and a clear night both contributed to the quick drop in temperature, and before he even dismounted, Reandn dropped the reins on Sky's withers and pulled his jacket from atop his bedroll; he'd sweated hard with the exertion over Elstan's fall, and he knew better than to let himself grow chilled beneath dried sweat.

Nican swung down from his horse and fumbled in his gear for his own jacket, muttering at Elstan to do the same—though so far Elstan simply sat atop his unmoving mount, probably too stiff to bring himself to dismount. After a moment Nican went to help him down, while Reandn quickly set to hobbling the hungry horses so they could browse on what little was available to them here. They'd end up chewing bark before the night was over; where the surrounding rocky slopes weren't covered with hard-bristled pines and scrubby brush, they held budding trees whose lower limbs had been well ravaged by fellow travelers over the years. Reandn hoped Kalena's escort had extra fodder with them, or her pretty little palomino was going to lose weight and polish by the time they met Damen and the supply cart. And Sky, always a bit on the touchy side, had a tendency to colic if he went hungry too long and then stuck his nose in a pile of hay.

He was, Reandn thought ruefully, thinking like a true wrangler. And lost enough in those concerns that he started when Nican came up to him and said, "Dan, after all the ribbing I've given you I almost hate to ask, but . . . I'll feel a lot better if there's two of us giving this place a scouting before we settle down."

Reandn didn't tell Nican he would have done it regardless; in fact, he didn't get a chance to say anything before his stomach growled with amazing volume. Nican grinned, his teeth standing out in the starlit darkness, and added, "I've set Elstan to starting a fire and cooking us up a little flatbread to round out the turkey jerky we got in Pasdon."

"Sounds like a feast," Reandn muttered.

"Doesn't it just. You'll do it, then?"

Reandn, former Wolf First of the Keep's deep night patrol, managed to shrug and say, "I'll do my best. It won't be what Damen would accomplish." That much was the truth.

"Your best'll be good enough," Nican said. "With Ardrith's graces, we have those troublemakers figured out properly, and we're safe for tonight. Just take a look around the Keland side of the pass, and keep an eye out for anything obvious."

"Like someone's knife sticking into my back?" Reandn said dryly, and was rewarded by Nican's snort as the Hound moved out to scout. Then, alone in the dark, Reandn stood tall, stretching muscles tightened by a day of riding, and then released the stretch, dropping into Wolfish movement. The excellent night vision that had earned him deep night patrol led him around the perimeter of the long-established camping site and some distance up the slope that towered beside them to the west; nothing there but an irate owl, huge and silent as it took to the air to look for a more private hunting ground. A screecher called from above him; across the natural cut of the pass and up the snow-spotted slope on the other side, another screecher answered. Reandn added his own call, outraging the territorial birds into more frequent and demanding cries—enough noise to cover any sound he might make as he moved across the head of the trail they'd come in on and eastward to the head of the longer road. A few days ago this area was probably a mixture of mud and the last vestiges of the season's snow, miserable for traveling—thank goddess for the recent handful of mild sunny days.

Long used to deciphering the grey-silver shadows of star and moonlit rock, tree, and brush, Reandn moved onto the road with assurance, circling far into that woodier portion of the mountain to look for the churned ground that any recent, clandestinely picketed horses would create. Nothing. He stood at the top of the road and looked down the slope, his gaze skipping over the patterns in the drying mud to look for any odd shadows that, under scrutiny, might turn into tracks.

And then he returned to the camp and slid right on by, to repeat the procedure on the Resiore side of the pass, riling the screechers up again as he went by. Come the end of spring, the roads to and from the pass would be dotted with nightly campfires, but now theirs was the only one within sight. Satisfied by what he saw, Reandn returned to the dispersing horses. Sky still needed a good grooming, and some grain—as did the other two saddle horses for the day—but it was better to let him relax and nibble what he might before the grain hit his stomach. Reandn checked his hobbles and scratched the horse's favorite spot beneath his thick black mane, listening to Elstan speculate that their wrangler had gotten lost in the darkness, since neither of them had heard or seen any sign of Reandn for some time. Nican seemed more concerned that the wizard would burn the flatbread, and from the smell of it, he was indeed close to doing just that.

Reandn dropped the Wolf as best he could, and took his wrangler self to the fire.

Chapter 6

The next morning dawned grey and without dew, and Reandn figured they'd seen the last of the sun for a while. Nican climbed to his feet and peered up at the sky from sleepy eyes, offering a dramatic groan.

"If we're lucky, it'll hold off till after Kalena arrives," Reandn said, not particularly hopeful.

"That's truth." Nican rubbed the small of his back and stretched himself into wakefulness. "And so's this—my body rues that ride we took up here yesterday. You'd think I'd never been on a horse before!"

"The horses no doubt feel the same," Reandn said. He'd been up just long enough to take an accounting of them, finding only Sky and the bell mare within sight. Tying them, he poured what was left of the grain into even, well-spaced piles, and gave the string of bells a hearty shake. The wooded Resioran area below them came alive with hurried little snortings and the rustle of horses moving through trees, awkward in their hobbles.

"They sound like an entire herd," Nican said, waking up enough to find some humor in the day; they both stood back while the horses sorted themselves out in front of the grain.

Behind them, in the mostly flat, definitely exposed area where they'd kept camp, Elstan groaned.

"Ah," Nican said. "Our wizard is awake." Pitching his voice louder, he said, "Can you move this morning, wizard? Or do we need to tie you to a horse and send you back down that road a ways to loosen you up?"

"Eat horse apples," Elstan growled at him, sounding more petulant than convincing.

"He's crabby," Nican informed Reandn somberly, shaking his head. "We can't have a crabby wizard. He needs breakfast, is what—and so do I, come to think of it."

"He did fine with that flatbread last night," Reandn said, putting on a thoughtful face.

"I like the way you think. You should have been a Hound, Dan, you definitely should have been a Hound." Nican missed the incredulous look on Reandn's face as he turned to regard the wizard with hands on hips. "Elstan, eating is just exactly what I have in mind. But you're doing the cooking, and whatever you come up with, you'll be eating right alongside me. So I suggest you stay away from horse apples and stick to some of that flatbread you so ably produced last night."

Elstan struggled up from his blankets; it only took a glance to see how badly he'd stiffened up from his tumble the day before. "And you'll be . . . ?"

"Doing another walk 'round," Nican said. "Making sure no one moved in on us during the night. Someone around here is all too aware of the impending arrival of our first official ambassador from the Resiores."

Reandn thought he'd do the same, but it could wait until after breakfast. He doubted that Kalena's party was up and moving yet, and if they were close they probably would have pushed on to make the pass the night before. So they had time, and if Nican was smart, he'd continue making his rounds during the day. Reandn certainly intended to.

While Elstan grumbled and stumbled around by the fire, Reandn haltered Kalena's palomino and rummaged in one of the packs, pulling out brushes and a relatively clean rag. He brushed the creature as thoroughly as he could, moving her downwind from the fire so her shedding winter coat didn't end up in his own breakfast. She had rolled during the night, of course, and he rubbed handfuls of sparse, slushy snow into the stains and scrubbed them with the rag.

Well. Maybe if the Highborn daughter-turned-ambassador didn't look too closely. . . . Then again, Reandn and his escort were a bit stained themselves; Reandn's tunic was splashed with the blood of the dead mare, and Elstan's torn pants maintained decency only by the judicious application of several rawhide laces. Nican looked the best of them, and that wasn't saying much. Reandn had a sudden image of Damen arriving fresh and unweathered and quite happily making them all look like brigands by contrast.

While Reandn'd been grooming the palomino, Elstan had clattered about with the cooking, making a great show of his efforts but unfortunately not paying enough attention to the actual process to keep the flatbread from burning. Nican climbed the hill from the Resiore road, wrinkling his nose. When Elstan saw his face, he merely said, "Cook it yourself next time, then."

"Nice try, boyo," Nican said. "But we all have to pitch in, especially when we're short a Hound. Which one of us wasn't busy already, hmm?"

Elstan sat on a thick, short section of tree trunk, legacy of some past traveler. He did so, Reandn noted, with extreme caution, leading Reandn to some speculation about just where Elstan had landed when he'd fallen off his horse. But Elstan's words recaptured his attention quickly enough. "The one of us who could barely move," he said. "That doesn't mean I didn't have something to do. I've got a spell I want to try—it should tell us better than any Hound eye whether we've got unwanted company."

Wonderful. More magic.

"Watch your mouth," Nican said, not sounding

particularly offended at the wizard's words. "If you have such a spell, why didn't you use it last night, when we were crashing around in the dark?"

"Because I was too tired," Elstan said with some asperity. He flipped the hair out of his face, and gave Reandn a sideways glance. "That is, I could have invoked the spell, certainly. But not protected our wrangler from it. I was in no mood to face his pique."

"Don't start," Nican said, making a cutting gesture. "Elstan, just cast your goddess-blessed spell, will you? And then get cleaned up. We *all* need to do that."

Reandn abruptly rose and crossed over to the other side of the flat. He doubted it would make much difference, but the further he was from Elstan, spell-casting, the happier. He stood by the palomino's quarters and pulled her tail over to untangle the remaining knots by hand.

Elstan set his wooden plate aside and put his hands in his lap, closing his eyes for a few moments of concentration; Reandn could all but see the magic gathering around him. And then he lifted his hands, and his fingers began to move in slow, deliberate gestures, a much more careful casting than Reandn had seen yet from him.

He was ready for it, or he thought he'd been ready, but the wave of magic emanating from Elstan rocked him back on his heels. A swell of angry sound in his head, a tightening in his chest—*breathe*. His fingers clenched in the mare's tail, and her steady quarters held him up. He tried just to let it happen, to endure the magic without giving way to the anger it so easily triggered, but just as he lost track of what was up and what was down and where the ground waited for him, the mare stepped uneasily aside. He found the ground, then, ending up on his knees and the ungainly prop of his arms.

He couldn't go all the way down, he *couldn't*—that would be giving up, and with the thought of it came a flash of fear, the knowledge that if he did, he'd never find his way out again. His anger came in a flood that washed over him as strongly as the magic, and he clung to it as though it were some grim lifeline.

At last, the magic stuttered and trickled away; it might have lasted only an instant, or maybe an hour—Reandn couldn't tell. At last, he had room to think again, and to feel the cold, damp ground against his palms and knees, along with the edge of a horse pile he'd nearly put his hand in, to hear the horses shifting around, the noise of their hooves far too close to his ears. With expanded awareness came a new trickle of fear, for he still struggled to draw a decent breath, and his tightly closed eyes stayed that way, as if adding more sensory input would turn his world into complete chaos.

"Ten'tits!" Nican was saying, near to Elstan, and with his voice lowered. "That's *it*, Elstan, no more magic for you until you figure out how to shield him." His words came over the sounds of hasty rummaging, and barely made it to Reandn's ears through the noise of his own battle to breathe. But he was getting his equilibrium now, enough to inch slowly, slowly up to sit on his heels. "Where *does* he keep that stuff?" the Hound said with exasperation, and then added to Elstan, "I hope you at least discovered something useful for your efforts."

"As much as I could," Elstan shot back at him, his own voice as low as Nican's but filled with hot resentment. "There's something interfering with my spells—there has been, ever since we started this journey."

"Just how much field experience do you have?" Nican said, and the sounds of his search—*whatever* he was doing—abruptly halted. Reandn, his eyes still unwilling to open, wiped his muddied hands on his thighs and tilted his head back, freeing his chest to draw in as much air as possible.

"*He* shouldn't—"

"That's *enough*! Of the two of you, Dan is the one who's done what's been expected, and more. It'd be nice if he didn't have a problem with magic, yes, but that doesn't change the fact that *you're* the one who hasn't managed your own spells! So what the Hells are you doing here?"

Elstan didn't answer right away; Nican resumed whatever he'd been doing and almost immediately muttered, "Ah, there we are." And then, "I asked that question to get an answer, Elstan."

After a moment, Elstan replied, and he was again as composed as any court wizard should be. "I've already told you. Malik trusts me. He knows what I can do. He requested my presence on this escort. It's not your place to question, just as you refuse me the right to question our wrangler's presence here."

Politics, Reandn thought. The bane of every Wolf who just wanted to do his job. The Hounds lived amongst it, some even thrived in the court atmosphere—and that was the difference between the two elite Keep forces.

Only this time, Nican didn't sound any more thrilled than a Wolf would be with Elstan's reply. "There's more to it than that, wizard—you think I don't know? I'll tell you this much—before we're done, I'll figure it out."

Silence, then, from Elstan, and by the time Reandn figured out Nican was moving, the Hound was already by his side. "Doing all right, Dan?" he asked, crouching beside Reandn.

Reandn didn't waste breathing time with a reply, not at first. But when Nican's hand landed on his shoulder, he said, "Doing." Which wasn't much of an answer, but he wasn't sure he had any answers to give. His hand closed around the amulet hanging at his chest, and for the first time he truly wondered if he'd have to use it.

No. Doing that would mean admitting just how crippling his allergies were, and how restricted the rest of his life might be. Maybe he was fooling himself—in fact, *probably* he was fooling himself—but for now, it was the only thing he could live with. His hand fell away from the amulet.

Nican caught Reandn's hand and pressed something cool and smooth into his grasp. "Thought this might help," he said. "I'm not sure how much good it does."

"Anything is better than nothing," Reandn said, speaking more freely as his breathing eased, and then recognized the thick-glassed elixir bottle. He found his eyes would open for him, now, and that the world no longer wavered in front of them; he wiped them with his sleeve and looked down at the bottle. "No matter what it tastes like."

Nican grinned, a sudden and relieved expression. "As long as you're talking like that, I imagine you'll be just fine."

Reandn worked the cork out of the bottle. "Not if he hits me with magic like that again." *Don't overdo this stuff*, Kacey had told him, and warned him to back off it if he started up with headaches, muttering about sneezebane and flowering manroot. At this moment, Reandn's concern for headaches didn't amount to much, but he took only a modest sip. It had to last. Wrinkling his nose at the taste, he made an expressive noise and then pointed his chin at Elstan. "For all of that, did he learn anything?"

"I'm still a little unclear about that point," Nican said, and raised his voice to include Elstan in the conversation—not that he couldn't hear the one they were already having. "What about it, Elstan? Just exactly what did you learn?"

Elstan spoke casually, as if he'd already put this incident, and its import to their group, behind him. "That Kalena's party is about half a day away. And that there *is* at least one other person besides Damen on the long road . . ." There he stopped, evidently not to say anything more about it, despite the way his sentence rang loudly unfinished to Reandn's mind.

Nican's, too, apparently. "And?"

Elstan tossed a scowl at them both, barely looking up from where he was pushing several hot fire rocks around with a stick, setting them up as a base for a small pot of water. Washing water, Reandn thought. He flicked a glance at Nican when it seemed the wizard might not answer at all; Nican gave his head a barely discernible shake. As if it was the cue Elstan had been waiting for, he said, "Whoever they was, I couldn't sense them clearly. I think they had some sort of shielding magic in use. I was about to find out when . . . *whatever* it was interfered with my magic." He looked up from his task long enough to throw Reandn a baleful look.

"What's *that* supposed to mean?" Reandn said, but he said it for Nican's ears only.

"He's got to blame someone," Nican said in Reandn's ear, pushing off Reandn's shoulder as he rose to his feet. "Leave it be."

As if Elstan's implication made any sense at all. Reandn said it with his expression, but kept his mouth shut, and this time when he made to rise, Nican extended a helping hand. "Whoa, steady there, Dan," he said as Reandn's world tilted slightly. No, wait—Reandn realized he was the one who was tilting. He rode it out, as Nican grinned at him and said, "A bit premature, boyo?"

"It's passing," Reandn told him.

Cautiously, Nican released his grip on Reandn's arm and stepped back a pace. "Hmmm," he said reflectively. "Well, if you weren't a mess before, you sure enough qualify *now*. With any luck our half day gives us time to clean you up."

"I'm just the wrangler," Reandn said, knowing he'd spend a good deal of that time in a wide patrol of the area, trying not to get caught acting the part of a Wolf. He gestured at the horse, which was indeed cleaner than he was, now. "Kalena won't even look at me once she gets her hands on the palomino."

"A handsome fellow such as yourself?" Nican scoffed. "No, clean yourself up. If nothing else, the two of us can distract her from the things about Keland that are sure to cause her dissatisfaction." He grinned, but then raised an eyebrow and an admonishing finger in apparent afterthought. "But say, you let *me* do the talking, ey?"

Reandn stood by the palomino's head and figured they looked pretty much the same, he and the horse. She had rain dripping off her forelock and down her face, and so did he, no matter how many times he finger-combed his hair back. Only an idiot would have his rain-cape hood drawn around his neck instead of up over his head . . . an idiot or a wrangler in the presence of Highborn. And Kalena was definitely Highborn, Highborn enough to suppose querulously that the steady rain had been arranged as some sort of insult.

The arriving Resioran party—Kalena, a personal servant in a wagon heaped with supplies, and seven honor guards, six of whom surrounded her loosely at all times—dismounted with little ceremony. The seventh seemed to serve as point guard and a sort of chaperon. Big and burly, he overtopped Reandn and outweighed Nican; his face was broad and close on homely, but his smile seemed genuine. He introduced himself as Vaklar and then presented Kalena as the new ambassador from the Resiores. "And the woman," he added, with the sound of a line that he'd memorized, one without his natural Resioran lowborn inflections, "who will bring our lands out of strife with one another."

Kalena smiled a perfunctory smile from beneath her large hat as one of her guards collected all the party's horses and took them off to the side. *Too young*, Reandn thought, looking at her. If she'd reached her twentieth year, he'd be surprised, and her face held none of the cultured wisdom many of the Highborn cultivated in their children. It was a young woman's face, full of a young woman's thoughts. Her smile, as brief as it was, revealed an overbite, although her chin was strong enough to turn the feature into a quirky asset. Her face held a distinct smattering of freckles, especially across her nose, which only enhanced her appearance of youth.

But beneath the shadow of her hat brim, her dark hazel eyes swept over the three Keep men without a flicker of friendliness.

"This is what your King has sent to meet his new ambassador?" she said, and her words—underlain with a distinct air of youthful petulance—clashed with the sweet tone of her voice. She should be a singer, then, Reandn decided on the spot, and only allowed to put someone else's carefully composed words to that voice.

Nican, his square features looking pinched in the chill rain, spoke as if he hadn't seen her eyes or heard the prickle in her words; his own were full of welcome, and casual confidence. "My name is Nican, meira. My partner and I are of the King's closest Hounds, and it will be our privilege to ride with you on the road to King's Keep."

"I see no partner," Kalena observed, although Elstan stood behind him. But there was no mistaking Elstan's bearing for that of a Hound, even if he'd had the uniform beneath his rain cape.

"As you may know, the roads on this side of the pass are somewhat more difficult to travel than your own. Damen is scouting the safest and most secure path for your travel. He'll meet us shortly."

Kalena gestured at Elstan, and then Reandn. "You left my Keland escort behind, yet brought these along with you? That's a strange notion of proper respect."

"Ensuring your safety is the highest respect we can offer, meira."

He was good. Reandn had to give him that. He understood anew why Nican and Damen had been chosen for this assignment—and realized how quickly he himself had shed what little ways of the court he'd ever had, once he'd left the Keep.

Nican was gesturing at their minimal campsite—the small tent they'd erected for her once the rain had started, the sullenly smoldering fire with tea water warming in the midst of it, their own blankets neatly rolled and piled under an oilcloth. "We'd have preferred to meet you with a much grander sight," he said. "But in deferring to your own wishes, we kept our number to a minimum."

"My father's wishes," Kalena said, a quiet aside that was nonetheless meant to be heard. Reandn could almost feel Nican's wince, and Vaklar remained as straight-faced as a man could be. If that's the way it was, nothing they'd done in accordance with the Resiore demands would satisfy this young woman, who'd apparently had other ideas altogether.

Nican cleared his throat and gestured at Reandn, who took the cue to move closer with the mare. "We did bring a gift we thought would best serve you on this trip," he said. "Her name will be up to you, but her pedigree is flawless."

Kalena's gaze flicked to the mare, and seemed to take in Reandn for the first time; carefully, he avoided looking directly at her, which was made easier by the necessity of lowering his head in a respectful gesture. She asked, "Did you assume there would be something wrong with my own horse?"

"In no way," Nican said, and the hastiness of his words was the first sign of his struggle to accommodate the woman. "We sought only to offer you variety, and variety of the highest quality."

Kalena walked slowly around the mare—who was, in truth, a lovely creature, blessed with the abundant, long mane and tail that most women seemed to like in a horse; if she was built delicately, she was also well put together, and would certainly hold up to Kalena's weight. Her fingertip tapping her lower lip, she said, "She *is* adorable, I suppose. If she just weren't so *wet*."

Reandn, his voice flat and unapologetic, told her, "It's raining."

Nican gave him a meaningful look—Reandn translated it into *Do you want to keep your tongue, boyo?* and added nothing more meaningful to his comment than sluicing rain out of his eyes and brows. But rather than taking offense, Kalena simply stopped seeing him. Not what he'd have expected, given her previous behavior.

Kalena looked thoughtfully at the mare, but no longer anywhere near Reandn. Just as well. Kalena, he'd seen at once, was the sort to bring out the worst in him, and was as Highborn as the Highborn came. She tapped her finger on her lower lip one more time, and announced, "I shall have to thank the King for his kindness. Will she be ready to ride tomorrow?"

"She's ready to ride this afternoon, if you want her," Nican said immediately.

"This afternoon?" Kalena said, glancing back at her point man. "I think not. This rain looks like it's here to stay, and I want to get out of it."

Despite the steady downfall, Reandn doubted she'd actually felt any water on her skin; she was draped with two oiled cloaks and topped off by that fanciful hat, the overwide brim of which kept the rain from her shoulders but would probably never look the same. Not a problem for her, he figured. She probably had at least one other with her. He had no idea how she was dressed underneath, other than the glimpse of rich colors he caught when she dismounted her fat gelding.

Nican, too, looked to Vaklar, as if appealing to the common sense he hoped to find there. "Meira," he said, and seemed to be framing his words quite carefully, "this is an exposed area. And as much as we welcome your arrival, not everyone is happy at the new arrangement. I strongly feel it would be more prudent to move into Keland and find a more protected area for the evening."

"Ah. Then you think my escort is unable to protect me. Or you lack confidence in yourself."

Vaklar, deferential and casual, put in his first words. "We all value your safety far too much to take the slightest chance with it," he said. He was an older man, well-seasoned in this role. To judge by Kalena's reaction to him, he'd been playing it since she was very young indeed.

"Very well," she said. "If Vaklar says it's for the best. But right now I insist on some hot food, and a short period to rest." She looked at the modest tent Nican had set up for her, and frowned in a manner far too stern for that young face. "Unload my tent, please, Yuliyana; Pawl will help you."

Nican said nothing, just glanced at Vaklar, who shook his head so slightly as to be nearly imperceptible. After a pause, Nican said, "Please allow my men to assist. Elstan is our guide, and Dan is handling the horses; they, too, are here to make this trip easier for you in any way they can."

The unplanned gesture drew surprise from Elstan, though Nican's quick glare instantly eliminated all signs of protest. Reandn was relieved enough to discover that Vaklar appeared willing to work with them instead of apart from them that he hardly cared about his consignment to grunt-work status. He tossed the mare's lead rope to Nican and waited for Kalena to accept Nican's offer.

She did so with a slight nod, and then, as she turned away, an obscure and indecipherable hand gesture. As one, Reandn, Nican, and Elstan turned to look at Vaklar. With just the hint of a smile on his broad face, Vaklar tugged at his upraised cloak hood, and Reandn wasted no time in retreating beneath the hood of his own oiled rain cloak. Followed by a grudging Elstan, he went to help Varina, Kalena's personal, and Pawl, one of the guards, with the ornate tent.

They exchanged a minimum of conversation in completion of the task, and when the tent was up, and the new ambassador had gone within to eat her midday meal and rest, Reandn removed himself from the fire circle. He stood with the horses at the edges of the camp, his mind abuzz with chatter and leftover magic; Kalena's retinue did not appear to notice him in the least, and after a few moments he slid away to check the roads, circling through the sparsely wooded slopes.

Water ran down the roads in small rivulets, weaving its way through preexisting divots and old tracks in the soft ground. The vestiges of snow evident the evening before were long melted away under the rain, and the roads looked like they'd make slow, sloppy travel indeed. But there was no sign of anyone lurking around the area.

Not, Reandn supposed, that he really expected any. Whoever had caused their trouble was no doubt lurking on the Keland side of the pass. With any luck Damen would spot them on the way up—and be smart enough to pretend he hadn't, until he got up here and could gather Kalena's guard to help dispose of them.

Reandn almost hoped they were Knife. The members of the Shining Knife weren't killers, whatever trouble they made. But nor did they traffic with wizards, and that spell along the rocks could easily have killed Elstan and had certainly been meant to maim him. Reandn wondered if Nican would reveal their previous trouble to Vaklar, and then wondered if he should do so himself.

And then he froze, realizing he was no longer alone in these woods. Someone was closing in on him, trying for furtive silence and not succeeding; the rain had eased into a sprinkle and left little sound to cover movement in the woods. Without even stopping to think about it, Reandn shifted smoothly to the side, finding himself a tree to press up behind. When a quick glance around showed him no one—which meant the other person couldn't see him at that moment, either—he backtracked to another tree, moving closer to that not-quite-quiet-enough someone. There he waited, listening, following the footfalls and then the breathing of whoever it was. And finally they passed his position, sticking to his original trail as well as could be expected.

When, boot knife drawn, he slid out from behind the tree, up behind the man—for it was indeed a man, and a large one—he discovered his tracker dressed in Kalena's guard colors of black and deep blue. Reandn hesitated, but then silently took the man from behind, jamming the back of the blade against his throat.

Vaklar. It was Vaklar, and he stifled his sound of protest so quickly it never made it all the way out of his throat. Reandn said, "Even a wrangler doesn't like to be followed."

"Peace, man," Vaklar said, his voice hoarse and strained. "I mean you no harm."

"Funny way you have of showing it." Reandn's mouth was at the man's ear, his voice sliding into the gravel of its deepest tones. "If *I* were after Kalena, the first thing I'd do is take care of her other escort. Is that what you're about, Vaklar?"

"Good goddess, no!" Vaklar shifted in his grip, and Reandn pressed the blade closer to his throat. "I'm here to talk to you, aya? Just testing out what Keland sent . . . wanted to see how long it'd take you to catch on I was here."

"Not very damn long," Reandn said. "I don't like games, Vaklar. I don't like them at all."

"Easy now, ladaboy. I'd nay'er done it, knowing you'd react so."

"And I don't like being patronized, either." Reandn tightened his grip. "I know what I'm about. It's why I'm here."

"I begin to understand so." Vaklar gave the merest of shrugs; it was all Reandn gave him room to do. "I came only for talking, wrangler. Thought I'd be able to get some real words out of you, whilst none from that court-tongued Hound back at camp. At least, you gave our meira so."

"For all the good it did," Reandn said. He removed the knife from Vaklar's throat, holding it out just long enough for the man to see he'd been using the back edge of the blade.

Vaklar snorted dark amusement. "Aya, then, ladaboy.

May be you do know what you're about. And if I'd been a true danger, then what?"

"Look closer," Reandn said, stepping around to face the man but holding the knife steady where it was. Up near the point, the back edge, too, was sharp. "Makes it a better throwing knife." He hefted it, switching his grip, and sent the weapon at the closest tree. It struck with the satisfying *thunk* of a solid throw, with perfectly judged distance putting it perpendicular to the tree trunk.

"And now you've just lost your only weapon." Vaklar's words held a touch of scorn. "You trust me that well?"

Reandn grinned at him, more teeth than mirth. "What makes you think so?"

Vaklar shook his head ruefully, but there was a twinkle lurking in his eyes. "Well enough to say we trust one another equally, then, ladaboy."

"Dan," Reandn said. "I won't ever answer to ladaboy, I can promise you that."

Vaklar raised an eyebrow. "No, then? It's not any insult, I assure you of that."

"Use it on Elstan, then." The thought amused Reandn; he figured Elstan was court-conditioned enough not to correct Vaklar, especially if Kalena was in earshot. "And say what you came to say."

"An' you're some wrangler, are you?"

"A good one," Reandn said. "Who happens to know how to take care of himself."

"And to care for the meira, as well. That's what you're about here, is it not? And what has you so worried, to send you into the wet woods while your Hound sees to Meira Kalena?"

Reandn looked at him a moment, weighing the consequences of telling the man—Nican's prerogative—and of *not* telling him. "We had some trouble on the way up."

Vaklar grunted, his wide mouth crimping in disapproval. "Shining Knife?"

"They didn't leave any convenient signatures," Reandn

said. "I killed one of them, and they came back anyway. So either we're up against two groups—both with magic-users—or the first one is persistent."

"Magic, then? Not the Knife. They have aught to do with magic."

"Doesn't make any difference, does it, as long as they're set on causing us trouble? Be a lot easier if we had the right escort—then we could keep her both safe *and* happy. Right now she's neither, no matter how good your people are."

"They're right good," Vaklar murmured. "Better than a wrangler, I would have said." He sighed, his gaze going distant for a moment before he refocused on Reandn. Making a decision, Reandn thought, just before Vaklar spoke again. "Understand this, lada" —Reandn raised his chin and eyebrows both, and Vaklar corrected himself—"Dan. Our Kalennie's a good enough girl. Smarter than she came across up there. She's just . . . young."

"I noticed," Reandn said, dry words indeed. At Kalena's age he'd been full Wolf, and entrusted with the lives of others. But there were far too many lives depending on Kalena, who seemed younger than Reandn ever remembered being. *Just turned thirty and already looking back more than forward.*

"Naya," Vaklar said. "Keep that voice to yourself, then, especially an' you talk to the others. They're younger than I, have too much energy to waste on quick offense. Kalena's a'right to a bit of a snit or two over this. Near just two months back, she's naught but the daughter of a Resiore Highborn Meir, an' him the Highest of all them wishin' to cleave to Keland. Come the start of the thaw, and all them on that side find they want to get a leg up on the Knife, you follow?"

"Not exactly," Reandn said, tripping over the man's thick Resioran speech patterns, the thickest he'd ever heard, or figured himself likely to. And tripping, too, on the fact that Malik had been preparing the Keep for Kalena's arrival since fall. Someone in the Resiores liked to plan ahead.

Vaklar made a flicking gesture, as if the whole matter was just that simple. "Knife knows that with the thaw comes interest from the Keep, new talk on Resioran obligations and the like. They want to shift us over to the Geltrians, aya. They say because the magic's not so strong there, for magic's a branding-hot subject for some of us, but there's else to it."

Nothing that was part of Reandn's briefing; he knew only that Elstan's skills were to be kept secret, and that he was forbidden to discuss magic of any sort with the Resiorans. "Like what?" he asked, retrieving his knife from the tree and turning on his heel to lean against that same tree, not bothering to hide the intensity of his curiosity.

"Coal taxes and tariffs, lad—Dan. The coal we haul to you all summer long, most of that's obliged of us, in return for Keep protection. What we have left to sell your way comes under mighty fine tariff; our valleys have been under Keep rule for so long, there's naya chance of changing that. So happens most of the Knife troublemakers come from the miners, up in the mountains. They figure maybe we go to Geltria, and start new, get a better deal on the taxes. Geltria proper's got its own coal supplies, doesn't need ours so bad."

"And Kalena's people?"

"More have the right of it, to my way of thinking. If Geltria nay'ent take it in coal they'll take it in something else, and leave us no better off. Double so, because any fighting over the matter is bound to happen on Resiore soil."

"Can't argue with that," Reandn said. "So for this they've taken a spoiled Highborn girl and set her to a task better suited to her elders?"

"Watch it there, now," Vaklar warned. "Naya say such things of her. She's a fine young meira, that one, and if you saw her on a better day you'd know just why they've sent her. She'll shine in court, outshine the Knife for sure. If she can talk the Keep out of a percentage of the taxes, just enough to show good will, things'll turn, our side of the pass. 'Sides that, she's just of the right age to find a match, there at the Keep. That'd be two things to tie us together, aya? A young couple spending half the year this side of the pass, half the time on ours?"

Reandn made no effort to tone down his skepticism. "There's more to making progress at court than determination." He knew *that* well enough. "And more to diplomatic negotiations than finding a mate."

"Spoken like a wrangler." Vaklar grinned at Reandn's glowering response. "Tell you this much, Dan. Kalena wants nothing more than to return home, and that's naya going to happen until the Keep listens to reason." His grin broadened. "She's used to getting what she wants, Kalena is."

That last, Reandn figured, was nothing but the absolute and unfortunate truth.

"She's a brat," Nican muttered in a fierce undertone as he tightened his horse's girth. Kalena was already mounted on her new mare, her guards in position around her. The delay had been much longer than a mere meal and rest had need to take; if Kalena was as skilled at arguing for the Resiores as she was in subtle procrastination the Allegients might yet have a chance. "A spoiled, heavy-handed brat."

"I wouldn't know anything about it," Reandn said. "I'm just the fellow who feeds the horses and keeps that adorable palomino looking adorable. Oh, and sometimes I put up tents in the rain."

Nican's look was as fierce as his words had been. "Damn, wrangler. Get that smile off your face."

Reandn was only partially successful. "Go ahead," he said. "Take it out on me. I told Elstan I was here because I was used to dealing with the Highborn, and when it's one like this, I know just what to do. Hide behind the horses."

He could afford to be in a good mood. After mentioning to Vaklar that Kalena's outrage was a certain thing if she happened to hear the casual way the guard had discussed her, the older man readily agreed it wouldn't be a good idea to relate the conversation to anyone, not even his fellow guards—and especially not the part where Reandn held the knife to his throat. That was one incident Reandn didn't want reaching Nican's ears, and he was reasonably assured it wouldn't. Not as long as Vaklar didn't want his charge to know he'd slipped and called her Kalennie, a childhood name gone bitter when the opposition used it to mock her age and her unearned new status.

"You're bloody damn happy all of a sudden," Nican said, his eyes narrowing as he regarded Reandn over the back of his horse. "That magic jar something loose in your head this morning?"

"Possibly," Reandn said, indeed all too aware of the magic that thrummed in his very veins—an unforgettable, underlying threat. "Or maybe it's just the fact that you've forbidden Elstan any more of it."

"It's not just for you," Nican said. "Until the man can shield you, the Resiorans are going to know every single damn time Elstan twiddles off a spell."

"Result's the same, as far as I'm concerned. Although I imagine he's going to try to get away with a spell or two, and before too much time passes."

"I expect you're right." Nican pulled himself into the saddle with a creak of leather and the grunt of his unprepared horse. "Not much left of today for him to do it in, though. Hardly enough daylight worth traveling."

Reandn mounted next to him; he was riding the bell mare today, and her round barrel felt strange indeed after Sky's deep-chested, slab-sided form; he had to use the thinnest of blankets to keep Sky's saddle from pinching her. "Why insist on moving out, then? We'll only have to set up that tent again."

From the head of the forming procession, Elstan called that they were ready to travel; that was Nican's cue. He lifted the reins. "To prove a point," he said, nudging his horse forward.

"What?" Reandn said. "That there's danger here, or that you're just as stubborn as she is?"

"Both!" Nican called over his shoulder.

Reandn grinned at Nican's retreating back, and checked behind himself to make sure the remounts had remained lined up properly, tethered to one another by a series of long lead ropes. Sky was in the back, since he'd shown early on that he wouldn't tolerate another horse that close on his heels. Reandn didn't even give him a chance to get studdy with one of the mares, and tied him behind a gelding. Not that there were many of them, now; Elstan was on one of the extras, and Kalena chose to have her fat gelding tied to the back of her wagon, rather than under Reandn's care. He ignored the slight; it meant he could pay less attention to horses who were getting to know one another under difficult circumstances, and more to the scrubby woods around them.

Under the overcast sky, the day went quickly from daylight to deep dusk, and Reandn figured that Nican had just barely made his point by the time they stopped for the night. Nican and Vaklar conferred on the site, one with signs of much use in the past. To the side of the road, a gentle slope kept the ground reasonably drained, and among the trees there was just enough room for Kalena's tent.

Better than pitching the thing in the road, Reandn thought. Not much more discreet, though. Too bad the tightly woven silks were dyed such garish colors. He tied the horses and eased around the wagon—it took up much of the road despite the care with which Varina, Kalena's personal, had maneuvered it to the side—so quietly that no one snagged him for tent duty, and found Nican and Elstan where they conferred on horseback at the head of the party.

Elstan greeted his presence with an annoyed look, but Nican seemed considerably cheered by their little traveling exercise. "Dan," he said, "how goes it with the horses?"

"About the same as the last time we spoke," Reandn said, amused. "I was thinking of saddling Sky and moving out ahead a bit, checking the road. Might run into Damen."

"Tsk," Nican said. "Escaping sounds more like it. Timely, however. I was premature in shutting down Elstan's magic; I'd forgotten the Keep expects to hear from him at this point in our trip. A little distance might be a good thing right now."

Reandn closed his eyes and schooled himself to patience. *Patience*. "Give me time to saddle Sky," he said. "And keep the Resiorans off my back if they decide to corral me for their set-up chores."

"Done," Nican said. "And I hope you find Damen. Be a lot easier if I had him around to take over when I've had enough of—" He broke off and raised his head a fraction, raising his voice as well. "Well, then, Vaklar, is the site to your liking?"

"As good as any, aya, though I'll like it better when Kiryl and Rufo finish scouting around." Vaklar, too, was mounted, approaching them at a leisurely walk. "I'm for moving on some, checking out the road ahead. Thought you might want part of that."

Nican gave a rueful shake of his head. "Until we meet up with Damen, I'm not leaving the meira. But Dan is a little restless, I think."

"Oh, aya, that I know." Vaklar's gaze met Reandn's, full of wry amusement. "Come with, then, Dan?"

"You couldn't stop me," Reandn said, pleasantly enough but meaning it. Nican frowned at him, but Vaklar just chuckled. "Come back to the horses and see if we've got one to take your saddle. Yours has done enough for the day."

Vaklar gave his horse a pat; it was a sturdy, well-muscled creature, but Vaklar was no small man, and it looked played out. "Truth enough, an' it be a kind offer."

"Come with, then." Reandn headed for the horses, ignoring Nican's appalled expression at his mimicry of the Resioran speech pattern.

Vaklar, he thought, had grinned outright, and he made no attempt to lower his voice as he reassured Nican. "Not to worry, ladaboy. Don't you come to find life gets boring without at least one of him around?"

Nican's muttered reply was impossible to decipher, loud enough for Reandn to know he'd made one. Deliberate, no doubt.

The remounts were happily rustling through individual portions of hay when he got back to them. He looked to the Resioran wagon and one of the guards there raised a hand; Reandn nodded thanks. Kalena might be a handful to deal with, but it seemed her escort deserved more credit. The hay wasn't much; the horses would still need to forage. But every little bit counted when you were trying to keep weight on horses under hard work.

He pulled Sky out of the string and offered him a spare handful of grain, just enough for the horse to think he'd actually been fed, which was what he expected and all he'd think about until it happened. He was tightening the girth when Vaklar finished untacking his own horse and came to eye the remounts, his saddle propped on his hip.

"Suggestions, then, Dan?"

Reandn eyed the topline of Vaklar's horse, and said, "Probably the mare I just unsaddled. They're built alike, and she hasn't done much today—Hells, none of ours have. Her bridle's over on top of the packs. I don't think she'll take to the one your horse works in."

"He's a stubborn one at times," Vaklar agreed, scooping up the bridle in question. Reandn, through with Sky, watched as the man set his saddle on the mare's back and eyed it for fit in the near darkness; satisfied, Vaklar fumbled beneath the mare's belly for the free end of the girth. "But he carries me through. Worth the trouble."

Reandn looked at his own horse. Sky stood rooted to the spot, too wise to jig away in his anxious eagerness about the ride to come—but his head bobbed up and down, the equine version of a nervous tick, and he was already drooling around the bit. "I know the feeling," he said dryly. He turned Sky's head to face uptrail and double-checked the girth as Vaklar tested his own and mounted up. "Give me a minute here."

Sky stood rock-still until Reandn's weight hit the saddle, and then bounded forward, heading out at his fastest rack. "You're going uphill," Reandn told him, his right toe still searching for the stirrup. "And you've already come down this road. It's boring."

Sky snorted hard several times, and seemed to come to the same conclusion. He soon lowered his head into the bit and came down into a walk, and when Reandn turned him back toward the camp, he complied.

Overcast as it was, the clouds had thinned enough to let the rising moon not only shine through, but reflect among them; for the horses and their superior night vision, it would be no more difficult than finding their way in daylight. It was certainly light enough to see Vaklar's grin as Reandn returned.

"Now, that *is* an interesting creature," he said as they threaded past the wagon and the other guards. "Might be I'd like to try out that gait myself."

Nican's voice came from a distance; there was no pinpointing where he actually was within the camp. "No, you don't," he called. "Trust me on this one!"

Reandn just shrugged. "Up to you," he said, and touched his calves to Sky's side. Sky surged ahead, still full of himself, and Reandn gave him a moment of it.

Vaklar cantered up beside him, and fell into a posting trot. "Maybe I'll not try him, at that," he said. "Now give an old man a break and slow it down where I can put this mare into a jog, aya?"

Reandn picked the reins up just enough for Sky to feel the bit tilt in his mouth; they slowed. "Old man," Reandn said. "You don't think I'm going to fall for that one, do you?"

"Naya," Vaklar said, sitting more comfortably on the mare. "It's not always the years that do the aging, is it now. On that score I'm guessing we might be near the same age."

Taken aback, Reandn nearly stopped Sky altogether; the horse faltered, but moved on with the mare when he received no more unintentional cues from his rider. "No," Reandn said. "That's not a conversation we'll have." To emphasize the point, he turned his attention to the trees on either side of the road. Even were there someone out there, Wolf and guard were unlikely to realize it— but Reandn's memory of the route and its most dangerous spots focused considerably tighter as he saw landmarks he recognized.

"Oh, now, ladaboy," Vaklar said, emphasizing the ladaboy just enough to let Reandn know he'd used it on purpose, "you don't be taking offense so easily."

"If I take offense, you'll know it," Reandn told him. And that's when Elstan's magic crept up behind him and wrapped itself around his body.

This time Sky did stop, stopped short and bobbed his head uncertainly, his ears flicking back to Reandn and forward again in constant, anxious motion. Reandn clutched at his thick black mane as dizziness struck and whirled around him, waiting for it to get worse, hoping to stay in the saddle, and ignoring Vaklar's increasingly urgent inquiries.

But it didn't get worse. Staying far below the pitch of magic it had taken Elstan to make contact from the inn, the thrum of it through Reandn's body peaked and faded; despite his increasing sensitivity to the effects of magic, his chest barely tightened around his lungs and the dizziness faded quickly. Puzzled, he cautiously straightened, and discovered he could indeed trust his own balance. Had they moved that far from the campsite already?

"All right, then, Dan?" Vaklar asked. His mare stood broadside before Sky, and Vaklar was pressing her closer; Sky had stopped paying attention to whatever Reandn was up to and was nickering at the mare, sounding a little bewildered at the variety of things happening around him.

"Stop it," Reandn muttered at him. To Vaklar he said, "I'm fine." And then, at Vaklar's frankly disbelieving look, clear enough under the bluish-silver aura of the clouds, he said, "It's . . . an illness. It comes and goes."

Vaklar looked at him another long moment. "An' it be something that can leave my meira open to danger?"

The sudden intensity in his voice opened a flood of memories that Reandn had learned to keep deeply buried. *Adela, challenging him in just this way, worried for him when his allergies were still just baffling symptoms in a world that wasn't supposed to have magic. Adela, dying at the hands of a bitter old wizard's stolen powers. And Reandn himself, torn from King's Keep, torn from his place in the Wolves, torn from everything that made his life whole.* All because of magic.

He blinked and discovered he was staring at Vaklar, his face aching with the clench of his jaw, his eyes narrowed and brows drawn. He took a deep breath, and wrenched himself away from the things that anchored his life to the one short period when everything had changed. It should come as no surprise that the memories lurked so close to the surface, not when once again he'd been torn from his life—this time as Wolf Remote, not Wolf First—and put in such an untenable position in an effort to regain what he'd had.

"I'm the remount wrangler," he told Vaklar, whose eyebrows had been slowly advancing up his forehead while he waited. "I'm irrelevant to your meira's safety, unless I put her on a rank horse."

Far from the truth, of course. The truth was that he

shouldn't have been in this condition in the first place,
that Elstan should have kept his magic from wreaking
such havoc. But he hadn't, and now Reandn could only
hope that his role in this escort remained that of a
wrangler—and a wrangler only.

"Aya," Vaklar nodded, though his face held no assent
at all. "The wrangler. For some reason, I do keep
forgettin'."

Chapter 7

Damen arrived the next morning, while Varina was still bustling in and out of Kalena's tent on errands for her meira. The rest of the camp was packed up and ready to go; Reandn was marking time by rechecking the balance of the two light pack loads when he heard Nican's undignified shout of greeting. He ducked his head to hide his grin; Nican was at wit's end this morning, trying to chivvy Kalena along without stepping out of his courtly role. Kalena's own guards stood by their saddled horses, surrounding the waiting palomino, their expressions stoic and loudly patient.

Damen was walking into it without even a hint of warning.

Too cruel, Reandn decided, hearing the bustle of greetings and introductions to which Damen fell prey, and knowing that in the wake of them, Nican would pass the job of rousting Kalena to Damen's unsuspecting shoulders. Vaklar's voice boomed as loud as Nican's had, and just beyond the wagon Reandn could see him gesturing at the guards, naming them. Yuliyana, Pawl, Kiryl, Rufo, Tanich, and Jasha—Reandn himself placed faces to names only tentatively, since the original introductions had been made only to Nican.

The second line of conversation seemed to be Damen's

inquiries about why they were still sitting here, so late in the morning. And to the side, where he doubted anyone else could hear, Kalena's voice rang briefly loud enough to come clearly through the silk layers of her tent. "I *won't* hurry, Varina. Nobody's going to bother us on this road, because no one takes me seriously enough to care that I'm here."

"But the Hounds say—"

"The Hounds are Keland-born! They know nothing of Resioran hearts—and they've not seen the dissidents who mock my name. Well, to the Lonely Hells with my father for putting me in this position, and to the Hells with the Knife who think they can take me so lightly. They'll learn better. Right now it's enough to show these Hounds who's *really* in charge."

"But—"

"Enough! If you don't mind your place I'll trade you for a Keland personal when I get to King's Keep."

Varina's gasp of dismay also came clearly to Reandn's ears. He glanced at the apparent chaos at the head of the party; the cart mule had added his voice to the fray, and from the sound of it the cart had taken a few solid kicks, probably in lieu of Vaklar's too-close horse that the mule couldn't reach while in harness. He had a sudden vision of all the mornings to follow, all proceeding exactly as this one, and closed his eyes on his frustration. *Patience*. He couldn't help but wonder if Saxe had known exactly what he was sending his wayward Wolf to deal with.

If only Kalena had been right, that the road ahead was safe and clear.

But she wasn't.

Eventually, Kalena ventured from the tent; her presence introduced another element of chaos to the camp, as her guards swooped in on the tent, hauling out the belongings still within and swiftly packing it into traveling shape. Kalena was introduced to Damen, whom she seemed to find no more impressive than anybody else. At last, Yuliyana led the palomino up to her meira, and Kalena, after Varina had made several last-minute adjustments to her riding clothes—a much more reasonable array than her over-done rain costume—begrudgingly mounted. Almost instantly Nican got the cart moving, mounting while his horse trotted along beside it.

For a short while, all was silent. They traveled at an active trot, with all the horses lowering their heads to snort at and accept the sudden change. Reandn slid into Wolf mode, unhappy to be at the back instead of leading point, but deep in the process of noting each sound and movement and assessing each potential danger as they approached. Sky was just relaxing beneath him when Damen stopped his horse at the side of the road and let everyone else pass him, moving in beside Reandn as they came abreast.

"Nicco tells me there've been some problems," he said, just loud enough to hear over the sounds of the horses' hooves. Reandn slowed Sky to put a little more space between himself and the wagon, with Varina, ahead of them.

Reandn looked at him a moment. Damen, tall and lanky and outrageously red-haired, looked like he'd taken the time this morning to clean up especially well in preparation for meeting Kalena. He thought of the days since they'd separated and eventually nodded. "Yes."

"You and Elstan have this conflict between you under control?"

Through a flash of resentment that Damen should bother to say this thing, Reandn asked, "What did Nican say?"

Damen shook his head. "I'm not fooling around with this, Dan. We've got enough to watch out for here. We need to work as a team."

But we're not a team. Out loud, Reandn said, "As long as he doesn't hit me over the head with his magic, I don't give an owl hoot about him. That leaves him two choices, since he lied about his shielding abilities—warn me so I can get some good distance between us, or don't use his magic. We're not supposed to have a wizard with us anyway—there's no telling if any of the Resiorans can feel it—so there's not much excuse to use any more magic just now."

"That's true," Damen said. "All of it's true. He did lie, and it's something the Keep'll hear about when we get back. I know that's made this trip pretty hard on you, but—"

"Look," Reandn said. "My priority is making sure Kalena stays safe and reasonably happy, even if I am just the fellow who tows the remounts along. If killing Elstan makes her less safe, I'm not going to do it. Is *that* what you wanted to hear?"

Taken aback, Damen just looked at him a moment, and then looked ahead to Elstan. Finally he said, "Was that supposed to be amusing?"

"No, it was supposed to end this conversation."

"Dan—"

Reandn didn't even let him get started. He turned on the man, and if his voice stayed even, it was only because he let his frustration burn in his eyes. "Every time that man uses magic, he threatens my life. Sooner or later, he's going to kill me."

Damen's words trampled the tail end of Reandn's question. "We don't *need* this, Dan, we've got enough trouble to deal with—"

"Then talk to Elstan!"

Damen's expression, set in a face flushed red, would have been just as appropriate if he'd been reaming out a very junior Hound in his own patrol. But he kept his mouth shut, and after a long moment he released his breath in a long, slow exhalation. Control. Reandn knew it well. "All right, Dan. I hear you. Can't say I'm not disappointed in you. Until now, I've found you more reasonable than Elstan in most ways."

"It's not in my hands," Reandn said. "Although,

speaking of hands, I suppose if it comes down to it I can just break his. No finger-twisting, no magic."

Damen gave him another long look that turned incredulous, and snorted. "You know, sometimes I can't tell if you say things because you mean them, or because you're just determined to be outrageous."

"With any luck, you'll never know," Reandn said, and then grinned at him.

The tension broke; Damen relaxed in the saddle. He glanced up to where Kalena rode, just before the wagon and surrounded by her guards. "Meeting up with this party is going to end up as one of the more memorable moments of my career, I think. One of those stories the grandchildren demand to hear again and again."

"You've got a family?" Reandn asked, surprised because he'd never considered it; two years in the Remote had done that to him, that and the fact that he worked so hard not to think about his own.

"Couple of kids," Damen said. "Hellions, they are. Nican's free and easy, though. Quite the ladies' man at court, though he doesn't overstep himself any."

"Doesn't surprise me, somehow." Reandn, especially now that he'd heard Nican in action with Kalena, could easily imagine the shorter man sweeping someone's personal off her feet, or even one of the borderline Highborn. "Kalena seems immune to his charms, though."

Damen eyed Kalena with some doubt. Today's outfit revealed her as a pleasingly if not outstandingly proportioned young lady, the sort that looked like she'd put on pounds too easily if she didn't watch herself. Maybe that's what made her so crabby, Reandn thought, having to do that sort of watching. And then he thought instantly of Kacey, who already had those pounds and who looked simply as though that was how she ought to be. Perhaps Kalena might be happier if she just let it happen. . . .

And then he thought of Kacey's quick tongue and

decided that it hadn't made a bit of difference for *her*, simultaneously resolving that Kacey would never get the slightest hint he'd ever thought it. You never knew what was going to get you in trouble with a woman, Highborn or not.

"I think," Damen said, still watching Kalena ride, "that our meira is probably immune to any charm whatsoever. A trait that will stand her in good stead, once she reaches court."

It did not, Reandn decided as they rode through the day—through switchbacks and places where the woods closed so tightly around the road that Sky danced in barely restrained worry at Reandn's tension—stand Kalena in good stead here on the road. They couldn't charm her into delaying their frequent stops, they couldn't cajole her into eating her prolonged midday meal more speedily . . . even Vaklar seemed frustrated by her, and when he and Reandn rode together that evening—minus any of the prying conversation Vaklar had offered during their first ride together—the Resioran freely admitted he wished he could give her a good shaking up.

"You need to talk to her," Reandn said.

Vaklar looked at him askance, but the night's clouds were lower than they had been the evening before, and his features were mostly obscured by darkness. They rode slowly tonight, picking out the terrain ahead with some care. The horses could see just fine, but they were no help when it came to spotting the features that made any particular spot more of a potential problem than any other. Not that it made any difference—they gave themselves nothing but false assurance with these little rides; there was plenty of territory they'd travel within the next day with no chance to scout whatsoever.

The last time Reandn had done this, it was as part of a patrol that rode ahead, beside, and behind the Highborn they protected—unseen by the travelers themselves. Now *that* was the way to protect someone properly in this area.

"Talk to her," Reandn repeated. "She can be a burr

up our butt once we get on the main road, if she has to. Tell her that."

"Naya, I will not!"

Reandn grinned into the darkness. "You're her man, Vaklar. Find other words to say the same thing." He patted the neck of the mare beneath him; she was such a steady thing, if a bit short of personality. "*Someone's* got to—"

He cut himself off, and straightened in the saddle, every sense alert. Magic thrummed in the air, just the faintest touch of it; enough to make him swallow hard and shift his jaw as though trying to pop his ears when he had a cold. It lacked Elstan's touch.

"Dan?" Vaklar said instantly.

"Someone's out there," Reandn said, a murmur that was as much to himself as anyone else.

Alarmed, Vaklar looked around them. "Sure?" he asked, puzzled, when he obviously discerned nothing.

Well, that was one member of the Resioran party they didn't need to worry would detect Elstan's magic. At least, not subtle magic, not that Elstan seemed capable of such. "Not close," Reandn said, removing the hand that had been hovering over his horse's neck. No need for it tonight; the magic had already faded. He amended, "Or if there *is* someone close, they're hunkered in pretty well. I just . . . heard something."

"An' you've better ears than I," Vaklar grumbled.

The magic disappeared altogether. Whoever was out there had no intention of making a dramatic appearance just yet. Reandn relaxed enough to give Vaklar a wicked grin. "That," he said, "is because I haven't spent any good part of my life listening to your meira."

Vaklar sputtered something; Reandn didn't give him a chance to make good on whatever precise threat the words represented. He turned the mare on her heels and cantered uphill to the camp, where Nican and Damen would no doubt greet his news with dour expressions indeed.

❖   ❖   ❖

Vaklar spoke to the meira.

Reandn heard the fringes of the conversation, early the next morning. Damen was already saddled up and heading out of camp, taking Reandn's news seriously enough to ride aggressive point. But whatever the guard's words had been, they weren't enough. Although Varina had Kalena dressed and out of the tent—she, it seemed, took Vaklar's words most seriously indeed—no one could do anything about the rate at which Kalena ate her breakfast. Once again, the horses saddled waited by Reandn, the guards waited by the packed wagon, Nican and Vaklar waited together by the cart, and Elstan hung around trying to look like he knew exactly which shortcuts to take today. Every so often he made a pretext of offering advice to Nican, but his words were merely lifted from whatever he'd heard in Reandn's most recent private report to the Hounds.

Sky jigged beneath Reandn, feeling all the tension from the camp and turning it into his own worry, and Reandn sat it out, knowing the horse would only worry more if forbidden his little dance. *Everyone feels it but you*, he thought silently at Kalena, and indeed, if she realized how anxious they all were to move on, she showed no sign of it. She broke her fast most completely, disappeared into the woods for a short while, and then returned to mount her fat gelding. Everyone finally rode out in silence, too concerned with making time to make conversation as well.

The morning, grey and chilly and with a gusting wind, remained quiet. Damen frequently rode back to touch base with them, and offered the cheerful news that they ought to make it at least halfway down the road before the day was out. Slow progress, indeed.

When Kalena started making noises about a midday meal, Damen fell into line next to Reandn and offered the news that Vaklar was determined to keep it a cold one no matter how the meira might fume. "And I've been thinking I ought to swap horses. This one's going to be played out soon, with the kind of ground I'm covering."

"Go through three of them, if you want. We need all the coverage we can get right now," Reandn said, eyeing the steep drop-off at the very edge of the road, the result of a recent ground slide. The rock rose up just as abruptly on the other side of the road, and the travelers tightened together, suddenly in a spot where there was just enough width to take Kalena's heavy wagon. "Besides, no need to ration them at this pace," he added, studiously maintaining a sober expression. "Sky wouldn't be quite so . . . fresh, otherwise."

Good old Sky. As if he knew he was being discussed, the gelding suddenly jolted forward, his head slinging up in the air and his quarters bunched. Nican just snorted amusement, but Reandn cut him off with a gesture from the hand that held the lead rope, abruptly serious.

"That was for real," he said. Sky grunted and started forward, desperately trying to listen to Reandn's steadying weight and legs but dancing in protest—and then Damen's horse started, too, and Reandn felt magic swirl around them and close in on his ears, his balance, his ability to think—

"Magic," he told Damen, as Damen's gelding kicked out angrily behind itself. But he hadn't felt the magic before Sky's strange reactions, so there was something else going on, too, but he just couldn't think enough to put it together and by now Sky was crowding the wagon, chest to wood, and Elstan was crying " 'ware," and the other guards were searching the woods around them. Something pinged off the wagon backboard and he realized then that it was a slingshot pebble that was meant to have hit horseflesh like the others before it.

"Damen, behind us!" he said, and then suddenly Sky, flinching and twitching under a quick barrage of the painful little missiles and finding no relief with jamming himself up against the cart, spurted ahead to go around it.

And ran out of roadside.

Downward they both plunged, with Sky just as astonished as Reandn, his hooves scrabbling at the vertical slope and getting just enough purchase in the soft dirt to control his descent into a series of bounding leaps. The cliff flashed by Reandn's head, the magic snarled through his veins, and with each of Sky's leaps came the terrified explosion of his snorty breath. They hit a true slope, dotted with trees the horse barely evaded in his out-of-control descent.

Above them, the sounds of fighting—and dying—rang loud and clear, piercing the haze of magic around Reandn. He found he could think, discovered he was murmuring comfort at his terrified horse, and that he could slowly angle Sky across the slope. As soon as Sky found his balance, the horse stopped on his own, all four legs trembling so hard Reandn threw himself out of the saddle, only then realizing he hadn't so much as lost a stirrup. Not much more amazing than the fact that he hadn't lost his life.

The magic flowed in currents above him, surging and folding around the fight—of which Reandn could manage only the barest glimpse. Elstan's magic had joined the mix now, too, and Reandn stared up the hill for only an instant before stuffing Sky's reins down the saddle gullet where he couldn't trip over them and scrambling up towards the deadly power, moving over a slope so steep he pulled himself up with his hands as much as with his feet.

One of Kalena's guards slid over the edge, a limp rag of muscle and bone skidding down the soft dirt of the cliff. Reandn hesitated there, feeling the magic close in on him again; he took the time for several deep, free breaths—quite possibly his last—and crept up the cliff, constantly slipping, losing ground, and scrabbling onward, until he finally made it to the top, right alongside the wagon. He threw himself up over the edge and rolled beneath the wagon, his vision greying, his temper failing him, another guard falling lifelessly directly before him. *Magic—always magic!* Taking so much from his life that he could barely fathom the loss, and still slamming away at him—his fury gave him strength, and when the next peasant-clad pair of legs ran by, he shot an arm out and snatched the fellow's legs out from under him. The other hand retrieved his belt knife and by the time the man finished falling, Reandn had buried it just below his breastbone not once, but twice.

Climbing out right over the body, he ended up in front of another man on a horse, making the horse rear with surprise and throwing the rider back against the saddle cantle, still ahorse only by dint of his cruel grip on the reins. Reandn snagged the man's jacket as the horse came down and he and the rider both ended up on the ground—but only Reandn struggled up to his feet again, whirling just in time to slash at the woman who was coming at him from behind. An arrow thunked into the wagon at his side, and someone screamed, and someone right beside him grunted with effort; someone else fell before him, and hot blood ran down his arm and slicked his knife hilt. In one moment he had hold of someone's well-balanced single-handed battle axe, and in the next it was gone.

All the while the magic closed in around him, until his vision became a narrow tunnel with grey haze closing in on it, but there was less screaming, and less chaos around him; he felt his knees going and knew at least that he'd done his best to keep Kalena alive—he saw her, then, struggling against the wagon with someone who gave her a brutal backhand. From his knees he threw his deadly boot knife, making an automatic adjustment of grip for distance and the knife's familiar revolution so the blade sunk deeply into the assailant's back just below his ribs.

Rough hands jerked him upright as he succumbed to the magic; Reandn had just enough wits left to see a descending club. But somebody roared in anger, and blood sprayed warm across his face—the hands flung him away and he fell, immediately smothered by a heavy weight.

Then came silence, or as near to it as possible in the aftermath of any battle. The magic stuttered away, and in its place was the sound of crying and moaning, and of someone offering up the harsh, incredibly quick gasps that always presaged death. Someone rolled him roughly onto his back; a sudden gust of cold wind hit his face— and snow, wet cold snow. "Any of that blood yours, then, Dan?" Efficient hands searched his blood-soaked tunic for rents and then gave him a rough pat, apparently satisfied. Reandn's vision returned in agonizingly slow increments; his ability to breathe freely remained elusive. "Nothing killin' that I see," Vaklar's voice came with relief and puzzlement. "Come, then, ladaboy, come on out of it, whatever fit you're into." Thick, calloused fingers gripped his jaw and tilted his head this way and that.

Reandn couldn't help the groan that rippled out. Just what he needed, his world spinning around for real. *Go away, dammit.* Weakly, he pushed at the man's hand, and of course his arm lost strength and he ended up hitting himself in the face.

"All right, then," Vaklar said, and the bulk of his presence disappeared from Reandn's side. "I've others to look to. We need your help, ladaboy, so pull yourself 'round if you can."

Breathe, Reandn told himself. That was the important thing. Beat the poisonous magic and breathe.

Teya's head jerked up; she wrapped her jacket more tightly around herself. Where an instant ago she had been nodding over her horse's lulling walk, now her heart skipped up to a pounding beat. Magic flared into action somewhere to the north; magic big enough to change the currents drifting quietly around her. Two unknowns, flinging around spells that never quite seemed to make it to completion, not past the first salvo. The spells themselves felt murky from start to finish, unlike the crisp ring of spells performed by the school masters.

She stopped her horse, dropped the reins, and quickly formed the gestures of the now-familiar spell that would probably only confirm what in her alarmed heart she knew to be true. *Where's Reandn?*

Right at the heart of the magic. Of course. How could she have let herself become so complacent, to be dozing along the road? Teya neglected to think of how carefully she'd been managing the horse, and how poorly she'd slept the night before, tossing and turning with nightmares of dying Wolves on a wet hillside, and gave herself a good mental kick in the behind. Gathering up the reins, she put the horse into a trot. With any luck it would last her, and she was only a few days away. *Let it be close enough*, she thought. *Ardrith, let it be close enough.*

Kacey drew water from the well in the front yard, taking her time with it. The still, warm day was giving way to gusting fits of cold breezes and taking on the air of late winter again, but for now it remained a day to be enjoyed. Especially since, at last, Teayo had hired a woman as full-time help. What luxury—to be able to see to her patients, without juggling them between laundry or cooking or cleaning or even running into Little Wisdom for foodstuffs. Why, if she'd been busy today, she could have sent Wenda to fetch this very bucket for her.

But she wasn't busy, and the day was so lovely—she ought to be giving the barn a thorough cleaning or making visiting rounds with her father, or making an inventory of . . . of . . . well, of *something*. Something practical. Instead she left the bucket on the stone well wall and wandered to the edge of the small woods, where the shy spring wildflowers, tucked in low and close to the ground, proliferated.

She wouldn't even think about Reandn today, or worry

about him, or wish he was here to see flowers with her. He was odd about things like that—always so intent on his goals, so focused on his patrol and his responsibility to them. And still harboring enough anger that Kacey yet found herself startled when he wholeheartedly immersed himself in some foolishness, like last year when it had been so hot, and they'd been on the road to Little Wisdom—and without so much as a wink of warning, he'd tossed both herself and Rethia into the small lake just outside town. And jumped in after them, she recalled, smiling at the great deliberate splash he'd made, and the water fight he'd gleefully instigated.

She'd been just as surprised to discover he knew the wildflowers as well as Rethia, and simply never said anything about them. Oh, once in a while he'd identify one of Adela's favorites, but not much more. Kacey wondered if he knew what her own favorites were.

Damn, she realized, crouching down to look at a soft-leaved carpet of tiny pink and white moss stars. She *was* thinking about him. Well, maybe that was all right, considering she was still smiling, still happy with the day.

A sudden splash by the well startled her; she jerked around, almost losing her balance, and discovered Rethia there, not paying much attention to the fact she'd just knocked into the full bucket and soaked her own feet. Kacey narrowed her eyes—Rethia distracted was one thing, but Rethia like this meant something else altogether. "I'm over here!" she called, coming out of the woods. "What's wrong?"

Whatever Rethia had to say seemed stuck in her throat, as though the urgency of it was just too much and yet at the same time her attention lingered elsewhere. Kacey ran to her, and gave her a little shake. "Rethia, come back *here*! What's wrong with you?"

At that her sister's eyes widened, though they were huge already and all but dominated her face with the intensity of their mingled bright blue and rich brown color. "Not me," she said, her words barely making it into sound. And then she closed her eyes and gave herself another little shake on her own, beating Kacey to it. When she opened them she was *there* again, in front of Kacey and giving her wet feet a quick, bewildered glance.

"Not you," Kacey said. "Father? Is Father all right?"

Rethia blinked. "Fine."

"Then *what*?" Kacey all but shouted. And then she realized, and tried hard to close her mind to it—unsuccessfully, of course. When had she ever been successful in keeping that man out of her thoughts, since the very first time they'd met and Reandn, delirious, had mistaken her for dead Adela and drawn her into a kiss she could still feel on her lips today if she thought about it. *When* she thought about it. "Not—" she said, and tried starting again, finding she could say it if she thought not of Reandn, but the amulet. "Not the amulet—tell me it's not the amulet."

"It's not," Rethia said, whispering again. "It's Danny himself."

Kacey, vexed and beside herself, bit the inside of her lip and took a deep breath. "I can't do this today, Rethia. Just *tell* me."

Rethia looked a little bewildered herself. "He hasn't broken the amulet—he's calling me. Oh, not calling *me*, just—I just *feel* it. I've got to go."

"But what happened? Is he all right? Is it magic, did it get to him?"

Rethia shrugged the questions away with a small frown, as though they were pesky flies settling on her shoulders. "I don't know. I just know he needs help."

"But then . . . it might not be magic at all. It might be fighting, and there's nothing we can do about that but get killed." Kacey hardly believed the words were out of her own mouth. What she wanted to do most was grab Rethia's hand and refuse to let go, so that when the Solace wizard sent Rethia to that little town of

Pasdon, there'd be no choice but to send Kacey, too.

Rethia gave her a look. Just a steady, *are you in your right senses* look, the one that Kacey herself had sent Rethia's way often enough. "He's been in plenty of fights in the last two years. I never felt them, did I?"

No. And they'd been much closer, too. "All right then," Kacey replied, and added what she should have said in the first place. "I'm coming, too."

Reandn blinked when a drop of mushy rain hit his face, coming suddenly and abruptly to his full senses. Still alive, still breathing—if not with complete success. Well enough so that he could think again. His vision was watery, as ever when he'd been hit so hard with magic; he dragged his sleeve across his eyes without thinking and the odor of fresh blood struck his nose afresh. Blinking down at himself, he realized he was soaked to the elbows with blood, that his entire tunic was splotched and dripping. He found the cleanest spot he could, down along the hem, and pulled it up to wipe his face.

The sound of Vaklar's voice filtered through the noise of crying, and moaning, and the hoofbeats of uneasy and shifting, untied horses. *Sky*, he thought briefly, wondering what had become of the horse. And then he took the deepest breath he could, rolled onto one knee, and struggled to his feet, pulling himself up the side of the wagon to get there. Once steady, he took his first good look around, shivering as the gusting wind hit him full on and plastered the clammy wet tunic against his skin.

Past the end of the wagon, Damen lay twisted and still, an arrow protruding through his chest, the shaft of it in his back, propping him up in an impossibly awkward position. At Reandn's feet, a number of men and women sprawled just as awkwardly, just as dead. One of them had Reandn's knife sticking out the side of his throat; carefully, he leaned down just far enough to yank it free, and then stuck it through his belt rather than clean it or sheathe it covered with gore.

In front of the wagon, between the wagon and the cart, he heard Kalena's rising voice—a cross between whining and true fear—and Vaklar's as he cut her off. "They'll be back," he said clearly, intractably. "*We can't be here.*"

Leaning heavily on the wagon, Reandn made it to the front wheel; Vaklar looked up at him and nodded with satisfaction. Kalena knelt with Varina in her arms; Reandn didn't see much blood but sometimes it didn't take much. On the ground between her and Vaklar was Yuliyana, her tunic cut away; Vaklar handled her like he would a baby, wrapping her arm and upper chest with bright silk, completely unheeding her nakedness. On his other side, Kiryl lay deathly still, bleeding from a number of minor wounds but untended aside from a garish silk around his head and half his face. The spitting slushy rain left the other half of his face glistening wet.

"Where—" Reandn started, but Vaklar didn't let him finish.

"Sit down here with the rest of us a moment, Dan. Nice to see you on your feet, mind, but I'm thinking you won't stay there long. I've moved them. We didn't need to have them among us just now."

Moved them . . .

"All of them?" Reandn asked, his words sounding just as strangled as they felt.

"Aya," Vaklar said, assessing his work on Yuliyana with a critical eye and, as an afterthought, taking a wrap around her breasts for the scant modesty it offered her. Yuliyana knew no differently; she was a rag doll in his hands. "Not your Elstan; he's up front with Nican."

No, Elstan was coming up beside the cart, his hands bloodied but very little else of him. "Dan," he said, his voice cold. "Vaklar said you seemed to be alive. I'm surprised you're even back among us, considering how well you don't handle that horse of yours."

"Bloody damn mouthy little man, you are then, Elstan," Vaklar said, standing to wipe his hands on his thighs—for what little good it did. Like Reandn, the guard's clothes were washed with blood, some of it his own. Looking at him, Reandn suddenly felt the stiffness of the dried blood in his own hair, the flakes of it drying in the corners of his eyes, and the pull of it drying on his skin. "That was some hellish riding, it was. And tell you this—had the horse not run off, Dan would be dead like Damen, an arrow in his back." To Reandn, he said, "It was distraction, then, Dan. Rile up the horses while their archer moved in and the others closed up around us."

"They . . . gave up? After all that? And with only a few of us left on our feet?"

Vaklar started to wipe his hand over eyes gone suddenly weary, as much with grief as fatigue. "They lost enough of their own. Panicked, like. Not career fighters. It's what I've been trying to tell the meira—they'll be back, aya. Soon."

Soon. Reandn knew better than to think he'd be as effective a second time around; the magic, subdued as it was, taunted him with moments of surcease and then surged up again to grey the edges of his sight. "Elstan," he said. "Do that again, and I'll break all your fingers."

"What're you talking about?" Elstan snorted. He seemed oblivious to the devastation around him, but his voice was high and had a brittle edge. "What do you think saved us?"

"Magic!" Vaklar said. "I thought I felt it! That'll take some explaining, ladaboy." But after one piercing glance at Elstan, he moved to the cart and began tossing supplies.

"Not your magic," Reandn said, answering Elstan's question. "I know the feel of a spell completed, and you didn't manage much of that."

"Neither did the enemy's wizard," Elstan said stiffly,

and he was right at that. "Besides, I've told you before, there's something interfering—"

Vaklar snorted, pausing in his task. "Elstan, boy, I'm sore tired of your voice just now. Put yourself to work rounding up the horses—they're plenty more than we need as mounts, but we'll need pack animals."

"But he—"

"I'm not hearing it! He turned this fight for us. Think me *you'd* have climbed back up that mountain to return to this slaughter?" Elstan opened his mouth and the older man brutally cut him off. "Naya, don't even try. Go round up the horses!"

For once, Reandn felt a twinge of sympathy for the wizard—albeit a quickly passing one. He grabbed the side of the wagon as a wave of dizziness washed through his body, and said, "You're leaving the wagon."

Vaklar nodded. "The cart'll carry our wounded. The wagon's too big for this road. Not fast enough."

"But my tent!" Kalena objected, though she seemed more dazed than outraged. "My things . . ."

"Your life is what you have now, meira, and give thanks to the goddess Ardrith for it." Vaklar appeared entirely unmoved by her distress; the only things left in the cart were the bedding, the small Keland tent, and the food packs.

"Seems to me the tent is already lost," Reandn said, nodding at the bright bandages on the wounded.

"You keep your place!" Kalena snapped at him, tightening her arms around Varina as if protecting her from Reandn.

"Dan," Vaklar said, "I don't know what's with you, but you're not in any shape to help me here. Your Elstan was up with Nican, said he lived yet. Don't know if it still holds true—but an' you can make it to him, do it."

Reandn's surge of hope died quickly, for there was none of it in Vaklar's voice. With careful steps he made it past the small group of survivors and around the cart, and found Nican as Elstan had left him, covered with a cloak and blinking slowly into the wet falling rain-turned-to snow. Whatever grievous wounds he bore were hidden by the cloak, but the scent of opened bowel could not be so easily hidden.

Nican didn't notice him until Reandn crouched gracelessly beside him, one hand touching the ground to keep himself from tipping over. Didn't notice him even then, not right away. Reandn watched his face a moment, glad to find Nican peaceful and not writhing with death throes. By the time he was ready to clear his throat, Nican looked straight at him and said, "Dan. What of Damen? Elstan couldn't say. Or wouldn't."

"Couldn't, probably. I never saw the wizard anywhere near us. But Damen . . . Damen's gone."

"They started it back there," Nican said, as though pondering it all. "Up here they had their wizard." He raked his gaze, a little sharper now, over Reandn, and said, "I told him to use his magic, Dan. I'm sorry. Had to let him try."

"Yes, you did. I made it through."

"Did your share of the fighting, I see."

"What I could. Not enough. But Vaklar's alive, Nican, and he's holding things together. We'll be away from this place as fast as we can; we'll get Kalena to safety." Reandn kept his doubts well hidden, but his weakness wasn't so easy. He put the heel of his hand against one eye, as if he could push away the dizziness, and as strong as he meant his words to be, they still came through the wheeze of his tight chest. Nican, he hoped, was beyond noticing.

"Not to worry about carting me around," Nican said. "I don't think I'll take that long to die."

Reandn snorted at him, but it was a mild sound. "Aren't you the cold son of a bitch."

"Aya," Nican said, a fair imitation of Vaklar. His eyes started to roll up, and Reandn grabbed his shoulder, pulling him back.

"Go with Tenaebra," he said, sounding much fiercer

than he meant to. "I'll do the Binding for you and Damen."

"Binding," Nican said clearly, as if the one word on its own had the strength to hold him. "You know . . . the Binding. *Who*—?"

Reandn grinned at him, a fierce look that Wolves—and Hounds—on the hunt often exchanged. "Reandn," he said. "Wolf Remote First."

Nican grinned back, a weak expression full of relief and wry amusement. "Too damn cocky for a wrangler," he said, and died.

Chapter 8

"I don't think I can do this," Tellan said, slumping onto Kacey's tall stool behind the workbench. Down at the end of the sickroom, their only patient made an obvious attempt to eavesdrop. Kacey spared the man a glance, thought perhaps it was time he had an enema, and took Tellan's arm to turn him till his back was to the row of beds.

"Of course you can do it," she said. "You know *how*, don't you? And isn't it much the same as blocking pain from someone who's been hurt?"

"Well, yes," Tellan said, apparently to both questions. He wiggled on the stool. "But I haven't even thought about it since I left Solace—not since before that, when my masters saw I had a gift for health work. And, Kacey—" He stopped, and eyed her uncertainly.

"What?" she said, impatience sparking in her voice. "*What?*"

"It's just that . . . well, if I do this . . . I mean—"

Rethia leaned over the workbench and inserted her first words into the conversation. "He's got to go back to Solace soon."

That's right, he did. A season of work in the field, then a short course of classes in which to enhance his practical experience, when the masters guided him to the new spells for which he would then be ready. That look on his face, those nerves—they weren't about accomplishing what she'd asked. They were for facing his masters after he'd done it. Kacey smiled at him, and Tellan drew back from her, wary. With good reason, she thought. "Tellan, dear," she said, oh-so-reasonable. "It's face them, later—or face me, *now*."

Rethia stirred as though to protest, but said nothing. On the floor beside her were two wicker-bottomed satchels, filled with herbs and salves and bandages— just in case—and with a few basic cooking supplies. Not to mention soap, two precious toothbrushes, and personal supplies that Kacey was sure one of them would need, on schedule or off, as soon as they embarked on a trip where it would be hard to get such things on the spur of the moment.

They, she thought fiercely to herself, and let the fierceness show on her face, watching Tellan react to it. For though only Rethia had been given her own amulet, one that would prepare her for the Wizard's Road and signal a Solace wizard to spell her from one place to the other, Kacey no longer had any intention of staying here at home while her sister and her—and Reandn—dealt with whatever had happened out near the pass.

Convincing Tellan was only the first step. Writing a note to Teayo went easily enough; the clinic was all but empty, and Tellan could well handle the case they had now, an elderly man who'd turned too difficult for his family to manage. As soon as Tellan figured out the best combination of medicines to keep the man calm without dosing him to death, the man could go home. After that, either Teayo would have to stay here and tend the clinic, or new patients would go to the less experienced healer between Little Wisdom and Solace.

Too practical again, Kacey thought; her scowl was for herself, but she was glad to see the effect it had on Tellan. The real problem would be charming her way onto the second leg of the journey, the spell from Solace to Pasdon. She glanced at Rethia, who shifted her weight from one foot to the other and back again; such a gesture from her quiet sister might as well have been a sudden shout of impatience. "Well?" she said to Tellan. "Which'll it be?"

"No matter what I do, I have the feeling I'm going to be sorry," Tellan muttered.

"Call it the price of being able to play with magic," Kacey suggested in a pointed tone. "And *do* it."

Tellan sighed hugely, an annoyed sound, and Kacey knew she'd won. "Are you really ready to go?"

Kacey gestured at the satchels. "Don't we look it?"

Tellan raised an eyebrow at her, looking a bit imperious. She let him have it, considering. "Not to put too fine a point on it, but I mean, are you really *ready*?"

"Oh!" Rethia said, understanding. "At Solace they told me it's a good idea to use the backhouse first. Just in case."

"Fine," Kacey grumbled. "No one told *me*." Together, she and Rethia hurried to the backhouse and took care of that pesky detail. When they returned, they found Tellan waiting for them outside the house.

"More space," he told them, and didn't explain further. In truth, Kacey didn't care. Now that she'd managed to convince the apprentice to prepare her for this strange journey, all she could think of was the way Reandn reacted any time the subject of the Wizard's Road came up. Anger, of course, and bluntly severe condemnation. But she knew him well, now, probably better than he'd like, and she knew what it was lurking in his grey eyes behind the flash of that anger.

Fear. Fear in the eyes of a Wolf who'd taken on all other opposition with feral mastery. And just now, especially *now*, she couldn't recall any other time he'd shown it.

But he hadn't traveled the Road prepared. Tellan would see to that for her. He certainly seemed to have taken over, now that he'd committed himself to do this thing. "Both of you pick up your things," he said, in a voice he'd never used on Kacey before; it didn't even crack. Turnabout, she supposed, was fair play. She hoisted her satchel and ducked under its shoulder strap, tugging her rucked up jacket free. Rethia, looking too slender and too serious in the long split traveling kirtle she wore, struggled to do the same, and Kacey shifted the thing for her, then looked to Tellan for the next step.

"All right," he said. "Once I do this, you're not going to see or hear or smell anything, Kacey, and you're especially not going to feel anything. So wrap your arms around Rethia now—that's the only way you'll get taken along with her, if you're as close to one person as you can get—and once I cast the spell, don't think of anything but holding on to her, even though you won't feel her."

"After I get to Solace, everything'll be normal again?" Kacey couldn't keep the doubt from her voice. Tellan, she thought, looked a trifle too full of himself in return. Ah, well. She supposed he needed an infusion of confidence.

"Perfectly normal," he assured her, in a voice that reminded her too much of Farren. "Ready?"

She'd already made this decision. So she nodded, and said, "Yes," for good measure. This time there was no doubt in her voice. But all the same, as she wrapped her arms around Rethia's waist, Kacey whispered up into her ear, "Break that thing just as soon as he's done!"

"Yes," Rethia agreed.

Sudden darkness closed in on Kacey. No sounds, and not only no feel of Rethia in her arms, but no sense of having arms at all. She was nothing but a disembodied speck of thought, she realized abruptly, right on the heels of the discovery that she couldn't even taste the mint of the last mug of tea that had been lingering in her mouth. Good goddess, what if Tellan got it wrong? What if nothing changed when she arrived in Solace? What if all the wizards of the school couldn't give her back the feel of being within herself? Would even Rethia be able to find her there, to feel her in the same way she felt Reandn? And how long could a body even live like—

Kacey squinted against the sudden brightness of a sunlit courtyard. Her ears, too, worked perfectly fine; she winced at the shout that hit them, and felt Rethia flinch within the circle of her arms.

"—*two* of them! No wonder—"

"Calm yourself. I can count." This age-touched voice came more quietly, and its calm gave Kacey the wherewithal to collect her thoughts and take in her new surroundings. Her first glance went to Rethia, and held a silent question; Rethia nodded. She, too, was all right. The second glance turned into one long look, a twist of her head in both directions, as far as it would go. This modest courtyard held nothing more than a square of carefully trimmed grass surrounded by a flagstone path, with a center diagonal of flagstones where they stood. Green grass? Already in need of trim?

These are wizards, she reminded herself. And . . . sheep. One sheep, anyway, grazing contentedly off to the side. A splash of color at its neck seemed to be . . . a scarf. A winter scarf. *Wizards who like strange pets?* she thought, and looked then at the wizards in question. One—the younger one—seemed to have followed her gaze to the sheep. Clothed in dark robes with thin piping around the sleeve that probably meant something, the young man wore a flush as well, one that crawled into the roots of his badly thinning hair. He cleared his throat, and said, "Mascot."

The other wizard looked up at him from her considerably shorter height and said, "No need to explain Woolly. *They're* the ones with explaining to do." To Rethia, the woman said, "Our arrangement was with you, not you and someone else. Do you know what sort of danger you put yourselves in, adding another person to this retrieval without telling us?"

"If we'd had a way to tell you, we would have," Kacey said. "But I had to come."

"You *had* to come?" she repeated, raising one finely shaped eyebrow into a heavily lined forehead. Not a natural brow, Kacey thought. Must be some new city style. The rest of the woman looked much the same—styled. A stiffened, unadorned headpiece pulled her grey hair tightly back, but let it fall freely between her shoulders; her spell-twisting hands had none of the chipped nails that frequented Kacey's fingers, and her simple robes with their rich burgundy piping looked as elegant as the best dress that Kacey—or Rethia, for that matter—owned.

Silently, Kacey reckoned her for a stiff-necked, power-wielding school official, and resigned herself to losing too much time here. Out loud, she said, "Reandn's in trouble. Had to."

The woman indicated Rethia. "She's the one who can help him, so you've told me nothing. However, I take it the amulet has been broken?"

"No," Rethia said. "I felt it."

The wizard only looked at her a moment, while the young man fidgeted behind her. "She does that sort of thing, from what I hear," he whispered to her, not quite quietly enough.

"Yes, that's my understanding. I'm not so eager to send her on without the signal, though. If there's no trouble, her arrival might very well cause some."

"Send *us* on," Kacey corrected, trying very hard not to sound annoying, or as annoyed as she felt at having the wizards discuss them like this. "Meira, if Rethia says he's in trouble, he's in trouble. And I have to go, too."

"It's true," the wizard said, her words coming with consideration, "that sending two or three people isn't much more difficult than sending one." She tapped her lower lip with one of those manicured fingers. In the corner, the sheep gave a quiet, contemplative bleat. "And you *just have to go*."

Kacey took a deep breath. "Please," she said. "It's important." And Rethia took her hand.

From the corner opposite the sheep, a small inset door banged open; the woman winced in disapproval. A tall man came rushing through it and straight to the center of the yard. "I heard," he said. "Why in Tenaebra's name are there two of them?"

"Why do men always swear by Tenaebra?" she countered. "And why do you Locals always stomp around these grounds with no sense of propriety?"

"There's two of us because it's better if we both go," Kacey said.

"Then that's how you should have arranged it in the first place. No way I'm dropping two of you into the Keep without them knowing about it."

"Please," Rethia said. "We're just wasting time. I'd like Kacey to come with me. She knows what she's doing. We both know what we're doing. It's no more trouble than sending one of us."

"No more trouble sending you, perhaps. More trouble when you get there, yes." The Local looked like he was settling into stubbornness.

"Rethia's right," the woman said. "We *are* wasting time. Addem, please take the good Local to Master Farren, since no doubt my own decision won't be satisfactory."

"But—"

"Do it, please. Now. Quickly."

Addem glanced at the Local, who indicated the young man should lead the way. "The sooner we stop this foolishness, the better." And then he didn't wait for Addem to lead the way after all, but set out on his own with the younger man hurrying to catch up.

"My sentiments exactly," said the woman to herself as the two men exited the courtyard. She turned back to Kacey. "Now. You tell me again why you have to go."

"To help my sister—" Kacey started, but the woman waved her words away.

"Tell me," she said, "why you *really* have to go."

"What?" Kacey said, glancing at Rethia to see if her sister understood the request any better than she did. "Because I . . . because he . . . he's in trouble, that's why. Because I can't just sit at home and wonder what's happened to him."

"Ah," the woman said. "Now that last's the truth, though from what I've heard, there's not much about this Reandn to inspire such loyalty."

Stung, Kacey said, "He's got a reason for everything he does!"

The wizard's voice gentled. "There, now, dear. Just surprised to find the man's so lucky." To Kacey's surprise, her face held complete understanding. "Don't worry about the fussy old Local. You'll be gone before he gets back."

"We will?" Kacey breathed, finding her knees a little weak with relief.

Rethia, sounding truly cross, flipped her braid behind her back and said, "Good. And don't send us to the Keep; I want to go to Pasdon."

"I was given that as an alternative destination," the woman agreed. "You're sure? Pasdon can send only one Local out with you."

"We've wasted too much time *here*," Rethia said, shifting the satchel strap on her shoulder. "We'll lose *days* if we go to the Keep. And we'll have to argue with a lot more people before they'll even let us go."

The wizard pursed her lips. "You're right about that. Let me just send them a warning that you're on your way, and then off you go." She favored them with a truly stern look, and added, "What you did here today was a foolish and dangerous thing. Don't pretend to understand the limits of magic you know nothing about."

"Don't blame Tellan," Rethia said suddenly, and then she stiffened, and looked down at herself in surprise, down where the amulet rested between her petite breasts. "Kacey—"

"He broke it," Kacey said, and looked at the wizard,

all her heart on her face for anyone to see. "He broke
the amulet."

"Well, then," the wizard said grimly, "let's not waste
any more time." And before Kacey could so much as
draw a deep breath, she plunged back into that senseless
state, with the bleat of the sheep echoing bizarrely in
her ears.

Gone. Reandn rested his hand on his chest, confirming
the fact. The amulet was gone. He'd had it before the
ambush, beneath his jacket; now he wore someone else's
shirt, and someone else's jacket, because his own had
been all but hacked apart in the fighting and Vaklar
had finished the job in order to check for wounds when
Reandn was down. A search amidst the churned-up mud
where the wagon had been yielded nothing, not even
when Vaklar took precious time to help him look—not
that he knew the exact purpose of what he was looking
for.

Reandn jammed the thick-glassed bottle of Kacey's
infusion into the new jacket's pocket, and stretched his
shoulders back inside their too-tight confines. *No amulet,
and the bottle three quarters empty.* Should he break
Elstan's hands now, or simply bind the fingers together
so tightly he'd never free himself?

But of them all, only Elstan bore nothing more than
a couple of scratches to show for the fighting. The only
one aside from Kalena herself, that was. Vaklar still
moved with tremendous force of will, reorganizing the
party into its new formation, but he'd lost blood, and
his energy wouldn't last. If any of his shallow wounds
got infected, he'd be no better off than Reandn, who
was breathing a tad easier thanks to Kacey's medicine,
but who found himself annoyingly prone to spells of
weak dizziness. The more conventional injuries Reandn'd
taken were merely irritating inconveniences, especially
the deep cut in his brow that reopened every time he
frowned—which seemed to happen far too often. Kacey

would fuss over that one, he realized, for it was going to scar.

He tried to remember the last time he'd pushed his tolerance to magic this far, and couldn't—because he hadn't. Even in Rethia's clearing, when magic had returned to Keland and Reandn had fought the rogue wizard Ronsin blade against magic, the overexposure to magic—as acute as it was—had quickly abated. So there was no predicting how things would go for him from here, just the certain knowledge that there wasn't much he could do about it.

Vaklar's call sifted through his thoughts. "Dan! You ready, then?" They'd wasted no time in gathering themselves; Reandn had looked up from Nican's death words to find Vaklar half done with gathering their dead; Elstan had helped without complaint, which spoke more of their danger than anything.

"Coming," Reandn told him, looking down the road to where the cart and horses waited. In the cart were their wounded—the two guards and Varina, beside whom Kalena stood, constantly touching her and soothing her. Tied to the back of the cart—for Vaklar no longer wanted Reandn himself tethered to them—an unmatched string of horses, as many of the enemy's as their own, bore ill-balanced loads of their pared-down supplies. Sky waited with them; the horse had returned on his own, though Reandn wasn't sure just where he'd found a spot to regain the road.

Between Sky and Reandn was the wagon, resting on its sideboards; beside it, in the lee of the increasing snow, their dead were laid out in neat rows. Too many to bury, not enough time for a pyre . . . their solution had been this, to turn the wagon over them and send someone back to finish the job. Whether it would be enough protection from scavengers remained to be seen, but it was the best they could do.

Vaklar stood next to the wagon, carefully scratching in his close-shorn grey hair and then frowning when his fingers came away bloody. "Another damn cut," he told Reandn. "Be finding the things for days, aya. You ready to turn this wagon?"

Reandn regarded the dead for a somber moment. Four Resiorans and two Hounds, Nican with that silly grin still on his face. He and Damen lay side by side, and Reandn thought of the Binding he would do for them, and the Binding he'd so recently done for his own patrol. All for Tenaebra, like most of the people he'd lost in his life. *All* of them. He suddenly realized he didn't have any idea what happened at a burial for one of Ardrith's own. If he'd ever been, he didn't remember.

He looked down at his hand at the sudden realization that he was rubbing his thumb over Adela's ring, and stopped. "Ready," he told Vaklar. "Be easier if we could get Elstan to help."

"He's writin' the note," Vaklar grunted. "And since neither you nor I can do that, we'll see to this."

"Remind me to learn my letters." Reandn moved in beside Vaklar and settled his feet, looking for solid ground beneath the slick mud. Bare feet would do better, he thought, finally finding tenuous purchase. He nodded at Vaklar, who nodded back, and together they pushed, grunting, feet slipping, trying just to dig the upper edge of the grounded sideboards into the mud so the wagon could tip over that fulcrum instead of sliding along in the mud.

When at last the edge caught, actually tipping the thing seemed easy. It hit the ground with a hollow boom, and settled into the mud, leaving Vaklar panting and Reandn struggling for air. The soggy snow quickly dotted the wagon undercarriage with spreading wet blots.

Elstan walked neatly between them and jammed his note—an identification of the dead and Keep-authorized orders to leave the wagon as it was—by the axle box, covering it with enough stones to protect it from the snow and make its presence obvious. "There," he said, backing out between the two men. "That ought to do it."

Reandn straightened carefully, keeping one hand on the wheel he'd been holding. "Assuming that, like you, whoever happens by can actually read."

"Everyone knows the Keep mark," Elstan said, removing himself from between the two of them, and especially, Reandn noted, moving himself out of Reandn's reach.

"I don't," Vaklar said, but he sounded satisfied enough. "All the same, it'll take a pretty determined bunch to set this thing right, an' you'll pardon my blunt speaking if I say no one'll even want to get near it after a couple of warm days hit this hill."

"I can do something about that," Elstan said in absent distraction, and lifted his hands.

Reandn was almost too astonished to react—but when he moved, Elstan didn't even see him coming. Reandn yanked the wizard up to the wagon, pivoting in the mud to kick his knees out from under him, and shoved him down against the wet wood, one knee on his back. Elstan's protest turned garbled as his face met the wood. "No more," Reandn told him, his voice grounding out in its gravelly lower registers. He put his mouth at the wizard's ear and repeated it, shoving against the back of his neck in emphasis. "*No more.*"

Vaklar merely stood there and shook his head. "Have you no wits, Elstan?"

"This is what I'm *here for*," Elstan said indistinctly and somewhat nonsensically. "To save her from this!"

"Naya," Vaklar said coldly. "That's what *I'm* here for. You're here to make sure we don't take the wrong road— or to give us a good one to hide on, should we need it."

"Wrong again," Reandn said, still on a level with Elstan's ear. "I'm the one that knows these roads." Ignoring Vaklar's surprised frown, he told Elstan, "Swear it, Elstan—no more magic. Swear it by Ardrith's mercy and Tenaebra's cold touch."

"But—"

"*Do it*."

Elstan hesitated yet, just enough to let Reandn know the vow would really mean something to him. "So sworn," he muttered finally, instantly following it up with, "but if the enemy's wizard comes at us again, there won't be anyone to stop him!"

Reandn released him, an exaggerated motion that conveyed his disdain. "We'll just have to hope you've been right all along, and that there *is* something in this region that's interfering with magic. Then that wizard's not really a threat, is he?"

Elstan moved away from the wagon, shaking his head at both of them. "You're mistaken if you think you can get us out of *this*."

Vaklar watched him stumble back toward the cart, pulling his horse out of line and mounting up to wait for them, making a great show of pulling his scarf around his face against the increasing bite of the wind and snow; the guard's expression was as much of bafflement as anything else. "Odd way to put it," he said, and then turned on Reandn. "You'll tell me what's up with this little escort your Keep sent, Dan—aya, that you will. Later, then, when we're some safer."

"Elstan's the one who came from the Keep," Reandn said, his only feint; he didn't expect it to work, and he was right.

"And you're just the wrangler," Vaklar finished for him in dry tones. "Oh, and the guide, aya? What else, then?"

Looking at him, Reandn shrugged, a response to his own thoughts as well as Vaklar's words; just at the moment, he couldn't think of any reason not to tell the man who he really was.

Except for the fact that the wind blew more insistently every moment, and the wet snow landing against his face and eyes was thickening just as fast. And that little tickle of Wolf in him said they'd already spent too much time here; no matter how sorely they'd hurt their anonymous enemy, that enemy would be back, and delighted to find them lingering so cooperatively.

Vaklar's eyes had never left him, and now the man grunted, a noise of dissatisfaction. "Later, then. Mount up, ladaboy."

Back to that, were they? Reandn held his protest and drew his borrowed jacket more closely around himself, wishing for the neck cape that went with his Wolf gear; he found his anxious horse and mounted up to trail the suddenly small traveling party down the switchback trail toward the main road and safety.

Or the safety they all hoped was there.

"I'm hungry," Kalena announced. "I demand that we stop *now*."

"My apologies, meira," Vaklar said. "But not just yet."

"You dare to ignore a direct order?" Kalena said, her voice rising in pitch. She was hooded against the weather, but Reandn could well imagine the look on her face—the one that narrowed her otherwise pretty eyes and turned her mouth into something pinched and small. He ran a hand down Sky's cold, wet shoulder and wondered when it might be safe to use more of Kacey's elixir.

"Yes, meira," Vaklar told the unwilling ambassador, his voice regretful but steady.

Reandn kept out of it. For one thing, he agreed with the man, no matter how his own stomach growled with hunger. Though hard to tell in this weather, dusk couldn't be far away, and were he Vaklar, he would push right on through. There were worse things than cold and hunger.

He pulled his scarf up over his ears and hunched into the jacket, wishing once again for something larger; this jacket was one of the women's, and as sturdy as she'd been, she hadn't had a man's shoulders. Reandn counted himself lucky that he wasn't sized as Vaklar—but then again, no one that size turned into a successful Wolf, an existence in which stealth and quickness counted as much as brute strength.

Reandn popped his jaw in a futile attempt to ease the magic in his ears, and suddenly realized he was hearing—or feeling—something else as well, something that ran under the magic like a sweet harmony. *Rethia*, he thought, but knew immediately that it wasn't. This had a deeper feel, like it could have been Rethia's magic in alto instead of soprano, and it carried an unfamiliar edge to it.

Still, it felt like a call from home, an invitation that would lead him to some safe place, where the magic would leave him in peace. A surge of unexpected longing took him by surprise; he closed his eyes against it. *Foolishness.* It could be anything, anything at all, and if he wasn't so desperately weakened by his allergies, he probably wouldn't have given its presence a second thought.

All the same, he couldn't help but wonder how far away it was.

Not much use in even thinking about it, he told himself, glancing down at their wounded in the cart beside him—*they* certainly couldn't afford the delay. Kalena rode on the other side, fuming—and Reandn gave thanks she was doing it silently—while Vaklar rode point and Elstan now trailed sullenly behind them. The cart mule itself, used to being led, followed Vaklar without much fuss. Twice now, Reandn had turned them off the main road to trails the wagon never could have navigated, shortcutting from one loop of the road to another; if he remembered right, there was another opportunity to do the same just ahead.

The strangely familiar magical voice distracted him again, luring him . . . an insistent voice in his head revealed sudden, puzzling alarm at the realization that he might just die without help, overburdened by magic.

It was a startling notion. Only two years earlier, he'd have embraced death in his quest for revenge against

Kavan and Adela's murderer; it meant only that he could start searching Tenaebra's Hell for them, and be with them that much sooner. But now . . .

Think about supper, he told himself. Damned escort duty was worse than the darkest hours of a long night patrol with nothing happening. Dizziness washed over him; he put a hand on Sky's withers to wait it out. At least, he realized wryly, it had gotten his attention. And then it occurred to him that it wasn't going away, that his body must have finally had enough—

Magic. Not his allergies surging up on their own, but new magic trickling in to kick them off.

"Wrangler, are you . . . are you all right?" Kalena asked as though she wasn't certain just how to go about showing concern for someone of his standing; under less trying circumstance he might have found it amusing.

Instead he ignored her, turning his head enough so Elstan would hear the sharp note in his voice as he shouted, "*Elstan!*"

"It's not me!" Elstan shouted back, and though Reandn's immediate inclination was to disbelieve him, the thread of fear in those words overrode it.

Vaklar stopped his horse and circled it tightly. "Don't be tellin' me—"

"Magic," Reandn said, blinking hard against it, trying to focus so that he, too, could search the woods, an area of shallower slope that might well hold an enemy. But dusk had crept upon them, and the woods were nothing but a blur of dark limbs against dark hillside, veiled by wind-driven wet snow.

"Take point," Vaklar said abruptly, reining his horse back around to flank Kalena's palomino. "Get us out of here *now*."

Reandn didn't hesitate. He sent Sky ahead at a fast rack, fast enough that the others broke into a canter behind him, running awkwardly downhill in the sloppy, uneven footing. He almost missed the shortcut amidst his dizziness and the darkening woods, and had to pull

Sky up cruelly short; the cart mule ran dangerously close to the bay's heels.

And then suddenly they all stopped. Sky pranced in place, his ears flicking madly around, his posture more of frustration and fear than that of disobedience. The magic rolled around them, and Reandn broke out into a sweat despite the cold. Magic held them here, and he couldn't fight it this time, couldn't hold himself together long enough to protect Kalena from the brigands it would bring with it; it was all he could do just to keep breathing, to stay ahorse. And still he had that nagging sense that as much as he didn't fear death, he just wasn't ready for it.

Nor was Kalena, who cried out in panic, or Vaklar, who cursed his horse, biting the words off hard. But as much as Reandn tried to summon the anger that often drove him through magic's insidious touch, he couldn't.

So he did what he never thought he would. "Go ahead," he shouted hoarsely to Elstan. "Use it!"

Elstan didn't take the time to gloat; his magic, feeling more focused than usual, flooded around them all, a backwash of the spell he aimed at their enemy's wizard.

"Ten'tits, they're right behind us!" Vaklar said grimly, filtering into Reandn's awareness only in the most distorted way. He lurched as Sky jolted forward, on the move again and hitting top speed on his own. They swept into the foreboding darkness of the side trail, and Reandn had no idea if the enemy saw them and followed.

He knew they were closer to that sweet harmony he'd heard just before this attack, the Rethia-like voice that called to him so strongly. He knew when Sky took a sudden swerve left, onto a branch trail he hadn't even seen, never mind had any intention of taking. The cart jounced along behind him, eliciting cries of pain from within; Vaklar's questioning shout came to him more dimly. Behind them the magic faded but its effects stormed through him as strongly as ever, and when Sky

dodged right and stopped short, Reandn stayed in the
saddle purely from coincidence.

The cart rattled to a stop on his heels; Vaklar pounded
past him, only then getting his horse wheeled about. If
the remounts were still with them, Reandn couldn't hear
them, and then Elstan, swearing at his mount, charged
up behind him and ran smack into Sky; the bay squealed
and kicked out with both hind legs, flipping Reandn
forward in the saddle.

Reandn had only enough presence of mind to note
that they were in the middle yard of a small farm between
the snow- and darkness-obscured barn and a tiny house,
and that someone was coming at them with lantern in
hand, followed by what was either a huge dog or a small
donkey. That when that someone spoke, her words
spilling over with fury and fear and unwelcome, it was
in a sweet, strangely familiar alto. And then he felt himself
stiffen, his body's last cry of protest before giving up.
Sometimes, it seemed, even when you weren't ready,
you were done.

Chapter 9

"We need to stop for the night!" Lamar, the young Local assigned to Kacey and Rethia upon their arrival in Pasdon, had to raise his voice against the wind. Kacey blinked so rapidly against the fall of snow on her cheeks and lashes that she could barely discern where they were going anymore, and she thought the man spoke pretty good sense. Darkness closed fast upon them, in any event.

But riding next to her, Rethia mutely shook her head, and Kacey sighed, trying to prod her horse to more speed.

Kacey missed her little black mare. This one was a livery rental out of Pasdon, and quite content to plod on in its own way no matter what she might be asking of it. Rethia rode on a similar horse and seemed oblivious to the creature's disregard for her; she didn't even bother with the reins, but kept her arms wrapped around herself, her startlingly odd eyes unfocused and unheeding of the snow that whipped against her face.

Neither of them had been prepared for the weather of this higher altitude; Lamar had quickly provided them with cold weather gear, chattering something about the changeable spring days. He didn't seem the least put off by his strange assignment—to accompany them and see to their safety, while letting Rethia choose their way—

and spoke freely of the other unusual incidents around Pasdon in recent days. Kacey immediately recognized Reandn's hand, but kept the news to herself. Rethia stayed deeply inside herself, giving no clue that any of Lamar's chatter meant anything to her.

Lamar pulled his horse out in front of them both and turned it sideways across the road. "We can't even see where we're going anymore!" he told Kacey, as though he sensed he'd get nothing from Rethia.

Rethia surprised them both. "I don't need to see where we're going," she said firmly. "I just need to *get there*."

"We can do it faster in the morning," Lamar said. "With a night's rest behind us and daylight around us. This road has a number of shortcuts and I'm sure we've missed at least one."

Rethia looked at Kacey, hesitating for a long moment. It finally occurred to Kacey that she was looking for guidance, but before Kacey could offer it, her sister said, "I can't get them separate. I need to go far enough to figure it out."

"Get them separate?" Kacey asked, frowning.

Rethia nodded, and her gaze went inward again; Kacey wouldn't have known what was happening in the dimming light if she hadn't been so familiar with it in the first place. Although such moments happened very rarely these days, she found she'd lost the habit of patience with them.

Lamar just looked at them both, completely baffled, as Kacey demanded, "Get *what* separate, Rethia?"

"Oh!" Rethia started, refocusing on them as though she'd only just realized that she'd wandered off in the first place. Kacey, pinned to the here and now by the cold wind and the snow on her face, not to mention the definite need to dismount and run behind a bush, couldn't imagine how her sister managed it. Rethia finally said, "The amulet is too loud. I can't get any sense of where Reandn is."

"With the amulet, I would think," Kacey said. "Rethia,

maybe Lamar's right. We'll never find him in this. It would be different if you knew the country, but—"

Rethia looked like she couldn't believe her ears. "Kacey . . . he *needs* us. Can't you feel all the magic? He's right in the middle of it!"

"I know," Kacey snapped, even though she couldn't feel a thing, and winced under the onslaught of guilt and worry. "But at this rate, we'll miss the right turnoff. Unless you've changed your mind about finding him on *this* road?"

Rethia hesitated, then shook her head. "No, not from the map I saw."

Had she seen two maps, or was she referring to the two Reandns? Kacey shook her head, more to herself than anyone else. It didn't really matter. What mattered was that Rethia was right; Reandn was in the middle of the kind of magic that would kill him. She shivered, and nodded, more to herself than to her sister. "All right, then. Let's try a little longer—"

"No." Lamar planted his horse across the road in front of them both. "I'm sorry, meiras, I really am, but we go no further tonight."

Kacey had an instant's rebellion, an urge to snarl *and who's going to stop us*—but before she could even think of acting on it, Lamar's horse was crowding hers, and his hands were on her reins.

"I'm sorry," he repeated, and looked miserable enough to mean it. "It's not safe, and we'll get nowhere for it."

Kacey glared at him a moment, and then looked away in frustrated acknowledgment of his truth. But she transferred her angry gaze to the shrouded woods and not anywhere near Rethia, whom she couldn't begin to look in the face. She knew she'd spend the night fighting her vivid imagination and its notions of what might have happened to Reandn . . . and whether they'd get there in time, or just one moment *too late*, while she wondered for the rest of her life if this moment was the one that made the difference, that she should have protested harder, kicked her horse past Lamar's, *made* him *see*—

"It won't come to that," Rethia said, all but inaudible. "It won't come to that."

But Kacey heard the fear in her voice.

"Help us," Vaklar said, in peremptory tones that were surely meant to be a request. Ought to have been. Reandn heard him perfectly well, and saw him, too. Saw them all, including himself, and only then realized where he was. *Not yet, dammit.* Vaklar pulled his slumping body out of the saddle, at the same time shouting over Sky's rump to Elstan. "Take Kalena into the house! And get that cart off the trail when you're done."

Does this always happen when magic taints a death? Two years earlier, in a clearing filled with charging unicorns and tumultuous magic, he'd been thrown into this same in-between place, on the verge of death. Just like this. Only . . . this time, there was no sign of Adela. Reandn looked for her, felt for her, yearned for her . . . and found nothing of her.

"You're not taking *anyone* into my house," said the alto voice, just as filled with anger as the first time Reandn had heard it. With newly acute vision—more acute, in fact, than normal—he looked at her, seeing her as well in the uneven light of her wind-rocked lantern as he might in full daylight. Young, furious, and frightened, with absurdly short chestnut hair puffing this way and that in the gusts that drove snow into her face, she stood in front of Sky and jabbed her finger at the road. "You're not welcome here!"

"You're a healer," Vaklar said shortly, jerking his chin at the post from which a small painted sign flapped in the wind. "We need healing." He held Reandn easily in his arms, and what a strange sight it was to see his own body dangling so limply, his head lolling without resistance as Vaklar shifted his hold. It was a body that still breathed, albeit in only the most strangled, shallow

way. Reandn looked away, and in the process spotted
Elstan escorting Kalena past the confrontation and into
the small, wattle-fenced yard around the house.

"I don't do *people*," the young woman spat. She turned
on Elstan and said, "Not one step further!" following
the command with a sharp whistle. In the open doorway,
the shadows shifted, and resolved in the form of a huge
dog. He stalked out of the house and stood just before
the open doorway; his rumble of a growl vibrated in
the air.

"Vaklar . . ." Elstan said, pulling Kalena behind him
despite the meira's gasp of outrage at being handled
so.

"Just don't move," Vaklar said, assessing the dog with
a flick of his gaze before turning back to the young
woman. "I don't care if you're a healer for pigs and
snakes. What you know might still save his life, and no
healer can just stand by and watch him—or the others—
die!" He looked back out to the road, and Reandn knew
he listened for sounds of their pursuit.

"You don't understand—I don't work on people—I
can't!" Her eyes narrowed, and she glanced out to the
road. "Someone's after you—probably right on your
heels. You brought them straight here!"

"It was chance," Vaklar snapped at her, looking at the
dog, the road, and Reandn in quick succession, while
his expression hardened in decision. "You might not want
us here, then, but we're *here*. Call off the dog and let
me get these horses out of sight—*now*."

She glared at him, but gave the horses a quick, worried
look. After a moment, she said, "*Kendall*," and the dog
came to stand by her side, his shoulders nearly as high
as her hip. In a gesture still full of indignant fury, she
pointed at the dark bulk of the barn.

Elstan immediately shoved Kalena toward the open
house door, though of course she did nothing more than
take a few resistant, stumbling steps before coming to
a complete halt. Elstan ignored her; he ran back to the

cart mule and began maneuvering the beast around in
a tight turn. "Your woman's bleeding again," he told
Vaklar, and Vaklar, in clear dilemma, finally put Reandn's
struggling body on the relatively dry ground beside the
wattle fence. "I'll see to them," he told Elstan, who
instantly grabbed the leads and reins of as many horses
as he could.

And Reandn, watching himself die, growled, "*Breathe,
dammit! Breathe!*"

"What's wrong with him?" the young woman asked,
hesitating between Elstan and Reandn, while from the
yard Kalena moved in closer, uncertain.

"Magic," Elstan said shortly, wrestling with Sky. "He
shouldn't have been on this trip. He's allergic to it."

Don't quit, not yet.

"To *magic*?" She looked at him askance, one hand
resting on her dog's back.

"Yes." Elstan gave up on Sky and turned for the barn.
"Are you sure you can't—"

"I *told* you," she said, and there was as much fear in
her voice as anger, "I can't!"

Elstan gave her nothing but a surprisingly grim look,
and led the horses away, with Sky trailing behind them.

Something closed down over Reandn then, a dimness,
a sense of the struggle he'd been watching in himself.
Damned Wolf, you've lived through this before!

"You could, if you tried," Kalena said, her first words
for quite some time. She pulled her fancy jacket closed
against the wind. "Go on, get closer. *Look* at him. Can
you do that and not even try? He's got some kind of
medicine with him—at least give him some of that."
Her voice shifted back to its haughty Highborn tones.

Miserably, the young woman said, "*I can't touch him.*
You do it."

A choking sensation closed in over his disembodied
throat; Reandn felt his fingers scrabbling over the wet
ground at the same time he saw himself do it—spastic
clutching movements, as though if he could just find

something to hang on to he'd survive after all. As though in the actual dying, his body drew him close again.

Kalena said, "Me? *Handle* a man like—like—" and then stuttered off, caught in her own argument. With an expression of some disdain, she came around the fence and knelt by him, gingerly patting over his jacket pockets. She found Kacey's elixir and pulled it out, struggling with the cork. And then she froze, staring at him. "He's not *breathing*!"

The young woman came closer as though despite herself, but stopped short, a clear decision. She whispered, "There's nothing I can do."

But she was close enough. Never one willing to take *no* for an answer, no, not Kalena. Her hand shot up to the woman's thin jacket, grabbed hold, and yanked. Caught off balance, the young woman stumbled and fell, thrusting her hands out to save herself—and landed on Reandn.

An astonishing jolt ran through both of them—Reandn felt it, he saw his body jerk in response, saw the woman snatch her hands away with a cry of surprise. His vision cleared; his body struggled anew, gaining a single successful breath. The woman looked at him, her eyes wide, her face filled with both fear and disbelief. She looked at her trembling hands, and slowly, ever so slowly, reached for him again.

The instant she touched him, he lost his strange dual existence. Crammed back into a body that suddenly felt too small, he drowned in sensation—his burning lungs, his fingers digging into the ground, the shout of magic in his head, the fear caught in his throat.

And then suddenly he was breathing, overwhelmed by the assault of sensations and devoid of rational thought. The fear in his throat turned into a cry of alarm, and he did what a Wolf was ever wont to do—improve his position, face his threats. Faster than thought, he rolled away from the two women and onto his knees and then up to a crouch—only his legs failed him and down he went to his knees again, heaving great ragged breaths with the catch of a sob buried within. Wild-eyed, he found Kalena—scrambling back from him—and the young woman, who knelt frozen where she'd been at his side. Just as distressed, her face full of shock, she stared back at him.

And met his gaze with startling blue and brown piebald eyes.

Chapter 10

"What did you *do*?" Kalena cried at the young woman, and didn't wait for a reply, turning to call for Vaklar in a high, thin voice. Reandn struggled for composure, knowing better than to try to get to his feet again, his mind's eye full of the young woman's haunted marbled eyes and his body slowly realizing it somehow still lived.

The young woman rose and slowly backed away from him, while the wind caught her short chestnut hair and flattened it into a fringe around one side of her face. Back she went, clutching her jacket closed with white-knuckled hands, back to the doorway of her house. There, she seemed to lose strength, and she slid down along the door frame and wrapped her arms around her giant dog.

"Vaklar!" Kalena called again, her voice steadier this time, full of its usual demand. Vaklar came around the end of the barn at a run, a dim figure in the darkness but full of intent and concern for Kalena despite the unevenness in his gait that spoke of his own stiffening wounds.

"You're to be in the house!" he cried at her, but then stopped short, close enough to take in the details of the scene and blinking hard into the wet, driven snow. "Dan?" he said. "What—how—are . . . you all right, then?"

"Alive," Reandn said, trying out his voice and finding it hoof-rasp rough. He made another attempt to get to his feet, wincing as he rose into the full strength of the wind, and nodded at the healer. "Her doing."

"Aya?" Vaklar said with distracted surprise, shifting uneasily as he glanced from the road to Kalena. "You're to be under bloody damn cover, Kalennie!"

He pulled her to her feet, ignoring her startled outrage, and marched her to the barn, leaving Reandn too dazed to do anything but stand and stare at the girl. The dog left off snuffling his mistress long enough to curl a lip at Reandn and snarl.

Vaklar emerged from the deep shadows around the barn. "You, too, Dan. Naya be standing there like a painted target."

"They lost us at the last turn," Reandn said, not thinking about the words. "Else we'd be found by now."

"There's sense to that, especially with the suddenlike way we took that turn." Vaklar narrowed his eyes, but let whatever the thought was pass. "Lucky the snow's melting as fast as it falls; they'll naya track us at night. But don't push it, aya?" One meaty palm fell on Reandn's shoulder.

Reandn didn't lift his eyes from the figure in the doorway. "She saved my life . . . I can't just . . . *leave* her like that."

"You're not thinking clear, ladaboy—"

"Do we know her name?"

"You don't," she said, her words so muffled they were almost incomprehensible. "Madehy." She gave a moist sniffle, barely audible in the wind.

"Madehy," Reandn murmured. He hardly knew what to think about first, his thoughts as buffeted by what he'd been through as his body by the wind. Some part of him was drawn to Madehy, and the rest of him latched onto the dangers they all faced. *Kalena's safety.*

But she *was* safe. And so were they all, at least for

the moment. *There's still a chance.* A chance to get the Resioran ambassador to the Keep, to carry out the orders he'd been given, as impossible as they'd become. One exiled Wolf, saddled with an ambitious but inadequate wizard and aided by a single Resioran guard who might or might not be willing to work with him. The wounded, he thought, would best stay here. Here, with . . . Madehy. "How do we stand?" he asked Vaklar, and then barely listened to the answer.

"The wounded are still alive—Ardrith's mercy, surely, after what they've been through this day. Horses are settled and covered—there were plenty of blankets in there, and not for you to worry, Meira Madehy, we'll leave it all just as we found it." Madehy appeared oblivious to them, and Vaklar turned a questioning eye on Reandn. "Tell me, ladaboy, just why *was* it we took that one? No shortcut trail, this, or I'm a Keep man."

Reandn shook his head, and froze in mid-gesture, closing his eyes. *Don't do* that *again.* "I'm not sure. You've seen . . . I don't take well to magic."

Vaklar frowned at him a moment, his broad, pocked features caught in a lack of understanding.

"It's an illness," Reandn said, quoting himself from their first evening together. "It comes and goes."

"Aya," Vaklar said suddenly, shifting sideways to the wind. "I have you now. Was magic, then, too?"

Reandn nodded. "Elstan, letting the Keep know we'd met up with you."

"I didn't feel naya a twinge of it," Vaklar said. "Ladaboy, that's a fair skill to have, an' you not being a wizard."

Reandn snorted. "It's a curse."

Vaklar nodded. "I've seen that, too. But I'm not seeing what it has to do with being *here.*"

Reandn shook his head. "Perhaps nothing," he said. "Or maybe everything." Under Vaklar's gaze he faltered, realizing the impossibility of sorting out the situation into a simple explanation. "At . . . home, there's a healer who helps me with it, and there's a certain . . . *feel* to her presence."

"Aya," Vaklar said, intent enough on the conversation that he ceased his constant glances back to the barn. "I'm with you, though not understandin' you at all."

"Madehy . . . has the same feel. I must have done something to make Sky think I wanted to come this way, toward that feel. I'm not sure."

"You mean," Vaklar said, a meaningfully incredulous look on his face that in the shadowed lamplight turned his face macabre, "we're here by *accident*?"

Reandn shrugged; it was a weary gesture, and full of more than just the day's efforts. Somehow it carried all the weight of his constant struggle to survive with magic insidious around him, and the strain of a Wolf trying to fit into a system that no longer quite accepted him. "It might be the best thing we could have done. We *did* lose them, whoever the Hells they are. That gives us some time. And I have to say I'm damned glad to find myself alive."

"The best thing!" Madehy said, her incredulous voice rising fast, surprising them all; Reandn hadn't even thought her aware of their conversation. "The best *thing*! Not for me, it's not! This is *my* place, my haven, and you came charging in and . . . and . . . and you made me—you made me—" Her words, progressively incoherent through sobs, dissolved altogether, and she hid her face in her dog's chest and cried without restraint, like a child. Gravely, the dog licked the top of her head, his brow furrowed; it didn't stop him from keeping a meaningful and menacing eye on the strangers in his yard.

"Oh, now," Vaklar muttered uncomfortably. "We didn't mean to cause you such trouble."

"Madehy," Reandn said, and took a few, hesitant steps toward her. The dog stopped his ministrations just long enough to growl, a deep rumble from the depths of his broad chest.

Madehy didn't even look up. "You stay away from me—all of you!" she cried. "You've done enough already!"

Reandn halted, looking back to find Vaklar just as uncertain as he. And Madehy cried. He suddenly wondered just how old she was, and why there was no one here to hold her but a dog. He took an unwitting step forward.

Vaklar gave him a wry look and said, "Naya, Dan, leave her be. That's her choice, and we've done enough already, aya?"

Aya. Right. Reandn dragged a hand back through his hair, gummy now with the fallen snow and dried blood. Vaklar said, "There's a forge shop off the end of the barn; we've a fire started in it and water heating. For all it's good to see you standing again, I've not much faith you'll stay that way. Come in, eat something, and get cleaned up some. And sleep. We all need that."

Reandn shook his head. "Later. I'm going to backtrack along the trail a ways, and make sure we didn't pick up any unwanted company."

"No," Vaklar said, and he meant it. "That's for me, this night. I may not have your ways among the trees, but I'm standing upright—and you're listing."

He what? Hells, he *was*.

Vaklar gave the barest of grins at Reandn's disgruntled response, and nodded toward the barn. "Eat. Clean up. Sleep. We'll have plenty to do tomorrow."

"You won't *be* here tomorrow," Madehy said in a ragged voice, but there was more desperation than confidence in her words. Reandn rubbed both eyes with one hand and deliberately, reluctantly, stepped away from her.

Sleep, he thought, might be long in coming tonight, no matter how heavy exhaustion lay on him.

Kacey woke to the earliest hours of a clear day and the sounds of Lamar saddling horses; she stuck her head out from beneath the blankets, awkward in a full set of clothes under it all, and discovered Rethia looking at her. Waiting.

"And?" she asked of her sister.

Rethia gave a little frown, and shrugged her shoulders in a gesture Kacey couldn't quite interpret.

She emerged abruptly from beneath the blankets, throwing them off altogether. "Is he *there*?"

"Hush," Rethia told her. "He's there . . . quietly. I just can't tell . . . Well, we're close, now, you know. If we can find the right trail, it won't take long."

A chill ran down Kacey's spine; she wasn't sure if it was the cool morning air—though this day seemed much improved over the last—or if it was fear and anticipation. What if they didn't reach Reandn in time? What if *quietly* meant it was already too late?

And what if things turn out just fine? Kacey scowled at herself and struggled to get a grasp on the practical outlook that had ever been hers. To her astonishment, it remained out of reach. She sat there in disarray, her mouth open, struggling with herself.

"Hurry," Rethia said, apparently unaware of her sister's emotional jumble, and ignoring the physical. She held out a lump of pressed nuts, raisins, and honey. "Find a bush and let's go."

A turnip has more wits than I do. Kacey struggled up from the bedding, grabbed the nut ration, and stumbled off into the woods, chewing. Behind her, Rethia attacked the bedding with purpose, and when Kacey returned, she found Lamar and Rethia mounted and waiting, and her own horse ready to go. Without comment, she mounted up, barely managing to swing her leg over the bulging packs behind her saddle.

Rethia didn't even wait for Kacey to settle in the cold saddle. "This way," she told Lamar, pointing northeast, where the road didn't go. "The amulet is there."

"We'll take the first trail that breaks off in that direction," Lamar said. "Or we'll make one, if we can't find one. Don't worry, meiras, we're almost there!"

Kacey took a deep breath, squashing down all her threatening misgivings. They would find Reandn soon, and then everything would be all right. *It would.*

Teya breathed deeply of the morning air, grateful beyond words for the warming, sunny day. All she needed was for the travelers ahead of her to move on; she'd followed them all the previous day and stopped when they did, unable to go further in any event.

Accordingly, she'd kept her morning spells quiet and direct, locating Reandn without any trouble—he hadn't moved from the night before. And whatever magic had been afoot the day before, there was nothing but bird song in the air, now. Either he'd done fine without her, or he desperately needed help; in either case, he probably wasn't going to be at all pleased to see her.

Not that it mattered; she was here. Teya mounted her worn horse and gently pulled its head away from the buds it was so desperately jerking off the trees, grabbing them almost faster than it could chew and swallow. "Soon," she told the animal. "Later today. Then I'll let you rest."

Assuming she didn't stumble into the middle of something too big to handle—or, worse yet, find Reandn already dead. She gave the horse a pat and amended her promise with a heartfelt, "I hope."

Reandn woke to silence. Or if not silence, the quiet shuffling and jaw-grinding noises of relaxed horses picking at their hay and the occasional low groan of someone in pain, subdued by medicines. Early morning, he thought, with everyone still asleep and all the questions of the day yet before them.

And then he opened his eyes and saw that, though the barn was swathed in only low, diffuse light, the daylight showing under the sliding main door shone bright and undeniable.

At that he sat bolt upright, instantly regretted it, and

sank back down to his elbows. What had happened? And why was he still in here sleeping?

Oh, right. Because he was just the wrangler, and no one else knew otherwise. Something it was time to change. More carefully this time, he sat up again, discovering again all the bruises from the fighting, and not a few dried cuts, well-buried beneath his clothes. Nothing deep, not as far as he could tell. Just that one in the midst of his eyebrow, and it was too late to stitch it now.

He meant to get to his feet then—and find his boots, for someone seemed to have removed them for him— but instead he just sat there, and considered the depth of his sleep, and the feel of magic in his system. Of the last, there was little, nothing but the ordinary background noise to which he'd grown accustomed. And he doubted Elstan would even consider using magic now, not when it would so neatly give away their position.

Heavens, it was nice to feel *right* again.

Except that there was something deep within him that said things were *not* right, that he'd lost track of something so crucial, so significant . . . nothing to do with Kalena or Elstan or even their unwilling hostess. The sense of it kept him sitting there, chasing his thoughts. He chased them from this barn all the way back to Little Wisdom and then forward again, through the intense memories of the day before. Finally, he returned reluctantly to the moments between life and death, to what had been missing there.

Adela.

Alone in the barn, Reandn froze, as though he could avoid the inexorable direction of his own thoughts. She'd been missing then—but had come to him in the night instead, holding herself unusually distant and distinct. Reandn found himself unable to voice his words directly—but she'd known the questions tumbling inside him. Why had she stayed away when he'd been so close to her through Tenaebra? Why hadn't she been waiting for him? Why wouldn't she touch him now?

You were going to die or live, no matter what I did or where I was, she'd told him. *If you'd died, I would have been here for you. But if you lived . . . then touching you so closely would only have done what I've done so many times before. . . .* Even with the distance she held between them, he could feel her distress, and he reached for that, too, to soothe it from her. She slid further out of reach. *Forgive me, Danny,* she said, and though he could no longer see her, he knew she was shaking her head. *I've been too selfish. Just remember . . . that I love you.*

And she slid away entirely, buffering her words with his exhausted and dreamless sleep. She wouldn't be back. She hadn't said as much, but Reandn knew it, knew it as well as he knew the ache in his heart. He drew his knees up, resting his forehead against them, awash in the equally familiar frustration of sorrow and yearning. As little as he'd felt of her over the past two years, somehow it had become enough just to *know*, to have that sense of her within himself. Losing it suddenly seemed like losing her all over again.

And then, in the center of it all, growing stronger despite his own resistance, new understanding spread stubborn roots. He saw her face again, not as he so often saw it, locked in terror at the moment Ronsin's twisted magic stole her life away—at the moment he'd failed to protect her—but saddened with regret. In an instant of clarity, he saw himself through her eyes, and realized that somehow, hidden behind the intensity with which he had flung himself into his role as Wolf Remote, tucked amongst the homespun moments, both light-hearted and quarrelsome, that came along with his tentative acceptance of Teayo's family, he'd only been faking it. Faking life.

Somewhat to his surprise, it occurred to him that had he died one dark night on Keep patrol, he certainly wouldn't have wanted Adela to live her days out alone in the small tower room they'd had together. He thought of her then, lost in the memory of all the delightful little things he'd seen in her, the silly giggle that made her sound like a little girl, the heat in her eyes when he did some Wolfish thing that, to his way of thinking, inexplicably and unreasonably angered her, and the entirely different heat in her eyes that still made his body long for her. Without him, she would have remained all of those things, and the thought of her without someone to recognize and appreciate those facets of her hit him as hard as any sorrow he'd endured in truth.

She wanted only the same for him.

She wasn't abandoning him, she hadn't stopped loving him at all. Years after death, she was finally letting him go—pushing him away, even—because she was as unhappy as he in the way their past had trapped them. Reandn held himself very still, very quiet, trying to understand the enormity of the concept. In the quiet of the barn, his heart pounded as if he had just run down a Keep Forest poacher . . . or as if Adela was settling into his arms, her panting breath cooling his bare skin and her eyes aspark with the pleasure they'd given one another.

Someone groaned, a pained and unduly loud sound against the silence of Reandn's thoughts, and Reandn jerked his head off his knees. For the briefest moment he felt like he'd been caught with the privacy of his passions spread bare to the world, but he took hold of himself, and then took a moment longer to realize he didn't have to *do* anything with those passions and those startling new realizations but let them exist while he attended to the world pressing in around him. Stiffly, slowly, he stood, and looked around the barn for his boots and half-chaps.

What he discovered was a small herd of horses milling in a sectioned-off corner in the big barn—noting with a grimace just how far into shedding season they were, now that the wind couldn't blow the loose hair away. He and the cart were crammed into the middle section of the barn, along with a plow, a harrow, and a pile of edged gardening tools. Wooden cabinets lined the back of the area, their doors ajar and supplies spilling out— blankets and soft, thick ropes and leg wraps; hobbles and bandages and jars of salves and powders.

I don't deal with people, Madehy had said. Obviously, she turned her talents to animals.

Reandn moved over to the cart, stepping carefully on the cold, packed dirt floor. In it, the two Resioran guards lay aflush with pain and fever; Varina was gone. Up and about, Reandn hoped, since her injuries had been the least severe—a cut on the leg positioned so that she couldn't ride, and a bad bump on the head.

For these other two, he didn't have much hope. But they'd obviously been treated, and aside from resetting the tangled blankets over them, there wasn't much he could do for them.

On the other side of the cart, just out of reach of several curious goats and a disinterested striped sow, he found cold flatbread—Elstan's particular hand, by the taste of it—and a handful of dried apple slices. He helped himself, washing the meager meal down with generously watered wine and, upon finding his boots, braced himself to go out in the cold to find the others.

Two things struck him as he slid the door aside just far enough to squeeze through: that the day was warm, a bright blue sky over just the hint of a breeze, and— startlingly—that Rethia was somewhere nearby.

Or . . . was it just Madehy? He frowned, trying to sort out what he felt; Madehy's presence, when he thought about it, played a constant undertone through whatever currents of magic drifted around the area. But wasn't there another presence in there, one with which he was more familiar? Just not as close, and not nearly as conspicuous?

After a few moments, he gave it up. Maybe he should ask Madehy. If she was even willing to talk to him.

Vaklar came around the corner of the barn and discovered him. "Dan! Fine day we've got here, aya?"

"You tell me," Reandn said. "Did that dog eat Elstan? That would be a good start."

"Oh, tsk," Vaklar said reprovingly, though his broad face seemed to be holding back a grin. "You ought to be in a good mood, for all we let you sleep."

Reandn found the sun, and blinked to realize it was halfway up in the sky. Vaklar watched his reaction and added, "In truth, then, Dan, we couldn't wake you. Stopped trying after a while. I went out and had myself a good look around the area."

"And?"

Vaklar shrugged. "Found no signs of anyone lurking around, though our own sign is plain enough. I had a go at muddling it, where we turned onto this path. You might have a see, yourself, if you're truly well."

"Well enough," Reandn said. "Kalena?"

"Wants to go home," Vaklar said, and the sun-hewn lines in his face deepened with his quick frown. He shrugged, and added, "She won't, though, not without an escort, and by Tenaebra's cold hand, I'm not about to lose so many of my own without something to show for it. I'll finish what I started, here."

"I did make a promise to the Hounds," Reandn agreed without thinking.

"A promise, was it?" Vaklar narrowed his eyes. "Come around to the yard, then. I think we've all got some talking to do."

Yes. They did. Reandn fell into step with the older man and walked around the end of the barn to the same yard they'd occupied the evening before. Kalena and her personal were by a well he hadn't noticed the night before, within the fenced area around the house. Kalena sat on the edge of the wooden well and chattered on while Varina, her leg propped awkwardly out in front of her, rinsed bloodied pieces of what had been the silk tent. At the fence gate, the dog sunned himself, relaxed and panting, and just as big as Reandn remembered. In the daylight he was a handsome creature, a short-coated, light fawn dog with crisp black points on his face, ears, and lower legs.

The dog appeared to remember him, too, for when the creature noticed him, his loose-flewed jaw snapped shut, and he repositioned itself to a posture of alert readiness.

Madehy appeared in the doorway to her small house, glanced at the dog long enough to say, "Kendall, leave him," and then marched to the well, glaring the other two women away from it. She grabbed the silk, stuffed it into the bucket she carried, and headed right back for the house.

"Bring that back here!" Kalena demanded, her voice edging toward shrillness.

"She's going to boil it," Reandn said. He eyed the dog warily, although the animal had returned to his previous sunbathing. "You'd be a fool to stop her."

Kalena gasped, a showy Highborn affectation, and turned her ready outrage on him. "Are you daring to call me—"

"Are you going to stop her?" he asked, not giving her any time to recover from his interruption. "No? Then I'm not."

Kalena fixed a cold eye on him, and her voice was Highborn ice. "You'd be dead if I hadn't done something about it."

"I know." His unrepentant response didn't go over well with her, either, but Reandn was thinking about Madehy. "Sometimes you have to let people make their own decisions."

"No," she said, not understanding him and not caring. "I'm not sure I do."

"You'll learn. The hard way, no doubt."

"Vaklar," Kalena said, drawing his name out into a

warning. "We can easily get a new wrangler, can we not?"

"Aya," Vaklar said, looking at Reandn rather than at his meira. "A wrangler, we could. We've some things to settle first, though."

"We've been through this," Elstan said with some irritation, anticipating Vaklar's next words. At the entrance to the farm was a hitching rail, and he'd been leaning against it, tilting his face to catch the sun. His skin was no longer quite the pale shade it had been when they'd first met in Pasdon. Not as clean, either, and his affected gesture of flipping his hair from his face seemed to have become one of true annoyance. "The Keep knows more about what's happening on this side of the pass than you do, and they decided to call me a guide and send me along even though you didn't want a wizard. Turns out to have been a good thing, considering what we encountered."

Right. Then they'd had *two* wizards running around flinging unsuccessful spells into the currents. But Reandn managed to keep his thoughts to himself, though Elstan gave him a wary and expectant look.

"You knew of him, then," Vaklar said to Reandn, stating the fact more than asking the question. "Because *you* were the one who really knew the roads."

Reandn shrugged. "The road was easy. Coming down with a wagon, there's only one way to go, anyway. It's the shortcuts and side roads that count. But yes."

"Well and good," Kalena said, her voice full of meaning. "Wrangler and guide, and we need neither of them anymore."

"What else, then?" Vaklar asked Reandn, and Kalena frowned at him for ignoring her.

"What are you talking about?" Elstan asked, straightening from his studied slouch. "He's the wrangler. And the thorn in my side, what with the way he carries on about my magic."

"Me?" Reandn said. "I've done what I said I could

do. Can you say the same? If you could, we'd have had no problem with one another."

"There," Vaklar said suddenly. "Talking about *that*." And he pointed at Reandn, who realized he'd drawn himself tall and tense and dangerous. Vaklar responded in kind, like the experienced guard he was. "What of that, then?"

Reandn relaxed, deliberately taking a step back from Elstan, and told Vaklar, "Wolf."

"*What*?" Elstan's shocked outrage filled the air, while Vaklar merely nodded, his eyes narrowing a touch more, his face hard but not angry. "You're a *what*?"

"Wolf," Vaklar said quietly, his eyes on Reandn. Kalena drew back a few steps, her expression turning thoughtful, her eyes watchful.

"I don't believe it," Elstan said, all traces of his languid court speech vanished into sharp, staccato words. "I live at the Keep, remember? I've seen all the Wolves."

"Believe what your eyes tell you," Vaklar said, a touch of scorn laced in his words.

A wry grin tugged at Reandn's mouth. "Wolf Remote," he told Elstan. "Wolf First, before that. You've been at the Keep how long, since your magic was good enough to get you there? A year, year and a half? I grew up there, Elstan. I led the deep night patrol for years."

Elstan went speechless for a long moment—not long enough, as far as Reandn was concerned. "They'd have told me!"

"An' who *did* know?" Vaklar asked Reandn.

Reandn said, "No one, aside from the Prime and the Wolf Pack Leader." As Vaklar's hardening jaw turned his wide face even squarer, Reandn shook his head. "Come off the pride a moment, Vaklar. You wanted to travel Keland with nothing but seven guards—you didn't know the territory, you had no protection against magic, and you were escorting . . . well, you were escorting trouble. What was the Keep *supposed* to do? And where would Kalena be now, if they'd done nothing?"

"And if things had gone well, I suppose we'd never have known about you," Vaklar muttered. He slid his thumbs into his wide leather belt, muting the aggressive hands-on-hips stance he'd taken up along with the conversation.

"Or me," Elstan put in, interrupting his own fierce scowl, the one Reandn had been ignoring. "But things didn't go well, did they? Fine job you did. Probably has something to do with the reason Wolf Remote was just kicked out of the Wolves."

"Foolish ladaboy," Vaklar said under his breath.

"Wrong," Reandn said. "They *kicked me out of the Wolves* because I stopped a Minor from manhandling an injured Wolf. Know what you're talking about before you start flinging words around, Elstan. Don't get this one wrong again."

"That doesn't change the fact that this escort fell apart around you, does it?"

Reandn's voice bottomed out to the grit of its lower registers. "No," he said, closing in so he and Elstan were all but touching, the intensity of his gaze as much of a weapon as the knife at his side. "It doesn't. Look to yourself as much as to me for that one, Elstan."

"The Keep shouldn't have sent someone who was allergic to—"

"You said you could shield me!"

"That's *enough!*" Vaklar snapped, moving in to shove them decisively apart. "Listen to *this*, ladaboys—no one of you put us here, and no one of you saved the day. Six of our dead prove it so. I won't have it said otherwise." He stabbed a finger into Elstan's chest. "You! No more magic! And *you!*" Vaklar said, turning on Reandn with the same stabbing gesture but pulling it short as he met the fury in Reandn's eye. After an instant's hesitation his demanding expression turned toward resignation and he said in a hard tone, "*You*—don't kill the wizard."

❖   ❖   ❖

"*You*," Madehy's angry voice came on the heels of Vaklar's injunction. "All of you. It's time for you to leave."

Startled out of their contention, all three men turned to look at her—her and her dog, standing by the gate of the little yard. Reandn took a moment to reorient, lost in the confrontation as he'd been, rocked with the high emotions of the last day and the last few moments. By then Vaklar had offered her an amazingly deferential protest.

"The wounded," he said. "Surely you know they can't travel yet, aya?"

"I'll send for someone to take them to Pasdon," she said, unyielding. "That's not far."

"Might mean the difference between life and death for Kiryl," Vaklar persisted.

"What makes you think he's safe here?" Madehy took a single step forward and stopped herself; to Reandn's eyes it was long habit and not second thought. The healer looked like she could use her own ministrations; her puffy eyes were bruised and haunted, and though from here their marbled blue and brown coloration was indiscernible, Reandn's vivid memory supplied it for him. Of her age he remained uncertain, though she couldn't be more than late teens. How she'd already built this life for herself, with a homestead that seemed well broken-in to her idiosyncrasies, he couldn't imagine. Nothing about her bearing gave him the impression of the indomitable will such an accomplishment would take. Instead he saw only fear, and a frantic sort of fear at that, here in this quiet yard where no one had made any move to threaten her. Madehy glared at him, as if she sensed his puzzled assessment, but returned her attention to Vaklar. "Whoever you are, there are people after you. Your wounded might just as well risk the road to safety as lie in my barn waiting for your enemies. I don't want you here when they find you."

"Do you even know who I am?" Kalena asked, a touch of astonishment in her voice. She slid off the well wall but, after a glance at the dog, stayed right next to it.

"I don't *care* who you are." Madehy didn't even turn around to look at Kalena; she kept her eyes on Vaklar. Reandn had the sudden impression that Vaklar was the only safe one to look at, and that he himself, of all of them, presented the greatest risk. Risk of what, he didn't know. "I want you gone. That's what I care about."

"Interesting attitude for a healer," Reandn said, just to see if he was right. Madehy looked at the ground when she answered.

"I told you—I don't work with people. I heal stock. And I can't do that while you're here. I can't do anything while you're here. So *go*."

Varina cleared her throat, a tentative sound, and said, "I'm no good to my meira as I am . . . I could stay with the others until someone comes for them, and then go to Pasdon with them."

"Be quiet," Kalena said, Highborn haughtiness in her voice and in the tilt of her head, so natural in her bearing that even with her stained clothes and ragged coif, she looked the role. To Madehy, she said, "What scares you so much that you're willing to ignore our obvious needs, when they are in truth the needs of Keland and the Resiores? But then, you don't even know that much—because you're afraid to ask!"

Madehy turned a quick glare on Kalena before fastening her gaze on her own hand, which absently stroked the bristling hair between Kendall's shoulder blades. "I don't need to ask," she said. "I don't care. I choose who I help and who I don't. You've already taken more than I care to give."

Reandn took a few deliberate steps forward, as far as he could go before the dog lifted his lip in threat. "Why," he said carefully, "do I have the feeling that *we* should somehow be helping you?"

"I don't want anything from you," she shot back at him, glaring fiercely at her hand. "I already have your griefs, don't I, and me with enough of my own!"

Reandn hesitated, trying to make sense of that and then realizing there wasn't any sense to be made. Impulse urged him to honor her wishes, to get them all gathered up and out of there. It was true that there was no point in hanging around this area. Whoever wanted Kalena wanted her badly enough to keep trying—Vaklar's trail muddling wouldn't hold them forever.

Reandn glanced back at Vaklar, reading much the same in the man's honest face. And then he tensed, alerted by the sudden scolding fury of a pine jay in the trees across the road, by the slightest rustle of clothing against leaves at a distance. Vaklar saw it in him, and immediately responded, stiffening to look around them.

A man emerged from the trees on the other side of the road; draped over his shoulders was a small spike buck, and though his legs were too short for his frame, his broad shoulders and easy movement under his burden made it plain that he could hold his own in any scuffle. The look on his face made it plain he was prepared to do just that, right now. He headed straight for Madehy's yard, his eyes fastened on Vaklar and Reandn. Once at the entrance, he stopped, planted his feet, and said, "The meira doesn't seem to want you here. I'm afraid that means I don't want you here, either."

"And your opinion means what to me?" Kalena said, not sparing him her practiced and arch sarcasm.

"About the same as your opinion means to me, I gather," the man said. He lowered his burden to the ground. "Madehy, this is from Arah, to pay for the healing you gave his cow and calf. He told me to bring a quarter back for him, though. That what you agreed on?"

Madehy nodded, looking no less distressed now that she had an unexpected supporter. If anything, she had become more anxious. "They're not trying to hurt me," she told him, winding her fingers around the dog's collar. Reandn was unreassured; he figured if the dog decided to attack, dragging Madehy's weight along would barely slow him down.

"Looks to me like they've done it anyway," the man said. "As far as I'm concerned, that's all that matters."

"We're not here by choice, aya?" Vaklar said. "We'll be going—"

"When we can," Reandn interrupted.

"Maybe you should go before you *can't*," the man said, shifting to face Reandn, his hand landing on the curved dagger at his belt.

"Stop it!" Madehy said, her words muffled by the hands she held clenched at her mouth. The dog, freed, did nothing more than gaze over at her with his almost comically worried eyes. "I mean it! I can't bear this!" And she turned and ran back into the house. The dog, torn between responsibilities, followed her halfway and then sat sideways on the narrow flagstone walk, swapping his focus from the house to the occupants of the yard and back again.

"You see there?" the hunter said, and he spat on the ground between them. "I don't know what you've been up to, but it's got her all set off. Won't take me long to round up a score of men and women to run you off, so you might as well save yourselves a beating and get on the road right now."

"I don't understand," Varina said softly. "We really haven't done anything at all. We needed help, that's all. Just shelter. We would have died last night without it."

"Be quiet, Varina," Kalena said through clenched teeth. "Mind your place."

The hunter shot her a scathing look, but it faded when he looked back at Varina. Then he assessed the three men again—although Elstan had remained conspicuously silent. "You're strangers," he allowed. "You might not know of our healer. She doesn't take to company, not at all. She's . . . special, needs to be treated special. I see her more than anyone, and this time is the first I've set foot in the yard."

"Why—" Kalena started, though Reandn wouldn't have bothered. No doubt protecting Madehy meant keeping the details quiet; the hunter had that look about him, and cut Kalena off to prove Reandn right.

"Not your concern," he said. "What you need to know is that she keeps our stock healthy, and she's stopped more than one family from going hungry in the winter because of it. She's important to us, you catch my meaning? We're not going to let anything disturb her."

Reandn said quietly, "We don't want to be here. We have our own problems. But we can't move on until we've taken care of our wounded."

Vaklar cleared his throat. "Madehy said someone local would be willing to escort them to Pasdon, maybe in a day or two, aya? Varina could care for them until then—"

"Varina is under my authority," Kalena said, but her voice held a petulant note, as if she half realized Vaklar would ignore her.

He did acknowledge her with a nod, but murmured only, "We do what we have to do, meira." To the hunter, he said, "Mind you, were my people treated poorly, I'd have to do something about it. But were I convinced they would be cared for in a proper way, we wouldn't have any reason to stay here and bother your Madehy." He glanced at Reandn. "You see it that way, aya?"

"Supposing I was convinced." Reandn gave the hunter a narrow-eyed look, waiting for the slightest sign of something to distrust. He didn't find it. In the man's cool green gaze there was only the same kind of stubborn intensity Reandn knew so readily from within himself.

"Whoever's after you isn't here now," the hunter said. He glanced down the road, where the drying mud held the story of their panicked flight. "Someone's done well enough covering your tracks at the turnoff. You might be well pleased to learn there'll be near ten head of beef going to spring pasture this day . . . on this road."

Welcome news. Reandn relaxed a little. "Tomorrow," he said again. "We'll leave tomorrow. I need a chance to scout these woods before we move through them."

And that's what they'd be doing, too—moving through the woods, not sticking to nice predictable roads.

The hunter said, "I'll be by to check on things."

"Don't ride our trail," Reandn said, half challenge, *I dare you to try and remain undiscovered*—and half warning, *you might not be the only one*.

The man shook his head. "I don't care what you're about," he said, "as long as you're not bothering Madehy. The others around here can deal with you themselves."

Reandn stared past the canine sentinel to the almost closed door of the house; for someone who wanted so much to be alone, Madehy was consistently lax about latching the door. Something about her lured him like a complexly woven trail, and he could neither understand the pull nor shake the conviction that she needed help. That *he* could help, if she'd let him.

Not likely. Tomorrow he'd be gone, off to fulfill the promise not only to Saxe, but now to Damen and Nican as well. He pulled himself back into focus. *Get Kalena to the Keep*. The sooner that job was done, the sooner he could wash his hands of her irritating Highborn ways . . . the sooner he could take his place back in the Wolves. His gaze slipped from Kalena to the departing hunter to Vaklar and back to Kalena, skipping quickly over the door of the house as if he might find Madehy lurking there—and all the while, some quiet, nearly inaudible inner voice wondered if, when it came to his patrol, he would ever fully trust Keep judgment again.

Keep your thoughts where they belong. Finish this assignment. It mattered; it had to. For if he didn't have any trace of Adela left, and if he lost his trust in the Wolves, what was left?

"You're sure?" Lamar asked Rethia, frowning into the woods. "There's no easy trail to get us going in that direction from here. Not even if we backtrack and come at it from a different direction."

"I'm sure," Rethia said. She sounded tired, and no

wonder. She'd spent the morning concentrating on the amulet, doing her best to work with Lamar's knowledge of the trails so that between them, they could find the quickest way to Reandn.

Kacey shifted impatiently on her horse, straightening her loose trousers where they'd twisted around her leg and wondering with irritation—again—what it was about this particular saddle and this particular beast that kept causing the faded brown cloth to inch its way from shin to calf, front to back, and then around again.

Or maybe it happened on her little black mare, too. Maybe she'd simply never gotten this impatient, this fed up, with the pace of her travel. *We're close now*, Rethia had told her this morning, with every expectation of its truth. Maybe they had been, as a bird might fly. But not as three horses, two women, and one escort might travel. "Just let her lead us," she told Lamar, trying not to take her inner agitation out on him. "We can't possibly get there any slower than we already are."

Lamar glanced up into the moderate slope of the woods and made a face, as if considering the truth to Kacey's words. After a moment and a sigh, he nodded. "I expect you're right at that. It'll be all but impossible to move quietly in there, though."

"I want to *find* Reandn, not hide from him," Rethia said absently, already turning her horse into the woods.

"We don't know the circumstances that brought him to breaking that amulet," Lamar said, his voice taking on the first sharp tones he'd used with either of them.

Kacey bit her lip, unhappy to hear the very same concern that had been cropping up in her own thoughts since late the evening before. But she'd considered it enough to satisfy herself, and responded to Lamar without hesitation. "It's been a day since then, Lamar— a day and longer. Whatever it was is over. Besides, we're no help to him for anything other than his allergies, and he'd never have triggered the amulet if it meant putting Rethia in danger."

"Of course he wouldn't," Rethia said, stopping her horse some lengths into the woods. "Are you coming?"

They traveled without discussion after that, until Kacey felt like shouting just to break the silence. Or singing, or quarreling, or *something*. But moving uphill through the woods on horseback demanded a certain amount of attention; branches came from nowhere to threaten her eyes and face, and the ground varied constantly, always a threat to her horse's legs and the security of her own seat. The effort came as an annoying astonishment to Kacey, who often rode her little mare bareback on the flatter deer trails around home and never considered that this experience would be so different.

She was hacking herself free of tangled greenbriars with her belt knife, muttering imprecations at her mount for its repeated efforts to forge ahead, when she heard Lamar's heartfelt oath. She felt like a juggler then, cutting the last vine away, checking her horse yet again, sheathing the knife—all the while failing to find that which had alarmed Lamar. As far as she could tell, the greenbriars were the worst of what they faced; Rethia, only her head and shoulders visible, had just surmounted a particularly steep outcrop on the slope above; at its base, Lamar hesitated, standing in his stirrups to look ahead.

"What?" Kacey demanded, prickling when Lamar didn't respond immediately. She opened her mouth to repeat herself just as Rethia cried a surprised protest.

"Lonely Hells," Lamar spat.

"*What?*" Kacey shouted, desperation lacing her voice, her irritation vanished.

He shouted back at her; she couldn't understand it. By then he'd driven his heels into his horse, snatching its mane high up on his neck and leaning forward in the saddle to free the animal's quarters for its sudden charge up the steep outcrop. One bound it took, two, and almost to the top—

A new voice rang out, a warning cry, and Lamar jerked

back with the sound of stone hitting flesh, twisting in the saddle, losing his grip on his mount's mane and inevitably yanking on the reins instead. Kacey watched with a fascinated horror as the horse fought the inevitable, teetering on its back legs. Like a falling tree, it slowly tumbled backwards on top of Lamar, rolling on him a number of times before both horse and rider came to a stop practically at Kacey's feet.

Stunned, she could only gape at him—until Rethia, no longer within sight, shouted, "Kacey, *run!*"

And by then, of course, it was too late. She finally saw what Lamar had seen, and what Rethia had known before them all—they'd met a small band of raggedly dangerous men, two of whom immediately scrambled down to take a look at Lamar. They grabbed Kacey's reins while she sat stunned by Lamar's death—for no man's head sat his neck at that angle—and unwilling to leave Rethia.

Something woke in her when calloused and dirty hands closed on her reins near the bit; Kacey took up the long trailing ends of those reins and slashed them at the two men, discovering only then that one of the men was a lean, worn woman under close-cropped hair. That same woman ducked behind her arm as the whipping reins came down on her face, and too late Kacey realized that the arm served as more than a shield; while her companion fought to hold onto the excited horse, the woman grabbed Kacey and yanked her out of the saddle. Pain shot through her ankle where it twisted, stuck, in the stirrup, and the horse's hooves danced next to her head as she hit the ground. Huge horse hooves, iron-shod hooves so big they were all she could see, her ankle all she could feel, and no thinking whatsoever going on in between, just the pure terror of her precarious position.

"Hold him, dammit," the woman snarled at her companion, jerking on Kacey's leg with no care for the damage she did the ankle, oblivious to Kacey's cries.

After a few agonizing moments, the foot slid free of both stirrup and the woman's hands, and Kacey rolled away from the horse, ignoring the rocks in her ribs. Her thinking started up in short jerks—*got to get away can't run then* crawl, *dammit*—little more than emotion-ridden concepts, and then, as she hit something warm and soft and her eyes flew open, stopped altogether. Inches from Lamar's face, her gaze glued to his own dulling, sightless eyes, Kacey lost her ever-tenacious hold on *sensible* and *practical*. She opened her mouth and screamed.

Chapter 11

Madehy looked out through the thin line of daylight at the barely open door. With translucent greased skins still over the windows for winter, this meager opening was all she had, the only way truly to keep track of what was happening in the yard. With the open door, she didn't have to watch for changes, for shifting emotions in her unwelcome guests. All she had to do was think about it, and feel it.

Never mind that *thinking about it* and *feeling it* were the very things she'd fought all her life to escape. Doing so from here was still better than being out there among them. And far, far better than being forced into contact with any of them. Bad enough that that woman had grabbed her, filling her with fear and frustration and unpleasant arrogance. Much, much worse to land on the dying man. As quick as Madehy was, she hadn't been fast enough to avoid the flash flood of his pain, of his weariness, of the very intensity that made him who he was. And underlying it all, the grief—for so many things. A woman. A boy. A way of life. It ran like water under ice, affecting all the things that might have touched him since, even the loyalties he felt and the good things he might have made from them.

Madehy grimaced; it had gotten worse. For she

especially hadn't been fast enough to avoid the realization of how her touch had affected him. That he'd responded to it, reached for it, renewed his struggle to live. And so she'd had to force herself to endure it all again, more afraid of living with herself if she let him die than of living with whatever else of him might pour into her.

As choices went, it had been no choice at all. But it was done. She'd given as much as anyone could be expected to give, and still they were here, invaders in her carefully arranged life. She healed animals. That's what she did, that's what she was. Straightforward creatures, barnyard animals. The complexity of the wild ones she helped were spice to her life, and the healed stock brought her food, and bartered muscle if she needed it. Only the hunter spoke to her, and he rarely enough; as if he understood her needs, he'd never even offered his name to her. He'd gifted her with his distance and his carefully cool disinterest.

For a moment there, she'd thought he might even clear out the barnyard. But no, not until tomorrow morning. She wondered how she'd make it that long, hiding in her own house, lurking at the door to spy on her own yard.

Except the last time . . . the last time, the one she'd touched, the one they called Dan, had looked over at the door. Had looked straight at her, as if he somehow knew she was there. He couldn't have, she'd told herself, he *couldn't* have, but she'd slumped back against the wall, unable to convince herself.

He was gone, now. Had been gone for some time, though she could feel him out there, a little spark of magical scent that everyone had, but that she usually managed to ignore. Not him, not after she'd touched him. He'd been out in the woods, traversing a huge loop around the farm, and now he was closing in on it again.

The others had been quiet in his absence. The big man was tired, more bruised, cut and battered than he'd let on to his mates; Madehy had felt that first thing this

morning, without much effort at all. He was in the barn
with the injured woman, showing her what to do for
the wounded for the days between his departure and
the escort to Pasdon. The woman had started praying
to Ardrith the moment she'd offered to stay; Madehy
supposed she was praying still. And well she might, for
although Madehy had provided some herbs—to fight
infection, to strengthen bone, to obscure pain—the man's
knowledge was of rough, battlefield skills, and the woman
had not even that.

The wizard was wandering elsewhere. Not long before,
there'd been the slight current of magic—faraway magic,
magic that had reached out to her farm and found this
man. She didn't know what it was about and she didn't
care, not as long as he didn't gather magic of his own,
revealing the fugitives to their enemies and bringing
them down on this farm.

The haughty woman slept, napping in the hayloft.
Madehy judged Kalena to be of her own age, though
she knew she herself looked much younger. She also
had no doubt that this mess revolved around her, for
she was as clearly Resioran Highborn as the older man
was Resioran country stock. Resioran freedom, that's
all she seemed to hear about lately. If they wanted to
be off by themselves, then let them go, that's what she
thought. No one should be bound to any society against
their will. She'd fought too hard to earn that freedom
for herself to take it lightly.

Dan was closing in on her. *No*, she corrected herself,
he's closing in on the farm. He wouldn't come into the
house, she was sure of that. For all the pain he'd caused
her, he also seemed to be the only one to understand
that she was truly *different*, that her strange ways were
based on undeniable need, not eccentric whim.

She reached out a little, trying to pinpoint his location,
wondering if she dared linger by this door any longer.
Kendall was already outside, positioned at the gate, his
tremendous size a comforting reassurance for her

sanctuary here. The woman Kalena would barge in if she could. So would that wizard.

There, Dan was close now. Too close. She withdrew her exploration the instant she focused on him, already moving away from the door—and then froze. He wasn't alone. He'd gone out alone, but he was coming back with another stranger, someone else she didn't know the feel of. Someone he chose to be with? Or someone who'd bring even more strife to her home? No matter how she felt about Resioran freedom, Madehy didn't want the struggle for it to happen *here*.

But warning Vaklar meant running out to the barn, actually being in the barn *with* him. She hadn't been able to stand in the same building with someone since the magic came back.

Madehy compromised as she could. She stayed by the door, and watched as the hair bristled along Kendall's spine. *Stay*, she told him, embracing his presence as she could never embrace any human touch. That he heard her distinct order was doubtful. That he felt her touch was certain.

Kendall stood, then, reacting to the two barely discernible figures walking down the road, one of whom led a horse. But he remained within the fence, and a rare smile hesitated at her mouth; he would stay as told, no matter how much he wanted to clear his yard of strangers.

The new one, at least, seemed to pose no threat. Madehy relaxed a little as she saw the expression on Dan's face; whoever she was, he knew her, as puzzled and upset as he was by her presence. And she bore no overt weapons, nothing more than the knife that most people carried. But the horse—

Madehy sucked in her breath and slid out of the house before she thought about it; Dan and the woman were just coming to the hitching post. "Bring that horse over here," she demanded of Dan, surprising even herself with the strength of her voice.

The woman looked at her with astonishment. The braid of her long brown hair was uneven and loose, her expression exaggerated by the dirt smeared on her face. Dan, too, hesitated a moment, but Madehy could see that he only made sure that she really meant it, that she wanted him that close. She held out her hands for the reins.

He took the horse from his new companion and brought it up to the fence, where he looped the reins over its neck and stepped back.

Madehy ran her hand down the horse's long, bony face; its eyes half-closed as it leaned into her. Its exhaustion trickled quietly into her own bones, and dull hunger gnawed her stomach. One foot ached from bruising, and a knee throbbed with some old, chronic pain. Nothing here that a little time and care wouldn't put to rights. Madehy scratched around the animal's ears, beneath the bridle, until the itch she felt disappeared.

She couldn't bring herself to look straight at the woman, but her words were direct enough, and hard with judgment. "You were cruel to use him so."

"I didn't—" the woman said, but cut off her nonplused response to replace them with irritation. "You don't know anything about it. Keep your words to yourself."

"Without my words, he has no one to speak for him," Madehy shot back at her.

"Madehy," Dan said, and waited for Madehy to quit looking through the woman and transfer her attention to him instead, "She used herself as ill. We'll care for the horse."

Madehy took her hands from the horse and stepped back, abrupt gestures with no understanding or forgiveness behind them. "That makes it no less cruel."

"And you can go to a cold and lonely hell!" the woman snapped at her, but Madehy took another step back at the undertone of tears in the woman's angry words, and hastily stopped herself from doing what was so instinctive, so reflexive as to be involuntary, stopped herself from reaching out. Until these people were gone, she had to take refuge in herself, to keep her healer's skills trapped inside her own body.

At least she'd sent those silly dog-mauled sheep home the day before she'd been invaded. There were no animals here that would suffer greatly from the lack of her attention, and her own animals were being fed by the big Resioran. He'd even turned out her small flock of sheep a short while ago.

To the woman she said nothing. To Dan, she also said nothing—but she managed to meet his eyes briefly as he came up to retrieve the horse, finding them just as clear, just as grey as the night before. She flicked her own gaze quickly away, bracing herself for the onslaught that such direct connection inevitably inflicted on her—

It didn't come. How—not her doing, but that meant . . . *how* had he—

Vaklar's voice shattered apart the thoughts she struggled to form; Kalena's demanding reply plunged her into a despair of sorts. Back to the house, then, back behind the door, which suddenly seemed all too flimsy a wooden shield. All they needed now was to add the wizard to this mix, and it'd be all she could do to avoid the swell of emotions and fears swirling around this small yard. And—oh, *Hells*, there he was, cheerfully trailing along, hefting her collection of old spare horseshoes that were hooked over his hand. Wanting them for spares, no doubt. With a last, desperate glance at Dan, Madehy fled.

"Who," said Kalena, with the contrived pause she often used to make her words sound more important, "is *she*?"

"The woods are clear," Dan said; Madehy knew he was talking to Vaklar and got herself in position to peer through the door crack just in time to confirm it, and to see Kalena's face redden. "I found a deer trail that heads back for the road."

"That'll make things easier," Vaklar said, and inclined his head at the woman. "My meira asked you a question."

"This is Teya a'Apa," Dan said. "Patrol wizard for the Remote."

Teya closed her eyes at the outburst that followed her introduction; she'd been expecting it. Anticipating it ever since she'd left King's Keep, in fact, and running potential scenarios over and over in her head, preparing herself to make the right responses, the ones that would stop Reandn's anger and make him willing to think about what she had to say.

But she was so tired, as weary as her overworked horse, used to extended travel but not without the support and resources of the patrol—and not since before she was hurt. Her shoulder ached, her legs trembled, and her mind turned to total fuzz, a pile of carded wool.

But Reandn hadn't greeted her with anger when he'd slid out of the woods behind her, startling both her and the horse. He'd been upset, yes, the kind of anger that meant worry—she could see that now. He'd asked a few short, sharp questions—was everything all right with the surviving Wolves, was *she* all right, had she been followed by anyone—and then simply allowed that she looked like she could use a good meal and a rest. And now, his seemed like the only voice that wasn't raised amidst the others' noise. The Highborn woman, her clothes soiled, her complex hairstyle as much a mess as Teya's own braid, the smaller man, his court hairstyle as out of place here as the woman's, and the big man— the really big man—trying to shut them both up.

Finally, the smaller man's voice rose above them all, filling the sudden silence as the other two abruptly gave up. "*You dared to call in another wizard?*"

He was a wizard, then. A court wizard. Teya gave him a swift look, and just as swift an assessment. She'd seen this sort before. Just old enough to enter serious schooling as magic faded, and not old enough to have had any real experience before it was gone altogether. In Solace, most of them resented every moment of reschooling they'd endured, and left as soon as possible, getting into positions through personal contacts and family clout. Though many of them had true talent, their magic tended to be rough around the edges, showy when possible, and narrow in scope, rarely matching their fervent ambition. In manner she found them almost universally unbearable, all the more so for the way they secretly begrudged the younger students who showed any flair or style.

"As it happens," Reandn said, in that carefully controlled yet still edged way he had, "she's here for her own reasons. We haven't discussed them yet."

"Then how did she know where to find you?" Elstan persisted. "You told us no one knows about this assignment."

"Are you always this rude?" Teya found herself saying, too tired to cater to this spoiled man. "I'm a wizard, meir. I know perfectly well how to cast a spell to find my own patrol leader."

"Ex-patrol leader," Elstan muttered.

"Teya," Reandn said, flipping the end of her horse's reins against the palm of his hand, "they've reason to be concerned."

Teya looked at him, more carefully than when they'd met on the tree-shadowed and sun-dappled road. She saw again the thick black scab through his brow, the bruises on his face, and the ill-fitting cut of his shirt. *Someone else's clothes.* She raked her gaze over the Highborn woman, who lifted her chin in response, lips tightening over her teeth. The big man met her gaze in a frank and equally scrutinizing look, but he held himself stiffly, and there was old blood crusted at the roots of his hairline, stubborn blackened glue that only a complete scrubbing would rid him of. She ran her hand over her own hair, worrying the strands that had escaped her braid. "I've been feeling magic for days," she said. "Yesterday morning . . ." She glanced back to Reandn. "I've been worried about you."

"With good reason," Reandn said darkly, giving the wizard a grim look. "But there's a healer here. She's . . . very much like Rethia, in some ways."

"I half expected to find Rethia here with you," Teya admitted. "Didn't you use the amulet?"

He gave his head a short, sharp shake. "Lost it in the fight."

"We're telling her all, then, Dan?" the big man asked, lifting an eyebrow as though it was a pointed reminder.

"She can help us. She's an experienced Patrol Wizard, the only one the Wolves have. And she can protect me from her magic."

"If she's that good, why didn't the Keep choose *her* for this assignment?" the court wizard asked.

"Teya, this is Elstan." Reandn said, acknowledging the wizard's words only in his dry tone, and then nodded at the Highborn woman. "This is Meira Kalena, and Vaklar is her personal guard—along with the two others in the barn who still live so far. Four others are dead, and we lost two Hounds as well."

"Over *what*?" Teya asked, aghast, closing her eyes to shut out the thought and finding her mind suddenly filled with the images of her dead comrades. She couldn't open her eyes fast enough then, even if it was to Elstan's unfriendly face and Vaklar's grim understanding of her reaction. She suddenly realized that for the rest of her life, she would face this unwanted intimacy between two strangers who happen to share similar horrors.

Kalena spoke up then, her manner coolly assertive. "Over me," she said. "The new Resioran ambassador to King's Keep."

"That's *that* decision made, aya," Vaklar grumbled. "You want the rest, then, Teya girl?"

"The rest . . ."

"A briefing," Reandn said, and gave her a grin, a comradely expression she wasn't sure she'd ever gotten from him before. "The parts you haven't seen, heard, or already figured out."

She stumbled over her reply, suddenly realizing that she and Reandn shared not only similar horrors, but the *same* horrors—and that it had forever changed the way they would work together. *Was Saxe right, wanting to split up the rest of us? Or is he more wrong than ever?* "Of course I want—that is, I didn't come all this way to sit and watch." *I came because I didn't trust another wizard with my patrol leader.* The thought came with a surprising wave of possessiveness. And it seemed she had been right to worry.

"She means *yes, please*," Reandn informed Vaklar. Vaklar nodded, squinting suddenly as the dropping sun took his face out of shadow and into the late afternoon glare.

A step sideways put him back into the shade again, and without further ado, he explained the situation, couching the facts in an accent so thick Teya had serious trouble deciphering his words. She was just tired, she decided, and then realized, so was he. At the end he added a few short words about Madehy, the healer who owned this farm, and Teya found herself looking around despite his comment that she was rarely to be seen.

All she found was a huge creature in front of the house, his fawn coat bright in the sunlight, his black-tipped ears cocked forward as if he, too, were following the explanation. "What kind of a dog is *that?*"

"Madehy's dog," Reandn said.

Vaklar snorted. "True enough. And also a Resioran breed, aya. Guard dogs, they are. Can't nothing get past them, and yet a family's babes can climb all over 'em."

"Wonderful." Elstan put his hands on his hips, horseshoes and all; the sudden clank of them seemed to remind him of their presence, but distracted him for only a moment. "But I don't want to talk about dogs. I want to talk about what we're going to do with her." He nodded at Teya.

"I don't expect we'll do anything with her," Reandn said, more mildly than Teya would have expected.

"She knows everything now—that doesn't mean she's part of this assignment."

"Relax," Teya said. "I have no intention of snatching away any of your glory." She had, after all, done nothing to prove herself in battle. The kind of help she could offer here would attend to the quiet things, the background work. If she did nothing more than protect Reandn from Elstan's magic—well, that's what she'd come all this way to do, wasn't it?

"You're too damn sure of yourself," Elstan said, but again, it was a mutter. He changed tactics then, and turned slightly so he addressed Vaklar more than either of the Wolves. Teya was just as glad. As Elstan made some comment about being safer here than leaving on the morrow, Teya leaned in close to Reandn and said, "That one's lost his judgment, Reandn. He's only thinking about one thing—how to get out of this mess with the least amount of blame stuck to him. I don't trust him a bit."

"I'm not sure I ever did," Reandn murmured back to her, without taking his eyes off Elstan.

"—heard from the Keep a short while ago, and there are reinforcements on the way," Elstan was saying. "I think we should stay right where we are until they arrive. We're safer here than on the road."

"We're not welcome here, aya?" Vaklar said, as if he were speaking to a particularly slow child. "Did you think that hunter was bluffing, then?"

"He might have been."

"Naya, there was no bluff in his eye, an' no offense to you, but I'm thinking I've had a lot more years at reading a man's eye than you."

Teya shifted, torn between her desire to find a quiet corner and sleep, and her alarm at Vaklar's changing manner. She noted Reandn seemed entirely disinclined to dive into the argument. Of course, he probably planned to go ahead and do things his way regardless. *That's not fair.* More likely, he knew the big man would not be swayed by anything Elstan had to say.

Surely Elstan felt it too, or he wouldn't be persisting with the air of a man who had nothing to lose. "We're safe here, and we've got shelter."

"And how long will it take them to find us? We're lucky to have had today! D'you think I'm leavin' my meira hanging out like a target all that time?"

Kalena inserted a chiding comment. "Your meira has a say in this, Vaklar. As it happens, I don't want to go on to the Keep." Elstan's face bloomed in triumph, just in time to herald her next words. "I want to go *home.*"

"*What?*" Elstan said, overriding Vaklar's surprised exclamation. "Have you lost your mind to fear?"

Kalena instantly flushed bright red. "No more than *you*, you sorry imitation of a wizard! Do you think the others can't see what drives you to hide in the healer's barn until your Keep soldiers can surround you?"

The words must have hit some mark, though Teya herself had seen nothing of true fear in the man. "Highborn bitch!" Elstan spat back at her.

Vaklar erupted. "Naya!" he cried, stepping in on the wizard. "You'll not speak so to her!"

"It's about time someone did!"

Teya stepped back, aghast at how quickly they'd descended into hot and dangerous words. Thank the Bright Goddess, Reandn had had enough; he moved up behind Elstan, his eyes catching Vaklar's and his body language carefully neutral, a quiet calm in the storm of their anger. Gently, he set his hand on Elstan's shoulder, opened his mouth—

Elstan whirled, anger distorting his face and his reason, his arm upraised. How Reandn dodged so quickly was beyond Teya; she had time to do nothing more than hold her breath, and then release it in a cry when Elstan's reach somehow turned unnaturally long. With a discernible crack of metal, Reandn twisted

and fell, rolling once to get his feet back under him—
and then he lost momentum and wobbled, looking
completely baffled. Blood ran down his face and
splattered the dirt as he headed back down again.

Elstan looked at the horseshoes in his hand, his
expression just as baffled as Reandn's.

"*Tits*," Vaklar snarled, pushing the wizard aside to get
to Reandn.

Elstan said hesitantly, "I didn't mean—"

"Shut up!" Vaklar knelt beside Reandn who, head
hanging, had ended up on hands and knees while his
blood pooled in the dirt beneath his head. Vaklar put a
less than gentle but entirely expedient hand in Reandn's
hair and pulled his head up; both he and Teya sighed
in relief. The old cut was reopened, deeper and longer
but no threat to his vision, and without any unwelcome
dents around it. A glancing blow, then, just enough to
addle him. Vaklar released Reandn's hair and absently
patted his shoulder, his meaning clear. "You were lucky,
then, ladaboy," he said softly to Elstan.

"Now?" Reandn said, indistinctly but strong enough.
"*Now* can I kill him?"

Kacey rode with her hands lashed together in front
of her and the reins in someone else's hands, unable to
put her twisted ankle in the stirrup. She wasn't sure
how she was going to dismount, but she had a strong
suspicion that someone would simply yank her out of
the saddle again. She didn't think she'd notice the new
bruises; her captors hadn't hesitated to slap her around
when she hadn't immediately answered their questions.
"Stupid," they'd told her, and then, when she'd felt blood
trickling down her chin and wiped it off to stare at her
fingers in astonishment like she'd never seen the stuff
before, "it's your own fault, lassagirl."

Lassagirl?

Rethia stumbled ahead of Kacey's horse, afoot and
in better shape. While Kacey'd been recovering from

her rough treatment, her questioners had moved on to Rethia, who promptly told them she and Kacey were looking for a friend, but didn't know the area and so didn't know the best way to get there. At Kacey's expression she'd added calmly, "There's no reason not to tell them. Why should they care?"

Kacey closed her eyes in the memory of it. If only she'd had time to think before they had hauled her to her feet in front of Lamar's body and started throwing questions and slaps at her, she, too, might have realized that telling the simple truth was the best response. As it was, her stubbornness—born of the immediate assumption that these people were tangled in whatever had happened to Reandn—had made them suspicious.

She still wasn't sure who their attackers were—or whether they'd really meant to kill Lamar.

The horse lurched, and Kacey clutched at the saddle, her eyes flying open. A fallen tree, that was all; she ignored the amusement from the man who led the horse and sat straighter in the saddle, removing her death grip on the low pommel. Her face burned with humiliation as well as with welts, which just made the man's smile wider. Silently, savagely, she wished wicked boils upon him. Ahead of him, as if she could feel Kacey's distress, Rethia turned to catch Kacey's gaze; the man planted a hand in the middle of her back and shoved.

"Keep your mind on movin', aya?" he growled at her.

Whoever they were . . . they weren't from Keland.

Eventually, they entered a sheltered dip of land dotted with lean-tos and blackened fire rings; at the back of it, the land rose steeply for a short distance, topped by a number of massive, jumbled rocks. In the center, in the deepest part of the gentle dip, the coals of a large central fire glowed and occasionally licked fire up the side of the charred wood. Someone dragged Rethia toward it, and the man leading her horse stopped and gave Kacey an amused and meaningful look—her one chance, she quickly realized, to dismount on her own— if she were fast enough.

In clumsy, aching movements, she swung her injured leg over the horse's rump to stand in the stirrup, jerking her foot out so she could land on it as well.

Momentarily, at least—for of course she fell back on her bottom, providing yet more amusement for the man. *Boils*, she thought at him, regaining a little of the spirit she'd lost during their encounter. *Many many boils*. And she chose several specific sites of affliction.

"C'mon, then," he told her, still grinning. "You've got more questions to answer."

And answer them she would, for Rethia had been right—fighting would only make things worse. And hurt more. As far as answering truthfully was concerned . . . that was another matter altogether. But then, so was getting to that fire ring. "I can't walk," she told him.

"Want I should drag you, then? Might take two of us, but it can be done."

Kacey bit her lip. "I—" she said, as he turned impatient, "Let me crawl. I can crawl."

"Do it, then," he said.

Jaw tightening on tears of humiliation, Kacey crawled. Bruising her knees on stones and roots, she made her way to Rethia's side, where Rethia pulled her into a quick and desperately tight embrace, murmuring, "Shhh . . ."

Someone jerked them apart, but—Ardrith's graces— allowed Kacey to clutch her sister's hand. She wiped away the unshed tears that blurred her vision, and lifted her head to see what they faced.

A small gathering of equally ragged men and women, including one from the band that had captured Kacey and Rethia. Three of them were sitting on a large log directly opposite Kacey, but none of them—for the moment—paid their captives any heed. The man in the center—a lean man, with a neatly trimmed black beard and the hardest eyes Kacey had ever seen, as well as clothes and a manner that didn't fit with the other, clearly lowborn people around her—continued his conversation with the worn-looking man beside him. "We should have searched for them all the night, if it took that long. We'd have them now—instead, they're probably holed up with one of these cursedly stubborn hill folk. You should have *backed me*, Fiers."

Who are they looking for?

"Naya," Fiers growled. "We lost more people than they. Everyone else took damage—even your bloody damn wizard couldn't stir magic. Not that it's done us any good in the first place, an' I'd be quit of it right now, could I."

The other man gave a derisive snort. "As if one who shuns magic could make such a judgment. What do you think kept you safe from their wizard's spells?"

"Aya, an' he yet lives, doesn't he?"

They glared at one another until the man said softly, "The point *is*, you failed me last night."

"Aya, but not my people," Fiers said, unperturbed. "Were they even able to track down our quarry in that dark night, there'd have been nothing left in them to do aught about it. Have your wizard spell out their location, an' you're so eager to use magic in our faces."

"*Stupid*," the man said, displaying dramatic patience. "No wonder my sponsor wanted me in charge. Their wizard would feel it, would he not? And then they'd be prepared—and so would whoever of these hill folk that took them in. We don't want this thing to grow, do we? No, now that you've prevented us from dealing with them cleanly, we'll at least try to take them by surprise when we *do* locate them. Or are you going to thwart me on this matter, too—and lose the support my sponsor brings?"

"Naya," Fiers muttered. He jerked his chin at Kacey and Rethia, instantly destroying the small spot of calm Kacey had built around herself. "See to them, then,

Arik, an' you're so eager to hold on to decisions."

The other man eyed him a moment, clearly unsatisfied. But inevitably, and all too soon, he turned back to Kacey and Rethia. "I see one of you wasn't very cooperative," he noted, and then glanced up to the man from the band. "What's up, then?"

"Found them in the woods, well off the path. Up to something then, aya? That one wouldn't talk. The other was smarter. Said they'd just got lost looking for a friend who lives around here—one of those trappers, most like. Reasonable enough . . . if that one hadn't have been so determined to keep it from us. Thought you might like a chance to talk to 'em."

"I was just confused," Kacey said, no trace of defiance in her voice—or in her heart, not at that moment. There was a hard edge to some of these people, and the kind of intensity she saw most often in Reandn. "I fell off my horse . . . and you'd killed Lamar."

"Local that was with 'em," the man explained to his compatriot. "Didn't mean to kill him . . . his horse fell."

"That's unfortunate . . . but we should be able to get the story from these two."

Arik's expression, while hardly benign, held no particular malice, either—although his calm certainty struck Kacey as infinitely more frightening. She tightened her grip on Rethia's hand, easing up only when Rethia gave an involuntary squeak of protest. "Why are you so sure there's a story to be had?" she asked, squeaking a little bit herself. She cleared her throat and tried again. "We're just looking for a friend. We're healers, and we got a message he was sick."

He raised an eyebrow and held it there until Kacey moved back against Rethia, suddenly very sorry she'd spoken at all. With one hand over his head, gesturing demandingly, he said, "You may well be telling the truth—in which case we'll hold you here until we're through with our business. On the other hand, the people we're looking for are probably all wounded in some fashion or other . . . so maybe you can help us after all, aya? Maybe they're one and the same."

At her chagrined expression, he burst out laughing. "Don't take it so hard. It doesn't matter what you say now. We'll have the truth out of you." No one had responded to his gesture, but he didn't seem to care.

"It's all right," Rethia whispered into her ear, though the cold and clammy touch of her hand belied her calm words. "We'll just tell them, and then we'll wait."

Kacey squeezed her eyes closed on desperate supplication—*Ardrith, save us for your own*—and opened them again to find that the man had moved closer, and that there were several others taking position behind herself and Rethia. And though she was dressed warmly enough for a pleasant spring day under the shade of the woods, she started to shake.

"Now, then," the man said, sounding harder and less amiable than he had. "Why are you in our woods?"

Their woods? With such slurred and chopped-off sounding words coming out of their mouths? Kacey didn't think so. Beside her, Rethia said softly, "We're looking for a friend."

"And who is this friend?" Someone handed him a steaming drink, and he took it absently, cupping his hands around it and never taking his eyes from his prisoners.

Who are you? Kacey wanted to ask. *Meant* to ask. But the words wouldn't come out, though her mouth was open.

Arik grinned at her. "You see? Not easy to say anything that doesn't answer my question, is it?"

She stared at him, not comprehending, until Rethia whispered to her, "Magic."

Someone *had* responded to that gesture. An instant of panic flashed through Kacey's shivers, stilling them. Arik took a sip of his drink, and then, just for an instant, she thought she saw his eyes turn cruel. Not just a man with a mission anymore, but something more—and something less at the same time. "Who," he said, turning each accented word into a separate, distinct statement, "is your friend?"

"His name is Reandn," Rethia said. "He's . . . he's more like a member of the family than a friend, I think."

He looked sharply at the woman sitting at his side, and she shook her head. "No one in the escort went by that name."

Kacey decided to get this horrible moment over with. "Look. He's just a friend of ours; he's here doing a job for someone and then he'll go home. But he was hurt, and he needs our help."

"How?" Arik barked at her.

"How . . . ?" Rethia repeated, not understanding the question any more than Kacey.

Again, he spoke in those distinctly separate words; it was as much an insult as a threat. "How was he hurt?"

Kacey shook her head. "We don't know." Which was the strict truth, but somehow she felt compelled to add, "Probably too much magic."

He frowned at her. The woman said, in quiet aside, "Sometimes the spell results in a little nonsense, Arik, you know that."

He frowned at them a moment longer, holding the last mouthful of the drink; instead of swallowing, he abruptly spit it out in the edge of the fire coals, raising a hiss of steam. Rethia grabbed Kacey's arm as they both started; what little composure Kacey had regained since their arrival fled her.

And then she saw the amulet. At the edge of the fire circle, blackened and cracked and discarded . . .

These people weren't random bandits. They were here after the escort; they wanted Reandn. They'd somehow been close enough to get their hands on the amulet—but not on Reandn himself, and once they realized who they had sitting in front of them. . . .

Kacey traded a quick, frightened glance with Rethia, who, from the look on her face, had followed her thoughts to the same conclusions. They couldn't be in any more trouble if they'd set out to find it.

Arik's impatience startled them. "You're lost. You don't know the area. How did you expect to find him here? Where is he supposed to be?"

"He's not supposed to *be* anywhere," Kacey said. Again, nothing more than the strict truth, and this time, when she felt compelled to add an explanation to it, she fought against it.

But she lost. She felt the words bubbling up even as Rethia, her body gone taught as a bowstring in her own effort to resist, said damningly, "I can feel Danny. I can find him, wherever he is." But she didn't say anything about the amulet. Not yet.

Kacey heard her tears, and lifted a shaking hand to rub her sister's arm. "It's all right," she said, whispering Rethia's own soothing words back at her, watching the man Arik.

He at first seemed taken aback, but his face soon cleared. "Ahhh," he said. "You can find him, can you? And can you find just anyone?"

Rethia shook her head.

"Arik," the woman said.

He ignored her. "You're sure, then?" he pressed, sounding a little too interested for Kacey's severely rattled peace of mind. Rethia nodded, not lifting her head from Kacey's shoulder.

"Leave her alone," Kacey said. "She's no wizard. You've got one of those already—what do you need us for?"

"*Arik*," the woman said, and this time he looked at her. "Didn't you hear her? *Danny*, she called him. You know as well as I that the biggest problem among them is named Dan. How much of a coincidence do you think that is, aya?"

Kacey had an instant's impulse to leap on the woman and shut her up for good, but one look at Arik changed her mind. He'd straightened, his prop of the beaten metal cup forgotten, his eyes on Rethia and his face

caught between narrowing eyes and a growing smile—
damning intent and his exultation at finding a way to
execute it.

"She can find him," the woman said, her own face
fiercely alight. "She can lead us straight to him—straight
to them *all*."

"No," he said, his soft words at odds with the intensity
of his expression. "No, we won't do that. Who knows
what kind of help they've found amongst these damned
hill dwellers. They'll fight just to be fighting."

She lowered her voice until it was almost seductive.
"They're holed up in some damp little den somewhere,
licking their wounds. None of them escaped unhurt,
you know that."

"Nonetheless." The single word stopped her next words
short; with more expectation than resignation, she
watched him. Fascinated by the depth of his dark elation,
so did Kacey. "The Knife has lost too many to this cause—
we'll risk no more of our own. And we'll have no need."
His gaze passed over Rethia and fell on Kacey; she
flinched at its unvarying and merciless probe, feeling
more like a tool or convenience than a person. "Aya,
lassagirl. You're going to be quite useful after all."

Goddess, what a headache. Reandn sat in the last of
the sunshine, the too-tight jacket open to the cooling
breeze, his back to the barn and his face to the modest
pastures beyond it, trying to relax the headache away . . .
with no success whatsoever. He'd have to depend on
Vaklar to get things ready, and hope that, come the
morning, he'd be out of the thick fog in which his
thoughts stumbled around. For now, all he seemed
capable of was aimlessly scanning the fields. A few
moments before, he'd spotted a vole working its
clandestine way from field to barn, dashing between
the islands of last year's stiff, dried grass clumps. Tentative
stalks of new growth added up to a fuzz of green haze
out in the fields, and it occurred to Reandn that by the

time he got back to Little Wisdom, he'd have missed spring on Teayo's land. In spring, Rethia lost herself in her meadow and in the woods, wandering as she pleased and never fearing attack by the forest predators. In spring, Kacey finally took some time for herself, walking the edges of their yard where the wildflowers reached for light.

In spring, when Reandn's patrol passed through the Little Wisdom area and he ended up at Teayo's, Kacey invited him on her walks. Never a planned thing, just the sudden lift of her head and a glance his way, and then he, too, would forget some of the matters that lay so heavily on his shoulders. He'd forgotten that until just now . . . or maybe not realized how much he liked it until he contemplated missing it.

Beside him, the big sliding door opened just enough for Kalena to come out, wearing Vaklar's jacket, the sleeves rolled up and the waist belted with rope. No doubt it was warmer than her own tasteful coat. If nothing else, it covered her bottom and came up around her neck.

Cupped in her hands, almost lost in the sleeves, was a steaming mug of something. She came to him, and, after a moment in which he said nothing in the way of greeting, held out the mug. "Madehy gave this to me," she said. "Or, more accurately, she shoved it out the door with the new poultices for Yuliyana and Kiryl. And one for Vaklar—he's got a cut that doesn't look good at all. Anyway, she said this drink would help your headache. Or, I *think* that's what she mumbled."

"Huh," Reandn said. "Wonder what made her think I might have a headache?"

Kalena looked away from him, out at the fields. Her lips pursed slightly, exaggerating the undercut of her lower lip. Reandn looked at her mouth and forgot to wonder why she'd bothered to come out here—though after a moment, he'd forgotten why he was looking at her in the first place. Realizing that, he gave himself a mental kick. *It wasn't that hard a blow. You're just feeling sorry for yourself.*

"I know what you were trying to do," she said. "I'm sorry it turned out like it did. So is Elstan, believe it or not."

"Not," he replied, not bothering to put much feeling into it.

"I've only ever seen you acting out," she said, giving him a quick glance before returning her attention to the greening fields. "Full of insolence, or giving one of the others a taste of your temper when it didn't seem the least appropriate."

"Not appropriate as far as you were concerned, you mean," Reandn murmured. "I always had reasons. You just never knew about them."

She gave him a sharp look. "There was a lot I didn't know, and I should have. That the Keep dared to perpetrate such a deception on me is something they'll hear about, make no mistakes. But I understand that you were only following orders."

"Generous of you." He closed his eyes to concentrate on the feel of the fading warmth on his face, and wondered what she was up to. He'd never heard so much civil commentary come from her mouth, and certainly not aimed at him. For a moment, he simply let the pleasant, sweet tones of her voice fall against his ears, and pretended not to notice that even in her civility, she scattered condescension and inadvertent insult. She'd have to watch out for that, if she was to be of any use as an ambassador.

"Are you listening?" she asked him. "Drink that potion, so you can pay better attention to me."

Ah. He'd almost forgotten about that, aside from the pleasant warmth of it in his hands. The first sip told him why the smell was familiar; it was one of Kacey's favorite brews for aches and pains, and no matter what she did to it, she wasn't any more successful than Madehy had been in hiding the bitter flavor.

"What I'm trying to say is that I've judged you more harshly than I might, simply because you didn't behave as a wrangler ought to. Now, I understand there was good reason for that. I can see that you do indeed have trustworthy and admirable qualities."

Reandn sighed. "Maybe you'd better just tell me what you want, Kalena."

"Meira Kalena to you," she said sharply, and then modified her manner to something more appeasing. "Well. I suppose I'd better have more time to practice before I reach the Keep."

"You'll learn fast," he assured her. "Just think of it as getting your own way, when it's something you really want, and don't try to be so . . . honeyed about it. If people aren't used to all that niceness, they're going to know something's amiss when you start up with it."

"As if I need advice from you," she said. "Do you think I wasn't tutored before I left?"

"Of course," he said, as if he hadn't heard her, "you *could* try being nice more often. Then people wouldn't notice when you were doing it to get your own way."

"You," she said tightly, "are very difficult."

He opened his eyes to confirm that what he'd heard was indeed the sound of her soft boot tapping against the turf, her irritation manifested in movement. Yes, indeed. He gave her a tired grin and said, "I know. Being nice isn't my strong point, either."

She stared at him for a long moment, pointedly shifting her gaze to the aching lump of a cut on his dark brow. "That's going to scar quite fiercely, I should think."

Reandn caught his impulse to roll his eyes and decided against it. It'd only make his head swim. Instead he drank more of the bitter tea. He'd wait.

After a few more long, silent moments, Kalena gave an audible sigh and said, "All right. Obviously you realize we're not going to have much chance for survival if we don't work together. I can see that, and I think our erstwhile wizard finally sees it, too."

"Vaklar's always seen it," Reandn said. "If it comes down to the two of us, we can still get you to the Keep safely, as long as Elstan doesn't keep bouncing horseshoes off my head."

"That's just it," Kalena said. "I don't want to go to the Keep. I want to go home."

That, he suddenly recalled, was what had started the argument in the first place. "I have my orders."

"And what are they? To keep me safe? If our attackers are from the Knife, the only way I'll be safe is if I return home. Surely you can see that. But Vaklar's determined to honor his fallen, and to complete his assignment to escort me to the Keep."

Over the lip of the tea mug, Reandn said softly, "They were your fallen, too."

Her lips tightened over her teeth, so that her upper incisors peeked out. "Vaklar respects you. If you talk to him about it, you can convince him I'm right."

But you're not. What if these people weren't from the Shining Knife at all? They had a wizard; the Knife would never use the very magic it abhorred. And the Knife was not known for its fighting skills; its members tended toward hit-and-run assaults—arson or rigged accidents or knives in the dark.

"Are you paying attention to me?" Kalena said, and that foot started tapping again.

"More than you'd probably like," Reandn muttered. He took a deep breath, gulped the last of the tea, and let his wrist rest on his knee with the mug dangling out of his hand. "Kalena, it probably hasn't occurred to you that I might have my own reasons for succeeding with this assignment."

It hadn't; the setting sun limned her surprised expression, speaking more eloquently than any words she might have used to express the same.

The Wolves, he thought to himself, but was startled to discover that there was a more important reason at the forefront of his thoughts. "I made promises, Kalena.

I'll not break them because you're frightened."

"How dare you—" she started, but faded away, watching Reandn with a mixture of curiosity and trepidation.

He didn't notice; he frowned, concentrating, and it only added weight to his unhappy brow. Had he felt . . . ? A glance at Kalena revealed that she still watched him, and he almost shrugged off what he thought he had felt, when another quiet slap of magic against his face made him start and drop the mug.

"What is it?" Kalena asked warily, glancing around for some threat.

Reandn climbed to his feet, one hand on the barn, waiting for the magic to run through him and wreak its havoc, and knowing he had to figure out where the threat was coming from before it took away what was left of his wits.

But it didn't. It continued to dance around him and skip on its way, almost as disconcerting as the havoc it usually wreaked on him.

"Dan," Kalena said, "*what*—"

"Magic," he interrupted quietly, still fully caught up in deciphering the enigma.

"Get in the barn!"

The call came faintly, from the other side of the barn, from a voice not used to shouting. Madehy? Reandn exchanged a puzzled glance with Kalena, who seemed mostly to have forgotten she was supposed to be haughty and Highborn, and who looked just as baffled as he— as well she might, since his reactions were her only clues.

"Do it," he told her, nodding at the barn door. "And send Vaklar out."

She went, but not without resistance—the Highborn in her rearing its head after all—and not without a number of perplexed backward glances. As soon as he was sure of her, he returned his gaze to the fields before him, the origin of the inexplicable currents. Was there movement on the far edges? A widespread ripple? He squinted, all too aware of his less than perfect long-distance sight.

Madehy came running around the end of the barn at top speed, avoiding the pitfalls in the lumpy ground with the ease of long practice; she didn't even appear to notice him, not at first. Not until she hesitated to climb over the post and rail fence, about the time Reandn convinced himself that the movement he'd seen was real, and growing closer. When she discovered him, taking a few unconscious steps toward the fence, she turned on him. "What're you doing out? Didn't you hear me?"

"Hearing and listening are two different things," he said. "And I'm not sure you should go out there."

She snorted at him. "One day in my yard and suddenly you know my life better than I do? Get in the barn."

"Strange dangers have a habit of following me," Reandn told her. "I don't want them to run right over you."

She laughed outright, startling him. "Funny you should put it that way," she said, raising her voice over the growing rumble coming from the field. "Now *get in the barn.*"

"Dan?" Vaklar stood in the half-open doorway, frowning at them both, a sleepy looking Teya at his side. "What's happening, then?"

"I'm not sure." Reandn squinted out into the field, finally able to make out a mass of moving bodies, pounding forward and down into the slight dip in the far field, surging over the fence between fields, bringing a growing rumble with them. The slanting sunlight glanced blindingly from scattered reflection points he couldn't identify. "And I'm not sure we can do anything about it, either."

"I *warned* you," Madehy said, and hopped over the fence, running into the field. She stood there with her arms outstretched and her head thrown back . . . drinking in the magic? For while the currents still went around him instead of through him, magic there was aplenty.

No surprise, then, that Elstan poked his head out of the barn as well, shoving the door open a little wider. "Who's—" he started, stopping at the sight of Madehy in the field and the imposing mass of animals charging toward her. "Get her *out* of there!"

Reandn shook his head. "She knows what she's doing. She must."

"Aya," Vaklar said, raising what might have been a mutter to a near shout to be heard over the sounds of a hundred hooves. "So you hope!"

By then, Kalena was back at the door, with Varina behind her—and Reandn knew what he was looking at, knew he'd witnessed it once before. It had looked much different then, with him on his knees, holding onto Kacey, trying to protect her from the dancing hooves of charging unicorns. Now, glancing sunlight resolved into raised, iridescent horns, and the mass of dark color divided into the separate forms of the massive beasts. They might have been huge draft horses had their coloration not all been subtly wrong for a horse— palominos that were more fawn than blond, chestnuts more auburn than comfortable fiery red, hair that seemed to darken instead of reflect diffuse light as it curved over muscle and bone, but made highlights out of the sun's last direct rays just as on any mundane creature.

No, they weren't horses. If their horns—pearly or ebony or deepest brown, shorter than one might have expected for an animal so large, and entirely functional— weren't convincing enough, there was the way the hair on their tails didn't start until a third of the way down the bone, the unusual circumference of bone in their legs, and the wickedly curved claw set on the inside of each foreleg, just above the fetlock. And then there was the look in their eyes—gleaming with intelligence, aggressive, fearless, brooking no insult, offering no mercy, suffering no fools. They were sturdy and powerful creatures built for carrying magic, for *generating* magic . . . for protecting it.

They'd left this world once, gone somewhere only Rethia could describe—which she never did. Hunted and harried—for to kill one was a great feat, and to capture one even greater—they'd scorned foolish humanity and found themselves a safer place.

But they'd come back. And now they were bearing down on the petite young woman who stood directly in their path, welcoming the danger.

"*Madehy!*" Reandn shouted, breaking into a run and then breaking off again just as quickly, because it was too late, and there was no way he could reach her before they swept over her. He watched with a horrified fascination, looking away just long enough to see that his companions—aside from Varina, who had covered her face—were doing the same. What had Madehy been thinking, when she ran out into that field? When she behaved like she knew just what was happening, and *still* ran out into that field? He shook his head, slowly, a gesture meant only for himself, an outward reflection of his baffled helplessness. Before him, only strides before the unicorns, Madehy's posture still cried welcome.

And then Reandn blinked, stupefied at the evidence that such massive animals could be so agile. Turning sharply aside only an arm's length before her, the unicorns split, thundering by her close enough to brush their sides against her outstretched arms. Those who'd missed her touch the first time circled around to make the run again, and the thundering unity of the herd broke into clusters of movement. Never did they collide, or squeal and kick with the inevitable scuffling of horses. Reandn felt his jaw drop open, and did nothing to alter his dumbfounded expression. It seemed to be the only appropriate one he could come up with.

Somehow, it didn't surprise him when one of the unicorns trotted up to her out of pattern, lifting its feet high in an expression of its spirit and power. He especially wasn't surprised at its bold, splashed pattern of deep, bark-brown over white. After looking into her eyes, the animal was nothing but familiar—and after seeing Rethia convene with the huge aged unicorn whose exact walnut hues echoed the brown rims in her own blue eyes, nothing less than he should have expected.

"Oh," Kalena said, sounding breathless, "if only the Knife could see this! They'd never fight the magic again!"

Vaklar growled, "Naya, fanatics aren't swayed by beauty, Kalena."

Elstan's reaction was full of the ambition Teya had so quickly spotted. "If she has this sort of control over them, maybe I can study them. We know so little about them, and if I—"

Reandn couldn't help his laughter, though he didn't take his eyes off the amazing scene in Madehy's field— she had her arms around the pinto creature's neck, and he wouldn't have imagined such tolerance from any unicorn—to see Elstan's reaction. "What makes you think she has control over them? Have you ever even *seen* a unicorn before?"

But then, one didn't have to look at Elstan to hear the heat in his reply. "No, but I've read—"

"Reandn," Teya interrupted, "I think you'd better get in here—"

In the field, the unicorns—there must have been fifty of them, capering and wheeling and even deigning to lower their head to snatch at the grass—were beginning to circle, to build up speed. Somehow Reandn had assumed they would go back the way they came, but now—

"Reandn," Teya said, loud and demanding above the renewal of the pounding hooves, while Reandn straightened, going to Wolf on alert, *"Reandn!"*

—they'd picked up an easy canter and broken off from the circle to head straight for the fence. Straight for Reandn.

No, he thought, taking a step toward them. *I know you. I know you all.*

"—kill you!" Teya's words, broken and nearly lost in the rumble.

If they wanted him, ducking into a barn wouldn't stop them. Reandn stood, lifting his head in the very same way they lifted theirs, and in an instant they'd reached him, splitting around him as they'd split for Madehy, ignoring Kalena's squeal as the tight quarters brought them in close to the barn. They quickly dropped down into trot, and before Reandn knew it, he was surrounded by them, once more aware of just how massive they were. He stood completely, Wolfishly still while they thrust their muzzles at him and lipped at his clothes, snorting and snuffling and behaving for all the world like curious horses—except not once did they jostle him. Their currents of magic went neatly around him, brushing him with cool, shiver-inducing caresses, and beneath the distractions of their attentions, something else touched him—an eager intent, and their desire to communicate . . . *something*. Except he got the distinct feeling that they'd already made their explanations, and were just waiting for him to understand.

What?

The pinto unicorn stood at the fringe of it all, waiting—waiting until he caught Reandn's gaze, and then holding it in a long look from his dark eye, a look so full of meaning, of challenge and acknowledgment and even traces of fury, that Reandn couldn't have broken its hold over him if he'd tried.

But he didn't. He had his own things to say, his own challenges, and even a silent snarl of victory—*I have lived through what your magic did to me.*

And then it was over. The pinto shook his head, his ears back and his eyes rolled in stallion threat. *We'll see*, the gesture seemed to say, and the creature lifted his head to give a short series of melodic whistles, a sound unlike anything a horse could produce. The herd moved away from Reandn, past the barn and around it, trotting in a bold and leisurely manner. The ground trembled beneath Reandn's feet, sending miniature shockwaves up through his legs and into his chest, tickling him into a cough.

When he straightened from it, the beasts were gone— and Madehy was striding up to him, planting herself before him with her hands on her hips and suspicious disbelief in her eyes. "They ought to have killed you."

Chapter 12

"They ought to have killed you," the healer said, and Teya wasn't sure what she heard in that voice—wary surprise, and resentment, and hiding amongst it all, curiosity. She glanced around to see it on all their faces, that wariness—and on Vaklar's, something more demanding as well.

She knew. But she was more concerned about Reandn than about making explanations for him, although he didn't seem inclined to deal with making them, either. If he'd even heard Madehy in the first place. He stood where he'd been, dazed, with his eyes fastened on the last of the trailing unicorns as its tail whisked around the corner of the barn.

And then he blinked, and seemed to come back to himself, catching their unanimous demand for answers. His gaze shifted from one to another of them, and he opened his mouth . . . and deliberately closed it again.

Teya couldn't stand it any longer. "Are you all right?" she asked. "Did they hurt you?"

In answer, Reandn looked down at himself and spread his arms away from his body, gesturing *see for yourself*.

"I don't mean like that," Teya said crossly. She held her hand out, fingers fanned against the currents of magic; her irritation faded away, replaced by fascination.

265

She'd heard of this phenomenon, although she didn't know anybody who'd actually witnessed it. "Unicorn winds," she said, full of wonder. "Magic. Are you all right?"

"They . . . sent it *around* me," he said, looking at her over Madehy's head as if the healer weren't still standing there with her fists balled up on her hips, waiting. And then the healer gave a sudden little gasp, dropping the assertiveness in her posture to reach for Reandn's face, stopping just short of his cheek while he looked down at her, bemused. She snatched her hand away and held it to herself as if she'd just narrowly avoided some terrible danger—but her gaze didn't waver from his face.

"Your head—" Kalena said, cutting herself off as suddenly as she'd spoken in the first place.

Reandn glanced to Teya, and she realized that her hand had gone to her own brow, mirroring the discovery Kalena had made. Where the angry, scabbing gash had split Reandn's brow, she saw nothing more than a whitely distinct scar, covered by a few grey hairs in that dark eyebrow. Sudden understanding lit his eyes at her gesture, and he reached up to touch his own face, to discover the healed cut and, from the way he probed it, no soreness at all. "No," he said, and gave her a quick grin, though under it she could see his disconcerted uncertainty. "I guess they didn't hurt me at all."

"Why?" Madehy asked, and this time it was a pleading whisper. "I thought I—"

He shook his head. "We've met before, the unicorns and I. Not the same ones, but . . ." And he trailed off with a frown, daunted at the enormity of explaining it all. But Teya knew, and she cut right to the heart of it.

"He was there when the magic came back," she said.

Madehy whirled on her, for one instant pinning her with a shocking marbled gaze. But her eyes slid to the side, almost as though she couldn't help herself, and her voice trembled. "What do you *mean*, he was there," she said. "You mean *he* brought the magic back?"

Reandn gave a short, sharp laugh; Teya could only begin to imagine what he was thinking. Madehy didn't need to know the details, she thought. Not here, not now. Not while her patrol leader was standing amidst clumpy spring grasses, all but surrounded by his odd collection of companions and yet somehow looking entirely and devastatingly alone. With a flash of understanding, Teya realized she'd seen that look before, a more subtle version of it that had sometimes washed across his features and moved on again before she or anyone else in the patrol could put a name to it. She told Madehy, "No. He was there."

Vaklar's deep voice broke into their conversation. "Aya. I've heard . . ." But he hesitated, meeting Reandn's sudden sharp glare with an even, direct gaze of his own. "I've heard things I'll have to think about, then."

Beside him, Elstan said nothing, and while his tight face and tense body shouted his anger at this unexpected revelation, Teya saw something else as well. Fear. His anger was born of fear and worry. For a fleeting moment, she wondered what Elstan knew that the rest of them didn't, but in the next she wasn't quite sure where that thought had come from.

Madehy looked away from them all. "I thought I was the only one they'd touch," she said brokenly. "I thought . . . they were the only ones who could touch *me*."

The others watched in collective bafflement as she turned and ran, rounding the end of the barn opposite the unicorns. Teya met Reandn's eye; he looked away. He knew. The anguished look on her face was only a reflection of the look she'd seen in his eyes, moments before.

Kacey sat apart from the rest of the camp, her hands tied together in front of her. They hadn't bothered to secure her to a tree; probably, she thought with burning mortification, they figured they could outcrawl her. And there was little enough cover to crawl to, in these strange rocky woods of sparse underbrush and moss, with bare-trunked pines littering their needles everywhere; there was a smattering of hardwoods—beech, some flint-oak, a few small ironwoods—and beneath those grew the mountain glories, clusters of thick-leaved bushes just starting to bloom. But mostly there was rock and pine.

Her ankle was a swollen mess in her short boots, throbbing against the leather confines of it and screaming pain at her anytime she unthinkingly shifted it; her jaw ached from gritting her teeth, and she tried not to think about how she'd feel if she saw a chance to get away and then had to sit there and watch it pass by. Meanwhile, *they* had two people watching her, a motley man and woman who didn't pay her much mind except to loiter at this end of the camp and look her way now and then.

They. Kacey had been here long enough to become quite friendly with this beech tree, and to find the best roots between which to sit. She'd watched Rethia stumble away, her face full of determination and her eyes full of promise to Kacey, and she'd been here long enough to cry about that, and to choke on the anger that grew out of her tears. Now, she just wanted to understand what she'd gotten tangled up in, when all she'd meant and expected to face was Reandn's exasperated ire at her for coming along in the first place. And she wanted to know who *they* were.

The woman treated her with scorn, doing no more than flicking a glance at her now and then, and offering a look of complete disdain the one time Kacey'd bumped her own ankle and cried out at the sudden flare of pain. For the first time, Kacey understood Reandn's capacity for cold-hearted justice, even his desire for revenge. She felt it herself, licking at her heart, growing each time the woman raked her with those scornful eyes, each time she had to endure the indignity of escort to her less than private toilet area, and with each increasing throb of her foot . . . she understood, now, she definitely understood. How strong would it be, she wondered, if they'd gone so far as to kill Rethia, or further manhandle them both? Too strong to live with, probably, and she wondered how Reandn managed.

The man, at least . . . Kacey wouldn't go so far as to describe the look on his face as compassionate. But his manner lacked the enmity of his partner's. So she waited, and the next time he came to her—offering a tin plate full of fried beans with a paste made from flour she wasn't familiar with—she simply asked him.

He seemed surprised that her question wasn't backed with rancor or spit, and didn't respond right away. In fact, he busied himself with checking her bonds and then making sure she could hold a spoon well enough to eat.

From where she sat at the fringes of the camp and ate her own meal, his partner grunted with her mouth full, "Don't have to tell her nothin', Wectir."

That seemed to make his mind up. "An' don't have reason not to, aya?"

She shrugged and turned her back to them, a too-thin woman with short dirty hair and not quite enough clothes to keep her warm in the settling chill.

"Look at you," Kacey said, keeping her voice low. "Look at all of you. You don't have enough supplies to stay in hiding out here. You've got wounded dying. Why are you doing . . . whatever it is you really want? Why have you sent my sister to find Reandn? Who *are* you?"

"You *are* pushy," he said, in a perfectly normal tone of voice. "No need to whisper. There's no secrets about who we are or what we want. The more that know, the better."

When he didn't go on, Kacey looked up from her struggle with the spoon and plate and food, and found him looking toward the single tent they had, the one that held the wounded.

As soon as he realized she was watching, he looked away from it, his face expressionless. He said, "You've heard of the Shining Knife, aya?"

Kacey lifted her wrists and used the very ropes that bound her to wipe away the food she'd just managed to smear across her chin. "Well," she said, not quite sure if this would offend or amuse him, "I have . . . but only a little. I just got here yesterday, and I live . . . well, out past Solace. So all I know is that you don't want the Resiores to renew allegiance to Keland."

Passion lit his eyes then, bright enough to see even in the deepening twilight. "Solace," he said, and then made a gesture that was completely unfamiliar to her, lacing his fingers and then turning his hands so those fingers were perpendicular to one another—some sort of superstitious warning. She looked at her hands and didn't even know if she could do it—supposing she were untied—with her short and rather stubby fingers. "All those wizards," he clarified. "And their magic." He spat in the dirt, but he was careful enough to bend aside as he did it, so Kacey wouldn't end up sitting in the results.

Kacey spoke without thinking. "But you've got a wizard here!"

"Not like them others!" he said sharply, coming down from his crouch to one knee, too close to her, and leaning over her. Kacey squirmed against the tree, suddenly wondering if she might not have been better off to stay ignorant and quiet, hoping for a rescue and a happy ending.

If nothing else, his breath was ruining what little appetite she had for this strange paste concoction. He hadn't shaved for weeks, and beneath the new growth of beard his face was dirty, and even held traces of dried blood—though it must have been someone else's. "I didn't mean anything by it," she said, surprised to find her voice stuck at just above a whisper. She heard the fear in it that she hadn't truly allowed herself to feel.

He sat back on his heel as suddenly as he'd leaned in on her. "Naya, I suppose not." But he was breathing heavily, his nostrils flared, his mouth tight with distaste. "None of us like it. But we have to protect ourselves,

aya? That's all any of our people ever do, is try to keep
Keland magics away."

Kacey frowned, but didn't feel the least temptation
to voice her doubts.

He must have seen them anyway; he moved closer,
if not as close as before. " 'Tis a great sacrifice for any
Knife to use magic," he said, aiming those earnest words
at her as if it was the most important thing in the world
that she believe them. "But *we got to protect our own.*"
He let her consider those words, and this time when
he sat back, he relaxed, bringing his upraised knee down
to join the other. "Right now, that means stopping this
ambassador who's with your friend. We'll trade you for
her, an' that seems right enough to me."

"But . . ." Kacey said tentatively, waiting for him to
nod before she finished, "what will you do to her once
you have her?"

He shrugged. "Use her against her father, what else?
Grezhir is the power behind those who want to stay
chained to Keland. But when he sees his precious
Kalennie in the hands of the Knife—well, then we'll
finally cut those chains for good. You can keep your
magic here, and we'll be safer with Geltria than ever
with you and your magic."

"It's not my magic," Kacey muttered, thinking how
lucky they were that the Knife hadn't learned of Rethia's
role in its presence here when they had their hands on
her. "I can't feel it even when it's been spelled right in
front of my face." She got down another mouthful of
the food and discovered him watching her, an appraising
look that made her flush, though she wasn't sure quite
why. "What," she said, and coughed on the dry paste
where it stuck in her throat. Her eyes were tearing before
she cleared it, and she wished he'd thought to bring
her water with the plate. "What," she continued through
a slightly creaky voice, "are you going to do with her if
her father doesn't change his ways?"

"He'll change," Wectir said confidently. "All of the

Resiores know of his love for her, and how he's spoiled and pampered her. He'll do anything he has to to see her safe, aya."

Just as she'd done what she had to do to see Reandn safe. She wondered to what lengths Reandn would go, to get her out of this mess. He'd never acquiesce to the demands of the Knife; she knew that with an abrupt certainty that left her drowning in unexpected fear, and in the sudden flare of pain in her chest and throat, where the fear gathered to clog her breath and her thoughts. She turned away from Wectir, who watched her with an uncomprehending frown, and couldn't ask him what she really wanted to know. Not, what would happen to this Kalena once the Knife got their hands on her. But . . . what would happen to Kacey if they didn't?

Reandn led Sky out of the barn and into the front barnyard, tossing the lead rope over Madehy's hitching rail in lieu of actually tying the horse. Once he started grooming, it didn't matter; in the deepening twilight, the horse half-closed his eyes and stuck out his lower lip and dozed.

Grooming in the dark. No wonder Teya and Vaklar had both tossed him a questioning look as he left. They were working on Teya's horse, grooming out the sweat-stiffened winter hair, going easy over bones that had come too close to the surface and letting the animal nibble undisturbed on a small pile of hay, protected from the scuffling of the other horses. Varina sat by the wounded, while Elstan hovered at the forge room at the far end of the barn, proving once more that he was the best cook among them.

Kalena slept, which was what she'd done most of the day, surfacing only for the few moments of excitement they'd had. Reandn's initial resentment at this—she was, along with Elstan, the only one of them not injured in the fight—eased when he'd realized she probably wouldn't have been much help, anyway. He couldn't see her grooming saddle sweat from the horses or puttering around the forge fire with Elstan. It'd been astonishing enough to find her rinsing out bandages with Varina that morning. And if she was well rested, it would be easier to get her through the next day. Maybe.

So here he was, trying to prepare himself. To focus. His mind was awhirl with thoughts and feelings, enough to make him dizzy. He ought to have been centered and ready to handle whatever came their way in the morning. Instead, as the others had understood that the unicorns were gone for good and had returned to the barn, Reandn realized that there wasn't near enough room in the barn for them plus him and his overcrowded thoughts.

Now he saw that there didn't seem to be enough room out in this yard for both him and those churning feelings, either. The magical currents from the unicorns still somehow bumped gently around him, all but obscuring even the unique feel of Madehy's immediate presence and constantly reminding him of the events of this full day. Adela's final good-bye lurked in the raw edge of everything that had happened, and Teya's astonishing arrival mixed up the rest of it. He still had no idea what had driven her to come all this way, especially given her penchant for long thought and unhurried decisions, and he had no clues but her indistinct mutters about Wolf loyalty and justice.

Damn the wizard. Elstan, that was. If he hadn't lost his head, Reandn would have had a chance to talk to Teya, instead of spending the afternoon in an aching fog. That would've been one less set of questions bouncing around in his head, and then maybe there would have been room to think about what the unicorns had been telling him. For he was sure they'd been telling him something, in their own twisted way. They weren't benevolent creatures, and had a justifiably jaded impression of humankind; that they'd made the effort to say anything to him at all meant *something*. He just had to figure out what it was.

And somehow, when for a miraculous instant he cleared his mind of all of these things, in would slip the nagging feeling that Rethia was nearby, though he couldn't begin to sense her presence over Madehy and the unicorn-tasting magic that bounced along at their heels, still going around him instead of through him. That, he thought, was part of their obscure message. Even so, despite the magic, despite Madehy, he kept expecting to raise his head and find Rethia standing next to him. He wouldn't be glad to see her if he did. Not considering what she was walking into.

Yesterday he'd have thought differently. Yesterday he'd been too sick to be of any more good to Vaklar, and only Rethia could have helped him—he'd thought. But now, between Madehy and the unicorns, he felt as well as he'd ever felt, even before magic had reinvaded this world. As he reached under Sky's belly to brush out big tufts of soft winter hair, Reandn couldn't help but smile, though there was no amusement behind it. Under other circumstances, he might well have found himself working with the Knife, fighting the magic. He wondered, briefly, if he traveled through the Resiores and then northward into Geltria, would he reach a place where the unicorns ran so thin their magic no longer bothered him?

And then he snorted, because he now had plenty of evidence of how deadly just one unprotected encounter with spelled magic could be for him. There might indeed be such a place . . . but he'd never reach it alive.

He crouched to reach the inside thigh of the hind leg opposite him, brushing gently against that thin, tender horseflesh, when Sky suddenly came awake, lifting his head high to snort inquiry at something. "Stand!" Reandn told him sharply, ducking away from the near hind leg as Sky shifted his quarters around. "Those unicorns just trampled anything that might have been interested in eating you."

Sky's belly moved in little quivers above Reandn as

the horse drew air in small huffs. Reandn ignored him and briskly scrubbed a cap of mud off Sky's bad hock. The bay ignored Reandn in turn, shifting and huffing air and then, finally, unexpectedly, nickering a greeting.

To *what*?

Slowly, in an evening that had faded to starlight over a clear sky, Reandn stood and tried to see what Sky had seen. Out of the darkness, over light footsteps on the road that were just now audible, Rethia's voice said, "Dan? Danny, is that you?"

"Goddess damn," he breathed, not believing what his ears told him, though the rest of him had already known. "Rethia . . . ?"

Her answer was to quicken her step, while Reandn ducked under the lead rope and headed for the road. He met her in the middle of it, and got nothing more than a glimpse of her face before she caught him up in a hug so sudden and fierce it literally knocked an *oomph* out of him. "What?" he said, when her indistinct words met up with his jacket and turned incomprehensible, and then didn't give her a chance to repeat herself, but took her by the shoulders and set her back a few steps. "What are you *doing* here? Why are you alone?"

She didn't answer any of those things, but what she said was infinitely more important. "They have Kacey," she said breathlessly. *"The Knife has Kacey."*

Madehy stood outside the barn, keeping that barrier between herself and the people within. The night air, chilly under a clear sky, wrapped itself around her and went for her bones, but there she stayed, invisible to them with the lamplight in their eyes, looking through the hand's width opening they'd left for fresh air.

These people were stretched to breaking. As little as she knew about them, she knew that. As little as she knew about *people*, she knew that. The big man and Dan, they could work together. And the new wizard and Dan, too. Through him, she thought, all three of them might do all right. And if the three of them held together, the other two might fall in line. But Dan was the keystone, and Dan was—

Madehy cut the thought short, not willing to take the slightest chance of opening up to him. At the other side of the barn, he stood by himself in front of her stock and horse supply cabinets, on the periphery of the conversation of which he should have been in the middle. As she watched, he raked his hands through his hair and exploded into movement, nothing so regular as pacing but not the swift violence that lurked so near the surface, either. His turmoil and fury leaked through to her no matter how hard she tried to close it out— though she thought, if he'd known she was there, he might have tried to keep it to himself; he seemed to understand that.

Another time, she would have fled it, unwilling to put up with even the slightest taint of another's self. But this time, she had reason to stay. That reason, very blonde, slender even through her several layers of outer clothing, had her back to Madehy, and hadn't said much since explaining who she was and why she'd come to the area—and then why she'd come *here*. Madehy had heard her without much thinking about the words, not even willing to imagine the worry this woman must have for her sister.

No, she lingered by this door for entirely selfish reasons, drawn by the way the second unexpected arrival of the day—Rethia, her name was—*felt*. Unlike the others, with their perfectly normal personal stamp on the magic around them, Rethia created an aura with the feel of unicorns and magic, tinged by something calm and light. Madehy had never felt anything like it before, though she had to tell herself that that wasn't surprising, given how assiduously she avoided people. She also told herself it was foolish to stand out here in the chilly night, with Kendall patiently leaning against her thigh and her face flirting with splinters from the barn door, but she'd discovered some time earlier that she didn't seem inclined to listen to that common sense part of herself.

Drawn by Rethia's aura, drawn by some hope she didn't really understand, Madehy waited. She crouched down and put her arm over Kendall's warm bulk, and she stayed out in the starlight while her hearth slowly cooled and her supper along with it, and she kept her eyes on Rethia, waiting for some clue to explain why she couldn't seem to tear herself away from this door.

When the answer came, she wasn't near ready for it.

"Just how many of your friends followed you here, anyway?" Elstan asked Reandn. "Didn't anyone mention to you that this assignment was supposed to be kept under silence? Did you at least *whisper* when you discussed it?"

"Ladaboy, that's no help to us," Vaklar said, but said in resignation; no one really thought they'd have any effect on Elstan's attitude, not now.

Reandn didn't care about Elstan's attitude. He wasn't really listening to Rethia—who, with Teya's help, was explaining her role in this tangled and botched assignment. Those two had obviously discussed this assignment at some earlier date, and though he'd find out when before this was all done, right now he didn't give a bloody damn where and how that had happened. What he cared about—what he *needed*—was to sort out the incredible chaos that Rethia's announcement had stirred up inside him. He needed to find Kacey, he needed to get Kalena safely to Pasdon, he needed to avoid trouble with Madehy's hunter friend and his cohorts, he needed—

He needed to hit something.

"It helps me," Elstan said to Vaklar. "It helps me greatly to be able to point out how badly our wrangler has hindered us here. He hasn't been much good for his friends, either—this Kacey woman wouldn't even be anywhere near the Knife if he hadn't tried to handle an assignment that was over his head."

Elstan. Reandn fastened his gaze on Elstan. The wizard needed hitting, he thought, driven so far past the point of fury that he felt almost detached from it.

"Yer a mouthy bastard, ladaboy. D'ye think pointin' yer finger Dan's way and talking loud at the other end of it will take our eyes from yer own failures?" Vaklar's deep voice came out thick with anger and his Resioran inflections, and he was about to stand up when Rethia beat him to it.

"Please," she said, her hands turned into two white-knuckled balls just peeking out the ends of her sleeves, held stiffly by her side. "Stop it. All of you."

And they did, shamed by her quiet voice and the strain that ran through it. Vaklar subsided and Elstan closed his mouth, if only for the moment. There was silence then, except for Varina's whisper of reassurance to Yuliyana.

Aside from Reandn and Varina, they sat in a rough circle around the dinner Elstan had cooked—more flatbread, on which he'd heaped cooked oats and a layer of freshly picked cress. Varina sat on the wheel of the cart, where she could see them all and still keep an eye on those within—for Kiryl had taken a turn for the worse, and she seldom left his side. Reandn stalked the space in front of Madehy's supplies, unable to force himself to sit still, full of energy from the unicorns and closer to breaking than any tightly strung bow.

Rethia, too, had met the unicorn herd; once she'd mentioned the fact offhand, Reandn wondered why he hadn't seen it earlier. She had too much strength for a woman who looked so bedraggled, and who'd already faced a band of antimagic zealots and then been forced to rush through the woods looking for help. Except that in her case, contact with the unicorn herd had obviously cleared her mind, not muddled it. Now, she was able to catch Reandn's eye in the lantern light and say, "Kacey makes her own decisions, Danny. She wasn't supposed to be here, and she came anyway."

Somehow that didn't help.

Kalena broke her long-held silence with astonishingly level-headed words. "At least we know for sure it's the Shining Knife. That helps. We know how they think and we know what they want."

"Aya, and from Rethia's description, we know we've hurt them almost as badly as they hurt us," Vaklar said, though Reandn could see it was an effort for the guard to keep his words even and his gaze from going dark when it touched Elstan. "Though I've my doubts it's truly the Knife. Not with a wizard."

Kalena lifted one shoulder in an uncaring shrug symptomatic of her evident conviction that her opinions just naturally mattered more than anyone else's. "What reason would they have to lie?"

"To make the Knife look bad," Reandn said, beginning to think again, though waves of emotional turmoil still beat against him. "To turn sympathetic support to your father."

Kalena frowned at him. Slowly, she said, "That would mean they'd have something to feel sympathetic *about*."

"They promised they had no intention of hurting you," Rethia said.

"And you *believed* them?" Kalena said, throwing Rethia a dramatically skeptical look.

Rethia didn't answer. It was Vaklar who said, "They had arrows, meira. They easily could have aimed the first one at you instead of Damen."

"Vaklar! You talk like you plan to go along with this . . . this absurd trade!"

Vaklar just looked at her. When he spoke, it was with a reproach of quiet words and formal dignity that made her blush. "You mistake me, meira."

"And you mistake me," Rethia said, a touch of pride in her voice. "I don't know you. I'm not asking for your help. I'm here to see Dan."

"Whoever these people are," Teya said to Kalena, drawing her attention from Rethia, "the more we understand them, the better prepared we'll be to counter them. That's part of what we're trying to do here— understand them. I think you'll know a decision when you hear it."

Kalena glared at her and said, "I'll know it, because I'll be making it."

"Don't kid yourself," Reandn said, compounding the insult with his distracted bearing. As the influence of the unicorns faded, and as he grew used to Rethia's presence, he'd become aware of a subtle tug, hitting him in that same place that had been so sure Rethia was nearby. He only glanced at Kalena as he added, "Vaklar and I will be making the decisions, at least until we turn you over to an official Keep escort—which, I promise you, will be large."

"Vaklar said it himself," Kalena retorted, "we've hurt them as much as they've hurt us. I can get home just as safely as I can go on to the Keep—maybe *more* so, if stopping the ambassadorial relations is what these people want."

Silence greeted her words, until Vaklar said, "It's naya happening, meira."

She drew herself up, and Reandn caught Teya rolling her eyes, but the ambassador-to-be abruptly sagged, and turned her face away from them all. With some part of his mind, Reandn was sure he heard a sniffle, but the greater part of his attention remained elsewhere. No one else said anything; indeed, they didn't seem to know what to say. Given Kalena's shameless determination, Reandn supposed they might have been wondering if this behavior was merely another ploy—and in any event, she'd alienated everyone but Rethia at this point, making it all but impossible to offer her sincere words of comfort.

And Rethia's eyes were on him. When he met her eyes, she asked, "What is it?"

It took him a moment to understand; he'd been

expecting something more akin to *but what about Kacey?*
He ought to have known better. Rethia, made whole
with the return of the unicorns and their magic, was
often harder to fathom than when she'd wandered
around in her own private fog. "I'm not sure," he told
her. "There's some part of me that seems to think you're
still out there," he waved a hand at the general direction
she'd come from, "instead of here in the barn. And what
I feel of you here in the barn . . . doesn't seem *enough.*"

"What are you talking about?" Elstan said, flipping
his hair out of his face and putting his features into some
subtle court expression that probably meant volumes
to someone in the Keep but made Reandn wonder if
there'd been something gone bad in Elstan's serving of
oats. In any case, he didn't bother with the distraction
of replying to the wizard, although no one in the circle
seemed to understand, either, and Kalena even cast a
red-eyed glance at him.

Rethia had to think about it a moment as well, though
her small frown told him she understood what he'd said,
and just didn't have an immediate answer. It didn't take
long for her face to clear. "I . . . don't suppose you
noticed, but . . . did it change? Since I've met you?"

Uncomprehendingly, he gave her a slow nod. "Over
time. But that was just because of the magic . . . wasn't
it?"

"Danny," she said, "you feel the ones you care about,
the ones who mean the most to you. You've always felt
me, because I . . . had reason to be different. And I know
you've said you've never felt anyone *but* me, but . . .
haven't you noticed, that when you visit, Kacey and I
usually aren't far apart? We put other things off so we
can keep you out of trouble together."

She slid into humor and actually smiled at him when
she finished, but there was sadness around its edges.
Reandn shook his head, sure he ought to have figured
out what she was driving at. "I haven't given it any
thought."

"*I* haven't changed," Rethia said. "You have. You started picking up on Kacey, and you didn't even know it. Strong feelings, Danny."

He looked at her without comprehension for a moment, waiting for her words to mean something. When they abruptly coalesced into understanding, he got a sudden glimpse at himself from within, and the enormity of the things he'd hidden from himself. He shook his head, then, a quick gesture, as though he was tossing off an annoying fly, and drew on the safe and familiar walls of anger. He growled, "Irritation is a pretty strong feeling." No longer did he fight the need to pace, the urge to run outside and *do* something *now*. Behind those walls, he was Wolf incarnate. Dangerous. Lurking, waiting for just the right moment, grey eyes brooding under dark brows.

Elstan only helped, repeating himself with annoyance. "What are you *talking about*?"

Teya straightened suddenly. "Auras, they're talking auras."

"Danny," Rethia whispered, making his name a plea, trying to get back the part of him she'd just lost.

Reandn didn't look at her. "Auras," he said. "I might be able to find her."

Vaklar shifted uneasily; Reandn couldn't tell if it was in reaction to him or to the slice the guard had taken along his ribs, the one that was looking worse instead of better. Vaklar's long, assessing gaze was answer enough. "Dan . . . what're you thinking, then? You've responsibility here, don't be forgetting that."

"And this assignment is your chance—" Teya started, stopping short at Reandn's sudden and piercing look. As if he had to be reminded of any of it.

"No one questions Wolf loyalty," he told Teya, though his words might as well have been directed at himself. "But if a Wolf can't be loyal to the people who matter to him—to someone whose own loyalty brought her here at risk—then Wolf loyalty means nothing. Being a Wolf means nothing."

Rethia understood. After a moment, she gave him the faintest of smiles. And after a moment, Teya, looking at him with dismay, nodded. Reandn said quietly, "But being a Wolf *does* mean something to me, Teya. It means everything. I'd rather lose that now and preserve the integrity of what I had than turn away from true justice, and live out a charade."

"Dan," Vaklar said, his wide jaw setting in determination, "Don't—"

"Tomorrow morning," Reandn told him, "I'm going looking for Kacey. I'll do it alone if I have to, but I'm not leaving her with the Knife."

"I'm with you," Teya said instantly. Rethia said nothing. She didn't have to.

"I thought you had promises to keep," Elstan said, his voice acid. "To those Hounds."

Reandn's attention remained on Vaklar, who rubbed a hand across his bristly chin, considering Reandn with anger in his eyes, but not on his face. "Naya, I'll not waste my breath. But I stay true to my own loyalties, Dan."

Reandn tipped his head at Elstan, still looking at Vaklar. "He's right. I made promises. I'll keep them if I can . . . if you'll let me. They're licking their wounds back at that Knife camp, waiting to hear from us—though they've probably got someone watching the roads in case we decide to abandon Kacey and run for it. You can hole up in the woods a few furlongs from here as easily as you can hole up here, and almost as safely." He hesitated, waiting for some reaction, and realized Vaklar was going to wait until he'd fully committed himself. "Wait for me. Give me a day."

"You'll get this woman back in a day, then? Cocky Wolf," Vaklar said, and meant it.

Reandn shook his head. "If I can't, it'll be because things went badly and I'm dead. She's not that far from here."

"And you probably have no idea what you'll do once you find her, aya?"

Reandn gave him a wry grin. "None at all. But I guarantee you this—whether I succeed or no, there'll be fewer of the Knife on your trail."

Vaklar snorted.

"Come with me," Reandn said. "I'm going anyway, but I could use the help."

Understatement to the extreme, and from Vaklar's face, he knew it. But he shook his head. "An' I'm hurt, who'll take my meira to the Keep?"

Reandn had answers for him—that Madehy's hunter was a man who took his responsibilities seriously, that they could bundle Kalena up in the cart with the wounded, no one the wiser, and have her wait for the less formal escort to Pasdon, that they might even be able to goad the prickly hill folk into driving the Knife out and making the roads safe for Kalena and Elstan. But he didn't offer any of those thoughts, because Vaklar was smart enough to think of them on his own.

And because he couldn't argue with the guard. In Vaklar's shoes, he'd have said the same.

"We'll wait," Vaklar said. "For a day."

Teya let out a deep breath, while Elstan threw up his hands in pained exasperation. Kalena snorted in a coarse manner. Lips pressed against her teeth, she said, "There's nothing so pleasant as watching your life being tossed around like a playing chip."

"Respectfully," Reandn said, not looking particularly respectful, "that's just what it is. That's why you're here in the first place."

Teya put her head in her hands. "Just when I think you've learned," she moaned, throwing Kalena off-stride, her mouth open hesitating on a no doubt scathing reply.

Rethia didn't appear to notice any of it. Her eyes were on Reandn, and had been, for quite some time. Now she stood, silencing the rest of them with the unexpectedness of the act, and, with the quiet self-possession characteristic of her movement, crossed the circle and left it again to put her arms around Reandn and hold him.

Only then did he discover how she trembled. "All right," he told her, and ran a soothing hand down her jacket-lumpy back. "We'll get her back."

Kalena let out a *hmmph* of sound. "Can't we at least try to talk to Madehy?" she said, sliding into the role of a spoiled child again. "Maybe she'll let me stay here for another day."

Vaklar and Reandn simultaneously shook their heads, but had no time to say anything. For the door flung open and Madehy stood just outside it, and she snapped, "Haven't you done enough to my life? If you're not gone in the morning, I'll—I'll—"

"We'll *go*," Elstan said hastily, no doubt thinking of the hunter's threats.

Rethia turned around and Reandn released her, leaving nothing but a hand on her shoulder. He wasn't prepared for the way she stiffened at the sight of Madehy, and he didn't know what she saw—but Madehy must have seen it, too. Slowly, moving with a dreamlike quality, Rethia walked toward her . . . and Madehy let her. Until they were standing all but face to face, when Rethia reached out and touched Madehy's hair, touched her cheek, tilted her chin up so she could see those marbled eyes. Reandn watched warily while the others kept a baffled silence; Kalena flinched when Madehy, finally getting her first good look at Rethia's own striking gaze, gasped.

"I've wondered about you," Rethia said. "I didn't think I was the only one."

Madehy whispered, "I'm not alone." Tears spilled out of her eyes and ran down her cheeks; hesitantly, she touched Rethia's arm, lifted her hand, and deliberately replaced it. "You don't—I can—we—" She shook her head helplessly. "I'm not alone!"

"No," Rethia said. "You're not." She turned to look at Reandn, a message of trust. She'd come for help;

she didn't need to cling to him to know he would follow through. "We need to talk," she told him, and he just nodded. Rethia followed Madehy out of the barn, and presumably to the forbidden territory of the house.

"That," said Elstan, "is the strangest thing I've ever seen."

"Stranger than unicorns crowded around a cocky Wolf?" Kalena asked.

Teya said, "Stranger than the Shining Knife arming themselves with magic?"

"Strange enough," Vaklar said decisively. Stiffly, he rose and closed the door Rethia and Madehy had left open, though to Reandn's nose the fresh air had been a boon. A small herd of horses, three wounded and a handful of tense companions made even the spacious barn seem closed in. And that wasn't even counting the sheep. Vaklar gave Reandn a speculative look and said, "About that friend of yours. I'm thinking on some things I've heard, aya—"

"Don't." Reandn cut him off with no apology in his voice, just harsh demand. "Don't even think it. Not with the Knife so close. They'd probably brave the Loneliest Hells to kill her."

Startled, Vaklar yet managed to consider his words. "Aya, I don't even have to think to know you're right on that."

Chapter 13

"How," Madehy said, starting badly, and while her first visitor in several years still gazed around the small house to orient herself. "How come you can . . . why are we . . . do you *know*?"

Rethia was taking in the herb collection in the rafters. "Interesting that we're both healers," she murmured. "Although not the same sort . . ."

Madehy gathered her thoroughly rattled wits and wiped the last of her tears off her cheeks. "One of us is going to have to finish a thought soon. I can't waste this time . . . there's so much I have to—"

"And you think I have the answers?" Rethia ran a finger along the edge of the tiny polished wood table in the corner, and helped herself to the chair beside it. There wasn't another; why would she have two chairs? Madehy sat by the back of the tiny room—besides the table and chair it held her cookstove—which was all out of proportion to her house and her personal needs, meant as it was for brewing up cow- and horse-sized batches of draughts and effusions and poultices—and looked at the house through someone else's eyes for the first time since fire had razed her family home and she'd had this house built to replace it. On the other side of the stove was a sleeping alcove, barely big enough for a narrow bed—though that was her one luxury, a feather bed she'd earned when she'd gotten several shepherds through a difficult lambing season.

The walls held nothing but shelves, filled with crockery and more herbs and three precious volumes of illustrated stock care and management, books she could barely read but often perused. Beyond the bed was another door, one that even Madehy had to duck through, and it led to an overhang against the back of the house. She kept the wild ones there, the occasional fox or raptor or even wolf—though inevitably there was a raccoon in residence, and for most of the year before, she'd had an infestation of chameleon shrews, the result of one she'd studied for a short while . . . before it escaped, settled in, and started a family.

Humble. That word described this house as well as could be done. Just barely big enough for herself and Kendall—who was currently sitting on Rethia's foot, leaning back against her leg to tilt his head straight back and eye her from that strange angle, doing his best to look as if he might die if his ears weren't scratched. Madehy regarded this stranger, this woman who'd instantly known her better than anyone else in her life, and said, "If you don't have the answers, no one does."

Kendall gave a little bass hum of pleasure as Rethia's fingers found just the right spot behind his left ear. "I don't have all of them," Rethia said, "and I imagine you have more than you think."

"Things weren't so bad until the magic came back." Madehy rocked back on her bottom and brought her legs up to wrap her arms around them, hugging herself. To be so close to someone, and be able to relax! She wasn't, though. She reverberated with tension and anticipation, fairly quivering as the answers she'd sought for so long suddenly seemed within her reach. "I just had to be careful, then. Even when my family died in the fire—"

No. That had been too horrible, a harbinger of what

her life was to become. She had felt their terror so clearly, out in the barn where she'd been massaging the leg of a lame horse with liniment and expert fingers. Had gone from hearing it to feeling it, until suddenly she had been crazed with it, and instead of running to help, she'd bolted away from the barn, out of her mind and out of control. When it stopped, when she finally crept home, only then did she realize what had happened. Only then did she understand that her mother and two younger sisters had been dying under the wicked flare of the thatched roof.

Madehy lived under shingles now, as time consuming and expensive as they had been to obtain.

"They ought to have known." Rethia withdrew her hand from the dog's head and folded them tightly in her lap. In the lantern light her pale hair glowed gold and, without the jacket she'd shucked upon arrival in the warmth of the house, Madehy discovered shadows of finger-shaped bruises on Rethia's forearms. Her eyes were a little too large for her face and her nose was a little too straight and long, and right now her lips were pressed together, making her face look thin and tight. "They really should have known."

"Who?"

"It wasn't so bad for me. I knew there was something missing, something wrong about my life, but no one intruded on my thoughts unless I let them in. I just couldn't . . . sometimes I . . ." She looked down at her hands. "I always felt like something was calling me."

"*Who* should have known better?"

Rethia flashed a glance at her from under her heavy bangs. "You see? It still has a hold on me. I suppose it always will."

Madehy tightened her arms around her legs and her inner hold on her patience, but, unlike her legs, patience only seemed to squirt right out of her grip.

Rethia's face went vague. "Who gives you the honor of greeting when they might kill another? Who came back with the magic?"

Unicorns?

Rethia nodded as though she'd heard the astonished thought. "When they left, Madehy, they left a home they loved, even if they didn't love humankind half as much. They wanted to make sure they could come back, if ever anyone cared enough to look for them. But in a world without magic, who would open their passage from this end? Who would even be capable of *looking*?"

Madehy, open-mouthed, suddenly flashed on the memory of her mother's face, a much younger version than the one she'd heard screaming death in her mind. Open-mouthed and startled, because since the night of the fire, Madehy had been unable to face any memory of her mother or sisters. Any thought of them brought back the terror of their death throes, and never had she managed to push past that.

Now her mother looked down on her with gentle affection and repeated her favorite story, the event that kept Madehy, her eldest, as her special one, her child who would be someone in this world despite her strange ways. "You were all of two seasons old," she would say, her voice taking on the lilt of a story well-known and oft-told. "I put down your basket on the edge of our farthest field, and went to pick trillium for dinner—a treat. I'd gone no more than a dozen paces away when something made me look to you—*and there they were!* Unicorns, Maddy, five of them! A pinto stallion and his mares, and you in the midst of them. How my heart wailed! Them so big, and you just a nub of nothing in your little basket."

They had nudged her and snuffled her and given her mother a terrible fright, while as a baby she had done nothing more than gurgle happily. And then the great pinto unicorn had lowered his head, his sturdy horn aimed right at her soft little self.

At which point her mother had fainted. Madehy had never cared before, but now she discovered intense annoyance that her mother had missed those moments, had not been able to tell her just what had happened. She opened eyes she hadn't realized she'd closed, and saw Rethia watching her, nodding.

"I was six when they found me," she said. "I was the last. I saw them go, all but the biggest of them. It was he who touched me." She gave Madehy a sad sort of smile. "I don't remember that part, though. I guess I never will."

"But . . ." Madehy tried to remember what she'd seen of Rethia, found herself thinking of the way Rethia had gone to Dan. She'd *gone to him*—not tolerated his touch, nor flinched at it. "You can touch people. You can *be with them*. I can't—touching Dan once, by accident, was more than I ever want to do!"

"He's not the best one to start off with," Rethia admitted. "But he's the one who understands. The others may pretend, but he knows."

"Because he knows you."

Rethia nodded, her gaze losing focus for a moment—but she brought herself back. "And because of what he's been through. But then, we all have our own stories, don't we?"

"Maybe," Madehy said, finding her mind suddenly full of people she knew and the odd little ways they had, just as suddenly realizing that those oddities were only signs of their own stories, just like her reclusive eccentricity spoke of hers. She thought of the people in her barn, all wrenched around by circumstances so that their oddities shone through the loudest. "I don't suppose I want to know that wizard's story, though. That Elstan."

Rethia laughed. "But Madehy, he's just frightened. He's more scared than all of them, and doesn't dare let it show. He's not up to this task. He never was."

Madehy looked at her, suddenly breathless. "You can do that? You can be with them, and let that much in, and yet keep it from overtaking you?"

Rethia nodded. "Now that I've worked at it."

"Then . . . then—" Madehy abruptly took that breath she had needed so badly and blurted, "Then stay here! Teach me!"

Rethia said gently, "I have a sister. Her name is Kacey, and she's everything to me, even if she'd never admit it herself. She needs me right now."

Blunt disappointment hit Madehy right in the stomach. Of course. Why was the woman here, after all? "Then, tonight. Stay here tonight—and tomorrow, the others can hide here tomorrow. That's what they want, isn't it? Can't you show me, before you leave?"

Rethia reached out to Kendall, who hadn't moved his bony rump from her foot. "I can show you," she said. "That doesn't mean you'll understand."

Chapter 14

Unsettled, unable to sleep, Reandn sat in the darkened forge end of the barn, his back to a tree-thick support post and his wrists resting on his upraised knees. The others were asleep despite the fairly early hour. In a Wolf patrol, he thought, there'd yet be plenty of activity, plenty of noise. Someone singing, usually—or trying to—and the scrape of knife against whetstone, the curse of someone trying to fletch by firelight even when he knew better . . . and laughter. There was always laughter.

The Hounds had been full of such things—especially the willingness to laugh at their own and each other's expense. It suddenly seemed much longer than a day and a half since their deaths.

Magic. Magic, gathering into a spell. Reandn lifted his head sharply, detecting Elstan at work. What the Hells? And lead the Knife straight to them? He was halfway to his feet when Teya called out. "I have it, Dan." And indeed, the feel of the magic retreated from him, leaving him free to stalk into the low lantern light unhindered by its effects.

Aside from Teya, who was just now sitting, half covered by a blanket with her eyes only half open, the others slept. Vaklar lay on his good side, awkward and uncomfortable-looking, while Kalena had claimed two blankets and the only pile of hay not in the loft. Rethia was still with Madehy, and the wounded . . . he had to do a quick double take to see that Kiryl still breathed.

But Elstan . . . he cast around and found the wizard sitting in the cart's shadow, his legs crossed and his eyes closed, his face composed and trancelike, his mouth moving in a low murmur Reandn couldn't interpret. Reandn stalked up to him and waited; for the sake of those who were sleeping, he kept his voice down, looming over Elstan to make up for it. When the wizard opened his eyes, they grew wide with alarm . . . no matter how quickly he tried to hide it. "What," Reandn said in a harsh whisper, "do you think you were doing? Sending out an invitation to the Knife?"

"Don't speak of what you don't know," Elstan said, nonetheless leaning back to put some distance between them, and finding his back up against the cart. "We're safe enough. And I thought the Keep should know for sure what we're up against. They're sending help."

"That's not for you to decide." Reandn closed the scant distance between them, crouching to put himself closer yet. "When Vaklar and I want the Keep to know something, we'll tell you. And if we should ever decide to send a signal letting the Knife wizard know just where we are, we'll tell you that, too!"

Elstan shook his head in protest. "I've no death wish, you oaf-headed Wolf! The whole area is still awash in the currents the unicorns created. The Knife wizard might feel my spell, but no one could follow it here."

"He's right." Teya, too, kept her voice low, and moved in close behind Reandn, the blanket settled about her shoulders. "About the unicorns, anyway. But there's no excuse for not warning us what you were up to. Now that I'm here . . . let me put it this way, my fellow wizard. If you try another spell without either protecting Reandn or warning me so *I* can protect him, you're going to discover the real differences between a court wizard and a patrol wizard."

"You looked tired. I didn't want to wake you."

Reandn put his hand on Elstan's chest, just below the dip of his collarbone, and gave him enough of a shove that his head made a sharp sound as it connected with the cart. "Do it, next time. Only next time—no spells unless you clear it with both Vaklar and me. You got that?"

"You're mixed up." Elstan glared at him, but it was less than convincing—the haughty tilt to his head had some uncertainty about it that made Reandn narrow his eyes. "I'm under no obligation to take orders from you."

"Then we'll leave you behind," Reandn said. "We're better off without you if you can't work with us."

"You wouldn't," Elstan retorted, but again, his confidence seemed more feigned than real.

"He would," Teya said, and yawned. "He definitely would."

Reandn watched the wizard another moment, eyes still narrowed, as he tried to pick out what was different about the man, for there was . . . something. Finally he shook his head and turned away.

Teya followed him back to the forge, and opened the blanket to its pleasant and fading heat. "He *is* right. No one'll be able to tell where that spell came from. I'm right here, and it doesn't quite feel right to me. Not like a spell aimed at the official Keep receiver." She shrugged. "But then, something didn't feel quite right about you, either, when I went to shield you from the magic. The unicorns really stirred the currents up . . . added a number of them on their way by, too."

Reandn didn't respond to her. He found himself wondering if those currents would affect his ability to find Kacey by the feel of her aura. Rethia had found him with no trouble . . . but then, she was used to using auras like that. He took a deep breath and let it out slowly, and Teya must have misinterpreted the reason for it.

"He's something," she said. "I can't believe how many of the school rules he breaks!"

Reandn lifted an eyebrow at her, and she explained, "Wizardly etiquette. They pound it into our heads how important it is not to inflict magic on those who don't want it, not to parade our abilities like a pennant on a standard . . . that sort of thing. It's all part of the effort to keep down the clashes over reintroducing magic into society."

"It didn't work for the Knife," Reandn said dryly.

Just as dry, Teya told him, "The Resiores don't have an official wizard school guiding their people, either."

Reandn leaned back against the thick post he'd been sitting against earlier and regarded her for a moment; she returned his gaze comfortably. No signs of her usual reaction, the way she'd flick her eyes away and then back again, the little signs that let him know she wasn't in complete agreement with him, that she wasn't entirely happy under his command. She still looked worn, and stiff in her shoulder, and right now she had that spell-working expression, a tiny bit of a frown in her forehead, a barely discernible narrowing to her eyes. . . .

"You must have woken up out of a sound sleep to work that shielding," he said.

"You don't know how many times I did that very thing at the school." Teya gave her head a rueful shake. "You weren't there, of course. But I became very good at catching students who were working magic out of the shielded laboratories."

Chitchat. That's all this was, chitchat. And not really what was on Reandn's mind. He went to what was. "Why are you here?"

"Why am I—what?" Teya's spell-working frown turned into the real thing.

"You've no doubt put yourself in a lot of trouble with the school and the Wolves. It couldn't have been easy to get here. So why did you do it?"

She seemed nonplused; he was used to that. It flustered

her if she felt unexpectedly pressured, made it hard for her to come back with a quick reply. Dakina had been the same, when he'd first met her, years ago. Swamplanders. They thought slow, but once they'd done their thinking, the answers were solid. "I guess . . . I guess I found out some things. About the patrol, and the Wolves . . . and maybe about me." She shook her head, but not at him. "No. It comes down to . . . just what you were talking about last night. Loyalty. The right *kind* of loyalty. I guess . . . I felt I owed it to you."

He responded without thinking. "That's absur—"

"No!" She put her hands on her hips. "Don't you dare take the heart out of what I did! Don't you make it worthless!"

After a moment's surprise, he grinned at her. "Not worthless, Teya. Not at all. Believe me, come tomorrow, I'll take every advantage of having you here."

She resettled the blanket on her shoulders and pushed the loose hairs of her braid out of her face. It was a crooked braid, canted off to one side as a testament that her shoulder still hindered her. "What do you plan to do?"

He lifted one shoulder in a loose shrug. "Don't know. Get there, scout it out. Make something up."

She moved to the forge, to the flat working stone off to the side where Elstan had been preparing food, and poked around for leftovers. Failing to discover any, she checked the floor, kicked aside a piece of fallen coal, and sat cross-legged on the floor, practically up against the waist-high brick coal pit. "I might be able to help."

"I'm counting on it," he said, quirking his brows together, puzzled. "Didn't we just have this conversation?"

She smiled. "No, I mean, *now*. I might be able to get you a look at the camp, *now*."

He hunkered down in front of her, putting himself on eye level. "Can you do that?"

He must have been too intense, for she drew back slightly, and so did he, trying to curb himself. She gave him a wry look. "I said it, didn't I? With this . . . connection you have to your friend, I might be able to scry them out. As long as we get it done before the unicorn currents fade."

"Then do it."

"You'll have to be part of it," she said in warning. "I can protect you from most of the magic, but not all of it."

"I'll handle it."

"Then sit." She pointed at the floor with a peremptory finger. "I worked on this spell at school this time—I knew it before, but didn't have the fine points."

Now was his chance, he realized, to stop things right here, a nod to his insistence that she have complete command over the spells she employed. Quietly, he asked, "Do you know it?"

She nodded. Not too quickly, and not with any hesitation. A matter-of-fact *yes*.

He sat. "Do you have everything you need?"

"This one doesn't need props. Well, I suppose it does— but as it happens, that would be you."

Reandn felt a brief tug of the absurd. "Imagine the look on Farren's face," he murmured to her, causing an undignified snort of laughter. She clapped her hand over her mouth and ducked down, peering under the cart to see if she had disturbed anyone.

Apparently not. Straightening, she looked at him with a mockly stern face. "Don't do that to me! You don't want me to lose my concentration, do you?"

No. Not if he was part of this spell. He checked his hands to discover that he hadn't fooled them with his moment of humor; they were clenched and ready to strike out. Deliberately, he relaxed them, and crossed his legs to match Teya's posture. "All right," he said. "What do I do?"

She sighed. "It's not going to be that bad, Reandn. I'll start the spell; I can protect you from that. You'll know when I reach out to you—even if you don't feel me, that'll be when I can't keep all the magic from you anymore, and you'll feel *that*. All I need you to do is think about that pull you get from Kacey. The aura Rethia was talking about." She looked at him, her expression changing into something he couldn't decipher. "Rethia was right, you know. Even wizards have trouble finding auras unless someone's truly close to them. I could feel everyone in the patrol, but only when they were nearby. I can feel you right now, but put you on the other side of Madehy's first field, and I'd have to use a spell to find you."

Reandn cleared his throat, unaccountably uneasy, and pointedly reminded her, "The *spell*."

She looked away, abashed. "The spell. All right. Once I find her, I can open scope to see the camp as well—you'll see it all in your mind, like a dream. Take a good look; depending on how good their wizard is, we might be detected, and then I'll have to close up without warning you." She waited until he nodded understanding and then closed her eyes.

He did the same. He wasn't sure why; he saw nothing but the insides of his eyelids, and they weren't particularly interesting. A better backdrop against which to see the camp, he decided, aware that Teya had drawn magic for the spell, bracing himself for the moment when she dropped the shield.

It sneaked up on him—she'd done it carefully—but then he found himself in the middle of it, and unable to stop the anger that always arose from the feel of magic thrumming through his head. He fought himself, and floundered, and clutched for control—

The magic snapped away from him. He sat there, paled, breathing fast, bent over his crossed legs; Teya's hand settled gently on his upper arm. "That won't work," she said, her voice in close to his ear. "You're . . . well, I'm not sure what you're doing, but I can barely keep hold of the spell, never mind continue with it." She took a deep breath; he felt her release it. "You've got to work *with* me."

Reandn took his own deep breath, and straightened; her hand fell away and when he opened his eyes, she was sitting where she'd been. And Elstan was leaning against the cart, watching them.

He saw he'd been noticed, and said, quite conversationally, "He always did that to me, too. He'll deny it, though."

Teya's eyes widened slightly; she glanced at Reandn, who shrugged. "I don't know what he's talking about, I'll say that much."

She looked at him a moment, then shook her head. "No matter. Somehow, you've just got to trust me, Reandn, or we'll go into that camp blind."

Trust her. He *did* trust her. Or he wouldn't be doing this in the first place.

As if sensing she'd get no more from him, Teya merely nodded to herself. "Let's try again, then."

He closed his eyes, this time wary and tense, finding it an effort to center his attention on the quiet tug of feeling that was Kacey. As before, Teya's magic crept in gently—and he went rigid when he felt it, fighting not to struggle against the swoop of sensations it brought with it, and fighting the anger that always came with them.

"*That*," Teya said, her voice low but emphatic. "*Stop it.*"

Stop . . . *what*?

The instant that his concentration broke, the magic flooded through him, knocking him away from his sense of self and triggering his struggles, his anger, anew.

"*Stop*," Teya hissed.

Goddess, he couldn't do this. Without his ability to fight, without his anger, all he had left was fear. No, nothing so mundane as fear, just pure animal terror, and all he wanted to do was run but this was for Kacey, she'd come for him and now she was in terrible danger and think about Kacey think about Kacey . . .

The magic trickled away into an unpleasant hum.

Reandn drew a huge ragged breath and felt himself do it, felt his fingers digging into the ankles he was bowed over. The initial casting, he thought, a dim recognition in some working corner of his mind, must be over. But he didn't see anything, as Teya had told him he would.

She whispered, "Take me to Kacey."

For a moment he thought he wouldn't be able to sense her over the magic in his system, but there—there was a little tug, a familiar and welcome feel that disappeared if he thought too hard about it. Out of the corner of his inner eye, then, just like details at night. Once he got the trick of that, the Kacey aura grew stronger, and larger, and pretty soon he could look straight at it and there was nowhere for it to go—and then he was looking at Kacey herself.

For an instant he shied away from the image; it came to him with the same eerie clarity he'd had in his half-dead state, when the darkness hadn't seemed to matter and even the distant details were sharp and clear—and it was nothing he wanted to see. He went cold inside, stiffening in outrage, and ignored the quiet pull that came from Teya and her magic.

Kacey was on her feet, returning from the woods to the camp, trailed by a man who was obviously her keeper. She clutched a crooked, makeshift staff with jagged ends, and limped profoundly, barely able to touch her foot to the ground. She'd been crying; tears of pain ran down her face even as he watched, sliding over several bruises on the way. As she neared one of the trees, she reached out to it with desperation and sank to the ground at its distant roots; the man grunted something at her and she crawled up to the trunk, her chin quivering in a way Reandn had never seen before. There she curled up on her side, and hid her face in her hands.

Teya tried to get control from him, to move the scrying elsewhere, but he couldn't take his eyes away from Kacey—Kacey who he'd never seen like this, defeated and helpless and abused, bereft of the strength that

seemed to carry her through life and keep her kicking
back at it with determination and that quick tongue.
Somehow his mind locked onto that other Kacey, the
bold Kacey. The one who laughed with him, and sang
songs to her mare when she thought no one was listening,
and occasionally made as though she might push him
down the well if he didn't mind his manners. The contrast
made the cold, hard knot in his stomach swell into pain.
"Kacey," he whispered, not knowing if he spoke out loud
or only within himself.

Someone from the Knife camp lobbed a rock in her
general direction; it bounced off the tree above her head.
"Shut up!" the rock flinger yelled, although she'd been
making very little noise.

She froze, peering over her hands with startled alarm.
When no more rocks came her way, she pillowed her
face in her arms, hiding the only way she could. He
thought she had stopped crying, then, until her back
quivered and she released a muffled snatch of a sob
and froze again, anticipating another rock.

That cold hard knot rose right up into his throat and
burst, breaking through his hard, safe walls and bringing
a flood of emotion he thought he'd never feel again.
"Kacey," he said raggedly, "I'm here. *I'm coming for
you.*"

And Teya jerked on him, hard. "I can't keep this up
forever," she said into his ear. "They're going to figure
it out. Now look around!"

Look around. Away from Kacey. *Look around.*

He did, taking in the disrupted state of the camp,
the number of walking wounded, the placements of their
sentries. And though his vision retained its preternatural
clarity and his mind catalogued the minute details before
him, still . . . all he could see was Kacey.

"I have an idea." Teya crouched beside her patrol
leader in the predawn darkness, chewing the dried meat
and stale trail bread of their cold breakfast. Their horses

were saddled and waiting; the others slept, or pretended to.

Teya, too, was pretending—pretending she hadn't been tied to this man by magic during his powerful experience with the scrying, and that she hadn't felt his anguish as he helplessly watched Kacey's abuse. At least she'd come out of the spell trance quicker than he had, and had composed herself before he could see her face. Not that he'd have noticed anything, in the state he was in, and the speed with which he'd bolted from the barn, but . . . Teya knew with absolute certainty that he must never even suspect how intimately she'd perceived his experience.

Then you'll have to be more careful. She flushed as she realized that he was certainly watching her now, and as astutely as he'd ever done. She cleared her throat. "I have an idea."

"So you said."

Best to distract him quickly. "It's Kalena they want. Let's give her to them."

"Don't say *that* where Vaklar can hear," Reandn responded dryly. But he took a gulp of well-watered wine and eyed her, waiting.

"Well, at least make the Knife think we're giving them Kalena. It'll be me."

He shook his head. "Don't you think at least one of them is going to know what she looks like?"

"I can use a glamour." Teya shifted forward to her knees, forgetting breakfast, intent on convincing that frown right out of those grey eyes. "Look. I braid my hair fancier—we can even have Varina do it. I borrow Kalena's jacket. And I use a glamour. I won't even be close to them, at least not at first. But I bet I'll distract them. It'll give you a better chance to get in closer."

Reandn shook his head again. "Just put a glamour on the both of us, Teya. Standard patrol practice, just enough to slide their eyes over us. We're Wolves, after all. Wolves in the spring woods on a morning with a heavy dew. You don't think we can sneak up on a motley Knife camp?"

Teya didn't answer right away, feeling the instant frustration that always came of working with Reandn's reticence to try new magic. On the other side of the cart, someone started a muttered conversation; they were no longer the only ones awake. The others, too, had a mission for the day—to leave Madehy's barn and her yard, and keep Kalena safe until Teya and Reandn returned.

She didn't want to argue about it in front of an audience. But the words that hovered on her tongue— her *I can do it*—begged to be spoken anyway. He saw it in her, she realized suddenly. He was just as aware as she of the old patterns between them, and the old frustrations; he met her eyes with a steady, neutral gaze, the same as ever aside from the thin white scar through his brow, the one she hadn't gotten used to yet, as she was used to the somewhat coarser one along the back of his jawline.

She looked away, suddenly abashed. That old scar had always made her think of how far he was willing to push himself to get the job done; it had been a close thing, the mark of a knife sliding up his throat. That he'd lived through it was evidence of his experience.

She had no scars, not even a surface mark to indicate her dislocated shoulder. Half a year of experience as opposed to . . . she wasn't even sure. Fifteen? It suddenly occurred to her that his resistance to magic didn't always have to do with the magic involved. That sometimes it meant the idea behind the magic wasn't as sound as it should be. Teya met Reandn's eye for an instant—all she could handle just at the moment—and nodded. "If that's the way you want it."

A scuffle by the cart interrupted them; Teya discovered Kalena there, leaning on the side of it in a most deliberately casual fashion. "It really *was* a bad idea." She rested her elbow on the cart and her chin in her hand, raising an eyebrow in a supercilious manner that made Teya bristle instantly. "Anyone who knows anything about me knows I'm not stupid enough to put myself in that kind of danger."

"Pity," Reandn said dryly. "You can't inspire your people to great things unless you aspire to them yourself."

She straightened, truly stung. "As if you'd know anything about it."

Vaklar came up behind her, and said simply, "Think about it, Kalena," a comment that drew a grave frown but at least distracted her. He turned his attention to Reandn and said, "I'm coming with you, then."

"What?" Kalena cried.

Reandn got to his feet. "I'm not pushing you, Vaklar. You had reasons behind your decision."

"Aya, and I've reasons to change it, too." Under Reandn's gaze the guard ducked his head and muttered, "I had dreams, I did."

Kalena turned to him. "You did?" she said, and must have realized how odd her intent question sounded. "I mean . . . so did I. Horrible ones. About some woman I've never seen before."

Varina's drowsy voice, coming from the ground on the other side of the cart, added, "So did I. And such . . . vivid dreams, too." After a moment, she appeared on the other side of the cart, her hair mussed and her eyes still filled with sleep.

Teya tried to make herself small and quiet, but Reandn looked at her anyway—though, thank the Bright Goddess, he said nothing. Not that she'd have had any answers. There was no reason that scrying spell should have touched any of the others, sleeping or no. Unless . . . well, she had never worked magic in the direct currents of a unicorn herd. And she'd never even imagined a herd as big as the one she'd seen the evening before.

Vaklar strode over to their breakfast spot and helped himself to a strip of dried meat, shoving his first bite over to the side of his mouth so he could talk. "Aya, I just can't . . . *see* what I saw in my dreams and not try to do something about it. Can't explain it better than that . . . except to say they were uncommonly real dreams."

"I imagine they were," Reandn said dryly. "And I'm grateful for all the help I can get."

"Leave the other one behind, though." Vaklar looked in the direction of the house, which left him gazing at the back of the barn. "She's been the whole night in that house. Ask Madehy again about staying here another day—my bet is that she'll say different, now. For whatever reason, she does want to talk to your Rethia."

At least he wasn't speculating out loud anymore. Teya knew, had put it together, and thought that with a little nod at the right time, Vaklar could do the same. But she also knew Reandn was right—that if the Knife so much as suspected who Rethia was, nothing would stop them from killing her.

Reandn, too, was looking toward the back of the barn. "I'll go ask," he said. "Saddle yourself a horse. I want to be on the move by the time we hit dawn."

Madehy watched Rethia's face, still slightly dazed by the fact that she could be in such close company without enduring an overwhelming barrage of someone else's emotions. For not too far from them, sitting against the side of the barn and sunning herself at a respectful distance, Kalena sat lost in some troublesome thought.

As was Rethia, and though Madehy well understood why, she herself was still lost in her little cloud of wonder. They sat together on the edge of the well, with Kendall between them, his eyes half closing in the early morning sun, his head drooping into a doze, if only until some noise reminded him that he was awake and desiring petting. Then he'd jerk his head back into some semblance of alert posture, and wait for Madehy to notice. It was enough, a satisfying kind of morning, after their work of the night.

They'd been up late, and Rethia, buoyed by unicorn energy, had taught Madehy the beginnings of protecting herself. It was not, she made clear, that everyone threw themselves at Madehy, but just that they *were*, and that Madehy didn't know how to shelter herself. The first thing she'd done was build, for herself, her well-practiced barrier against the pain of her patients—something Madehy had never been able to protect herself from, not even when her patients were animals. Rethia had called it a dome of white light, but when Madehy tentatively looked for it, she saw nothing. When she tried to make one for herself, it failed utterly. It wasn't until she noticed that any contact with Rethia gave her a funny feeling in the center of her chest that they had made any progress.

Madehy no longer tried to build any domes of light, white or otherwise. She looked for the feeling, and in stuttering patterns of success and failure, built herself a barrier with that. And now she practiced, discovering how quickly she could do it—and how fast it fell apart when she became distracted. Even now, she felt a hint of the unrest that swirled behind Kalena's serene expression, the one that seemed to say she was so Highborn as to be aloof from and unaffected by what anyone else might say or do. Madehy strengthened her barrier and turned back to Rethia, wishing—to her own surprise—that she *could* feel some of what Rethia was thinking.

But closing others off meant closing yourself in, and Rethia seemed to have been doing just that, at will, since she was a young child. Or not doing it, when she chose, and in the power of choice felt no threat in the vulnerability of being so open.

At the moment Madehy found her completely inaccessible, and she could no longer stand watching the variety of subtle frowns that crossed Rethia's face. "They'll take care of it," she said, little enough reassurance as it was.

Rethia looked at her in gentle surprise, as if she had forgotten there was anyone else near. "Now I know how Kacey feels," she said, which Madehy didn't find enlightening at all; she wrinkled her nose.

Rethia sighed, and there was plenty of frustration behind it. "My sister," she said. "She's so practical. She's too sensible for her own good. And I . . . I guess she would say that I'm too much the opposite. Always wandering off, she'll say, always being willing to follow the moment and forget about the day—and what needs to be done. But sometimes . . . lots of times . . . she wishes she could come along with me. She feels left out. She frets." Rethia ran a slow hand down Kendall's back and admitted, "For the first time, I know how she feels."

"What?" Madehy said. "You want to go?"

Rethia nodded. "I don't know what good I could do. I can't fight, and I'm not very strong. But this . . . this is awful. This waiting, and wondering, and worrying."

Madehy gave Kendall's head a series of firm pats. He always took on a pained expression when she did that, but when she quit, he never failed to turn to her to ask for more. Now she obliged him and said, "Then don't do it."

"Don't worry?" Rethia asked, incredulous.

"Don't wait here."

"I imagine I'll worry wherever I am."

Madehy gave her a skeptical look; had she been that long gone from human contact, that she couldn't make herself understood anymore? Deliberately, she said, "Go to the camp, Rethia. You can at least throw stones at them, can't you?"

"Not with any chance of hitting anything," Rethia said, blunt in her self-assessment. But she turned thoughtful, and after a moment, added, "But I do know this lullaby. I use it on our patients sometimes—the young ones, who get so homesick. . . . I've never tried it on more than one person."

"I've got something similar." Madehy stood up and

faced Rethia with her hands on her hips. "If yours is like mine, it won't work on them once they're riled up. But if we can get there first—"

"We? You'd come with me?"

Rethia's surprise made Madehy stop and think, take a look at herself. What was she doing? What did she care about these people? Rethia was the only one who really mattered to her.

"If it didn't matter," Rethia said, "you wouldn't care so much when you *do* know what other people are feeling."

"Don't do that," Madehy said, feeling Kalena's piquing interest as her newly achieved barrier slipped in the midst of her momentary fuddle.

"I didn't," Rethia said. "It's obvious enough without leaving myself open to you all the time."

Madehy frowned, trying to sort out what she really felt and what she really wanted, and in the end gave it all up and went with her original and still strong impulse, recognizing only the reluctance to let Rethia go on her own. "I'll come. You need me. And I can get us to the camp before the others."

"Can you?" Doubt shadowed Rethia's face.

Madehy snorted. "How many places around here do you think look like what you described to me? I know just where they are, and I know the shortest way to get there. From what I gathered, your Dan is fumbling around trying to follow some aura, and he's never done it before." She hesitated, and then rushed forward with her words, trying to hide her sudden realization that she really ought to have offered to help Dan find the place that morning, when he had asked again if Kalena and Elstan could stay the day. She hadn't even considered it at the time, far too locked into her habits of avoiding unnecessary exposure to other people. "If we leave soon enough, we'll get there before he does. Maybe we can't do much . . . but if a few lullabies can make that Knife camp sleepy and slow, it'll be better for your sister than if we do nothing at all."

Slowly, Rethia nodded. She looked down at herself, as if evaluating her stained split skirt and the laced boots on her feet, and knelt to retie a bootlace. "I'm ready."

Madehy grinned. How good it felt to be making decisions about what she was going to do, instead of feeling trapped into decisions she didn't necessarily want! "I've got a bow inside," she said. "And I'll get some water."

She grabbed Kendall's collar—she'd shut him up in the house, rather than risk losing him; he was a companion first and guard dog second, and not ever a war dog—and headed indoors. But at Kalena's clear, loud voice, she stopped short, and slowly turned around.

"I want to come with you."

Madehy exchanged a quick look with Rethia, and found her new friend equally as surprised.

"I mean it. I want to come."

Madehy frowned, and let her barrier fade just enough to feel the truth in Kalena's words. "Why?" she asked, earning a quick scowl. "And don't look at me like that. I don't care who you are."

"Are you turning down help?" Kalena stood up and brushed off the seat of her . . . well, Madehy wasn't quite sure what it was, though Kalena had been wearing it since her arrival. A strange combination of trousers under a long skirt that was open in the front and split two thirds of the way up in the back. A Highborn riding costume, she supposed. Kalena stared back at her and pointedly said, "Well? Are you?"

"Are you going to be of any help?" Madehy asked, just as pointedly. She'd seen how Kalena treated the others; she'd had a dose of it herself when the woman had jerked her down into contact with Dan. "Trying to boss the Knife around isn't going to do us much good."

Rethia sighed. "I suppose she earned that, but . . ."

Madehy didn't turn her gaze from Kalena. "She's not used to it when things don't go her way. All we need is to have her squawk some kind of protest when we're trying to keep Knife eyes away from us."

"I won't." Kalena took a few steps closer; what truth Madehy hadn't sensed came through strongly enough in her face. "I don't know what I can do to help. But I've got to try."

Madehy glanced at Rethia again and, in silent accord, they waited. Kendall sat and leaned against Madehy, forcing her to take a few balancing steps, and Rethia sat back down on the edge of the well, and they waited. Finally Kalena gave an extraordinary fidget and said, "I . . . I've been thinking about what Dan said this morning. About being a leader. It's true I don't want to be here . . . I'm just a token, and almost everyone but the Knife seems to know it. They don't expect me to be any good at it. It's just a first step, my father told me. They're all willing to play games with my life, even when they don't really expect anything to come out of it!" She glared at them, as if they were the cause of her troubles, and then seemed to catch herself.

"It's an important step," Rethia said. "If it weren't, the Knife wouldn't care."

"I don't know why they do. I never expected them to, or I would have taken the Keland Hounds seriously when they said we needed to move on, to get out of the pass." She stopped, then, troubled; Madehy didn't have to let Kalena's feelings in to know she was thinking about the dead they had left behind. But she didn't dwell on it; she quickly turned brusque again, her color high and her stubborn chin lifted. "I haven't had any choice in this—up till now. Now, I have a chance to show them all how wrong they've been about me. To really make a difference for the Resiores. If I walk into that Keep having helped to rescue Kacey—a stranger kidnapped because of my presence here—I'll already have done more than expected. It would be a far better thing than limping into service after being pathetically rescued by Keland forces."

"Well," Madehy said after another long silence. "That's truthful enough. Sounds more like what I've seen of you."

"I liked you better when you hid from us all the time,"
Kalena said archly.

Madehy snorted. "It's all right with me, then, if you
want to come along. Though if you give us away, I'll
put an arrow through you myself."

"I won't." Kalena busied herself by fussing at her waist,
tugging at and twisting her clothing until she found the
ties that secured her overskirt. "And I won't get in the
way. I just want to be there—that'll be enough."

"It's up to Rethia." Madehy gave Kendall's collar a
pull, and the big tawny dog rose, unsuspecting, to follow
her into the house. "It's her sister."

"It's not up to *any* of you." Elstan stood at the corner
of the barn, leaning against it in an exaggeratedly casual
manner, his arms crossed. Startled, Madehy took a
moment to accept his presence; before she'd learned
her barrier, no one ever could have been that close
without her knowledge. Elstan took advantage of the
general silence. "Kalena is supposed to be here; I'm
supposed to be watching out for her. She's too important
to trot off on a fool's errand. The rest of you can do
what you like."

Kalena edged closer to Rethia and Madehy, who
stopped just short of tucking Kendall into the house.
From the dour and determined look on Elstan's face,
the dog might yet come in handy. Murmuring just loudly
enough for Madehy to hear, Kalena said, "All right, I've
got another reason, too. I don't want to stay with him.
I don't trust him."

"Why not?" Rethia said, responding in a nearly normal
volume.

Kalena sent her a frantic look. "Keep your voice down!
Why should I? As far as I can tell, he's a self-serving
Keep wizard who so far hasn't completed one major
spell for us. He doesn't care about anyone else, not really.
Just himself. He's worse than me."

Even Madehy had to smile at that blunt self-assessment.
At the barn, Elstan straightened, frowning at them and

their private conversation, and looked like he might just
walk up and make himself part of it.

"Besides," Kalena said, as if sensing they weren't quite
convinced she was worth the trouble, "he called me by
my nickname once. My little-girl name. The only people
who do that now are the ones who're mocking me for
who I am. For being my father's spoiled daughter. Except
for Vaklar, who just keeps forgetting I hate it." As Elstan
started toward them, she added, "How would he even
know it?"

"Maybe he heard Vaklar use it," Rethia said, and by
then Elstan had breached their privacy. Madehy found
it necessary to bolster her protection, for the wizard
flew his tense determination like a flag in the wind, and
she was definitely downwind.

"Don't even bother to plot about it." He put his hand
around Kalena's upper arm. "We've already had enough
go wrong on this trip. She shouldn't even be out here—
just because the Knife is waiting for our response doesn't
mean they're all twiddling their thumbs at their camp.
They could be scouting for our hiding place right now."

"That's true," Rethia said, but there was a hint of
something hidden in her normally forthright eyes; one
moment Madehy was sure of it, and the next she could
find no sign of it.

"What?" Kalena stared at her, building up a good head
of outrage. "I'm not under his orders, and I've no
intention of—"

"Go with him," Rethia said kindly. "You're safer in
the barn for now. And Madehy and I have a healing
method it would be good to practice before we go. I'm
almost certain we'll need it."

"Don't touch me!" Kalena jerked her arm well out of
Elstan's grasp. She favored Rethia with a particularly
vile glare, and stomped off toward the barn. Elstan
started to follow, but hesitated long enough to toss advice
to Rethia, as well.

"You should get out of sight, too. They might have

an idea of what Kalena looks like, but you, they've seen up close."

Rethia averted her eyes from him. "I have every intention of getting out of sight. After all, Madehy and I have that spell to practice."

Elstan waved them inside. "Do it, then. Work on your little spell. Just don't bring those Knife zealots down on *us*."

Madehy caught Rethia's eye, and this time she didn't need to feel anyone's feelings but her own to know just what her new friend had in mind. Yes, they'd practice their little spell all right. And Elstan would be the first to know if it worked.

Chapter 15

"You might have warned me," Kalena informed them, clambering up a short but difficult rise between Madehy and Rethia. Rethia trailed the other two, reaching for a tree to help pull herself along, and Madehy was at the top of the rise, evaluating their position. Too busy for idle word swapping, both of them.

Though when Rethia had joined the other two, Madehy waited for her to catch her breath, and grinned. "That was easier than I thought it'd be."

"He was only one man." Rethia said, unbuttoning her jacket in the warming morning air and pulling a twig from her hair. "There are at least ten of them at the camp, and that's not counting the wounded."

"But we learned it's not so hard to pick and choose who we aim it at—if Dan's there ahead of us, we won't accidentally put him asleep."

"I appreciate being the one you experimented on." Kalena straightened her trouser's bloused leg and made a noise of disgust at the tear she discovered. "Nice to know I might as easily be back there with Elstan, snoring away."

Madehy wasn't impressed with the complaint. "So?" she said. "It was the best chance you had. And if we'd put you to sleep, too, then at least you wouldn't be fretting."

But Kalena *was* fretting, and Madehy took a moment to shore up her barriers, wondering how long it would take before the process became as automatic—and as effective—as Rethia found it. Even now, Kalena's worries came through, enough so Madehy resolved not to depend on her if they got into a tight spot.

Not that she planned on that happening. She knew the place the Knife had chosen to camp in, all right. A short, wide jut of a cliff backed the camp, the face of which was composed of striated, flaky shale layers and impossible to climb. From Rethia's description of the camp layout, the top would be the perfect place to nestle in and work their unicorn-given skills. There'd be a sentry up there, of course, but they knew it. They'd deal with it.

In the shallow bowl of land before the cliff, the camp had shelter from the winds, and the brief rise of the edges of the bowl would be prime spots for a few more sentries. It also meant that anyone approaching the camp from below wouldn't actually see it until they were almost upon it. That worried Madehy, that Dan would blunder right into them, but Rethia seemed to have the utmost confidence in her friend . . . and there wasn't anything Madehy could do about it now, anyway.

"We'll have to keep silence, soon." She didn't need to see Rethia's nod, but she held Kalena's eye until the ambassador mumbled understanding. "I'm going to bring us in from uphill. There's a good place to hide, off to the side. Unless they cut the old tree down."

"You just let us know when we're close." Kalena gave her trousers one last twitch and straightened, waiting. Rethia, too, looked ready to go. Madehy nodded at them both—*all right, then*—and struck out up the hill.

Reandn crouched behind the swelling flower buds of a bushy mountain glory, only furlongs from Kacey. Most of her was hidden behind a tree, but he could see the foot she kept out in front of herself, and occasionally a movement of her hand. So close—the tingle of her aura had grown, feeling more and more like the one he'd always called Rethia—and yet . . . he wasn't ready to move in yet.

He ignored the thrushes fluttering through ground cover and the hopeful bee hovering near the glory buds, and centered his attention on the bowl of the camp, just in front of the short, wide cliff he'd seen in the scrying. This time of day, there ought to have been plenty of activity. Cleanup from the midday meal, conversation, even some signs that the Knife readied for further action. Instead, the loudest sound remained the rustling of the birds, with only the muffled hint of conversation coming through. A man wandered between one lean-to and another, a woman poked at the central campfire without any visible goal, and a low groan drifted up from the only tent there, a three-sided structure with two bodies wrapped up beside it.

He had dealt with only two drowsy sentries, tying and gagging them with supplies pilfered from Madehy's cabinets. There was another up on the cliff—Teya had found him with a quick, quiet spell—but there'd been no sign of him yet. Ten others were scattered sleepily throughout the camp. Why hadn't these people set up an entire web of sentries? Why hadn't they seeded the woods with people in anticipation of a rescue?

Without answers, he put them all at risk by going in. And yet . . . there sat Kacey. So close. *So close*.

Reandn pinched the bridge of his nose. *Think*.

Or maybe . . . stop thinking. *Do*. "It's strange, aya," Vaklar had said when they had reached the top of the rise and knelt together, considering what they saw. "But good opportunity all the same. Go get your Kacey, and we'll wait by." For they had quickly decided that their best chance was to use only Wolf wiles, and to avoid anything but the subtlest of Teya's spells. Otherwise, the Knife wizard would cry alarm before they were even started.

They waited now, opposite the cliff and still crouched on the rim of the bowl he had crept along, probably wondering what had delayed him, ready to grab Knife attention. Teya, he knew, would be sifting through her spells, always keeping the quiet, eye-slipping glamour right at hand; it was far better for her to fade back and cast her spells unseen if it became necessary. She'd cast it on him, too, if she deemed him at risk.

In the camp, the man closest to Kacey—the one Reandn had seen in the scrying—turned away from her and yawned, settling himself into a more comfortable position.

Yes. Do. Reandn moved, sacrificing some of his silence for speed, leaving the cover of the scattered mountain glories for the beaten brush at the perimeter of the camp. No one stirred.

And then Kacey saw him. Her mouth fell open, and after an instant of shock she took a deep breath, ready to cry out to him in relief and then realizing better of it before so much as a sound passed her lips.

Easy! he thought at her, motioning her to stay put, pushing the palm his hand at her to repeat the gesture when she yet sat rigid and ready to move. And at the same time he had to take his own deep breath, fighting the immediate desire to sprint the scant distance between them. He pressed his back against the rough bark of the tree that hid him, unable to take his eyes from hers.

But then her gaze darted away from him and back, widening; the hope on her face fell into desperation and then faltered, seeking something more neutral. Even from where he stood, Reandn could see a quiver in her chin, giving her away. Giving *him* away.

But the sudden slight hum of Teya's shielding instantly fell over him; only an instant later, Kacey—his mirror for what was happening in the camp—widened her eyes again. She dared a quick glance at him—he could only hope she wasn't being watched—and her eyes were full of question. Someone cried out, and then someone else, and finally a man's deep voice, coming from the center of camp and full of satisfaction, said, "Kalena."

What? Impossible. But the babble of voices only rose as the camp came to life at his back. Kacey, both panicked and astonished, looked to him for explanation so overtly that it was clear everyone else's attention was on something else.

"Stay where you are!" The cry was thin and wavering, full of nerves. And it wasn't Kalena, oh no, that was Teya, Teya come all this way to help him and now blatantly disregarding his orders. *Stay out of sight. No fancy spells. Don't put yourself at risk.* And now, if he was to believe his ears, she was out there in the open, masquerading as Kalena.

"Stay where you are!" Teya repeated. "I'm not alone."

"You're close to it." The same man, the one with confidence; by his voice, he had shaken off the malaise that seemed to grip the rest of the camp.

"I just came to talk to you, so keep your distance. That's all, I just want to talk."

"I bet you do."

Not to talk. To grab the attention of whoever had been about to discover Reandn. And, as foolish as she, he was wasting the gift. *Kacey.*

Reandn eased out from behind the tree, just far enough to see a Teya-sized Kalena standing outside the camp, Vaklar at her shoulder and not looking any happier than Reandn felt. The members of the Knife were moving toward her, but not rushing, not looking as though they actually knew what to do—aside from the man who stood at their head, his arms crossed, his head cocked, eyeing Kalena. *Teya.*

Whoever. Reandn pulled his knife and sprinted for Kacey.

But he'd waited too long.

"*Magic!*" A woman's voice took up the cry and repeated it. "Arik, they're using magic!"

"See to it," the leader snapped.

Reandn's world came crashing to a stop. Stretched by her concurrent spells, Teya's shielding failed; raging magic, a wizard rising to battle, hit him as hard as any blow. He gurgled an involuntary protest and fell, but didn't stay down. Not this time. Not with the strength from Madehy and her unicorns behind him, not with Kacey so close before him. One crawling lurch forward, and her foot was within reach, and he almost grabbed it before he remembered how badly she had hurt it. She shouted something; he couldn't decipher it, hearing only the fear in her voice. Beyond the cries of the Knife and screaming wail of magic, he heard a roar of defiance and thought it might be Vaklar. *Damn* the Knife wizard, anyway, he wasn't going down like this, he wasn't going to fail Kacey. Not now. Not after two years of failing her in other ways. Reandn grabbed at his building anger, the inevitable fury spawned by magic, and honed it into something more of determination.

And blinked as the magic backed off, almost too astonished to take advantage of it—but not quite. He threw himself at the tree and the stout rope circling it, sliding in, stretching almost full length to slip his knife under it and jerk the sharp blade through in one swift cut.

"My hands, my hands!" Kacey thrust them at him and he cut those, too, getting to his knees at the same time. Freed, she grabbed him; he held her while he tried to sort out the chaos around them, to find their best retreat. Teya—looking just like herself—and Vaklar both stood at the upper edge of camp, crouched and ready and with two men down in front Vaklar already. The rest of the Knife were out of reach, hesitating between camp and Vaklar—and then the tenor of the shouting changed and they *all* looked to the center of camp, where an astonished woman slowly lost her hold on the slumping man who had fallen back on her, a feathered shaft jutting from his breast. Beside her, the leader jerked his gaze from place to place, searching for . . .

Who? Who the Lonely Hells . . . ?

Reandn gritted his teeth against the angry magic in his head and fought to find the focus that had gotten him this far. The startled wizard, whoever it was, wouldn't leave him this slack forever. He had to get Kacey away before someone saw him—

Kacey clutched at him as someone shouted out and flung a hand to point; in an instant, the Knife were all following that hand—but not, as it appeared, to look at Reandn and Kacey. The Knife wizard's rough spellmaking died completely; even Teya and Vaklar appeared startled. In astonishment, Kacey said, "Dan!" and Reandn finally dared a quick glance away from the Knife, up to the cliff at which they all stared.

There stood Madehy, half-concealed behind a tenaciously growing tree on the edge of the cliff, bow in hand and dismay on her face. In the gap of silence that followed her discovery, she looked behind herself and quite clearly if inexplicably said, "Better start looking for rocks."

"Rethia," Kacey said faintly, getting the same brief glimpse of a pale blonde head that Reandn did.

Can't help her from here. Couldn't do anything from here but get caught. Reandn stood, shoving his body through the leftover tremble from the magic. He tugged Kacey up, steadying her as she wavered, curling his arm around her waist and prepared to all but carry her out of the camp. His eyes were back on the astonished Knife, watching as someone scrambled for a bow, as someone else sprinted for the place where the diminishing edge of the cliff faded into the rim of the shallow hollow before it—and as someone else's eyes finally fell on him and Kacey. The leader of the Knife, his head lifting and his jaw setting, as if Reandn's presence was the final insult in this unforeseen tumult.

Reandn froze, and then slowly eased his grip on Kacey. Quietly, almost casually, he asked, "Can you walk at all?"

"No," Kacey said, and her voice held unexpected and dark irony. "But I can crawl."

"Then be ready to do it." Reandn shifted his grip on his knife and eased away from her reluctant grasp, leaving her only an arm to hold on to and steady herself.

"Dan . . ." she said. "Dan, no. Please don't—"

He turned on her, fierce in his eyes, harsh in his voice. "And if not, what?"

For that she didn't have an answer, and though her chin gave a quiver and her eyes filled, she slowly released his arm, wobbling on one leg for an instant before turning away and reaching for the ground.

"Stop this!"

Kalena. Not some wizardly imitation, not Teya grasping at straws. Kalena, standing in clear view at the top of the cliff, set apart from Madehy and Rethia . . . and shaking visibly, just as her voice quavered around the command she tried to put in her words. "Stop this!" she said, but the two on the cliff kept coming, and Madehy was at no angle to aim at them. *Don't fight*, Reandn thought fiercely at them. *Don't fight*. Madehy glanced at him, pale and stiff and frozen in place, but the man who closed in on her looked very much like he was simply going to jerk her right over the edge of the cliff anyway.

Until an arrow sprouted from his side, causing a stumble, a misstep—and it was he who tumbled from the cliff, hitting the ground with a thud that again silenced the entire camp, silence enough to hear a small trickle of shale follow him down. No one moved; no one dared.

Reandn saw him first, on the rim of camp opposite where he had sent Kacey. Madehy's hunter, bow in one hand, another arrow in the other, coolly waiting to see if anyone else needed stopping—though the bowman who had been heading for Madehy had an arrow nocked and ready, and an easy mark on the hunter.

The Knife's man Arik held a hand high over his head, and called, "Hold!"

And everyone did. Even Vaklar and Teya, who looked more than equal to handling the two Knife left to engage them. Two more had been headed for Reandn; they hesitated where they were at Arik's cry, halfway between Reandn and the center of camp.

Arik pointed at the hunter, his voice raised only enough so the man could hear. "Consider yourself out of this, now. Or else die."

The hunter lowered his bow, his eyes more on Madehy than Arik—and the arrow still in his other hand, ready to nock.

"Watch him," Arik said shortly, and turned his attention back to Kalena. "Well, well," he said. "Now *this* is our Kalennie."

Kalena pinked. "Not yours."

He shrugged. "Soon enough, I think."

"I didn't come here to end up in your hands." Kalena's voice wavered; she hid her shaking hands by crossing her arms across her stomach, and lifted the chin that so sharply defined her lower lip. "I came to put a stop to this. What do you think you're going to gain by taking me? More dead of your Knife, I think, and there seem to be plenty of those already."

"What we hoped to gain in the first place," Arik said, with a slow grin and plenty of confidence. "You don't matter to us at all, Kalennie. Not really. Getting the attention of those idiots at home who're bound on ruining the Resiores, now—*that* matters."

"This isn't the way to do it!" Kalena took a stumbling step backwards, as if pushed by the glint in his eye.

"They haven't listened to anything else, now, have they then?" called another man, one of the more ragged of the lot.

"Perhaps," Kalena shot back at him, "they didn't think you had anything to say aside from demonstrating your joy in setting fires! Or could it be that they mistook those actions as statements of your heartless disdain for our mountains?"

"By the Bright Lady." Arik cocked his head and squinted up at her. "You already talk like a bloody-damned ambassador."

He was only playing with her. Reandn wondered if Kalena realized it, and thought that the sudden desperate look in her eye might indicate she did. He glanced down at Kacey, whose baffled expression reminded him that she knew little of the details around her own unexpected adventure; he thought to tell her to go while she could, but caught sight of the two men closest to him, and the unspoken threat in their eyes. It sparked against his lurking anger, the helplessness he'd felt the evening before, unable to do anything but watch the scrying. He drew himself up then, his eyes narrowing into shadows of grey and the challenge spreading to the crooked grin that never meant anything but trouble. They had hurt her, they had terrorized her, and now he wasn't about to let them stop her flight—however slow it was—to safety.

No. A wrong move now, and he'd end the tenuous hold Kalena had on the Knife, that hold on the restless violence simmering between them all. Kacey whispered his name; he discovered that she had gone frozen, that she was as afraid of his reaction now as she had been of the Knife before. He hesitated, holding her gaze—holding on to it. Leaning on it. The one that was practical, and always thinking of consequences, and that now so feared the consequences she saw before her.

To ignore that fear now would be as much a betrayal as never having come for her in the first place.

Reandn lowered his hands and rested the knife against his leg, stepping back; he shook his head at the two men. Not now. Maybe soon, maybe within the next few moments, but not just now.

Kalena had been staring at Arik, and her flush was different now, a touch of the temper Reandn had so often seen. "I *am* an ambassador," she said. "Whether you like it or not, and despite what the Allegients expect of me. Do you think they won't send someone else after me? Do you really think you'll do any good here? You'll get attention, yes, but who's going to take you seriously? The Shining Knife, dedicating to cutting us off from the evil influences of magic, and here you are with a wizard in the midst of you!"

Another man stepped forward—slighter, older, hair going grey and face worn, he moved in beside Arik but, somehow, didn't quite align himself with the man. "Naya, we'll have only the truth about that, then. The woman's only with us for defense against whatever your kind might throw against us. And you—once we have you, then both Keland and the home hills will be forced to listen to what we have to say. You'll naya listen otherwise, you've already proven that."

Arik gave him an annoyed glare, and pointedly stepped forward so that his back was to the man.

Pay attention, Kalena. Dissension within the ranks. Use it.

Goddess bless, she did. She ignored Arik and said quite sweetly, "For a wizard whose purpose is to defend, she certainly throws a lot of magic around in response to a simple glamour, doesn't she?"

Teya picked right up on the cue. "I worked no magic against the Knife. I disguised myself, that's all."

"She mistook it, then," the man said.

"That would be like mistaking your mother for your father." Teya put just the right note in her voice, the casual assurance of truth.

"On the road, then!" A woman spoke up, moving in beside the second man. "That other wizard, the man—"

"Was forbidden magic, because I didn't know he had it," Vaklar rumbled. "And I'd have squashed him like a bug if I'd known. I've no use for magic that causes more trouble than it solves."

"He used it only after he was attacked by your wizard," Kalena said, and looked suddenly, wickedly triumphant. "Do you want the proof?"

"And what proof could you possibly have?" Arik's scorn filled the camp, and was echoed by half a dozen voices.

Reandn got the uneasy feeling that he wasn't going to like what came next . . . and he didn't.

"We've a man among us who falls ill at the use of magic." Kalena didn't have to point at him; all she did was glance, and suddenly everyone was looking at him. Reandn glared back, but reserved the heat of it for Kalena. "Do you really think the Keep would have sent him to fight alongside magic? The Keep wizard was with us for communication purposes only."

"Prove it," Arik said, planting his feet in a defiant stance.

"Naya, they don't have to," the other man said with sudden understanding. "That's the wrangler, the bloody-damned fellow who killed so many of us. Those who lived through that fight remember well enough—aya, he fought like a man with too much drink, and at the same time like a man with none at all. When he fell there at the end, I thought someone else had got through to him. But none of us claimed it. You, then—" he looked straight at Reandn. "Was it the magic, then, that took you down?"

Reandn met his eyes for a hard minute and then growled, "Yes, dammit. Keep it to yourselves."

Unnerved by his belligerent response, Kalena lost some of the certainty she'd gained, but the Knife man seemed to gain strength of purpose. He nodded at Reandn. "We've a problem, then, Arik."

"You certainly do." Kalena was too eager to be subtle; the slight tremor was back in her voice. If she lost them now, there'd be no second chance. "No one's going to take your concerns seriously if they know you'll throw magic around when it suits you. When it's convenient."

Arik turned away from her in a show of boredom. "This conversation grows absurd. Who's got a bow? A sling? What we *want* is standing right there in front of us."

"That's right," Kalena said, too quickly. "Without me, you'll never get a speaker into the Keep. If you want to be heard, that's the way to do it."

"A *bow*," Arik snapped, putting out his hand. But no one responded, until a woman stepped up behind him, wearing the same look of inflexible tenacity he bore; he snatched the weapon out of her hands and nocked an arrow, swiftly raising it to draw aim on Kalena. Kalena shrieked and jumped back, losing her footing and crab-scrambling away from her exposed position.

The camp erupted in a crowded scuffle; even the man who was halfway up the cliffside, holding an arrow on the hunter, leapt back down to throw himself in the fray. Madehy disappeared from beside the tree; Reandn thought he caught a glimpse of Rethia's hair as they ducked away from the cliff, but he was busy enough grabbing Kacey up, setting his jaw at her cry of pain and hustling her away from the camp.

He didn't take her far. In a mad rush of ducking brush and stumbling when their weight came together off-balance, they climbed back up to the rim of the hollow and halted, panting. The distance between them and the Knife was as much symbolic as truly effective, although high ground was always nice. They turned to put their face to the enemy and stood panting as Reandn grabbed a tree to steady them both. Below, the scuffling had taken on patterns and was all but over; the Knife man held Arik's bow up high in his victory. Reandn stared down at them all and tried to figure out just what had happened to divide them so suddenly and decisively.

"I think . . . I want . . . to sit," Kacey panted, and he discovered with some surprise that he'd never let go of her, that his arm was still wrapped firmly around her soft waist and that indeed he'd been drawing some reassurance from the fact. But when he released her she yet held his shoulders for balance, and he frowned down at her, holding her eyes as if he might find some

kind of answer there. Still breathless, she returned the
frown in kind. "What?"

He didn't have an answer for her. He didn't even have
an answer for himself, and found he was thinking not
in words or concepts but in feelings, long buried and
long denied. So he did the only thing left to him, and
took her face between his hands and kissed her deeply.

When he released her he found her eyes wide open,
staring at him with a vague kind of comprehension, a
little frown drawing her eyebrows together. He just
looked at her with his mouth open and no words coming
out. *I—*, he almost started, and then *You—*, and even
We—, until he finally gave up and just shook his head,
still unable to look away from her.

"Reandn!" Teya's call filtered through the woods like
an intrusive, foreign thing. Suddenly, although neither
of them had moved, they didn't seem to be standing so
close together anymore.

"We're here," Reandn said, raising his voice but not
quite shouting, and not quite yet able to look away from
Kacey's eyes. But in the next moment he did, and
discovered Teya and Vaklar running to join them from
one side, and Rethia and Madehy sliding down the
diminished cliff where it sank down to meet the rim of
the hollow, joining them from the other.

"Kalena?" he asked, suddenly alarmed, as Rethia ran
to her sister, catching her in a fierce hold—a study in
contrast, with her pale hair up against Kacey's brown,
her slenderness distinct against Kacey's full form; Reandn
tore his eyes from them. "Where's Kalena?"

Teya pointed, and Reandn discovered Kalena venturing
back out to where she'd been. On the top of the cliff.
Exposed to sling and arrow, still pale, still shaking. Below
her, the Knife man had moved closer to the cliff, making
conversation more convenient—and correspondingly less
available for anyone else's ears.

"Bloody damn!" Vaklar cursed with great feeling, and
set his hand on his belted dagger, his skin once more

stained with drying blood. "Down we go, then, into it again."

Reandn stepped away from Kacey, his hand trailing down her back in an absent and wistful gesture. "Let's go, then, ladaboy."

Vaklar gave him a meaningfully cocked eyebrow, but it seemed to Reandn that he was hiding wry amusement as well. All for the good if he was still able to find amusement in anything, after this day.

Together they returned to the camp, making no attempt whatsoever to conceal themselves; the Knife were down by two more and had three on Arik and the woman who seemed to be their wizard; the odds remained dismal, but less dismal than before. Almost right up to the gathered Knife they went before stopping under the gaze of the ragged man. Vaklar crossed his arms across his broad chest. "She's under my protection, aya?"

"And mine," Reandn added, more quietly, just as assertively.

"And *mine*," said Madehy from the side of the hill, her bow propped on her knee, an arrow hanging casually from her hand. She looked at the hunter, who merely nodded.

Teya the wizard wisely kept silent.

The ragged man shook his head. "You're wrong if you think the Knife will walk away from this fight."

"No one's asking you to do that," Kalena said. "So let's do this another way, meir—what's your name?"

"Fiers." He proffered the name in a flat tone, with no hope and clearly no expectation that she had anything interesting to say. "And naya start up with this *going to the Keep*. You know we'd never live to see the day."

"Under my protection, *you* would. And under my protection, you would have a voice at the Keep. That's been your problem, hasn't it? Most of the Knife are lowborn, and the ones that aren't hide themselves behind anonymous donations of supplies or coin . . . none of

the Highborn, Resioran or Keland, feel much obliged
to listen to you. It'd be different if you arrived with
me."

"Naya, you must take me for a fool." The man's rough
anger stirred his followers; Vaklar took a step forward,
and Reandn, standing hip-cocked and casual, put a hand
on his knife. "You'd not give away such an advantage,
were it a true one."

Kalena put her shaking hands behind her back and
said, "I see great advantage to getting out of these woods
with my life intact. And frankly, I can scarcely consider
the Knife a true threat in anything other than the
random mayhem and suffering you provoke. Politically,
my position—and that of my countrymen—is quite
secure, whether you come to the Keep as an official
representative of your group or not."

Fiers' eyebrows all but climbed up his forehead.
"Snotty little Highborn bitch, you are."

"Yes," Kalena said, without a whit of humility. "That's
why I'm here, isn't it?"

Fiers glanced at the men and women around him,
an unspoken request for their opinions. No one said
anything; no one gave him anything but expressions of
grave and skeptical doubt. Kalena stepped back from
the cliff edge a pace and glanced behind herself,
obviously eyeing the fastest retreat.

Into their silence, Reandn sent his own matter-of-
fact words. "If you'd liked the way things were being
handled before, we'd still be talking to Arik and his
wizard."

"That wizard was none of our doing!" Fiers said, and
was echoed by the mutters of *naya* from his depleted
Knife. "We wanted none to do with her!"

Reandn took a long look at the vanquished leader, at
the cut of his clothes and the trim of his beard, and
said, "He's not one of you. Not really."

"Naya," said Fiers. "Came with a big lot of money
behind him, though. Too much to say no to."

Reandn exchanged a glance with Vaklar, and then looked up at Kalena, who seemed to be wavering between curiosity at his line of thought and great offense that he dared to step into this conversation. Finally she snapped, *"What?"*

"Just thinking," Reandn said. "Be interesting to know where that money came from. Might be more interesting to know who first came up with the idea of taking Kalena. And who decided that the Knife would start to kill?"

Everyone looked at Arik—and then Fiers glared at Reandn. "Naya," he said. "Don't think to distract me."

"From what?" Reandn said. "Taking Kalena because that's what you set out to do and you can't see beyond it to what she's offering now? Although I feel obliged to point out, you're all but outnumbered, now."

Kalena cleared her throat. She was, Reandn noticed, another step or two further back from the edge, and oh-so-casual about it. And she seemed to have no notion of the fact that Teya was inserting herself, Wolf quiet, into the sheltered spot that Madehy had so recently vacated. "Look. You can try to take me, in which case more of you are going to die, and you'll still have little chance of getting back through the pass with me. You can quietly go away—we won't stop you—and return home to continue burning storehouses. Or you—just Fiers—can come with us and use the chance to tell your side of things at court. Once they're listening here, they'll have to listen at home, too. No Resioran Highborn will let themselves be outdone by Keland's Keep."

Fiers grunted. "That much, we have in common." He glanced at Arik's scowl, and then gave a meaningful look at Reandn and Vaklar. "Were anything to happen to me, the Knife at home won't stop at burning coal anymore."

Coolly, Kalena said, "So I assumed."

"Well, then." Fiers looked around at his fellow Knife, and got shrugs and mutters. Finally one of the women muttered, "I never did like that we started killing."

"Aya, and getting killed," a man said. "We're not

fighters, then, are we? Not a signed-out Dragon among us."

No. If they'd been fighters, this whole series of events would have gone much differently. If Knife inexperience hadn't evened the odds, one of them—or both—might be stiffening under the wagon with their dead.

"But they'll take more notice of us, now," someone pointed out. "Once they know we've this much strength behind our convictions."

"Oh, they already know," Reandn said. "But I'm not sure it's the kind of notice you want."

"Even a fool can kill for his beliefs," Kalena said. "But it won't convince anyone of anything other than the fact that he's a fool."

One of the Knife instantly scooped up a small rock and winged it at her; Kalena gave a small shriek and retreated further. Vaklar stiffened, but Reandn only smiled, a small and tight smile as he shook his head. As impressive as she'd been up on that cliff, as persuasive and quick-thinking, she was still . . . well, she was still Kalena. Or, as the Knife were wont to call her, Kalennie. Spoiled Highborn bitch.

"Here, now," Fiers said mildly, not looking particularly concerned about the rock throwing he remonstrated. "Leave off a minute, at least until we decide. What's it to be?"

"You've been at the head of us since the start, leastways till Arik came in," the woman said. "We'll stand by your decision."

Fiers gave Kalena a long and pensive look, and then did the same to Arik—who, bound and guarded, returned the favor with cold regard. "Your way's no good," Fiers said. "And I'd not be following it naya more—of cert, not until we find out more about the money that came with you."

"That didn't seem to concern you when I offered it to you."

"Naya. Might be that was a mistake on our part, and

maybe no little one." Fiers turned to the woman who had stayed by his side through all the scuffling. "Calova, 'tis your job to wrench some truth from this man and his wizard, while I'm gone."

"Gone?" said the woman, her impassive face looking like it came at a price.

Fiers nodded, glancing up at Kalena. "Oh, aya, we could all go back to the hills and keep on as we've been, but over the last two years that hasn't gotten us far, has it? Have we anything to lose with tryin' something new?"

"You," Calova said pointedly, but offered no other protest.

Arik snorted. "Fool."

Up on the cliff, backed up into a mountain glory, Kalena seemed a tad less pale, but not inclined to close the distance between them again. She sighed loudly. "Good. Then let's end this."

"Not so fast." Fiers moved a few paces away from his Knife to assess them, and then nodded at a man, who stepped forward from the others. "I'll have my own escort, then. Comin' with ye isn't near the same thing as trustin' you."

"Oh, Goddess Grace," Kalena snapped, setting her hands on her hips with such feeling that Reandn thought she might give herself bruises. "Do you think I'm going to lose every bit of honor I have by luring you off into treachery? What kind of future will I have as ambassador if the very first thing I do reeks of betrayal?"

Fiers ducked his head; it seemed to Reandn that he hid a smile in his weathered face, albeit a small and wry one. "I take your point. And I'll take my escort, regardless."

Kalena flung up her hands in dramatic display of exasperation, completely destroying the effect of her ambassadorial dignity. There was, Reandn thought, nothing better she could have done at that moment, for it was honest and human, without any trace of calculation.

Fiers actually chuckled, as quiet as it was, but when he spoke, it was all business. "Calova, see what you can do about quietin' the other Knife squads. Won't look good for us if the raids continue while I'm tryin' to impress the Highborn."

"You want me to return home . . . to leave you alone?"

"I'll have Pevro here," Fiers said brusquely. "And you take care with that wizard."

"Wrap her fingers together," Reandn said, and earned a scathing look from the woman. "Most of them can't put a spell together without the finger-twisting."

Fiers assessed the woman, ignoring the fury on her face. "Aya, I suppose we might drug her at that."

Teya's voice startled them all but Reandn; as one, Knife heads swiveled to locate her where she casually crouched beside Madehy's tree. "She'll be fine without. Her magic's too coarse to come from anything but mnemonics."

"Took you on well enough," the woman said scornfully.

"Startled me, that's true. But it was—" Teya closed her mouth on whatever other words had been hovering there, giving Reandn an enigmatic and somewhat accusing look he all but called her on right then and there.

But magic whispered in the air, just enough that he unthinkingly worked his jaw—and then realized what he'd done. "Teya—"

She made a quick gesture, and the tingle of her shielding dropped over him; other than that, she just waited, the one calm soul in the middle of a suddenly tense camp. After a moment, she gave a hint of a smile, and the shield dropped away. "You see? She's not school trained. The lack does more than leave a wizard without ethics schooling—which," she added, looking at Fiers, "you might want to consider. I wouldn't want to be in the Resiores with magic, either, not if the wizards weren't schooled."

The woman only smiled tightly. "You're not half so smart as you think you are. You'll see."

Fiers snorted at Teya, ignoring the other woman. "You don't really think any of the Knife would consider *inviting* formal magic schooling into the hills, d'ye?"

Teya shrugged. "Magic is here, Fiers. Schooling it is one way to control its use."

Fiers merely shook his head, amused at the very outrageousness of the suggestion. "We've said what we need to, here. You," he looked at Reandn, "take your wizard and your Highborn and set yourself to wait up at the top of the hill. I'll be along shortly—Pevro and I."

Across camp, the hunter tipped his bow at Madehy, and moved off into the trees. Reandn glanced back up the hill behind him. The woods looked empty, but he knew Kacey waited for him there.

Chapter 16

Kacey winced as Rethia eased her boot away from her swollen foot and ankle, and tossed the useless footwear—for of course they'd had to cut it off—at Madehy's scrap pile near the supply cabinets. Rethia gazed at the limb and made a sound of dismay.

"Don't *tsk* at *me*." Kacey scowled and tried to get a glimpse of the ankle herself. "*I* didn't do it."

Reandn, a handful of bridles slung over one shoulder as he moved from the horses to their meager jumble of supplies beneath the cart, hesitated, crouching to rest his hand lightly on Kacey's knee and look at the offending limb. "Tsk."

Kacey narrowed her eyes at him, searching for the best response. In the end she stuck her tongue out and turned away. The ankle already felt better, free of the boot and under Rethia's innately soothing touch.

"I don't know if it's broken," Rethia said. "It might just be a bad turn. We'll poultice it tonight and wrap it tight for travel tomorrow . . . and you're not to walk on it. Not at all."

"But . . . Rethia!" Kacey lost her veneer of composure, for she'd been wondering where Madehy's privy was ever since they had returned here.

Reandn leaned in close and kissed her forehead, shocking her into silence. "I'll get you there," he said. Curse him, anyway, for knowing just what she was thinking. And for knowing just how to throw her off balance.

Although she wouldn't have taken that kiss back for all the bent-up ankles in the world.

"How did you do that?" Rethia pushed Kacey's trouser leg up as far as it would go, and worked a rough towel under her ankle, twitching straight. She glanced up at Reandn. "At the camp, I mean."

Reandn stood, hip-shot and much more tense than that casual stance would suggest. "Do what?"

Rethia only looked at him a moment, as if confused that he didn't know. From the other side of the cart, Elstan's exclaimed protest briefly punctuated the air; Vaklar had taken it upon himself to explain their new arrangement with Fiers and his fellow Knife. Teya had hovered around them for a while, harboring an obvious need to talk to Reandn. *Later*, he'd finally told her. Madehy was elsewhere—had, in fact, disappeared before Reandn had made it back up the hill outside the Knife camp. She'd had enough, Rethia had said, more than enough, for her first day back among people, and she supposed they wouldn't see her again before the day was out. And Kalena . . . Kacey had seen her head for the barn loft, and thought she was off in a corner crying somewhere.

Not such a bad idea, now that she came to think about it. But *after* a visit to the privy.

"Manage the magic." Rethia, too, stood; she was eyeing Madehy's cabinets with a speculative gaze, and Kacey knew right then that she was going to get a horse poultice. Rethia's gaze returned to Reandn for a brief and piercing moment. "When Teya lost her shield and you were trying to get to Kacey."

"Manage the—" Reandn didn't even bother to finish. "I *didn't*. If you'll remember, I went most of that distance on my hands and knees. I'm not sure, but I think there were a few moments of bellying, too." His bitter voice reminded Kacey of days past, when he'd arrived with Farren at the clinic and could think of nothing but revenge upon the rogue wizard who had killed his wife.

"Well, yes." Rethia took his strong reaction in stride. "But that woman—what a sloppy wizard! She stirred up far more magic than she needed. You may have been with unicorns yesterday, Danny, but it wasn't enough to protect you from that woman."

"How—"

"Just trust her," Kacey interrupted. "You should know that by now."

Rethia tipped her head in a brief gesture of annoyance. "If there's one thing I *do* know, Reandn the Wolf, it's how much magic you can handle."

Reandn seemed as though he didn't know whether to look irritated or abashed. "Not this time, then. Unicorn winds, Rethia, blame it on the damn unicorns. This whole mess is their fault to begin with."

"*This mess* is human fault," Rethia said sharply, and didn't give him a chance to reply before heading for the supply cabinets.

"It's not easy to make her that mad," Kacey observed. "Now, quick—before she ties me down with that poultice—help me outside!"

Madehy lay in the dark with her eyes open, her arm trailing over the edge of the bed to rest on Kendall's back. Absently, she scratched along the back of his ears; he groaned happily.

Above her, vague and shapeless shadows hinted at the dried herbs tucked in her rafters, resolving into forms only at the outer edges of her visions and coyly fading away when she turned her eyes directly on them. She played this game for a while, testing the limits of her night vision. She stared into the darkness, naming the shapes like she might name drifting clouds on a lazy afternoon.

What she didn't do was close her eyes. What she definitely didn't do was try to sleep, to allow her thoughts to lose structure and wander where they would. She'd slept plenty when she had arrived home before the others, after quickly tending her sheep—out and back again before Elstan, freed from the sleep compulsion and lurking in the barn with dark anger hovering around him, even realized she was home—and mixing up the handful of potions that had been requested of her. Hops poultices with sangrel root and scrubgorst for Vaklar and his people, and then a handful of other remedies—pentstemmon effusion for a wary 'steader expecting two cows to calve, several mixtures of powdered balmony and flagroot for those who hadn't gotten around to worming yet. All one- and two-word requests written by the lone man in the area who could read, and left in the small, flat copper box by her gate. For two years, those notes and an occasional word exchanged with the hunter had been her sole contact with the people in her world. Sometimes she caught sight of someone leaving off an animal; sometimes when she gathered herbs she discovered others, doing the same. But they never saw her.

For two years, this house had been a barrier against all others, protecting her from their unwanted intrusions of self. Now, lying in this bed, awake after hours of dream-plagued sleep and having no desire to return to it, she had come to realize that the house had never been any barrier at all. That she, like Rethia, had determined her own way to deal with the unwitting threat other people represented to her. She'd thought the house a barrier, and in doing so, had made it one.

Madehy gave Kendall a final pat. He lifted his head and gazed at her in the darkness, recognizing finality in the gesture before she did; she had to give him another pat for that. Then, carefully, searching for a place she might stand without stepping on some part of the lounging dog, she slid from the bed and took herself barefoot through the dark house. At the door she hesitated, but only for an instant, and then she was through it and out into the middle of the yard, the ground gone from mud to night-cool dirt after two days of sunny warmth. She fancied she could feel the oval ridges of a hundred overlapping unicorn tracks beneath her toes.

In the barn, everyone slept, their emanations of self muted and soft. Madehy let them wash through her, and then imagined that the house was around her, applying her newly learned sense of *barrier* to the image.

The night turned quiet around her, offering only the rustle of some furtive thing in the woods across the road. That persistent spiny possum, no doubt, heading for the small garbage heap behind her privy. But of those in the barn, she heard nothing. Felt nothing.

She opened the door to her house; just a crack. Quiet whispers of exhaustion, of murky dreams and leftover fears, made her heart quicken. And then she closed the door, and it quickened even more. The whispers silenced utterly.

The answer had been here within her all along.

Instead of elation, Madehy found herself struggling with sudden and overwhelming sorrow—sorrow for the lost time, the hiding and the unspeakable, incomprehensible affliction left to her as a babe. If only she had tried harder to understand . . . if only *she'd* been the one to call back the unicorns—maybe then her life would be different.

Or maybe not. Deliberately, in defiance of the swelling pain in her throat, Madehy again opened the door to the house, the door to herself, and opened it wide. So much easier when they were asleep, and muted, though she hated to think what it would be like to get caught in a nightmare. She had done that all too often, as a child, before magic's return had made a nightmare out of her waking life as well.

She oughtn't to have thought it, she oughtn't to have even *thought* about thinking it. With only the barest flash of a warning, Madehy found herself reeling in a sudden onslaught of pain and fear and humiliation, Kacey's captivity come back to haunt the both of them in dreaming. *Hands tied, foot full of anguish, huge and faceless guards chasing her from tree to tree*—Madehy slammed the door closed and watched in horror as it sprang open again—*while everyone laughed and she lurched along on hands and knees, crawling, groveling, trying to fend them off.* Madehy threw herself on the door, curling her toes against the plain wood boards of her imaginary floor until only the barest crack of an opening remained, a whisper—*they laughed and loomed over her and surrounded her*—and with a only a quiver of warning, the house shuddered, it creaked, and it split wide open, disintegrating around her, leaving her fully exposed as ***their hands plucking at her clothing, pulling her hair, pinching her breasts and bottom.* . . .**

She threw her arms over her head and screamed, slowly collapsing into the smallest possible hedgehog ball, and in her mind the other selves awoke, sharp alarm and confusion and above all, Dan's rising concern. She was all of them all at once, Elstan and Kalena's annoyance and Teya's empathy, with the touch of her own common nightmares, death and dying on a hill. . . . The splinters of Madehy's own house lacerated her soul, and she was Dan's fury and worry, and Kacey's broken-hearted sobs, and she was her own overwhelming grief, left alone in the dirt with nothing more than the ghost of Dan's arms as they went around Kacey, arms that weren't meant for her and meant nothing *to* her.

Until, through the pattern of her sobs, Madehy heard the soft, swift sound of bare feet, running feet, and felt the touch of someone's hands, felt the arms that encircled her and hugged her and rocked her, wrapping her mind in a soft warm quilt of silence. Rethia's arms. Rethia's silence.

The only peace, true safety, Madehy had ever known. And tomorrow it would be gone.

Chapter 17

One young ambassador, badly used and starting to fray around the edges; her only remaining Resioran escort, a big man with the age to know his job and know it well, with the marks on his gear and his person to speak for just how many times he'd had to prove it within the last handful of days. Filling the road around them, an unlikely assortment of companions: in front, a man in an ill-fitting and blood-stained shirt, his eyes ever wary of the road before them and his horse a tad unpredictable. Beside him, a substantial woman on a smooth-moving horse, one foot hanging beside where the stirrup belonged, if it hadn't been flipped up over the horse's withers. Every once in a while she gave him a good, long, searching look, and every once in a while he gave her a rakish grin; both were expressions of great promise.

Ranging restlessly from spot to spot in that group rode a man whose light brown hair had once endlessly flipped into his face; those side locks now hung in two stiff and uneven braids, and somehow suited the uncertain expression that often settled over his features, usually while he was wavering between uncertain amiability and quiet concern—though for what, it wasn't quite evident. His reputation, perhaps.

There was another couple of sorts, a stranger couple; two men who rode in the middle of the group without ever actually being part of it. They answered the questions put to them and offered opinions when they were needed, and had the look of two men committing an act of great and desperate foolishness.

And then there was another woman, someone who had started this journey with her sister, and who now had a new companion—two of them, in fact. The young woman and her huge tawny dog had ridden up from behind on the group's fifth day of travel, two days out of Pasdon, and since then these two had ridden together, their heads often close in conversation. The party's string of laden pack horses—reprovisioned in Pasdon—followed the two of them without lead or word.

Today, Teya rode behind them all, as she often did, and while her eyes watched her companions, her mind imagined how they might look to the Dragons and Wolves Elstan had summoned from the Keep to meet them.

Unexpected, she finally decided. Extremely . . . unexpected.

So far, given the personalities involved, they had all gotten along amazingly well on this journey. One day to Pasdon, and two days of rest and shopping for Kalena, and now they were a day out of Pasdon and heading for the Keep, expecting to meet the Dragons at almost any moment. The weather, while fitful, had given them nothing worse than this day of low, gloomy clouds and occasional cool gust of wind—and anyway, they'd not have felt the sun on this road, where the trees arched to meet overhead—a rare sight in this part of Keland. Aside from the inevitable daily delays Kalena caused—and those delays weren't near as bad as they'd been, Teya was given to understand—the travelers all seemed to be lost in their own thoughts, in their own anticipations—or fears—of what was before them in the Keep.

For herself, she figured she'd be lucky to escape serious trouble for taking the Keep's horse—even if she *was* returning it. She seldom thought of that problem, though. Instead, her thoughts tumbled around with the circumstances of Kacey's rescue, battering her for her performance at the Knife camp. Or her lack thereof. That which she'd wanted to discuss with Reandn for days, and never seemed to find the right moment.

Elstan slowed his horse, letting Rethia and Madehy—and their little following of horses—move past him. When Teya drew alongside, he let his mount out in the same free-swinging walk they'd held in for days now. No hurry; there was no one on their heels anymore—Teya and Elstan's magical sweeps had convinced even Vaklar, if not the two Knife men—and there were enough Keep forces on their way to counter even the most determined human obstacles between here and the relative security of Norposten.

Somehow, they had even managed to keep from tearing one another apart, largely due to, Teya thought, Elstan's relative silence. What concerns he had—and to judge from the little frown that constantly played around his eyes, there were plenty—he kept to himself. Not something that he felt he could do anything about, then. Or that he could bully anyone else into doing something about.

"Relax," she told him, finding that very look on his face right now. "Sometime today we'll meet the Dragons, and then who's going to stop us from delivering the new Resioran ambassador?"

Elstan gave her a dark look. "After the way this assignment has gone, I'm surprised you dare to say such a thing. Although I forget—you weren't here for all of it."

"Just as well." Teya gave her horse's neck a studious examination, fussing where a cowlick kept the mane flipped up at a funny angle. "I wouldn't have been of much help."

"What?" He said it as though he didn't believe what

he'd heard. "What're you talking about? Do you know how much easier *he's*," and Elstan's chin jerked forward, no doubt meant to indicate Reandn, "been to live with since you showed up?"

"That's just because I can protect him from the magic," Teya said, and then thought again of the Knife camp. "Well, usually."

He regarded her with great skepticism, and no apparent awareness that one of his unevenly woven braids was sticking out to the side at an odd and unfortunately humorous angle. "You're a patrol wizard," he said. "The wizard in that camp wasn't anything special—her magic spilled all over the place. The two times she came after me, it was all force and power and no finesse. I can't believe you had any trouble with her." *I didn't*, he seemed to want to add, and didn't. The restraint made Teya wonder; until they'd started this trip back she'd seen nothing at all of restraint in Elstan.

So she used restraint as well, and didn't mention that as far as she was concerned, his own magic came in rough and unpolished form, a characteristic problem with wizards who started spinning spells for the sake of the magic they could pull up, and not for the sake and presentation of the spell itself. The Knife wizard . . . that had been like running into a brick wall of magic, and while it hadn't been shaped into anything dangerous—not for lack of trying, just lack of success—the pure assault of it had startled Teya away from her own spells. Her glamour had fallen, her shielding had dissolved—and she had watched Reandn go down.

After that, the Knife wizard's magic had only increased in intensity without focusing in intent . . . and Teya, try as she might—and oh, how she'd tried!—had never been able to regrasp even the shielding spell she knew so well.

Patrol wizard, yes. But not one you'd want watching your back when there was offensive magic flinging around. Sadly, she thought of all her drills, all the practicing she'd done in Solace. True, she'd kept her head this time. She'd known what spell she *wanted*—a nice little hotfoot, to keep that wizard thinking of something else, as well as getting her own shielding rebuilt—but she hadn't been able to carry through on it.

She realized, then, that she hadn't ever responded to Elstan, but when she finally glanced at him—a quick glance, for she was certain he'd read the failure in her eyes—she did it twice. He, too, seemed to have gotten lost in thought, whichever thought brought his own worry. Teya stifled the smile that threatened to play around her mouth; here he was, looking actually human and approachable, and there was that . . . *braid*. Someone was going to have to tell him.

But it wasn't going to be Teya.

She put a sensible expression on her face instead, and said, "What's the worry, Elstan? Don't know what to give Kalena for lunch?"

"Tenaebra take Kalena's opinions about eating on the road," Elstan said with a scowl, but it lightened up as he saw she was poking fun at Kalena, and not at his predicament in his newest role. If he'd started this trip as a wizard pretending to be a guide, he'd ended it as Kalena's official journey cook . . . a demonstratively thankless task. After a moment, he gave her the real answer. "The Knife," he said. "I don't think they're a good idea. Even supposing they're just about what they say they are, bringing them into the Keep is going to cause trouble. Bloody Hells, introducing them to a bunch of Dragons is going to cause trouble enough!"

Teya's first reaction was to brush his words away, for after she'd heard what he'd put Reandn through, and after she'd seen him lash out, unthinkingly lost in his pride and with a horseshoe-loaded fist, she'd become almost automatic in dismissing his reactions. But something sensible within her noted that Elstan wasn't blustering, or shouting, or shoving his magic where it didn't belong. He was simply and truly worried.

She tried to sound matter-of-fact. "Dragons can be

rough, but they're as loyal as any Wolf. They'll behave themselves. At least when they're against someone, it's easy to tell—unlike what little I've seen of court."

"There is that," Elstan agreed, his flat voice completely unconvincing.

It occurred to Teya to wonder if he might know something she didn't. After all, alone of all of them, he *did* have recent Keep court experience. And so she began to worry, too. And to sift through her arsenal of memorized spells, looking for some small thing she might hope to pull off in the midst of trouble.

"I want to ride back to Little Wisdom with you," Kacey said, in that implacable way she had. She didn't look at him; she didn't look down at her horse. She watched the road with dogged determination in the set of her jaw.

Reandn knew better than even to consider saying *no*, and didn't bother to argue the point. At least, not head-on. "It's fourteen days of steady riding," he said. "That's a lot for someone who can't even put her foot in the stirrup. And I have no idea when Saxe will let me leave. There's a lot to sort out."

"The longer it takes, the stronger my ankle will be for the trip."

"Kacey—"

"Reandn." Her voice came out lower than normal, and her eyes turned much too serious for the conversation; the combination cut him short. "Dan . . . if I go back with Rethia . . . that is, if we put all that time between us—"

"You're afraid." The realization came with something more akin to shock than surprise. "Kacey, you're *afraid*."

"I am not."

He had the notion that if he'd been of a mind to test it, they could have continued with "are too" and "am not" for far longer than would have been amusing. For whatever Kacey had been about to say, whatever she'd been about to confess to, she'd locked it back behind those brown eyes of hers, putting distance between them.

Nonsense. Not after what they'd been through. Not after the vast shift in thought he'd finally taken; he recalled Adela's last good-bye with affection now, and as sacrifice instead of abandonment. And he knew she'd been right to leave. He nudged Sky over so his leg bumped her horse just before hers, and her leg fit in behind his. Neither horse thought much of the arrangement. "If you think I'm going to show up at your house having conveniently forgotten the things we haven't yet said out loud, you're mistaken. I've traveled an even longer way to get where I am now . . . you're one of the few who know just how far. I'm slow, Kacey, but I know how to follow a trail. I'm not going to lose my way now."

Kacey gave an audible and pointed sniff, but wouldn't yet look at him, no matter how he crowded her horse. "Well," she admitted, quietly enough so that he wouldn't have heard her if he hadn't been so close, "maybe I am afraid. Which is worse, do you suppose—being afraid you'll never have something, or being afraid of losing it?"

That question didn't take much thought. "Having something and not knowing it."

"Well, then," she said, the starch returning to her voice, and her eye on him turning bright and wicked, "you ought to feel Goddess-blessed to have *it* by your side all the way to Little Wisdom. There *are* worse things than having to spend a long stretch of early summer days alone with someone who . . ." and here she seemed to surprise herself, but said it anyway, "who loves you."

Reandn lowered his voice and said, "If you keep looking at me like that, I'm going to get distracted and stupid, and probably fall off this horse."

"Wouldn't want that." She adjusted her reins with an air of innocence, and then quite deliberately . . . *looked* at him.

Reandn closed his eyes and groaned. Now here was a side of Kacey he'd never seen before. Something, he supposed, he'd just . . . have to get used to. Somehow.

He found the thought cheering and opened his eyes to give her his most rakish grin. But she was, he discovered, already looking at something else.

Red. Movements of red in the curving road ahead of them, standing out brightly in the shade of the spring green roadside growth. "Dragons," Reandn said. "Squad of the Reds, it looks like. That's odd. The Blues usually handle the north." Not that he minded; the First was bound to be along, and Blue First and he had . . . a past full of grudge.

"Maybe someone warned them they'd be meeting *you.*"

He gave her a quick frown. "I'll regret telling you about that incident, I think." No, he was sure.

Rethia called ahead to him, nothing but his name, but there was something in her voice that made him halt Sky, taking Kacey by surprise. Another moment and they were all stopped, and all wondering; Reandn quickly threaded Sky back through the group to where Rethia, tense and alarmed, watched Madehy's paled face. Behind them, Teya waited, concerned and uncomprehending, while Elstan slowly took his horse a few unwilling steps backward. Reandn narrowed his eyes at the wizard, perfectly willing to end their uneasy truce. "What's going on?"

"She'll be all right," Rethia said, managing a comforting touch on Madehy's shoulder before Kendall crashed out of the brush to investigate the delay and the horses shifted apart.

Sky sidled away with a great snort of roll-eyed drama, and Reandn gave him a thump with his heel. "Not now, Sky." And, with another glance at Elstan before he reassessed Madehy and found her already sitting straighter, if refusing to meet his gaze as always, he said, "We can move on, then? The Dragons are just ahead, and we'll get a chance to rest, then."

"No!" Madehy's exclamation burst out of her as if

against her will; she bit her lip and looked away, not even meeting Rethia's eyes this time.

"That's just it," Rethia said. "The Dragons. As soon as we realized they were there . . . well, Madehy wasn't ready for it. She'd had her door open. We were practicing . . ." She stopped, as if realizing she hadn't managed to tell him the actual problem yet.

Madehy deliberately raised her head, catching his eye for the merest instant with her marbled gaze. He knew the effort it had taken, and he knew how serious she was. "He's afraid," she said. "He saw they were Reds, and he's afraid."

Reandn didn't have to ask who. Even Teya understood, and gave the other wizard a glance that turned surprised when she realized how he'd removed himself from them.

He seemed to notice what he'd done for the first time, as if betrayed by a horse who was paying too much attention to his body language. His defiant words were nothing against the flush of his face. "I was expecting Blues, that's all."

Teya cocked her head at him, her matter-of-fact tone leaving no room for argument. "You've been worried for days, Elstan."

"You've definitely kept your attitude to yourself lately." Reandn had been relieved enough not to question it before, had assumed that the wizard regretted his lack of participation in Kalena's grand first accomplishment as Resioran ambassador. To be entering the Keep with the first of the Knife willing to do anything besides play with fire and destruction . . .

But then again, Elstan was of the court. He'd have known how to put the right spin on it, the things to neglect mentioning . . . soon enough, everyone would have forgotten just exactly what his role had been, and only that he'd been there.

"Danny," Rethia said. It's all she *had* to say, sitting so tall and still on her horse, looking at him so intently. *This is important.*

"You'll have to do better than that, Elstan." Reandn moved Sky up, close enough that Elstan backed his horse another few steps, a few very deliberate and self-aware steps this time. "You've had your own plans for this trip right from the start, and they had more to do with what *you'd* get out of it than with getting Kalena safely to the Keep. Otherwise, you'd never have pretended you could shield me from your magic; you'd never have done anything to compromise the escort in any way."

"Dan?" Vaklar called from the front of the group. "What's up, then?"

"I'm about to find out." Reandn didn't take his eyes from Elstan, didn't give him a moment's peace. "Until then, we don't want to get too close to those Dragons." And he smiled at Elstan, a grim and humorless expression. "Do you know what Vaklar will do to you if you know of some new danger to Kalena, and you don't tell us about it?"

Teya moved in beside him, her voice just as cold. "I know how many of us are just going to watch Vaklar do it."

"Bloody Hells," Elstan muttered, with plenty of feeling behind it. "It could be nothing, *nothing*. You don't know what they'll do to me—"

All right then. They didn't have any time to fool around with this. "Vaklar, I think you'll want in on this. Bring Kalena; we're going to fall back before they get too close." Then he turned to Teya, and said, "See? I don't always break their noses. With any luck, I won't even lose my temper."

"Vaklar ought to be enough, from what I've seen of him," Teya observed soberly.

Vaklar trotted up to them, Kalena by his side; Kacey now trailed the group and they slowly backtracked their path, forcing Elstan to do the same. "Ten'tits," Vaklar said, pulling up beside Reandn, "what the Lonely Hells're you up to, Dan? Tormenting Elstan again? *Now*? What're those Dragons of yours going to think when they see us moving away?"

"That's a good question. Elstan might provide the answer."

Vaklar's bafflement turned quickly to something more serious; it took only another moment before he'd assessed the situation. "Aya? What's the good ladaboy got to tell us?"

"The Dragon Blues usually handle any action up this way. Instead we've got the Reds. And thanks to Madehy, we know how much this discovery upsets Elstan."

"Ah," Vaklar said, and frowned. "But naya *why*, am I right?"

"Oh, for the Goddesses' sake," Elstan snapped. "You can stop playing your intimidating little games. You're right enough—I think the Reds could mean trouble."

Reandn raised an eyebrow. "Because . . . ?"

"Bloody damned Wolf," Elstan muttered. "Because Malik's associated with the Reds, and Malik's trouble."

Kalena's initial perplexion quickly turned to Highborn irritation. "If you're going to lie, do a better job of it. Malik is my father's friend and business associate. He *offered* to come out here last fall and finalize the arrangements for my arrival—before I even knew about it, mind you—and to make sure everything was handled properly upon my arrival."

But Reandn had gone still and cold. He repeated flatly, "He *offered*." Elstan's mixture of relief and dismay told Reandn he was on the right track. Kalena shook her head in pure denial, and said again, "You're wrong."

Vaklar watched the byplay between them all, and demanded, "Dan, what—?"

"Malik," Reandn said. "He's made the arrangements; he set this whole thing up. What do you want to bet he knew Elstan didn't have the magic either to shield me or truly protect Kalena?"

"I had all the magic he needed," Elstan snapped, flaring

into self-betrayal. Silence followed his statement, as he realized what he had said.

"It's over now, ladaboy," Vaklar finally said, deceptively quiet; he moved his horse around to block the road. Ahead of them, the Dragons, now in plain view, had noted their strange behavior and halted; several of them were in deep conversation. "Give over with the rest of it."

Elstan looked at them all, one by one; they had him effectively surrounded, and while they weren't pressing in on him, he found no understanding or sympathy among them. Teya's reins rested loosely on her horse's neck, her hands ready to twist up magic if Elstan tried anything. While Reandn watched, Elstan worked from defiance to defeat, from tension to resignation. He sighed, and dropped his own reins, but it was a signal of surrender and not a precurser to spell-working; he kept his fingers quiet with the same deliberate passivity that Reandn would use to show an empty hand instead of the knife that many of the patrol's quarries feared. Quietly, Elstan said, "I never planned for any harm to come to Kalena, or anyone else."

Vaklar's eyes flashed; Reandn felt his own go hard. "That didn't exactly work out, then, did it?"

"It wasn't my fault!" Elstan's response seemed almost automatic; and for once no one argued with him. They just watched him. Even Madehy; though she watched his throat instead of his face, and although she'd known none of the dead, her face was just as grim as those of the rest. Their silence condemned his words as well as anything could. "I tried!" Elstan said, desperate for belief. "I really tried! But something kept throwing my spells off." He gave Reandn a bitter look. "I know you think I've no magic of worth, but the truth is, except for the shielding I never learned how to do, I've never had any trouble. And I honestly thought I could learn the shielding."

Teya said coldly, "There's a vast difference in the precision needed for the level of spells you probably used at court and spells that have to work in the field. People are so awed by magic, they don't notice the flaws around the edges of a flashy spell. It *matters* when you put those same flaws into spells you want to protect someone. Believe me, I know."

He had been preparing to strike back at her, bitterness intact . . . but her last words stopped him cold. As did Vaklar.

"Ladaboy, the Dragons are waiting now, but they won't wait forever. And we've no more idea what you're about than when you started talking."

"Just tell us," Reandn said. "Don't bother with the excuses. You'll have plenty of chances for those, later— if you're lucky."

"If we're *all* lucky," Madehy said, giving the Dragons a wary glance over her shoulder.

Elstan fidgeted; he lost all traces of court poise and affectation. "After Malik arrived in the Keep, he spent some time with all the wizards there, and in the end, he settled on me. He asked me if I wanted a chance for independence from the court—from being on stage all the time, with no real chance to learn magic."

"The school is free to anyone who qualifies, which you most certainly would." Teya wouldn't even give him that much of an excuse.

"Later," Reandn murmured, and she subsided.

Elstan limited himself to a glare of response. "What he wanted was someone to travel with the escort . . . someone to keep the Knife wizard informed about our circumstances and progress."

"Those times you contacted the Keep," Reandn said, "you weren't talking to anyone at the Keep at all."

Elstan rubbed a dirty finger across the bridge of his nose. "Well, sometimes I was. But not always, no. Sometimes it was Malik; sometimes it was the Knife wizard."

"No wonder you wanted nothing to do with the rescue," Teya said. "She'd have recognized you instantly."

Nodding, Elstan said, "I don't know why Malik conspired to do you harm, Kalena. But I never intended to let it happen. I thought . . . I thought it would be the perfect opportunity to prove myself. I'd play along, and then when the attack came, I'd be the only one truly ready to fend it off. And I *was* ready. I studied battle spells. I just . . . wasn't expecting Dan to need as much shielding as he did. Or for the spells to keep breaking apart. We . . ." he said it as if realizing it for the first time, "we'd have been dead on that road, if the Knife wizard's spells hadn't turned out the same way."

Vaklar grunted. "We're bloody-damned lucky not to be dead on that road anyway, boyo."

"We might end up dead on *this* road," Madehy said, and there was a tremor in her voice. Rethia took her arm and murmured a suggestion; Madehy took a deep breath, closed her eyes, and muttered something under her breath. When she opened her eyes again, she was visibly calmer. All she said was, "Don't doubt his word, Dan. Whatever he may have said before . . . this is the truth."

Kalena clutched at her saddle pommel, as if it were the only thing keeping her upright—and as shaken as she was, Reandn thought that such very well might be the case. "Malik," she said. "I've known him since I was a *girl*—"

"But he's been borderline Highborn all his life," Reandn said, recalling Saxe's words. "He's in coal, and most of the coal families lean toward Geltria."

"You think he'd betray me for the coal families?" Kalena couldn't fathom it.

"It'd be one way to get over that border between merchant and Highborn," Vaklar said soberly. "Aya, they'd owe him that much."

Kalena gave up half her grip on the saddle to point at Elstan. "You called me Kalennie. That's how he's always known me. I thought you were . . . I thought you were being deliberately rude, back at Madehy's. You as much as told me you were working with someone, and I didn't catch it!"

Elstan had the grace to look abashed. "He does call you Kalennie. But it didn't matter by then, anyway. I'd betrayed them, and the Knife, at least, knew it. I don't think Malik does."

"I knew the wizard woman was working with someone," Fiers said. "Only Arik knew the details, him and his sponsor. By Tenaebra's Hand, I wish I'd stayed to see what my people learned from him. It might well help us now." That statement got Vaklar's attention, and Fiers gave a short laugh. "We're in worse danger than your ambassador, I'd say, if any of Malik's men realize who we are." His companion shifted in the saddle, fingering the sling he wore on his belt.

Reandn nodded—two more hands, then—for they would certainly fight with determination if not skill— and went back to watching the Dragons, who were again moving in on them, not far at all now; Reandn lowered his voice. "How many Reds does Malik have?" He eyed the squad, caught by a familiar snatch of brown in all that red. "Did they say anything about bringing Wolves along with them?"

"Two of them, I think," Elstan said. "I don't know how many Reds are loyal to Malik. As many as he could buy, I suppose. No more than a handful."

Reandn considered the Dragons, and wondered about the Wolves. Once, he'd have sworn that no Wolf could be bought . . . but his blind faith had eroded some in recent days. "A handful. Then they can't *all* be trouble."

"Dan, you say that like you've got a thought." Vaklar scratched his square jaw. "You have a mind to share it?"

"If they're not all his, then some of them will be here to do just what we need—to protect Kalena."

"And the rest of us, I hope," Kacey said, but it was clear she didn't take it for granted. No one spoke to reassure her. Once the loyalist Dragons figured out who Kalena was, she would be their priority, and no other.

"The problem," Reandn said, finding it a great effort not to simply take Kacey's hand and tell her he'd keep her safe—false reassurance, given the odds, "is figuring out who's who."

Vaklar snorted, his gloved fingers tightening on the reins; his horse flipped its head up and down until the guard realized what he'd done and offered some slack. "They'll deny any accusations."

Reandn nodded, watching the slowly advancing group—for the closer they got, the more certain he was that one of the Wolves was Faline, once Wolf Third to his Wolf First. They hadn't worked together for two years, but he trusted her; the other Wolf would be from her patrol, and also likely to be trustworthy.

Furthermore, she would know him, and listen to him—and believe what he might say, with as few words and as little time as he might have to say it. Looking at her, assuring himself it was indeed Faline—lanky, short-haired and quiet-spoken—Reandn couldn't help but grin at all the new possibilities she opened up for them.

Teya gave him a sudden wary look. "What're you going to do?" she asked suspiciously, raising her hands as if she could—or would—stop him with some spell.

He shrugged. "What I do best," he said. "Make trouble."

Chapter 18

"Naya, I don't know I like the sound of that." Vaklar rubbed a hand over his jaw, frowning as Reandn dismounted.

"Why don't we just . . . run?" Kalena suggested. "We have horses. They seem to have only one among them."

"We could." Reandn hesitated next to Sky, one hand still on the horse's withers. "That wouldn't really solve anything, and then we'd never know just who Malik has in the Dragons. Eventually you'd land at the Keep, and you'd never know who to trust. Be a lot cleaner to handle this problem here."

Kalena made a face. "There are many more of them than there are of us."

"They're not all Malik's," Kacey said. "They couldn't be. Especially not the Wolves!"

Elstan stared down the road at the squad, where the heated discussion between Faline, the Red that Reandn presumed to be their Squad First, and the single mounted man had ended. The man clambered off his horse—not a graceful man, no, one with a comfortable belly and not many hours in the saddle—and walked slowly toward them. Elstan watched the man with trepidation. "That looks like Malik. I had no idea—"

Reandn went to alert, watching as the approaching man held his hands away from himself in that universal gesture of *no harm meant*, and eventually stopped halfway between the two groups—which were no longer all that far apart. "Kalena! What's wrong?"

Reandn cocked an eyebrow at her; they were close enough that he kept his voice low. "Well? Here he is, Kalena. I can flush his Dragons out for you . . . or not."

"If we don't," Vaklar said, his deep voice gruff in its whisper, "I don't think me that we'll see the inside of your Keep. Not an' we travel with these folk."

Reandn took that as a decision made. "Teya, I want you ready. With any luck, the Reds'll handle their own, but if not, do what you can to protect them." He nodded at Kalena, but he meant them all—the three who'd spent their lives healing, and not fighting—Rethia, Kacey, and Madehy.

No. Not Madehy. She'd brought her hunting bow, and even now dismounted so she could string it—though she did it behind her horse's haunches, where she wasn't likely to be spotted, and she'd already leashed Kendall to a tree.

Elstan had slipped back into his antagonistic self, ready to protest as soon as Reandn's eyes fell on him. Reandn cut him short. "Elstan, with any luck, we'll at least be able to stir Malik's Reds up, enough to spot them. I want you to hold them, if you can."

"I—oh," Elstan said, belatedly realizing he hadn't been counted as useless after all. Possibly it jarred something loose in him, for in a much lowered voice, he said, "I'll do my best. It's not a spell I've used on more than one man at a time before."

And probably then only for his own amusement, Reandn thought, but had moved on to Vaklar. "Trust the Wolves," he said. "The woman is Faline. I know her."

Malik stood before them a moment, all but upon them, and when no one responded to his presence, said, "Kalena? Goddess grace, girl, what's wrong? Why do you stand back and greet me only with furious whispering?"

"Did I mention?" Elstan murmured. "He likes the play of words on his own tongue."

Reandn handed Sky's rein to Kacey and moved forward, stopping just before Malik but standing to the side, his attention on the squad and not Malik. Though Faline's eyes were narrowed in the struggle to identify him, she hadn't done it yet, and no surprise; she probably hadn't given him any close consideration, and was used to seeing him in uniform at that—a uniform, and longer hair in back, the way Adela had always done it. Kacey cut his hair now. "Faline," he said. "It's Dan."

She saw him then, and her eyes went wide. "Dan!" she blurted. "What the Lonely—"

"Part of the escort from the start. Listen, Faline—I need you to trust me here. I need you to hold the Reds back."

The Red next to her—red-shirted, pot-helmed, armed with the shortest of swords and covered with a boiled leather vest that held his Squad ranking—looked startled, and recovered quickly to aim a scowl at Reandn for his presumptuousness. Faline took his arm, whispered a few quick words, persisted when he shook his head. When he subsided, it was with the expression of a man unconvinced and uncommitted, but he wasn't arguing anymore, and that, Reandn thought, might be as much as he'd get.

"And who *are* you?" Malik said, drawing his eyebrows together into an exaggerated peak that made his drawn-out face and the curved nose that went with it look even longer than they were.

Reandn gave him a predatorial smile, and spoke so only Malik would hear. "I'm the one who's going to make your life difficult . . . starting now."

Malik frowned at Reandn as though he were examining

a noxious bug, and then made a *pfft* of dismissal, waving his hand in Reandn's face. "Kalennie, come here and talk to me, child. I know you've had troubles, but I'm here, and this is the end of it. Elstan will protect you; I sent him along especially with your welfare in mind."

"So we heard." Reandn put himself directly between Malik and Kalena. "She doesn't want to talk to you, Malik."

Beneath the frippery of his courtly manners, Malik's eyes, a brown so dark as to look black, were cold and calculating. "Red First," he called, looking away from Reandn for only the briefest of glances at the Dragons, "I think we'll need your help to come to some kind of understanding here."

Reandn caught Faline's eye and shook his head, the tiniest of gestures.

"Kalennie, dear, I'm getting just a bit annoyed at you," Malik said, making another one of his waving-off gestures, his fingers all but brushing Reandn's nose.

Reandn snatched the hand before it left his face and turned it, twisting the thumb around and forcing a pained and astonished cry from Malik.

"Meir!" shouted Red First, and hard on the heels of it came Faline's sharp command.

"No! Hold your place!"

Malik went to his knees, hissing protest, furious but too stunned to truly understand what the strange turn of events meant. Reandn leaned over him. "We know, you see. Those two men, standing behind Vaklar? They're Knife. We've had some nice long talks, and Elstan had some things to say, too. Did you have anything you wanted to add?"

"Fool," Malik grunted, and then cried out like a man in agony and in fear of his life. "Please—First! Ardrith save me for her own! Save Kalena from this man! Get Kalena!"

"Hold!" Faline shouted.

"No Wolf commands me!" one of the Dragons cried,

and with a chorus of roars, a handful of the Dragons broke rank.

"First! Control your men! Dan is one of *us*, you tell them to *back off*!"

Red First roared in fury. "Back in ranks! Fall back!"

But the Dragons came on, drawing steel; Reandn lifted his head and met their charge with a grin, shoving Malik aside, wondering if Elstan would—

There. Magic sang through the air, Teya's shielding and the resonance of Elstan's strong magic right through it. The Dragons faltered, astonished; five out of the twelve Reds were held frozen by the spell, with the remaining men still in formation, restless and angry and resentful, glaring at Faline. Red First looked the same, but Faline had rank on him, and he kept his hands out to either side, a reminder and barrier to those men behind him.

Reandn tried to ignore the thrumming magic and leaped to grab the showing steel of those five caught Dragons, flinging each weapon into the brush, knowing from the men's expressions and their trembling but definite movement that he didn't have long. Tried to ignore it and couldn't, couldn't help the flush of anger, a reaction so ingrained that it was as hard to fight as the magic.

"Reandn, no!" Teya cried. "Don't do that!"

Startled, struggling against building dizziness, he glanced back to see nothing except that her spell was holding up well, a weird eye-twisting glamour that made it hard to locate anyone behind it—but that she hadn't included herself in its protection. Couldn't have, and still been able to perceive the events before her. No one else seemed to notice, for Vaklar and the Knife blocked the road in front of the distorted group, ready to take on the Dragons if they broke free of Elstan's spell.

If. *When*. With a sudden gust of magic that went ragged even through Teya's shielding, the Dragons broke free;

two of them landed on Reandn before he could twist
out of the way, and the others roared and rushed for
Vaklar's line. Reandn squirmed in the dirt, trying to keep
his knife out of a Dragon's reach, all the air slapped
out of his lungs and too much Dragon weight on him
to get it back. They hindered each other as much as
they hindered him, but it was only a matter of time;
his arm was caught beneath him and there was sudden
fire low in his side—with a curse he realized he'd missed
someone's weapon.

But the Dragons' triumph in first blood turned to stiff
astonishment as more of Elstan's magic trickled through
Teya's shield; they froze—at what Reandn didn't know,
but he took the moment to claw his way out from under
one of them, twisting sideways, still unable to free his
arm before they came back to themselves and grabbed
at him, confusing him with the uncommon amount of
green their movements revealed.

And then Teya cried out, surprise turned to shrieking
agony, and magic crashed down on Reandn harder than
the Dragons; they followed it up with knees and fists,
blending pain into magic's crippling touch. Beneath the
haze of it he heard Faline's command ring out, and Red
First's echoing bellow.

In moments he was free of Malik's men and
surrounded by the clamor of Dragon fighting Dragon,
hearing Vaklar's battle roar and thinking *Goddess,
they'll lose track of who's who* and *Teya!* and where
was Malik? Magic-dazed, stepped on once too often
and dragging himself out of the battleground, he found
Teya on the ground before him, writhing with her hands
over her face and blood pouring out from between
her fingers.

Behind her, Kalena, Rethia and Kacey—fully revealed—
fought to turn too many horses in too little space, targets
for any knife or arrow; Elstan stood before them with
his fingers in a wizardly stutter, stuck in mid-spell, unable
to channel the magic that still flowed around them all—

but from the determination on his face, still trying. Beside him, Madehy pulled ineffectively at her bowstring, her arms shaking too hard to manage while the nocked arrow slowly slipped off her finger and her knees gave way to the onslaught of high emotion around her.

And Malik? *There*, lurking by the side of the road, the intended victim of Madehy's faltering arrow, the target of Elstan's attempted defiance. Something in his hand, something glinting and wickedly slender—a dart, a heavy throwing dart—*Goddess, is that what he used on Teya?* Reandn's hand found his boot knife, for the other was lost in the struggle; he closed his hand tightly around it, all his focus on Malik, all his intent on reaching the man before he launched that weapon. Kacey saw it, too, and she tugged on Kalena's horse, grabbing after the reins while Kalena, senseless in terror, only screamed Vaklar's name over and over. Already spooked, Kalena's horse reared up and dumped her, slamming into Kacey's horse on the way down. Kacey's horse lurched up and back, throwing Kacey toward her bad side and, without a stirrup to catch her, she kept right on going, hitting the ground to roll frantically aside from still-dancing hooves.

Knife still in hand, clutched by white-knuckled fingers, Reandn found himself pinned by Elstan's magic, the magic and the lightning pain in his back that kept him from lurching on anyway. *Kacey!*—on the ground and terrified, a stunned Kalena crawling backward into her until they were one target, not two. *Not Kacey*. But there was Malik, shooing off the horses between them, ignoring Elstan, and ignoring the fighting behind him.

Which is worse—never having something, someone, or having it—and losing it. Not again.

"*Malik!*" Reandn bellowed, and the man glanced back only long enough to slide behind Sky as magic turned the world grey and Reandn's chest tight.

Bloody-damn the magic, bloody-damn what damage

the Dragons had done him, he wasn't going to let this happen, he wasn't going to lose Kacey. His frustrated anger turned hard and cold and determined and on the fringes of it he heard Rethia cry, "Danny!" as if she'd made some startling discovery. And Elstan cursed, his magic faltering even further.

And Reandn suddenly understood. He'd been so sheltered from magic since its return—shying away from cities and villages where it would be in use, turning on anyone who thought to invoke any small spell in his presence, and, of late, counting on Teya to protect him. He'd never allowed himself to be trapped into simply enduring the progression of a spell—not until these last weeks—and where he might see the results of his reactions to it. Elstan, fumbling even the small spells he ought to have been able to handle. Teya, struggling as he'd never seen her struggle, saying *You've got to work* with *me*, the certainty in her voice only moments ago—*Reandn, no—don't do that!* He understood the unicorns—they'd tried so hard to tell him, flowing around him, shifting in their own currents, none of it ever touching him.

Start with the anger. *Kacey, unable to run, facing Malik with Kalena in her lap and terror in her eyes*. Take away the haze of it, turn it cold. *Wolf-clear thinking, the heat of anger's fire turned into the steel it tempered*. Add the *feel* that lurked within him, that thing that came with his determination, that thing that had taken him from kitchen boy to Wolf First and then Wolf Remote. *It felt like a growl, down deep in his chest, something that had been stuck there a long, long time*.

Let it all go. No more harboring it all, like he'd harbored his grief for Adela. Let it go, and move on—parting the currents of magic like the prow of a ship as he moved.

Elstan stilled his hands and gave up, slowly backing away; Malik laughed, short and harsh, knowing only that the wizard had failed, unable to perceive the true significance of it. "Kalennie," he said, hefting the heavy throwing dart and reaching for his knife instead, "you should never have come."

Reandn slid his knife in front of Malik's throat, the blade barely kissing skin. "Neither," he said into the man's ear, the words throaty with promise, "should you."

Chapter 19

"I'm fine, I'm fine," Kacey said at Rethia's query, shooing her sister away and all but shoving Kalena off of her lap. Elstan ran around behind her, gathering up loose horses; Reandn caught Kacey's eye only long enough to assure himself she had meant what she said to Rethia, his hand tight around Malik's flabby upper arm, and then turned to find Faline.

She was striding up to him through the disorganized aftermath of Dragon against Dragon, Red First by her side, and though he opened his mouth to speak to her, open it stayed, while he stared at the subdued Dragons before him. "Green," he said, when he realized he should say *something*. "They're *green*."

"So they are." Faline planted her feet and crossed her arms to aim her steady gaze his way. Her whipcord frame and plain, spare features seemed at once familiar and yet out of place, in this here and now. "I expect you know something about that? In fact, I expect you can explain *all* of this."

"Green," Elstan said, on his way by with a packhorse. "I did it. School prank. Thought it would help identify them." He shoved the horse's lead rope into Kalena's hand, ignoring her gasp of protest, and went off after the fading rustle of brush and leaves that marked another mount's travel away from them all.

Faline raised an eyebrow at Reandn, her silent request for elaboration. No, more of a demand, he thought, shoving Malik at Red First and trying to decide where to start, absently noting the warm gush of blood that his movement released, past his belt and all the way down the back of his thigh.

Teya's whimpering moan instantly stole his attention; he pivoted to find her, his movement jerky, his back newly afire. She lay curled up at the side of the road, her hands still over her face and blood soaking into the ground beside her. Rethia reached her side as he did, and Kacey wasn't far behind; Reandn stayed out of their way, resting a hand on Teya's leg as Rethia soothed her and Kacey patiently but firmly pried her hands away.

She didn't look long; one hand resting on her patient's hip, she said, "Washrags. Water, and a fire to warm it on. And my packs, I need my packs."

Reandn glanced at Faline, who immediately gestured to the other Wolf. "Clon, get whatever they need; use our supplies if they don't have enough."

"What's he done to her?" Reandn asked, gently squeezing Teya's knee—although with any luck, and with Madehy joining Rethia's effort, his patrol wizard couldn't feel it anymore.

Kacey only glanced at him, accepting the canteen and rag that Clon thrust at her and murmuring, "More. And warm."

"Fire's being built," the Wolf assured her, and went off to query Elstan about the supplies she'd demanded.

"Kacey?"

"I heard you the first time. He's put out her eye, that's what he's done. I'll have to get her cleaned up before I can tell if it's any worse than that. Don't get in the way."

Her eye. Reandn grimaced, watching for a moment more before admitting to himself that there was nothing he could do *but* get in the way, and then stood, awkwardly and wincing, returning to Faline.

"You're losing a fair amount of blood yourself," she told him, prodding him in the side with an ungentle finger.

"Ow! Be careful!"

"That was just to stop you from growling *I'm fine* at me," she said implacably. "You're not. But you're on your feet, and you'll stay that way for a while . . . long enough to let me know *what's happened here.*"

"A huge miscalculation, that's what," Malik said. "I don't know who this man is, but he's in very serious trouble, as are you all if you don't immediately address the error you've made here. Release me this very moment! This man attacked *me*, if you'll recall." He made an attempt to jerk his arm free of Red First's grip, and settled for a disgruntled and, under the circumstances, impressively dignified expression.

"As I recall," Faline said, cocking her head and amused, if anything, "you were waving your hands dangerously close to his face and he stopped you. The distinction you've neglected to make, meir, is that if Dan had *attacked* you, you'd have been unable to, say, order your corrupted Dragons to attack, or to maim that young woman over there, or" —she held out her hand, and Reandn obligingly dropped Malik's remaining throwing dart into it— "even to think about throwing this dart at the ambassador we're here to protect."

"Exactly what did you need me to explain?" Reandn wiped road dust from one eye and discovered it did nothing to remove the haze that had appeared in front of Faline.

"All of it," Faline said firmly, ruffling her short bangs away from her forehead and favoring him with exasperation. "From the beginning. Only sit down, first. From the looks of you, the one thing I've gotten wrong so far was how long you'd be on your feet."

"You'd best listen to me," Malik said. "Before it's too late to save yourselves from the consequences of what you're doing here—"

Red First gave him a sudden shake that popped his teeth together. "Shut up, meir. You think I didn't see my Dragons—*my* Dragons—break orders to do your bidding? Someone at the Keep might listen to you, but I'll not."

"See here, First—"

Red First didn't bother to repeat himself; Malik turned pale as the Dragon rested one gloved hand on his short, serviceable sword, and tightened the other around Malik's arm. Reandn blinked as the two men hazed to grey.

Faline gave him a shove, just enough to set him off balance and stumbling toward the edge of the road, where he sat. One of the Reds came up, murmured to Red First that because the corrupted Reds had been disarmed, their worst injury was a broken arm, and left, taking Malik with him. The Red crouched in front of Reandn and took his plain pot helm off, tucking it in the crook of his arm and scrubbing his fingers through his sweaty hair. "Now," he said. "I'll tell you the opposite of what I told him. Talk. And you'd better hope I listen—and that I believe."

So Reandn started with the original escort and their concerns about Kalena's safety, and told them of the trouble they'd hit in Pasdon . . . and then the ambush on the pass road. He told them of Teya's arrival, and Rethia and Kacey, and of how Kalena had talked them out of the Knife camp alive. With his mouth going dry and his stomach starting to turn, his shirt gone cold and clammy against his back, he put the two Knife representatives under Dragon protection, mentioned Madehy only in terms of identifying her, and then, after making sure Faline realized there would be wounded waiting at Pasdon, he told them of Elstan's folly.

"Elstan," Faline said, looking at the wizard where he stood in the middle of the road, holding onto the reins and lead ropes of half a dozen horses; Elstan didn't even try to hide the fact that he'd been eavesdropping. He only lifted his head a fraction and pushed one skewed braid out of his face. "But he did turn those men green, didn't he."

"My men would have gotten them anyway," Red First said. "As soon as they broke ranks, they were marked." Grudgingly, after eyeing the wizard another moment, he added, "Made it quicker, though. And that green—" He glanced over at his men, then ducked his head and snorted. "I don't guess they'll have much luck trying to lose themselves, will they? 'Less that green fades."

Elstan shook his head. "Not until I remove it. I confess I don't remember that spell as readily as the first. I'll have to think about it."

"Don't waste too much time on it," Red First said. "Not yet. But . . . come deliver yourself up, meir wizard. Those at the Keep'll sort out where you stand in all this."

Elstan stood there another moment, his face blank, unsurprised but somehow not quite resigned to it. Madehy, still red-eyed and flushed, walked up to him and held her hand out—and then patiently kept it there. Finally Elstan took a deep breath and deliberately passed her the horses. "Couldn't get your bay," he said calmly, on his way by Reandn.

"He'll be back," Reandn responded, not much thinking about his words, not much thinking about anything— except maybe of the many explanations yet to come, and how very far away he still was from home.

Home. Yes, that felt right.

"Danny." Rethia knelt beside him, laden with rags and ointments and bandages. "You're scaring Kacey. Let me see."

"I'm all right," he said. "Or, I will be."

"I know," she said, pulling his shirt out from beneath his belt and lifting it to peer underneath. After a moment, she put it back down again. "Not bleeding anymore. I'll leave it for Kacey, if you promise to stay here."

"Promise." As if he were going to hop up and start ordering people around. This wasn't his game anymore;

it never really had been. Just a role he'd slipped into for a little while.

But Rethia was still there, and looking at him. Studying him. "You know what you did, don't you?"

He didn't have to ask what she meant. He thought of the moment Elstan's half-woven spell had started slipping around him instead of through him, leaving him to move in behind Malik hampered only by torn flesh and not the ravages of magic. "Yes," he told her, and then changed his mind. "No. I suppose. It's not something I understand. Me, working magic."

"You weren't." Rethia's short braid slipped over her shoulder as she tilted her head, watching him; her hand crept up and fiddled with the end of it. "You just made a place where it wasn't."

Reandn snorted; his back twitched against it. "Ow, dammit. No, never mind. Don't try to explain. I have the feeling I'll have to work it out for myself, anyway. How's Teya? Will she lose that eye?"

"She already has," Rethia said, standing up. "But like you, she'll figure it out."

One of these days she was going to make complete and total sense, and he'd expire from the shock of it. For now, he just nodded, and his attention drifted away from her. He thought about Teya without an eye, and whether she'd still have a career with the Wolves after quietly defying both Saxe and Farren—although, as he understood it, she'd never been told *not* to come after him. He thought about why he'd gotten involved with this assignment in the first place, and wondered if, after all of this, Saxe would still offer him back the Remote . . . and then he wondered if he would take it if they did.

Chapter 20

One day out of Norposten, with far too much traveling beside a squad of disgruntled and unhappy Dragons, Reandn found a small clearing and made himself some torches. One for Damen, who wouldn't get to tell his children stories of the spoiled Resioran ambassador after all, and one for Nican, who had taken the antics of his odd wrangler with as much forbearance as could be expected of anybody.

He had promised them Kalena would make it to the Keep; she was nearly there. And he had promised them a Binding. With Kalena, he'd had plenty of help. This, he did alone. He held the torches high for Tenaebra's dark eyes, and he then wove them together with cord. *Find each other*, he told them silently, in place of the usual, spoken words, while the oil-soaked torches hissed and sputtered into the darkness. *Don't walk her hell alone*.

Then he jammed them in the dirt together and watched the flames, heedless of what it did to his night vision in these strange woods. Properly done, there would be more people here. Properly done, the torches would be in a frame, and not awkwardly wrapped together. *Properly* done, the right words would have been spoken. But all that would happen, once the Hounds had their own Binding. This one, though . . . this one had the heart of someone who had been there.

Though, to judge by the noise in the brush behind him, someone who was no longer alone. Noisy steps were only a prelude to the *snap* of someone running into the dead lower branches of a pine. "Ouch, dammit!"

Teya's voice. And, a moment later, Teya beside him, muttering, "Sorry. I didn't mean to interrupt like that."

"You shouldn't be out here," Reandn said, not looking away from the torches. No point, not when he'd just see their leftover images instead of Teya's face. And he knew well enough what her face looked like of late—pale, usually, with thick padding held over her eye by rakish strips of linen. From below the padding peeked the end of a stitched wound, where the throwing dart had hit the flat of her cheek and skidded up into her eye. And as much as Kacey and Rethia tended to it, there always seemed to be something weeping down her cheek, as though pale serum had taken the place of the tears that eye would no longer cry.

"I know I didn't know them—"

"Out in the woods, I meant. After dark. Until you get used to looking at things with just one eye."

"—but I had to talk to you, and I just haven't found the right time—"

Reandn snorted gently. Not the right time, no.

"And at least you're alone. I need to talk to you alone."

And that, Reandn had to concede, *would* have been hard to accomplish, these last days. "You'd better take the chance while you've got it, then." The torches were guttering; Teya hesitated, shifting from foot to foot, until they diminished into quiet flames licking around the edges of cooling wood.

Then she said, "I just . . . wanted to say that . . . I'm sorry."

"Sorry for what?" Reandn said with some surprise.

"I tried . . . I really tried. I'm just not good enough to depend on in a fight."

He didn't say anything. He didn't know quite what *to* say. For she was right. She couldn't think fast enough, couldn't pull up the right spells at the right time. As if she'd heard his thoughts, she said, "I know you said not to masquerade as Kalena at the Knife camp, but they were about to find you, and it's all I could think of—I just wanted to distract them—"

"Teya," Reandn said firmly, wishing it was Rethia here and not him, and hearing the rising note of despair in her voice, something he had to stop *now*—"Teya, it *did* distract them."

"But I lost it. I couldn't hold on to it. And I couldn't follow it up with anything."

He looked at her directly now, his vision readjusting to the darkness. "We've pretty much decided some of that was my fault, I thought."

She was silent at that, and she turned her head away. He waited. Eventually she said, "They won't want me back, will they? The Wolves, I mean. Even if I *hadn't* taken that horse. What're they going to do with a one-eyed patrol wizard?"

Reandn took a breath. A deep one. And he let it out slowly. "I don't know that they will. But I also don't know if that's really your question."

"What do you—" Teya broke off, as though she knew both what he meant and what her answer was, and couldn't face it.

"Listen," he said. "You're right. You're not at your best in a fight; you don't think things through when you're crowded like that. You probably won't ever be a really good combat wizard no matter how hard you try." She stiffened. Surely she hadn't expected him to soften the words. He moved around in front of her, into her line of sight. "You're good with the subtle things, Teya. You're really good. I like having you at my back, and if you don't think it pains me to say that then you don't know me very well."

"Even after . . . after I left myself open to—to *this*?" She gestured at her face.

"Yes." He was silent a moment, trying not to let his own decisions rub off on the things he said about hers. "The question isn't, *will they take you back*. You're plenty good enough, as long as you don't accept assignments you know you're not up to. The question is, *what do you want to do*? Just keep in mind . . . sometimes, knowing who you aren't helps you define who you are."

She took a step back and gave him a skeptical look. He only grinned at her. "Too thoughtful? You'd rather I just went ahead and made some kind of decision about things, no matter what anyone else thinks about it?"

"Well," she said, "maybe not. Maybe I'll just think about this on my own for a while. But I'd like to know. What you're going to do, I mean. Success on this assignment is supposed to get you back into the Wolves . . . isn't it?"

"Define success," Reandn said dryly. "I'm not sure this is it."

Teya grumbled at him, reached up to touch her bandage, and lowered her hand with a self-admonitory sound. "Evasive," she accused him.

"Pushy," he responded. But he thought again of why she'd been on that road in front of Malik's dart in the first place. "I think they'll offer me Wolf Remote again," he said, and made his own exasperated sound, rubbing the bridge of his nose with his finger. "I don't know that I'll take it."

She looked at him with shock, and then slow comprehension. "The things you said at Madehy's. About being true to what a Wolf really is."

"To what it's always been for me." Reandn looked back at the extinguished Binding torches. He'd always been bound to the Wolves, to what they were, and what they did. And most of it hadn't changed . . . but it seemed to him that somewhere, something had. Something was missing. And he thought it might be time to go looking for it.

Kacey dreamt. She dreamt of feeling safe, and of lying in someone's arms, quiet and happy and feeling loved. Dan's arms, they were, strong ones . . . confident arms, that circled her without hesitation. She dreamt of being kissed, a long unhurried kiss, a tender thing. The kiss of a lover, with the taste of mint and an odd overtone of bitter tea.

She woke slowly, happy to carry the feelings of the dream to her sleepy wakefulness, finding the aftertaste of bitter tea in her own mouth—she'd taken some the evening before, feeling tired and cranky and particularly vexed about her ankle—and finding, too, that the ground was just a little too hard beneath her back.

Reandn sat not far away, his back to a tree and a sprig of something in the corner of his mouth. "Hello," he said, and she thought he looked just a tad . . . smug. Yes, that was it. Smug.

"Hello," she replied, somewhat warily. "You look like you've been up for a while."

"Long enough." Not only smug, but suspiciously cheery. He took a nibble out of the sprig and removed it from his mouth, letting it dangle from the hand he rested over his knee.

"What's that?"

"This?" He glanced down at the little green thing. "Spring mint. Rethia found it."

Mint. She narrowed her eyes at him, but he only smiled back, until she had to drop her gaze, blushing much more hotly than she'd like. Distraction. She needed distraction. She pushed the dew-covered blanket off her legs. "Breakfast?"

"The inn's still serving." He nodded at what seemed to be nothing more than a particularly scrubby patch of woods, but just beyond it was the Highborn-catering inn at which they'd all chosen not to stay.

They'd been just outside Norposten for a handful of days now, as close as Reandn could get to the Keep and its city without going crazed from the constant buzz of spelled magics—for his newly learned and unperfected technique for diverting magic turned out to be something he could sustain only for a short while, and even then it took a profound amount of effort. It had been that, and not any significant blood loss, which had given him the shakes after their clash with Malik and his men.

But that cut on his back had scored his ribs, sliced into the muscle of his lower back, and jammed short against his belt, leaving him sore and unable to ride more than short distances. Like the Dragons, he'd walked his way back from the north.

Here, they'd been given the woods of the King's land in lieu of the crowded inn rooms none of them wanted, anyway—for news of Kalena's arrival preceded them, creating a festival atmosphere and packed inns. Kalena was already holding forth in the Keep, making herself available to the Keland Highborn and impressing them with her poise in the aftermath of her terrible experience.

Like Reandn, Kacey was just as glad to be in the woods—although she figured now was her one chance to attend Highborn fetes, and had been to several, both with and without Reandn. And once she'd heard a minstrel, thinking himself alone behind the inn, fashioning a song around Kalena's brave confrontation with the Knife. She'd almost marched up to set his facts straight, but in the end had decided that correcting the one wouldn't do anything about the dozen other songs under construction that very hour. Besides, she wasn't up to marching yet. Call it a hop-limp-drag instead.

It didn't matter. The Keep had done right by them all, or right enough, anyway. Their provisions were paid for, their horses well-stabled, their needs seen to. One of the Keep's best wizard healers watched over Teya, ensuring that the wound stayed free of infection and keeping her comfortable. Under other circumstances, Kacey might have felt miffed to have had a patient usurped like that . . . but just now, she had plenty of other things clamoring for her attention.

She'd have preferred to have had a long talk with her sister, whom she'd hardly seen at all; Rethia and Madehy spent their days together, learning more about what they could do together, and working on Madehy's ability to protect herself from the sensitivities that had driven her into isolation. Reandn, too, had been hard to pin down—restless with the constant threat of active magic around him, unsettled about his future with the Wolves, waiting for Saxe to break away from the Keep and for the discussion they needed to have. In the meantime, he was seldom to be found around their little camp— always off on the prowl, or taking Sky for such short rides as he could. And Kacey—frustrated, tied to the camp by the slowly healing ankle the Keep wizard healer had declared a sprain—ached to talk to Reandn, to reassure herself that the things he'd said and done had more meaning to them than the desperation of the moment.

Except . . . now she looked at him, and at that withering spring mint dangling from his fingers, and she ran a thoughtful finger over her lower lip.

Maybe she had her answers already.

Reandn, watching her, smiled again. "You want help getting to the inn?"

"No," Kacey surprised herself by saying. "I'd like it if you'd just bring breakfast out to me."

He tossed the mint away and got to his feet, though not with the natural effortless movement that made watching him so easy; that was his strength, she'd learned, and an indication of the intense energy that lay hidden inside him. Now it was hobbled by the scabbed wound on his back, but it would return. Kacey wondered where it would take him next.

"And would you be wanting the Highborn setting, or what the rest of us commoners broke fast with?" he asked.

"I'm sure I'd get sick on whatever fancies the Highborn ate this morning," she said, waving her hand in a dismissive gesture closely imitative of Malik under stress.

"Will eat," Reandn said, mockly serious. "If you're going to do this Highborn mien, get it right. None of them are up yet."

Kacey said promptly, "Then I'm going back to sleep. I can't imagine what woke me in the first place."

"That would have been me." He looked down at her with laughter around his mouth, and something more serious in his grey eyes. "And I'd be glad to show you just how I went about it."

"Umm," Kacey said, feeling her eyes widen.

"Or is it that breakfast you want?"

"Umm . . ." she said.

"Then I get to choose."

Kacey missed breakfast.

It was over lunch that she learned what she had truly missed, early that morning—that Saxe had arrived in Norposten late the night before, and sought out Reandn in the dew and bird song of the arriving morn. She sent a cross look his way over the table of the inn. Like the inn at Pasdon, it was replete with intricately carved doors and mantles, fine sheer laces and fabrics, and plenty of food. There were musicians in every room, and they knew when to play and—more importantly—when to stop. But none of it was on Kacey's mind just now. "Saxe was *here*? How could you not tell me?"

Completely unrepentant, he tore a piece from the small loaf of bread they shared. "I was busy. Thinking about other things. Enjoying myself."

Kacey cleared her throat, neatly bounced out of her grump. "Hmmph. Well, then, tell me *now*—will they let you back in the Wolves?"

"They want me." Reandn spent an inordinate amount of time dribbling honey over the buttered bread, spreading it, and then studying the damned thing. Finally he allowed, "I said no."

Kacey slowly lowered her spoonful of sweetly marinated rabbit and rice. "You . . . what?"

"Said no." He took a bite out of his bread, as if his statement had been the most ordinary thing in the world. Reandn, Wolf down to his bones, Wolf in every gesture and in the authority he wore like a second skin. Wolf to the death, defiant of anything else. Kacey just stared at him. After a moment of it, he reached out and wiped some imaginary bit of something from her chin. "It's the right thing, Kacey."

"How can it be?" she all but blurted, tempering her reply at the last minute—although the tastefully appointed dining area was all but empty of other customers for the moment; most of the inn's residents had just finished breaking fast.

Reandn shook his head, though she decided it was in response to his own thoughts, and not to her. "Things have changed. I'm not meant to dance with the Highborn . . . I've got to do my job, and do it right. That's not what the Keep needs right now. I won't do them any good."

"They wouldn't want you back if they didn't—" Kacey said, but stopped, still stunned by the enormity of his shift in thinking—although, recalling the last eight or nine days, she could see that it had been coming.

Reandn shrugged. "Maybe I've learned something about keeping temper in its place, maybe not . . . but I'll never stop short of looking for justice. That means stopping a Minor who's shoving around my injured patrol wizard, and it means stepping on Highborn toes when they're getting ready to stomp on a lowborn head that doesn't deserve it."

"Well," Kacey said, and took another spoonful of her lunch, suddenly calmer than she'd expected of herself. "I guess I wouldn't want you if you were anything other than that particular Reandn."

He gave her a slow grin, a pleased and somewhat self-conscious expression. *Good*, she thought, gladdened to know her words had that power over him, after so much time of watching him make sure that they didn't.

"Saxe isn't convinced." Reandn pushed his rice around with what was left of the bread, like a boy with the fidgets. "Said he'd be back to try again."

"I'm not surprised he's not convinced," Kacey said. "After all this time . . . and all the effort you've put into staying with them."

"If he'd been with me for the last two years as much as you have, he'd know that the same things that once drove me to be a Wolf now drive me away from them. I want to do it right . . . and I can't do that with them anymore."

She just looked at him a long moment. "You amaze me," she said. "I didn't know if you'd ever realize that."

"I'm slow sometimes." He looked at her with that same grin, only this time there was a little more wickedness than self-consciousness. "There are a lot of things you probably figured I'd never realize. But when I get there, I do it with feeling."

Kacey cleared her throat. "So I noticed." She ate for a moment, savoring the level of cooking she was never inspired to reach for herself. Reandn, without the Wolves . . . *doing it right*? She shoved her bowl aside, jumping only a little when a server materialized to remove it, and shortly thereafter replace it with a pastry sweet. "You won't have the Wolf authority behind you anymore," she said slowly. "You won't have Wolf Rights." No more replenishing supplies at the Keep's expense, not after the ones that would get them home; the new tunic shirt, cuffed and collared and fitting him perfectly, would be his last on the Keep's dole. "If you knock down another Minor, you really *will* end up in trouble, probably right back under Wolf Justice."

"Then I'll just have to stay away from Minors," Reandn said evenly. "Kacey . . . there are a lot of people in Keland who feel like the Knife. Like *I* feel. They don't like magic, and they can't tell when it's being used. They worry about their livelihood, about being cheated or even attacked by magic when they're simply trying to go about business."

Kacey took a cautious bite of the pastry, discovered it far too sweet a thing, and pushed it aside. She looked at Reandn just as warily. "And?"

He sat back in his padded and ornate chair, shifting a little. That, Kacey understood. She found the things just as uncomfortable, and she didn't have a half-healed knife wound in her back. "And," he said, echoing her. "And I'm the one who can feel spelled magic before most wizards do. I'm still what I was, Kacey—still a Wolf. But I'm more, too. I'll do fine on my own."

Kacey folded her hands around the fine linen napkin in her lap and stared at them. Reandn, on his own, without the patrol to back him up.

"Teya won't be able to stay with the Wolves," he said, picking up a new thread of conversation when Kacey wasn't quite sure she was through with the old one. "And she doesn't want to go back to Solace right now." Not surprising. She knew little of Reandn's patrol wizard, but she knew the look of someone whose foundations of life had been rattled. She'd seen it too often on Reandn not to recognize it now.

"She wants to work with me," Reandn said. "For a while."

Kacey didn't say anything. He cocked his head slightly, watching her. She felt his gaze, and steadfastly stared at her fingers; she'd crimped the napkin into a twisted semblance of its former self. She didn't need to look up to see him, to know exactly the expression in his eyes, to picture the way his dark brows drew together, even to see the impossibly new and never-explained scar that cut through one of them. She knew his mouth would be open a little, that he was working his way up to saying something; she wasn't at all surprised when he raked a hand through his hair, the dark blond going streaky sun-kissed already.

But she didn't know what he was thinking. She didn't know where she fit in.

"Kacey."

I'm not looking at you. She couldn't. So much had changed, and all at once she realized that her life would never be the same, either . . . and just at the moment, she had no idea in which direction it was headed.

Trust him to get her attention. His little boot knife made a lazy arc and landed in front of her plate, quivering slightly in its neat, point-first landing. Kacey instantly yanked it out of the table. "Are you crazy? You can't do that in here!" Furiously, she rubbed the spot where it had been, as if she could smear away the tiny slit in the tablecloth.

"Kacey," he said, and there was something in his tone that made her stop her futile effort, hand frozen in place, and look up at him, the scowl still on her face simply because she hadn't replaced it with anything else. The corner of his mouth twitched and stilled in some private humor. "Kacey, I need to know if that's all right with you. I'll be on the road some, but not always; there might even be some times you can come along, if you want."

"If it's all right with me?" she repeated, sounding just as stunned as she felt.

His grin was wry. "It's the first real decision I've made about my life in a long time—as opposed to letting circumstances make the decisions for me. I thought you should be part of it. Unless you'd rather just finish shredding that napkin."

It was a Highborn establishment. Kacey supposed one didn't launch one's hobbled self from chair to chair and into the arms of another any more than one tossed knives into the tables. But she did it anyway.

Questions Answered

Rethia stood beside the inn and waved—again—as Dan and Kacey rode away from Norposten. In truth, Dan had already ridden away from the inn once this morning, and at quite some speed. Sky, of course. Silly horse. Madehy had petted his nose and told him so when he'd come back looking sheepish and a little puzzled, with Dan grinning just as sheepishly in the saddle.

Madehy wasn't here now. Ever more adept at protecting herself from unwanted spillover of everyone else's feelings, she still chose to absent herself from situations she knew would bring high emotion. And though Rethia would be returning to Solace on the Wizard's Road, probably to reach home before Kacey even though she didn't plan to leave for some number of days, this did somehow seem like something more than a simple separation. She and her sister both had other things besides home, the clinic, and a little family of three in their lives now. Kacey had . . . well, she had Danny. She'd had him for a long time now, even if neither of the two had quite known it. Rethia imagined her father's expression when he saw them together and smiled. He'd know right away, Teayo would; for all he left his daughters to make their own decisions, for all he was away from home and tending his human flock around Little Wisdom, he knew the unspoken things in their lives, and he'd been worried about Kacey for some time.

He wasn't likely to be as happy with Rethia's plans. Oh, Madehy had to return to her farm—the hunter wouldn't care for those sheep forever—and Rethia would return to the clinic, but soon enough, that would change. Soon enough, she'd start looking for the answers to her own questions. She had wondered about the other children who might have been touched by magic, as she was . . . the ones who didn't know why they were different or have the means to understand themselves. And now, through Madehy, she knew she could no longer just wonder. Together—later this year, early the next, whenever it happened—they'd look for others.

Danny, after all, was off searching for his special kind of justice, helping people deal with the magic. It only seemed right that Rethia do the same.

Doranna's Backstory...

Doranna Durgin spent her childhood filling notebooks first with stories and art, and then with novels. After obtaining a degree in wildlife illustration and environmental education, she spent a number of years deep in the Appalachian Mountains. When she emerged, it was as a writer who found herself irrevocably tied to the natural world and its creatures.

Doranna lives in upstate New York with an old hound and his irrepressible Cardigan companion, and a young Lipizzan gelding who thinks too much. You can contact her at:

doranna@sff.net

or

PO Box 26207
Rochester, NY 14626
(SASE please)

or visit http://www.sff.net/people/doranna/